Other Books by Lexi Blake

Courting Justice
Order of Protection, Coming June 5, 2018

Masters Of Ménage (by Shayla Black and Lexi Blake)
Their Virgin Captive
Their Virgin's Secret
Their Virgin Concubine
Their Virgin Princess
Their Virgin Hostage
Their Virgin Secretary
Their Virgin Mistress

The Perfect Gentlemen (by Shayla Black and Lexi Blake)
Scandal Never Sleeps
Seduction in Session
Big Easy Temptation
Smoke and Sin
At the Pleasure of the President, Coming Fall 2018

URBAN FANTASY

Thieves
Steal the Light
Steal the Day
Steal the Moon
Steal the Sun
Steal the Night
Ripper
Addict
Sleeper
Outcast, Coming 2018

LEXI BLAKE WRITING AS SOPHIE OAK

Small Town Siren
Siren in the City
Away From Me
Three to Ride
Siren Enslaved
Two to Love
Siren Beloved
One to Keep, Coming August 7, 2018

The Dom Who Loved Me

Masters and Mercenaries, Book 1

Lexi Blake

THE DOM WHO LOVED ME
Masters and Mercenaries, Book 1
Lexi Blake

Published by DLZ Entertainment LLC

Copyright 2011 DLZ Entertainment LLC
Edited by Chloe Vale and Kasi Alexander
ISBN: 978-1-937608-92-7

McKay-Taggart logo design by Charity Hendry

Acknowledgments

No book gets written in vacuum. It takes a team of people to write and produce a book, and I'm grateful to have such a support group of people around me.

Thanks to Shayla Black, who edited an early version of this book. *The Dom Who Loved Me* wouldn't have come out without your support. To Kris Cook, my lovely rock of support. You listen to my every moan and whine without complaint. To the best PA and friend a girl could have, Chloe Vale. To my kids, who put up with the fact that mom is always typing.

And to my husband, because none of this would mean a thing without you.

Chapter One

Sean Taggart watched the quiet one. Of the three men sitting across from his team in the cool, ultra-modern conference room, the dark-haired man who hadn't spoken once snared his attention. He was perfectly silent, listening in what appeared to be a submissive fashion. That was only right and proper since he was supposed to be a lowly assistant. Except that he was a lowly assistant wearing thousand dollar shoes. Sean had been in the covert business long enough to know that the little details usually gave a person away.

"The bastard has hit three of my facilities in the last year." Elliot Lincoln, the head of a lumber consortium, slapped at the heavy wooden table.

Sean hid a small smile as he risked a glance at his brother. Ian's right eyebrow was practically in outer space.

Anyone who knew Ian Taggart would have backed off, but the CEO just kept on. His fist came down on the table again. "That son of a bitch isn't costing me another dime, I tell you."

Oh, but he would if Lincoln hired McKay/Taggart Security Services. That bastard, as Lincoln called him, would be costing his lumber company far more than a dime. Sean looked briefly at the men and woman who formed the core of the very selective security team. Ian sat at the head of the table, with his partner Alexander McKay at the other end. McKay looked vaguely amused at Ian's annoyance. Liam O'Donnell sat to Sean's left. O'Donnell's eyes were red. He'd almost certainly been on another bender. They happened more and more often. It wouldn't affect his work, and that was all that mattered. Eve St. James, resident tough chick, took a long drag off her ever-present latte and drummed her perfect fingernails on the table. Only Jake and Adam had been permitted to miss this little mess of a meeting.

"Perhaps you would like to explain exactly what you need, Mr. Lincoln." Ian's voice sent a wash of icy disdain across the room. Big brother was not in a good mood. Sean saw that his brother was also looking at the tall man in the expensive suit. The man was pretending to stare at his notes, his eyes surreptitiously glancing around the room, taking in everything. Sean exchanged a glance with Liam. The Irishman rolled his eyes and shook his head. Sean knew just what he was thinking. Government bureaucrats couldn't do undercover to save their lives.

Lincoln waved a hand at the second man he'd brought with him. It was the arrogant command of a boss to his lackey. The lackey smiled good-naturedly and passed out folders. "Hello, everyone, I'm Gene, Mr. Lincoln's personal assistant. I have dossiers on both of the Wright brothers. Matthew is the younger of the two. He's the one we're asking you to investigate, though obviously we're trying to get to Patrick."

"And Patrick Wright is a member of the Earth League." Ian's statement was made without a hint of question behind it.

Gene responded with an apologetic shrug. "My research isn't perfect. That's why we felt it was important to bring your firm in. As far as I can tell, Patrick Wright is the head of the Earth League. The group sprang up about ten years ago. They started out benignly enough, protesting pharmaceutical companies, lumber companies, big real estate developments, and SUV manufacturers. Then Patrick Wright joined up and took over. You have to understand, this guy changes names and identities as often as the rest of us change underwear. The police have questioned his followers, and the name of the group's leader always changes. He's probably had plastic surgery as well."

Lincoln's voice filled the room. "That son of a bitch! Fucking monkeywrenching cost me five million in the last three years alone, and now he's threatening to bomb my goddamn house."

The businessman continued to rant. Sean could see Ian's patience was wearing thin. It would be nice to see big bro toss this asshole out on his rear. The last thing Sean wanted to do was sit outside this jerk's house trying to catch some "Save the Earth" whackadoodle. He had better things to do with his time, like perfecting his gnocchi recipe. It was almost there. It just needed a little more oomph to put it over the top. Sean forced himself to focus on the job at hand rather than his hobby. Despite the fact that he couldn't stand executive types, they did pay well. And he was curious about the government man sitting so still across from him.

He turned to Liam. "Monkeywrenching?"

Liam spoke softly, but Sean could hear him even over the moans and complaints of Lincoln. "It's a term for the way ecoterrorists mess with big business. They spike trees marked for cross cutting. It destroys very expensive saw blades. Often they destroy machinery. And sometimes they flat out torch places. E.L. is known for getting into places the timber industry thinks are secure and lighting it up. They're branching out a bit though. Other types of businesses are getting hit."

Sean nodded at Liam and settled back in his chair to glance through the myriad of photos Gene had collected. There was an old photo of Patrick Wright. He was a large guy in a band uniform. Sean chuckled to himself. If they were using his high school yearbook photo, this Wright guy was damn good at keeping off the radar.

There were several pictures of Matt Wright. He was thirty-nine, a well-dressed businessman. He was blandly good looking, in an all-American-apple-pie fashion. The photos were obviously taken when the subject didn't know he was being photographed. PI, Sean figured. His hand stopped on one of the pictures. It was Matt Wright walking out of his office building. A woman walked behind him, her head down. She looked a bit plump, soft. Of course, Sean couldn't tell for certain, given the bulky clothes she wore. Everything she wore was dark, from her slacks to the voluminous sweater that hid every curve. Her eyes were covered with sunglasses, and she carried a nondescript briefcase. The one bit of color on the woman's body was the bright yellow of the stilettos peeking out from her sensible trousers.

Fuck me shoes. Damn. Any woman who wore those shoes had a streak of the unexpected. He wondered what her underwear looked like. Something delicate and lovely?

Suddenly interested in the case, Sean sat up, flipping through the file looking for any pertinent information. It was well put together, filled with carefully thought out analysis. It almost certainly hadn't come from that prick Lincoln. "Matt Wright runs a temp agency?"

Lincoln was guzzling down coffee. It gave Gene a chance to respond. "Yes, one of the largest in Texas. His base is in Fort Worth, but his people work all over the state, as well as Louisiana and Arkansas. A couple of years back, he started brokering deals with temp agencies in India for information technology services. He's branched out to include everything from temporary white collar workers to janitorial services. He's been very successful."

"Who is this?" Sean slid the photo of the woman in stilettos Gene's way.

A smile tugged at Gene's thin lips. He pointed to the woman in question. "Grace Hawthorne, Matt Wright's admin. She's worked for him for six years."

"Nice shoes." Liam's accent sounded flat and Midwestern.

Sean stared at him for a moment. Liam wouldn't want to give the U.S. government a damn thing to tie him back to Ireland. Only a select group of people got to hear his native lilt.

Liam wrinkled his nose, obviously dismissing the photo. "The rest of her is a bit boring, but it looks like she's got nice breasts. Is anybody going to have to pork the assistant? She's older than my usual."

"Asshole." Sean stopped just short of punching him. The Irishman wouldn't know a real woman if she slapped him across the face, and given his predilections, that had probably happened numerous times. Sean enjoyed Liam's company, but he was a jerk when it came to women. If a woman wasn't barely eighteen and serving hot wings in shorts that rode up her ass, she wasn't really female to Liam. Sean far preferred women over girls. If Liam wasn't eager to take Grace to bed, Sean would be more than happy to.

There was a lot of boring back and forth. He ignored it and stared at the picture. Later, he would read Grace's bio, all the little numbers, facts, and dates that made up her life, yet told him nothing about who she was as a woman. He wished there was a picture of her without the sunglasses. He'd like to know what color her eyes were. Green, he bet, or hazel. Her skin looked very fair, almost luminous. She'd pulled her darkish hair back in a pony tail. In the picture, her style appeared somewhat nondescript, just like everything about the woman. *Except those shoes.*

"You suspect that Wright is laundering money for his brother's group?" Liam's question brought Sean out of his thoughts and reminded him there was a job at hand. He flipped the file closed.

"Suspect is all they can do," Ian murmured. "Otherwise they wouldn't be here." He turned his icy blue eyes to the elephant in the room. "And what does the CIA want with Mr. Patrick Wright?"

Lincoln gasped, but managed to hold on to his coffee cup. Sean turned his attention blatantly to the "lowly assistant" in the expensive shoes. Now that Sean really looked at him, he noticed the man's watch was a Rolex. Another tell.

The man in question flushed deeply. "I should have changed my shoes."

"It wouldn't have mattered. You look like a spook." Ian spit the words, as if that was the worst thing a person could be.

"He's not a spook." Liam yawned as though the entire conversation bored him. "He's a paper pusher."

The man in question sighed and leaned forward. "Look, you guys are all ex-military or ex-agency. You know the drill. You've worked for us in a quiet capacity before. Feel free to refer to me as Mr. Black."

"Original." Sean had known several Mr. Blacks over the course of his military career, and he'd learned not to trust a single one. The CIA always protected the identities of its agents, even from the military personnel who did their dirty work.

This particular Mr. Black seemed unfazed by Sean's disdain.

"I'll leave a cell phone number in case you need to contact me. I'm not officially here, and if anyone asks, I'll disavow any and all knowledge of this operation."

"Yeah, you types are good at that." Sean heard the bitterness in his own voice. He knew what it felt like to have his own CO stand in front of a military judge and flatly lie about the men he was charged to lead.

The spook ignored him. "The CIA is interested in certain connections Patrick Wright potentially made on a trip to Chile a few years back."

"Drug cartels?" Liam asked. He seemed much more interested now.

"Jihadist groups. They're popping up all over South America, and it seems they have mutual interests with our homegrown terrorists. I can't prove anything, but I believe Wright is potentially acting as a go-between to facilitate meetings between the South American groups and the Earth League."

"That's a pretty big leap," Ian frowned as he studied the man in front of him.

Mr. Black sighed and seemed a little weary. "You're not the only one who thinks that. No one believes me. Until I have concrete proof, I can't do anything. Because my proof is more than likely here on American soil…"

Sean knew this drill well. "You need someone without the strictures of the Agency. Why not the FBI?"

"And deal with all the interagency crap? No. Mr. Lincoln is amenable to bankrolling this whole op if it gets the Earth League off his back."

Sean chuckled. "You get the proof you need for a much wider op, and he gets to continue to rape the planet without interference."

"Fuck you." Lincoln looked like he was going to come over the top of the table.

"Sir." Gene tried to contain his boss.

"I wouldn't if I were you, Lincoln." The spook's voice seemed to make the CEO think twice. "That man you're about to assault is Sean Taggart. He's a former Green Beret. His brother is the gentleman at the end of the table. You read the file on both of them.

I doubt he would kill you here, though you might wish he had."

The CEO sat back, the arrogance on his face fading for the moment. "I just want you to catch the bastard."

Ian's fingers steepled as they often did when he was thinking. "I can't promise you anything, Mr. Lincoln, but if Matthew Wright is involved with his brother's activities, we'll do our best to bring them both down."

* * * *

Two hours later, Sean sat looking at the file.

"I'm sending you in, Sean." Ian stood over his desk, his shadow long, but Sean was used to being in his big brother's shadow. Though he was thirty-two years old, six foot three, and weighed two hundred twenty pounds, everyone on the team still called him Little Tag. Ian was Big Tag.

Sean tapped the photo he'd been staring at for an hour. Something about the set of her mouth fascinated him. He'd learned she was forty and a widow. She'd raised two boys and seemed to have no life outside her family and her job. According to the file, some of her co-workers whispered that she was sleeping with her boss. "She's the key, you know."

Ian leaned his big body over the desk. "Of course she is. You get to her, you find out everything about the place. An admin knows everything about her boss. It's why I don't have one."

Something made him hesitate. She looked almost sad in the photo. "Maybe you should send in Jake and Adam. Their pretend gay act always wins the women's trust."

Ian burst into a rare fit of laughter. "I'll be sure to let them know you appreciate their undercover efforts. As it happens, Jake and Adam will be your backup. If you can't manage to get close to the woman, perhaps they can. A lot of women like to be in between those two."

"I'll handle it." No way was he letting those two get close to Grace. There was something about her. "I'll get what you need." *Let that be it. Walk away now, big brother.*

"You need to think about dating." Ian's voice grated like broken glass underfoot.

"Fuck me." Sean's head hit the top of his desk.

"Yes, that would be the point. It's been a year since you last took a sub."

Sean groaned. "Would it work if I told you this is absolutely none of your business?"

Ian shrugged. "Probably not. I just don't understand. Rona was a lovely sub."

Rona had been a clingy, whiny painslut who didn't want the heavy burden of anything so difficult as choosing her own clothes for the day, much less having an actual job or ambitions. "I'm not like you, Ian. I don't want a slave."

"You don't want the responsibility." Coming from Ian, it sounded like an accusation.

Sean felt his eyes narrow. His brother just didn't understand. Not everyone was as utterly hard-core as Ian. "I love taking care of a woman, you know that. I'm just not attracted to the clingy ones who need me to do everything for them. I want her to need me, but not need me for everything, know what I mean? I want a smart, independent woman who just happens to enjoy submitting to me sexually. Is that too much to ask?"

There was a snort, and then his brother's sarcasm came spilling out. "It can be your eHarmony ad, bro. Wanted: smart, independent woman to play at D/s. Must like handcuffs, spankings, and anal sex."

Sean fought the urge to growl. "Don't make fun of me. At least I haven't run through every submissive at the club."

Ian's easy shrug let Sean know he wasn't getting to him. "Some of them twice. Unlike you, I have realistic expectations about how a relationship is going to go. It's best to keep things short and sweet, with a contract in place, so everyone knows how to behave."

Yes, Ian would think that way. Of course, he hadn't always thought like that. Ian had been engaged once. No one talked about Holly anymore, not if they wanted to keep their head attached to their body. "Just stay out of my love life."

"As you don't seem to have one, I think that will be easy." Ian stood up. His blue eyes were not unkind as they looked at Sean.

"I'm going to head out to the club. I'm meeting the rest of the team there. Why don't you come with us? You don't need to start this tonight. Your meeting with Wright won't be for another few weeks or so. You'll be in deep cover. I talked to a friend in Chicago, and you're all set. You're going in as a man negotiating a contract for labor services. You'll need to work at Kelvin Incorporated for a few weeks to make it look good."

Yes, a couple of weeks as a corporate drone sounded very exciting. He should go to the club with Ian. He could pick up a sub for the night and spend a few hours forgetting the fact that the next several weeks would be dull as dirt. Of course, the last couple of years had been long, tedious jobs punctuated with the occasional person who tried to kill him. He was used to boredom. His hand found the file, and the words were out of his mouth before he could stop them. "No, I want to read over this."

Ian shrugged. "All right, little brother. Jake and Adam are heading to Fort Worth tomorrow. I've already gotten them interviews. Luckily, Wright is always looking for sales staff. Liam is going down to do recon and set up a little base of operations. They'll make contact when you get there. We can go over it tomorrow. Don't stay here all night."

Sean huffed to let his brother know he didn't need the parenting. One by one his co-workers came by and offered to keep him company. They said goodnight when he turned them down. Sean smiled and went back to his research. She was the key. Grace Hawthorne would break the case; Grace with her sad mouth and those intriguing yellow shoes.

It was a long time before he left his desk.

Chapter Two

"Hello."

The deep masculine voice brought Grace's attention up from her work. She lifted her head up, and up, and up. *Wow*. The man was huge. She couldn't help but stare. He was dressed in an impeccably-cut dark suit. His snowy white dress shirt stood out against the black of the suit and emphasized the brilliant blue of his silk tie. His shoulders were so broad, she would bet he'd had the suit cut specifically for him. His shoulders tapered down to a lean waist and hips that flowed into legs that she bet were powerfully muscled. All of that she could handle, but then she got to his face.

His jaw was perfectly cut, as though someone had sculpted him from granite, chiseling away all the unneeded bits to leave him with a stark, masculine perfection. His blue eyes were icy, though not cold. As he stood looking down at her, he ran a big hand through his blond hair. It was slicked back, though some of it fell over his brow giving him a boyish charm to go with the utterly male sexuality he exuded. He shouldn't be in a suit. He should be wearing one of those helmets with horns on it, wielding a sword while he raided villages. He was a Viking god, and his lips quirked up faintly as she looked up at him. It emphasized the unbearably cute cleft in his chin.

"Hi." It was all that would come out of her mouth. Several other greetings leapt to mind. Please take me roughly was one of them. She decided a simple hello might be the best way to go. She'd been reading far too many romances. She needed to cool down.

"Hello." The Viking god had a slow, Southern accent. "I have a lunch appointment with Mr. Wright."

Grace laughed. She couldn't help it. Grace had learned long ago that she wasn't very good at social deception. She glanced down at her calendar. "Of course you do. You must be Sean Johansson. I'll let Mr. Wright know you're here."

His hand shot out as she was reaching for the phone. A grin played on his unbelievably sensual lips. Men shouldn't have lips like that. "I have to know. What's so funny? Is the suit bad? I admit I can have terrible taste in clothing. I usually wear jeans and T-shirts. My mother once accused me of buying all my clothes at concerts."

She shook her head and tried not to think about how her skin tingled where he'd touched her. She sighed. Men were needy creatures. She decided to treat the Viking god like she did every other male in her life, with an amused nonchalance. "The suit is more than fine, and I think you know that. Your eyes appear to function, Mr. Johansson. Tell me, did the girls at reception faint when you walked in?"

A slight flush stained his high cheekbones. "I don't know what you're talking about. I was perfectly nice to them."

"I bet you're nice to all the girls." She winked as she said it. It was a little fun flirtation. It livened up her day. She'd discovered men liked to flirt with a woman who had absolutely no expectations of them.

His expression took a serious turn. Those light blue eyes pinned her, and for the briefest of moments, Grace felt like a rabbit in the company of a hungry wolf. "I prefer women."

She swallowed once and then was saved by the door to her boss's office opening suddenly. The sound cracked through the air. Grace hadn't realized just how quiet it had been before. Evan Parnell strode out of the office, his boots making angry contact with the hardwood floors. Matthew Wright followed him.

"Damn it. We need to talk about this." Matt's voice held an

edge of desperation.

Evan stopped and held out a hand as though to stop Matt from speaking. Matt's mouth closed. Grace could feel the tension between the men. She got out of her chair and started to walk toward them, hoping to calm the situation, but Sean Johansson was suddenly in her way. His big body was a wall between her and the arguing men. He'd moved fast. One minute he was in front of the desk, and then next he was a bulwark between her and whatever he apparently feared was about to happen. Grace tried to push her way around him. He turned to her, and the command was there, written plainly on his handsome face.

Stay where you are.

Grace thought briefly about arguing. Johansson's eyes narrowed, and she backed down. She tried not to think about what the dominant look on his face did to her. Yep, she was going to stop reading romances. She was seeing things that weren't there. Johansson was simply a gentleman who didn't want to see her get hurt.

Evan's muddy brown eyes swept across the room. Grace had never understood why Matt had hired Parnell in the first place. He was rude, difficult to deal with, and far too intense for Grace's tastes. His face was always flat, as though the world was never enough for him, and he found not an ounce of joy in it.

"We'll talk about it later. But I mean to have my way in this, Mr. Wright. You won't like the consequences of backing out of our deal." Parnell's voice was dark, like molasses running over concrete. He turned to Grace. "Grace, I'll take my check now."

She looked to her boss. "But…"

"Just get the check, Grace." Matt's entire body was tight.

She wanted to argue that Parnell wasn't due a check until the fifteenth, but something about her boss's body language sent her to the locked drawer of her desk. The minute she sat down, the Viking eased up. He leaned casually against the side of her desk.

While Grace wrote out the check, Matt seemed to figure out that they weren't alone in his elegant office. He straightened his suit as he checked out Sean Johansson.

"I'm sorry. Is Grace helping you?"

Parnell moved to the door, waiting. He didn't look back, merely stood there, his arms crossed over his chest. He was a thin man, but strong. He wasn't dressed in anything like a suit, but that didn't surprise Grace. He always showed up in jeans, a flannel shirt, and a trucker hat. She supposed that was why he had to use Wright Temps to contract his janitorial services. He wasn't a very professional man.

"Grace has been very helpful." The Viking's tone was smooth and calming. Grace knew it was a trick of her own libido, but she thought she could hear approval in his voice.

Grace tore the check out of the ledger. She stood up. "Matt, this is Sean Johansson. He's your lunch appointment."

Matt shook his head as though clearing it. His hand shot out toward the big Viking. "Of course. Please forgive me. You're with Kelvin, right?"

"I am. I'm here to get the best deal possible out of you."

Grace moved to get around Mr. Johansson. He looked down at her and, without asking, took the check out of her hand. He crossed the office in two strides. Parnell's eyebrows arched, but he took the check. He wasted no time in leaving the office.

Johansson turned and smiled at Matt. "Now, I seem to remember we had a lunch appointment. I made reservations at Blue Moon. I find negotiations go so much smoother with a good margarita, don't you?"

Matt let out a long breath, the previous tension leaving his body, and in its place was the charming man Grace knew so well. "Absolutely. I can tell we're going to get along, Mr. Johansson."

"Sean, please."

"Of course, and I'm Matt. We should probably be on a first name basis since we'll be calling each other bastard and asshole by the end of the month."

Sean threw back his head. His booming laugh did things to Grace's insides. She was deeply surprised because she was pretty sure she'd buried the sensual parts of her with her husband. She turned away from the sight of Sean. He was just a kid. He looked to be roughly thirty years old. He was only a few years older than her sons.

"Come on into my office, Sean. We can talk for a minute before we get to those margaritas." Matt held open the door, and the Viking walked through. Grace felt the absence of his presence immediately. Matt's well-coiffed head poked back out. He grinned at her. "Gracie, can you clear the rest of my appointments, babe?"

"Of course." She glanced down at the calendar she kept on her desk. There was only one appointment, and she could foist that off on a manager or take it herself. Matt gave her a thumbs up and disappeared.

Grace laughed. It was utterly ridiculous, but she could breathe again. She quickly called one of the more competent managers. He was more than happy to take the meeting for Matt. It would be nice to have a quiet office for the afternoon. She thought of all the things she could catch up on. There were any number of projects she need to work on, so why did she find herself sitting at her desk, staring into space, listening for the sound of Sean Johansson's voice?

"Holy crap, Gracie, did you see that?"

Grace looked up into her best friend's face. Kayla Green's mouth was hanging open. Grace was just waiting for the drool to start. There was no question in Grace's mind that Kayla was talking about Sean Johansson. Grace shushed her. "He's in Matt's office."

"Are you serious? Can I go in?"

"No. Back down, girl. He's a client. You can't jump the clients."

Kayla set her hip against the desk and a saucy smile covered her sweet face. "I bet that one is used to getting jumped. I swear, I thought I was dreaming when he walked in, Grace. He looks like a...I don't know what he looks like, but that man is sex on a stick."

"A Viking." The words were out of her mouth before she could call them back.

Kayla's brown eyes went wide. "Oh my god, has your libido come back online? Hallelujah! Now, I think the Viking is a little much to start with, but I have some men in mind."

"Whoa! Don't you start on that." If she didn't put a stop to it, Kayla would have her own version of speed dating going in under five minutes. She would be fielding calls about dates from everyone from Kayla's deadbeat brother to the UPS guy. Kayla collected single men's numbers like others collected bobblehead dolls or stamps. "I'm old, not blind, Kay. I'd have to be blind not to notice that young man."

"He isn't that young, Grace. And you aren't old. Forty isn't old."

"Forty with two kids in college sure as hell feels old. I doubt that puppy in there has even contemplated having kids. He's a boy."

Kayla shook her head. "You were wrong about being blind. That was a man if I ever saw one." Kayla looked like she wanted to argue further, but simply sighed. "Fine. I get it. You're willing to read about dirty, nasty sex, but you won't let yourself have some. One of these days you're going to wake up and realize that life has passed you by. I'll be right by your side telling you I told you so."

"Gee, that sounds lovely, Kay." And possibly prophetic.

"If the boss is busy, what do you say we go to the salad bar for lunch and then get our toes done?"

Grace smiled up at her friend, eager to accept the invitation.

"I'm afraid the pedicure is going to have to wait, ladies." Sean Johansson stood in the doorway, his big body filling the space to bursting. He leaned negligently against the wall, and Grace had the sudden worry that he'd heard way too much of their conversation. "Grace is going to join us for lunch."

"I am?" The words croaked out of her throat.

His smile was steady and sure. "You are."

Sean moved out of the way as Matt walked up behind him.

"Come on, Grace. Sean here thinks we need your brilliant brain to help us poor males out." He was already pulling off his tie. If this was anything like Matt's other lunchtime meetings, he wouldn't come back to the office. Grace really hoped he would be sober at the end of the day. "And Gracie, bring something along to take notes."

Matt was out the door and waiting by the elevator before Grace could grab her purse.

Sean Johansson waited patiently by her desk. His hand came out gallantly to take the large briefcase she carried just about everywhere. He briefly introduced himself to Kayla, and then his hand came out again to help Grace from her chair. His big hand enveloped her small one as he steadied her. He held her hand for a second or two longer than needed. When he let go, Grace felt the loss of his warmth. He offered her his arm as though they were a lord and lady from another time.

"Shall we?"

No. No. They really shouldn't. It was a bad idea. Grace shook it off. He was a businessman looking for a good deal. She was the boss's admin. Every halfway decent corporate executive knew the admin was the lifeline to the boss. Grace plastered a bright smile on her face and gave Kay a wink. She could flirt just as well as Sean Johansson could.

"I believe I could use a margarita, Mr. Johansson."

"It's Sean, Grace. I've heard this place has the best in North Texas. The drinks better be good because I would hate to disappoint you." He started to lead her out. "And Grace, nice shoes."

She looked down at the purple peep toes she'd selected this morning. They were the only color in her outfit. She was wearing a black skirt and gray top. The purple seemed to give her a little personality. Now she wondered what those purple, four-inch heels would look like propped on Sean Johansson's shoulders.

She was definitely going to need that margarita.

* * * *

Evan Parnell strode outside the building. He looked up and down the sidewalk and then carefully planted himself behind a large bush. He pulled out a cigarette, just another guy on a smoke break in a city that didn't let a man's vice inside its sanctified walls. He watched as the Mercedes pulled out of the parking lot with three occupants inside.

Damn it, he didn't like this. They were so close, and Matt had to try to reel in some asshole corporate account? Matt should be concentrating on the goddamn Bryson Building. That was where they would score. Everything else was a distraction.

And distractions cost lives. Of course, they could be helpful on occasion. He chuckled as he thought about the last distraction he'd created. He'd enjoyed his brief time as an "ecoterrorist." It had put the Agency off him and gotten him a small army of devoted "soldiers." He had a couple of true believers, and they made excellent pawns. All he had to do was start a couple of fires, ruin some equipment, and suddenly no one was worried about his real activities.

He let his eyes drift across the skyline. He could see the Bryson Building. It was a large, nondescript building like most of the structures that made up Fort Worth's skyline. It was absolutely perfect because it housed the Texas Natural Gas Corporation. Not that he actually gave a damn about TNG, but it was the perfect cover. He couldn't see the west side. It was in a small office on the west side of the building that he would make his final, biggest score, and then he could retire.

In another week or so, he would be in Southeast Asia soaking up the sun and fucking as many girls as his dick could handle. Well, he would be if his brother didn't screw everything up.

Evan took a long drag off his cigarette. He wasn't looking forward to another round of plastic surgery, but it would be necessary. Evan Parnell would have to disappear the same way Patrick Wright had, and this time he wouldn't have Agency resources. They'd trained him well. Maybe if they'd paid him as well as they had trained him, he wouldn't have gone rogue.

He thought about the check in his pocket. Grace Hawthorne might not know it, but she'd been laundering his ill-gotten gains for years. She knew an awful lot about his banking practices. If his ex-handler ever caught up to him, she was a weak link. If Eli Nelson found him, he was screwed, and what Grace knew or didn't know wouldn't matter. Still, maybe he should think about taking her out. An accident. Yes, that could be arranged. He pulled out his cell and quickly called one of his loyal soldiers.

Grace taken care of, Evan tossed the cigarette aside, not bothering to put it out. He didn't care. He had a check to cash.

* * * *

Sean stared at Grace over the empty plates. She was flirting with the waiter. The young idiot was new to his job and had fumbled his way through taking their orders until Grace had turned her vibrant hazel eyes on him and starting talking to him in that ridiculously sexy twang of hers. He'd almost immediately calmed down, and the rest of the meal had been smooth sailing.

She was something else. The photos of her didn't come close to doing the woman justice. In the photos, he'd seen a woman approaching middle age. The clothes she'd worn had made her seem a bit plump, and the expression on her face had been a little sad. The pictures didn't show how her skin glowed in the late afternoon light. Her hair, which had seemed a flat brown before, was actually more red than anything else. It was pulled back in a ponytail, but Sean was sure it would reach far past her shoulders when he took it down. Little tendrils, waves of auburn, kept escaping from the brutal captivity of the scrunchie to frame her face. He was fascinated with her throaty laugh. When Grace Hawthorne smiled, she could light up a room.

Sean found himself slightly jealous of the attention she was fawning on the waiter until he realized she didn't mean a thing by it. Years of training as a Dom had taught him to read a woman's every nuance. She viewed the waiter almost as a little boy she was being kind to. There was nothing truly sexy about the way she flirted with the server. She wasn't thinking about finding a quiet place and tangling herself around the kid. She wasn't considering wrapping that gloriously glossed mouth around the kid's cock to see how fast she could make him come. She certainly wasn't wondering how to get the damn waiter's mouth to close over her wet pussy.

Sean was thinking about all of those things, although he'd placed himself as Grace's partner instead of the waiter, and it was making it very hard to concentrate. The way Grace smiled at the waiter and patted his hand put Sean at ease. Then set him on edge when he figured out she viewed him the exact same way.

He needed to fix that little problem and damn soon.

"You need to think about moving a good portion of your project development to Chile."

Matt Wright's declaration had Sean's mind wrestling control back from his cock. It reminded him he had a job to do. "Chile? I hadn't considered it. I thought most IT offshoring went to India these days."

Wright's hand came out in a negligent gesture. It was sloppy, and his speech was becoming slurred. "It does, but South America is trying to get into the game. There are a lot of highly-educated South Americans looking for good work. Many of the people at the location I'm thinking of actually have degrees in programming from American colleges. I can give you the numbers and backgrounds, of course."

Grace dutifully made the note, but Sean hadn't missed the slight tightening of her jaw when her boss had introduced the topic. She had misgivings about the South American projects. He would remember to question her about it later. She wouldn't say anything in the middle of a meeting, he guessed. She seemed very loyal. Sean wondered if her loyalty would transfer from her boss to her lover.

Sean played hard to get. He needed to be a bit elusive to draw out these negotiations. "I don't know. We've been pretty happy with the Indian offices."

Wright waved a disdainful hand and took another drag off his drink. He was halfway to stone drunk. "I can cut your labor costs by fifteen percent and keep your workers in the same time zone."

Sean nodded and pretended to consider it. It was interesting that Wright was trying to sell him on the idea of Chile. According to his research, Wright's agency had brokered several deals to offshore IT departments to India. Chile had only come up in the last year. "I'd like to see those numbers."

Sean's hand curled around the margarita he'd been nursing for an hour. He noticed that Grace had finished her raspberry swirl, but politely declined a second. Wright began to extol the virtues of cheap South American labor, and Sean allowed himself a moment to ponder the problem of Grace.

He wasn't going to be able to keep his hands off her. He didn't see why he should bother. It was clear to him that she wasn't the boss's mistress. She behaved much more like his long-suffering wife than a mistress. Wright might depend on the lovely widow, but he wasn't sleeping with her. He was almost sure of it. Sean had detected the slightest hint of jealously from Wright when he'd led Grace to the elevator. It had been little more than a flaring of his eyes when Matt noticed the courtly way Sean was leading her. It was gone by the time they reached the lobby. Ever since, Wright had called her babe several times and taken the seat beside her in the booth as though it was his right, but he didn't touch her. Sean had been happy to slide into the booth across from the object of his study. It gave him the chance to really observe her.

He had many questions for Grace, but they would have to wait until he had her in a much more intimate setting. He would give it a day, and then invite her to dinner with him tomorrow. He'd watched the pleasure she'd taken in her food and the sweet drink she'd ordered. She'd savored every morsel. Her eyes had roamed the large platter of decadent desserts, but finally she'd said no. It was clear to Sean that she hadn't wanted to say no. She was most likely giving in to the pressures of social constraints. She probably thought she needed to diet.

If they had been alone, Sean would have ordered the chocolate cake and fed her himself. He would have convinced her that taking pleasure in the dessert would please him. He would have watched the way her tongue came out to taste the bittersweet frosting before enveloping the cake in her mouth. Then he would kiss her, long and slow, the sweetness transferring from her mouth to his.

Better yet, he would simply cook everything for her, each course another level of his seduction.

He answered Wright when the man seemed to require Sean's participation, but his eyes rarely left Grace. He would be good for her. She was very lonely. She needed someone to shake her up a little. Sean would be good to her in and out of bed. When the time came, he would gracefully leave her. He would keep it light and fun. She wouldn't regret sleeping with him.

Grace smiled at him as the waiter took the check. Sean couldn't help the little hitch in his breath.

It was almost four when he helped Grace up from her seat. Matt stumbled a little. They made it to the car and stuffed Matt in the back. Grace tried to get in with him, but Sean held the passenger door open. After the barest of hesitation, she slid in, and he shut the door.

"I guess I'll drive him home." She looked out the window as they drove back toward downtown from the Stockyards.

"You could leave him in the lobby." It was an eminently logical solution to Sean's mind. Matt Wright had been all business at the start of the meal, but he'd ordered drink after drink. It was completely unprofessional.

"I'd just have to deal with him in the morning." She sighed, and he sensed a deep tiredness in her. She turned her hazel eyes on him. "He's a good man."

Sean doubted that. "I'm sure he is. Is he a good boss?"

Now there was no hesitation. "He's a great boss. He was the only one willing to take a chance on me. My husband died a few years back. I hadn't had a job the whole time we were married. The insurance paid for a lot, but I still needed to go to work. Matt was my thirty-first interview."

"That must have been a relief." It explained her loyalty to the idiot.

"You have no idea." She glanced into the backseat. Matt's head was back. "He can't handle his liquor. It's the bane of my existence. I keep hoping he'll get married, and his wife can deal with him when he's drunk."

"Just give me his address, and I'll make sure he gets home." It would serve a dual purpose. He could help out Grace and potentially search the bastard's house.

She shook her head vigorously. "No, I'll do it. I appreciate the offer, but it's my responsibility. Maybe next time, don't let him keep ordering drinks. We could have moved the meeting back to the office two hours ago."

He gave her a rueful smile. "I promise to give that great consideration. I have to say, though, that it tends to slide the scale in my favor."

"Not really. He never signs anything until he's sober. Trust me, I've been around him long enough to know not to ask him for a raise after a couple of martinis."

Sean pulled the borrowed Benz into the parking lot. He found a space a row over from Grace's little Honda hybrid. Of course, he didn't let her know he knew which one she owned. She pointed out her car and started herding Matt toward it.

"You won't regret working with us." Matt's words were firm

even as he wobbled on his feet a bit. He leaned heavily into Grace, his arm winding around her waist. "You're so good to me, Gracie. I won't let anything happen to you."

Matt slumped forward into her passenger seat. Grace closed the door, and a wan smile crossed her lips. "He really is a good man. Don't let this affect your opinion of him. He's alone in the world. He lost his parents and then his brother."

Sean allowed his eyes to go soft and sympathetic. So Matt had told her his brother was dead? "Really? He's young to have lost a brother."

"His brother was the only family he had left, and from what I can tell, they weren't very close. Matt told me his brother, Patrick, travelled a lot. He was killed in Europe. Anyway, it affected Matt." Grace opened her trunk and placed her briefcase inside. She slammed it shut and awkwardly put her hand out. "It was nice to meet you. Thank you for lunch and everything."

A thousand questions perched on the tip of his tongue, but he decided to play it cool. He would only lose her if he pushed her too fast. He took her hand in between both of his. He stood very close so she had to look up. "I enjoyed it, Grace."

Her voice was a little bit breathless as she stared up at him. It wasn't anything like the sure, flirty voice she'd been using before. "I did, too. And I'll get those numbers ready for you. Anything you need, just give me a call."

"I promise." He intended to call her a lot.

Sean let go of her hand. She started to walk around him to enter her car when a motorcycle roared through the parking lot. It came out of nowhere, a bullet on a path to destruction. The loud rev of the engine blasted through the quiet late afternoon. The scene played out in his mind like a little movie. The motorcycle was on a direct, unwavering path. It would hit Grace, and her body would strike the concrete at an alarming rate. Listening only to his instincts, Sean launched himself at Grace, placing them in a roll that threw them into the car parked beside her Honda. Grace didn't fight him. Her arms wound around his chest. She was soft and compliant against him. It made it very easy to maneuver her the way he wanted to go. He twisted as hard as he could so his back took the brunt of the impact.

The motorcycle sped off without stopping, an angry insect pissed off that it hadn't stung someone.

Sean turned to try to get the license plate number, but Grace's voice stopped him in his tracks. Her hands were on his chest, her fingers like little butterflies caressing him through his shirt.

"Thank you, Sir."

Everything inside him stilled at that one word. *Sir*. It wasn't polite. It wasn't the kind moniker one placed on a stranger. This "Sir" was breathy and held a singular promise. It was the habit of a submissive to honor her dominant partner. Every ounce of blood in Sean's body rushed straight to his cock.

Grace laughed. It seemed to break the spell. "What a jerk. He didn't even stop to see if we were okay. Thanks again." Grace pulled out of his arms before Sean could protest. Her alabaster skin was flushed a vibrant red as she quickly got into the Honda and pulled out of the space.

Sean was left with an aching hard-on and the knowledge that the next few weeks were going to be anything but dull.

Chapter Three

Three hours later, Sean slid into a booth at the back of the dive bar where he was set to meet Adam and Jake. He selected a booth at the back corner that gave him a view of the room. Brewski's was just the kind of crap bar one would expect in the suburbs, but then he wanted to drive by Grace Hawthorne's house later tonight. He'd already driven past Matthew Wright's. It always paid to know the lay of the land.

He thanked the waitress who brought him a longneck. He didn't dare order a Scotch. He doubted what they would bring him here would even vaguely resemble Scotch, though he passed a glance over the menu. He wondered what Grace was doing. He wondered who Grace was doing and if she'd had her gorgeous body tied up while they were doing it.

He didn't like the jealous feeling in the pit of his stomach. Grace was a sub. He knew it. She was someone's submissive. He doubted it was Wright. The man wasn't a Dom. Sean fully intended to find out who owned Grace's loyalty. It couldn't possibly be too serious. She didn't wear a collar, not even a small necklace to signify that she belonged to someone. No Dom worth his whip would let a sweet subbie like Grace walk around completely uncollared.

The door opened and Jake and Adam walked in, their entrance punctuated with a blast of wretchedly hot air. The September night hadn't cooled off a bit.

But then neither had Sean.

Adam immediately walked to the bar and started to flirt with the woman there. Jacob Dean's razor-focused stare found Sean. He moved through the crowded bar with the grace of a predator. Those dark eyes scanned the bar for any potential threats before he slid into the booth. Sean was surprised at how nice it was to see his former Army buddies. They had been on assignment and out of the office for much of the last year.

"Hey, Sarge. Good to see you again. I sent our report directly to your e-mail, coded, of course, sir." Despite the fact that they had left the Green Berets years before, Jake had never gotten out of the habit of deferring to him. Sean had been Jake's warrant officer in their Special Forces team. Jake had been the intelligence and operations officer, while Adam had been the sergeant in charge of communications. "How did the meeting with Wright go?"

Adam Miles had two beers in his hand when he sat down beside Jake. He handed one to his partner and took a long swallow of the other. Adam was a different story. He had never shown much respect in the first place. He certainly didn't bother to now. "Who gives a fuck about Wright? Tell me how the meeting with our luscious little Grace went."

The longneck hit the table with more force than Sean meant to use. "Don't play your games with Grace." The thought of Grace with Jake and Adam made his hand itch to beat the shit out of his two closest friends. "She better think you're gay."

Jake laughed. "Oh, she does. But then they usually do."

"Right up to the point they find themselves in between us, howling as we show them the pleasures of double penetration." Adam held up his beer in a mock toast. His lips spread in a decadent grin. "You would be surprised how well the gay thing works, man. Women open up when they think you're gay. They fall a little in love. Sure enough, the next thing we hear is something about how she wishes we weren't gay and bam, wish fulfilled."

"Sometimes we don't even need to play the gay card. We only do that undercover. Sometimes honesty works. There are women out there who like to be shared. Lots of them. That little lieutenant sure liked it." There was a warm affection in Jake's brown eyes as he obviously remembered the good time.

Sean had to roll his eyes. "I can't believe the two of you joke about that. What am I saying? You joke about everything. Most people wouldn't joke about the incident that got them dishonorably discharged."

Adam shrugged. "I thought we were very honorable. She came at least four times before we went off."

"The general wasn't happy when he walked in on us. I think he'd been planning to make a move on her himself. Asshole." Jake sighed. "Anyway, I like this job better. Big Tag doesn't care what we do in the bedroom, and he's better armed than the US Army."

Big Tag didn't have any right to question other people's kinks. He had enough of his own. Of course, so did Sean. He was just going to make certain Grace Hawthorne indulged in his kinks, not the ménage boys'. "Have you made contact with Grace?"

Sean didn't like the grin that crossed Adam's face. There was far too much intimate knowledge in it. "While you've been in the Windy City, we've been here. We've been her happy hour buddies for the last several weeks. She apparently likes to take new employees under her wing, show them the ropes. She quickly decided that Jake and I were of a homosexual bent and introduced us."

"I'm playing hard to get." Jake said, taking a drag off the longneck.

"As if. We flipped a coin, and I have to be the softie this time. I hate that, although it seems to work with Grace. Anyway, she's very happy with her matchmaking. This last weekend, she invited us out to her place for dinner. She made a heavenly lasagna. It wasn't as good as yours, of course, but I was more than willing to spend an extra hour or two in the gym to work it off. Of course, I would have preferred a different workout."

Sean leaned over. He hoped his face was as intimidating as he felt.

Jake put a hand between them. "Stop it, Adam. He's got it bad, and you know why. She's a sweetheart." Sean sat back. "And he hasn't gotten laid in a long time."

"Hey." What was up with everyone commenting on his love life, or lack thereof? It was starting to get annoying. "This is a job, and I think I'll fare better with Grace than the two of you."

Adam ran his free hand through his curly brown and gold hair. "What makes you think that? We can be very charming when we want to be. We've been pretty good at getting close to her so far. You didn't receive a dinner invite yet, did you?"

"She's submissive." He was absolutely sure of it now. The way she'd clung to him when things got physical and that breathy little "Sir" sealed the deal. She might be intensely competent in her workplace, but she would submit in the bedroom. She would be soft and sweet and utterly obedient. She would need it. Sean took a long drink. The beer sucked, but he needed the cold. Just thinking about being the one Grace submitted to was making him hot as hell. "She's either been in a D/s relationship before, or she's thought about it."

Jake's brown eyes widened at the thought. "With Wright?"

"Hell, no." Sean couldn't stand the thought of that bastard touching her. The man obviously had no control. Sean couldn't think of a worse trait in a Dom. He didn't care what Grace said. Her boss was in this mess up to his neck, and the sooner Sean brought him in, the better for Grace. She would be out of a job, but Sean already had plans for that eventuality. He was sure he could find something for her to do at McKay/Taggart. That way, she would be close in case he wanted to continue the relationship. "Maybe it was her husband. She's very sure of herself. She has a self-possession that only comes from being very well loved. It's intensely attractive. I suppose she could just be naturally submissive. But there was something about the way she called me 'Sir' that makes me think she knows her way around D/s."

Jake sent Adam a long look that let Sean know something was up. Adam shook his head, but Sean knew them way too well to let it go. "If you know something, spit it out."

Adam rolled his eyes. "Fine. But if this weren't a mission, I would tell you to go to hell."

Jake leaned forward. "We took a sneak peek at Grace's eReader while we were at her place."

"So, the lady reads. What does that have to do with anything?" Sean asked.

"The lady reads a lot about bondage," Jake said with a chuckle. "She seems to love romance novels about BDSM, with a heavy slant toward the D/s side. I don't know if I would peg her so much as a trained sub. She's more like a very curious lady. I took a look at her pictures when we were at her place. She's never wearing a collar."

Sean felt his groin tighten. A tourist? A sweet, curious, innocent little tourist. Now that was something to think about. If Grace was really interested, he could show her a thing or two. Maybe satisfying her curiosity was a way to get close to her. But Adam and Jake didn't need to know that. "Now tell me what you've learned. I know it's going to come as a shock to you, but we're here on a job, not to get laid." It was a reminder he could use, too.

"Says the man planning on getting laid," Adam shot back. "Fine. Jake and I are working in sales. It was easy enough to get in. It was also fairly easy to get access to the personnel files."

Jake sighed. His brown eyes heated up. "Tonya in HR. She thought we were gay, too."

They gave each other a quick fist bump before Adam continued. "We turned over the files we copied to Eve. She hasn't come up with anything yet, but she just got them yesterday. We've managed to keep our ears to the ground and come up with a few choice tidbits. First, Wright is a drunk."

Sean huffed. "Tell me something I don't know."

"Fine. He's completely dependent on Grace. She's involved with every meeting he has, except the ones with Evan Parnell. She never attends those. Parnell is a subcontractor who seems to have some sort of hold on Wright. Normally Wright specializes in white collar temps, but Parnell runs a small-time janitorial service. Three years ago, Wright brought him in as a way to get into the lower end of the temp services."

"Why would he want to do that?" It didn't make sense to Sean. "He has to make less money off janitorial services."

Jake took over. "His higher-end business took a dive when everyone started offshoring their IT departments. He started out offering IT services here in the States. It was too expensive and companies started looking for cheap labor. He's making a comeback. As you know, he's started acting as a broker for Indian and South American companies, but the lower-end work saw him through some lean times. The question is, why hasn't he cut Parnell loose? He doesn't need him anymore. The other employees aren't exactly sure what it is Parnell does. Gossip has it that Wright owes him some gambling debts."

"Do we have his financials?" Eve should have run those. Sean pulled out his Blackberry and looked for the pertinent e-mail.

"Don't bother, man." Jake sat back, relaxed. "His personal finances have done nothing but increase in the last few years. He has to be hiding something. Get on Grace's laptop. I bet everything you want to know is there."

Sean thought about the careful way Grace had packed up her laptop before leaving for lunch. She had made sure she had it with her when she left. It was important to her, and he would have to get very close to get on it. He thought back to what Jake had said about his lasagna. Cooking was a pastime he'd taken a lot of ribbing for, but maybe it would come in handy with Grace. Maybe it would allow him to get very close to her. "I'll download the hard drive the first chance I get. Now, tell me what I need to know to get into her bed as soon as possible."

A long sigh escaped from Adam's mouth. He exchanged a glance with his partner that let Sean know he'd thought this problem through. "If we have to give that sweet thing up, at least she's going to someone we like. Here's the skinny on little Grace…"

Sean leaned in. He didn't want to miss a word.

* * * *

Grace tried to concentrate on the eReader in front of her but found it utterly impossible. Normally, she would be eating up the tale of a lovely submissive and her Master, but tonight the words swam before her eyes like a playful school of fish. They swam this way and that and inevitably ended up looking like some scrumptious bit of Sean Johansson. First, it was his sensual lips. The bottom lip was slightly larger than the upper, giving his mouth a ridiculously sexy shape. Then she couldn't seem to get the sight of his backside out of her brain. His trousers hugged that ass in all the right places. She wondered what he looked like in tight jeans. And nothing else. She leaned back against the headboard. The eReader fell out of her hand. She didn't need a book. Her imagination was flying.

He would leave the top snap undone, exposing the place where his hip bones would be perfectly cut. She would love to run her fingers across that valley. There would be a line of light hair that travelled from his navel down, disappearing into his jeans like an arrow pointing the way to the Promised Land. The tent in his jeans would be impressive. His cock would be hard from the minute he looked at her.

She would get on her knees in front of him, naked with the singular exception of her heels. He would insist on the shoes, of course, and as he was the Master, he would get what he wanted. Her hands would slip inside his jeans, pushing them down over his hips, his cock bouncing free. He would order her to start at his bellybutton and lick her way down until she took the head of his cock just inside her mouth. His taste would be salty sweet on her tongue, and she would lap him up. He would want her to take him deep. It would be hard because there was so much of him, but she would try. She wouldn't complain or tell him it was impossible. She would just relax her throat and breathe through her nose. His masculine scent would be arousing in and of itself. He would taste so good. She would love the hard feel of his hand tangling in her hair as he fucked her mouth.

The shrill ring of the phone brought Grace out of her fantasy.

Grace sat up. She wasn't sure when she'd slumped down in the bed, probably the same time her hand found its way into her now awfully wet panties. Her finger had been circling her clitoris as she'd thought about sucking Sean Johansson dry. She glared at her phone. It had been a long time since she'd even wanted to masturbate. Shouldn't she be left to do that in peace?

Grace looked down at the caller ID and sighed. *Naturally*. He couldn't just sleep it off. "Hello, Matt. The aspirin is on the nightstand."

There was a shuffling noise. "Oh, thanks, Grace."

Grace could hear him fumbling, the cap to the aspirin obviously challenging him. If he kept this up, she would have to start pulling out the proper dose so he didn't have to do anything so complex as opening a bottle.

"Are you all right, Matt?" Despite the burden he had become in the last couple of years, she had a hard time forgetting that he had been the one to save her from working at a fast-food joint. He had also been the one to offer her health insurance. Matt had been the one to understand when she needed to work from home or take off a little early to attend her sons' baseball and football games. Matt had been an anchor after her husband had died. She took a deep breath and banished her annoyance. He had a lot of leeway with her. "How do you feel?"

"I feel like shit on several levels, Gracie." He sounded past sober now. He would be going into his "woe is me" phase. "Tell me, did I scare off Johansson?"

She thought about the way Sean had pulled her into his arms before the asshole on the motorcycle could take her head off. There had been no hesitancy to him. He'd been masterful in the way he saved her. It had done all kinds of things to her pink parts. "I think it would take a lot to scare Mr. Johansson."

She blushed when she thought of the instinctive way she'd called him "Sir." She'd been fantasizing about him all afternoon. She was damn glad he couldn't possibly know what that meant to her. He would probably run screaming from the building if he knew she viewed him as her dream Dom. Not that she'd ever actually had a Dom. Her husband had laughed when she said she wanted to try. She'd loved Pete, but he'd been very vanilla. He hadn't even liked her reading about BDSM.

There was a long pause on the other end of the line. "He was flirting with you pretty hard."

"I'm sure he flirts with everyone." She had reminded herself of that little truth over and over again. Sean was beyond hot. He was smoking and completely out of her league. Even if she'd been twenty years younger, that man would be playing a different ball game from her.

"He seemed very interested in you. He was the one who insisted on bringing you along." Matt's voice was a gravelly mess. There was no mistaking the hint of accusation in it.

Grace sat up a little straighter. She wasn't used to that tone coming out of his mouth. From day one, they'd had a strange relationship, she and Matt. They were friends, more partners than boss and admin. Now, he sounded like she'd done something improper. "Well, it's a good thing. I was able to drive you home. I don't think it would have made a very good impression on the client if he'd had to take you home. Your place is a mess. What happened to your housekeeper?"

"She quit. I haven't found a new one."

That explained it. Matt was a bit of a pig. She made a mental note to find him a new service. "It's a disaster area. It looks like a tornado hit your living room. And you need to do some laundry."

"It's not that bad. I know where everything is. Well, I know where all the important things are." He paused for a moment. "Son of a bitch. I think I've been robbed. Think Grace, was the door open or locked?"

"It was locked. I had to use my key. I didn't notice anything missing." There hadn't been. His monster TV had been in its place, along with his plethora of electronic equipment. His laptop had been in its bag with him. She hadn't checked the safe.

"Damn it." He sounded like he was running. "Damn it to hell. Where's the thumb drive? I had the thumb drive on me. They couldn't have taken it."

"Matt, calm down. Are you talking about the thumb drive that was in your pants pocket?" She'd found it when she'd helped him undress. It had fallen to the floor with a little bounce.

He breathed heavily into the phone, relief apparent in his tone. "Yes. The thumb drive that I brought home with me tonight. I put it in my pocket before we left for the restaurant."

"It fell on the floor. I picked it up."

"This is very important, Grace. Where did you put it?"

"I put it in my purse," Grace replied. "You have a habit of

losing thumb drives, then I have to find whatever important data you've managed to misplace. Do you know how long it took me to replace the payroll data the last time you lost it?"

Matt growled. "I don't give a shit about the payroll data. Just get over here and bring me that drive."

Grace looked at the phone like it was a snake that might bite her. He'd never spoken to her that way before.

"Grace?"

She put the phone back to her ear. "I'll be over as soon as I can change. I was ready for bed. It's almost midnight, after all."

"Gracie, I'm sorry. I shouldn't have yelled like that. It's been a trying day, but I shouldn't take it out on you. You're the only one on my side. Won't you please bring me that drive? It's got some info I need for the Kelvin bid. I thought I would stay up awhile and get some prep work done." He was all syrupy sweetness now. He sounded much more like the Matt she knew.

She took a firm hold on her temper. She didn't see what was so important it couldn't wait until the morning, but she was through arguing. "All right. I'll be there in a bit."

He agreed. Grace hung up her cell and rolled out of bed. Her nice night of dreaming of hunky executives was blown. She pulled the thumb drive out of her purse. "Stupid little thing. You're costing me sleep and some special quality time with Bob."

She needed to get a life, she thought as she pulled on jeans and wrestled the girls back into a bra. She'd named her vibrator. It was a sure sign that she'd taken a wrong turn. Of course, she also referred to her boobs as the girls, when they were obviously mature women, so she had to forgive herself for being fanciful. She pulled on a T-shirt. It occurred to her that he could still lose the damn thing. It made sense to download the data before she turned it over to him. She turned on her laptop and had whatever data it was that was so important tucked safely away before she left the house.

* * * *

Matt's street was very quiet as she turned into his driveway. Grace checked her rearview mirror and breathed a small sigh of relief. There wasn't anyone behind her now. For a while, she'd thought she was being followed, but given the time of night and how tired she was, she brushed off the feeling as paranoia.

Soft lights broke through the dark night. It looked like Matt had every light in the house on. The minute she opened the car door, Matt was striding out of the house. He was dressed in pajama bottoms and a T-shirt, his feet bare. His hair was wet from a recent shower. Even in the dim light, she could tell his eyes were red.

"Did you bring it?" His hand was out as he walked across the yard.

Grace practically threw the damn thing at him. "There's your thumb drive."

She turned to get back in her car. Matt's hand was on her shoulder in an instant.

"Come inside. Just for a minute. I want to talk to you about something, and it's best we don't do it at the office." His voice had softened, and the hand on her shoulder ran down her arm. "Please?"

Grace sighed and followed him inside. It seemed like the night was never going to end.

She walked through his entryway and into the living room. It looked as though he'd tried to straighten up the place. The pillows were back on the couch, and the papers that had been strewn all over were now in a neat pile on the coffee table. Matt shut the door behind them and gestured to Grace to sit down. She planted herself on his sofa and hoped this would be over soon.

"What is it, Matt?" Grace asked, trying to sound somewhat interested in what he had to say. She bit back a yawn. She needed her beauty sleep. Sean Johansson would be back in the morning. She didn't want to look like a hag. She wondered briefly if she had a low-cut blouse in that closet dungeon of hers.

"I need to talk to you about this Johansson guy."

He had Grace's full attention now.

"I don't want you to make a fool of yourself over him. You have to see he's not really interested in you. He's interested in getting a good contract." Matt stood over her like a father talking to a recalcitrant daughter. His mouth was a flat line as he regarded her.

"I know that." Grace felt her face go up in flames. She wished she didn't have such damn fair skin. She couldn't hide her reactions. She did know Sean wasn't really interested. She'd told herself the same thing. Hearing it put so bluntly, though, made her feel like an idiot for the little daydream she'd had before.

"Do you? You can't possibly believe he wants you. He's ten years younger than you and looks like he could have any woman who caught his eye. Don't try to tell me you didn't notice. You were practically drooling over the bastard the minute he walked in the door," Matt said on a low growl.

Humiliation washed over her. Grace stood up, blinking back tears. She was not going to cry. "It wasn't drool. It was a product of my advanced age. Now, if you're done, I'll take my elderly bones and ugly face and get the hell out of here."

"Damn it, I'm fucking this up." Matt's face fell. He reached out to grab her hand. "I'm sorry, Grace. I can't get anything right today. Number one, you're not old. You're forty, a year older than me."

She held herself stiffly. It was different for a man. She knew it. He knew it.

His words were soft and cajoling now. "And there is absolutely nothing ugly about you. God, Grace, sometimes I think I stopped dating because I figured out I was never going to find anyone as lovely and amazing as you."

Grace snorted. She knew it was a horrible sound, but she couldn't help herself. He couldn't possibly insult her like that and then think she would buy his compliments. "Don't feed me a line of crap."

Matt straightened up. "It's not a line of crap. It's true. Maybe seeing how that big blond bastard affected you is making me come to my senses. I need to get off the fence, or I could lose you. I really care about you, Grace. I think we make a good team. We work well together. We like each other. Well, I like you and you tolerate me. It's not a bad basis for a relationship."

"Are you still drunk?" Grace leaned in to get a good whiff of his breath. It wouldn't be the first time he attempted to get over a hangover by starting in on a new drunk.

Matt leaned over. One minute Grace was trying to discern her boss's recent liquor intake, and the next his lips were shockingly pressed against hers. Grace was stunned into stillness. Matt's hands found her waist, and he pulled her close. Her chest was smashed against his. Matt's dry lips nibbled at hers almost hesitantly, then with more force as his hands began taking a bold voyage toward her rear end.

"Matt!" Grace pushed at him, the feel of his hands on her ass pushing her out of shock and into action. "What the hell are you doing?"

He smiled sheepishly. "Something I should have done a long time ago." He held his hands up in mock surrender. "And I'm moving way too fast, as usual. Look, I just wanted to warn you about Johansson. I don't want that bastard to break your heart. You've been through enough. You need a man who'll take care of you."

Given the way she'd spent the entire evening dealing with Matt's shit, she seriously doubted he was the one to take care of her. A million and one thoughts flittered through her head, each trying and not finding purchase. She was flustered, and it must have shown on her face.

Matt pushed back a piece of hair that had come loose. "Let's forget that whole kissing thing happened, okay?"

Grace nodded eagerly. She was more than willing to forget that bit of idiocy. She'd never once thought of Matt in any terms other than friend and boss and sometime burden. "No problem. We can blame it on the tequila."

He nodded. "But I want you to think about it, Grace. I think we could make something work. I think we could be happy."

"Matt…"

He put a finger over her lip. "Hush. I just asked you to think about it. Can you do that?"

Grace nodded. She doubted she would be able to think about anything else.

Chapter Four

Grace set her laptop bag at her feet as she scooted into the booth at O'Hagen's. The small pub was half a block away from the office, making it the perfect place to end the very long and frustrating day. When Adam had shown up at her desk at four, she'd leapt at the chance to spend a little time with him and Jake.

"Hey, do you want me to move that over here?" Adam asked, indicating the heavy bag.

Grace shook her head. "No. It's fine. I like to keep it close. It's kind of got my whole life in it. I never let that sucker out of my sight."

Adam leaned back, his masculine beauty a study in negligent grace. "I bet it's not your whole life, sweetheart."

She sank into the comfortable booth, every muscle in her body relaxing after a taxing day. She needed this. She needed to sit and talk to friends and drink a glass of wine. It reminded her that she really did have a life. "You would be surprised. My kids are in college. I live alone. Work is pretty much my life."

And she'd been all right with that for the last few years. After her husband died, sinking into work and family had been comforting. But lately, she'd felt how alone she was. Watching

Adam and Jake connect was a bittersweet reminder of how much she'd missed having a man in her life.

"Two Cosmos." Jake smiled down at Grace as he passed her a frosty pink drink. He set one in front of Adam as well. Grace noted that Jake already had a beer sitting in front of his seat.

"Seriously?" Adam asked, staring at the drink.

Jake grinned at his new boyfriend. They were so cute together. "I remember you talking about how much you loved Cosmos. And I know Grace likes them. Look at how cute she looks with a pink drink in her hand. Very festive."

Grace took a sip. She really did love Cosmos.

Adam reached out for his. "Nice beer you have there, Jake."

Jake slid into the booth next to Adam. He picked up his beer and tipped it toward his partner. "I'm not as urbane as you, love. I'm afraid I'm still a country boy at heart. I just love a nice, cold beer."

Adam's eyes narrowed briefly and then he smiled that sweet, smooth smile Grace was coming to love. His shoulders came up in a negligent shrug. "Well, it's your ruggedness I find truly attractive." He turned to Grace. "Although softness is infinitely appealing, too."

She rolled her eyes as she took another sip of her icy cold drink. Adam was a ridiculous flirt. He seemed to prefer to flirt with women though, she'd noticed. She supposed women were safe to flirt with. Jake didn't seem at all jealous as Adam's hand found hers across the table and entwined their fingers together. Adam really was a tactile person. He was always hugging her and taking her hand.

"I'm not so soft, you know," Grace countered. "Just today, I had to put a man in his place."

She grinned, thinking about it. Sean Johansson had tried to maneuver her into spending the afternoon with him. He'd had all kinds of excuses for why she should sit in on the meeting between him and Matt. She had only really needed one reason to not sit close to Sean. Last night's episode with Matt had her thinking. She had to keep Sean at arm's length. He was too tempting. If she let herself go along with his playful flirtation, she was going to end up the laughingstock of the office.

"I heard that big blond guy was hitting on you pretty hard," Jake said. He'd taken off his tie and unbuttoned the top two buttons of his immaculate dress shirt, showing off several inches of tan, muscular skin. No wonder Adam was so into him.

Grace waved off his words with the hand Adam wasn't holding. "He's a man after a good deal. I think he's figured out the way to the boss's heart is through his admin."

"Then why was Kayla playing admin today?" Adam asked.

That had been her solution. Kayla had been more than amenable. Sean had told her that he required someone to take notes and type them up so he would have a hard copy of all the meeting's high points. Grace had given him Kayla, who was more than happy to stare at the gorgeous man all day long. Grace had beaten a hasty retreat, holing up in the supply closet doing an inventory that wasn't really due for another two weeks and that should have been handled by someone else.

She'd run like the coward she was, and she wasn't ashamed. "I had some other things to do. Kayla didn't mind."

Adam chuckled a bit. "Give him hell, sweetheart. Don't you let that big bastard charm you. I know the type."

"Really?" Jake asked, staring pointedly at Adam.

"I do. He looks like the 'love 'em and leave 'em' type. He's not right for our Grace." Adam's hand stroked across hers sweetly. "Grace needs someone different. She needs someone who's in it for the long haul."

A long shadow fell over the table. "What are we hauling? Dare I take a wild guess?"

Grace pulled her hand back from Adam's. Sean stood at the head of their table, his jacket held over one shoulder. Like Jake, he'd ditched the tie and looked gorgeous and casual. He stared down at Adam, a fierce frown on his face.

Adam sat back. If he was intimidated by Sean's caveman act, he wasn't showing it. "I was just telling my dear friend here how she has to watch out for men who would take advantage of her."

"Yes, she should be careful of that. She's a beautiful woman. There are a lot of liars out there. There are a lot of men who would misrepresent themselves in order to get close to a woman like Grace."

Grace looked between Adam and Sean, trying to figure out the weird tension between the two of them. "Do you two know each other?"

Sean's face changed in an instant. His smile grew wide, and he ignored Adam. He laid his jacket over the back of the booth and held out his hand. "Not at all, sweetheart. I'm just jealous that you avoided me all day, but you seek him out. Dance with me, Grace."

She actually felt her heart speed up. O'Hagen's had a small dance floor, but despite the music playing, almost no one ever used it. The song had switched from a bouncy pop tune to a slow, sexy ballad. No one danced to music like this. This was the type of music a man used as an excuse to plaster himself all over a lover in public. "Oh, I don't think that's a good idea."

His jaw hardened, and his voice was deeper as he spoke to her. "Grace, it would please me greatly if you would dance with me."

He knew exactly what to say to her. She started to slide out of the bench. Sean took her hand and helped her out. She stood, and he was standing so close she could feel the heat from his body. She had to tilt her head up to see his face.

"Thank you, Grace." His voice seemed deeper. His lips quirked up in a sexy half-smile. "I'm not so bad, you know. You don't have to hide in a closet to avoid me."

She felt herself flush. She'd hoped he hadn't figured that out. "I had to do inventory."

His eyes narrowed, and she felt like he could see through her. "I would prefer honesty, Grace, but I don't suppose we're there yet. Fine. I can play the game for a while." He looked down at Jake. "When the waitress comes by, could you order me a beer?"

Grace barely heard Jake's "yes" before Sean was leading her toward the dance floor. Her hand felt small engulfed in his large one. God, he made her feel petite, and she wasn't small in any way. Grace glanced around the bar. No one else was dancing. Everyone was going to be watching the big girl and the guy who was obviously out of her league.

Sean halted in the middle of the floor and pulled her close. "Stop it."

"Stop what?" She was doing as he asked. She just wasn't a very good dancer. "If you would prefer someone who knows what they're doing, please feel free to choose another partner."

She started to pull away, her face flaming. She should have known better. Sean's arm tightened around her waist, pulling them closer together. "That wasn't what I meant. I meant for you to stop stressing about what everyone else thinks."

"How did you know?" she asked, trying to follow his lead. It was obvious she wasn't leaving anytime soon.

His arm relaxed as though he understood she was resigned. His hand found the small of her back, and she could feel him leading her gently. "I watched you. Your shoulders come up when you get stressed or nervous. And your jaw locks when you lie."

"I didn't lie."

"You said you didn't want to dance with me. That was a lie. I saw the way your eyes flared and your jaw clenched when I asked you. You were looking at me the same way you looked at that decadent piece of chocolate cake at the restaurant, and you turned me down the same way you turned down dessert yesterday."

He was right about that. She was horrifically embarrassed that he could see through her so plainly, but there was a part of her that was amazed he'd learned so much about her. Her husband, God rest his soul, had never figured out those things. "Well, I think you're both bad for me."

He surprised her by laughing, the sound as rich as any chocolate. Yep, he was bad for her. He had her thinking all kinds of dirty things. "That is such bullshit, Grace. Everyone needs a little decadence. It makes life worth living."

Sean moved her around the floor, his grace and rhythm evident in his easy motions. Grace gave over and stopped fighting him. She let him lead. The only problem with chocolate was that it was highly addictive. Once Grace had a little taste, she wanted more. She was pretty damn sure Sean Johansson was going to be very similar.

"So says the man without an ounce of fat on him," Grace grumbled. Not an ounce. So close to him, she could feel how cut he was. She tried to keep her hands still, but his every muscle seemed rock hard. He enveloped her. She was surrounded by his heat and his very masculine, clean smell. Despite her every misgiving, she found herself relaxing into him. It felt so good to be close to someone.

She felt him sigh, and his arms left their proper dance position and simply wrapped around her. He swayed to the music. "Is that what the problem is? Grace, love, do you look in the mirror?"

"All too often," Grace replied.

It was time to let him know she was onto his game. She turned her head up, and found him staring down at her with the sweetest smile on his gorgeous face. It took her breath for a minute. Maybe it wouldn't hurt to just dance. She wouldn't let it go any further. If she was careful, she could enjoy a night out with an amazing man and not get hurt.

"I don't think you're looking at the same thing I am," Sean said. "Now, relax. Are you enjoying yourself?"

"Yes," she answered honestly. She liked being close to him far too much, but it felt so good to forget about all the reasons she shouldn't be here and just dance.

"I'm glad. I don't think you have enough fun, Grace." His hand moved to cradle her head. He pressed her gently to his chest.

The music swelled around them, and Grace simply forgot about all the people watching them and let herself feel. She wanted. She'd wanted for so long.

The music changed suddenly to a faster pace. Grace reluctantly brought her head up. That hadn't lasted nearly as long as she'd hoped. She gave Sean a smile.

He shook his head and held her hand. He winked as he twirled her around and brought her back into his arms. "I can do this all night long, Grace. Dance with me."

Grace felt a smile spread across her face as Sean picked up the pace. The man could dance. Grace relaxed and followed his lead.

* * * *

"What do you mean you didn't go through her briefcase?" Sean asked. The words came out more harshly than he'd intended, but it had been a rough night.

He'd spent at least a full hour dancing with Grace, her lovely, curvy body pressed against his. He'd been in agony. His cock had been harder than iron, and he'd had to keep himself carefully angled away from her body. He wasn't sure what Grace would have done had he followed through on his instinct which screamed at him to rub his cock all over her and make sure she was absolutely certain of his interest.

Adam took a long pull off his beer. The minute Grace and the others had disappeared, Adam had ordered a beer as fast as he could get the words out of his mouth. "Kayla showed up. What did you expect me to do? Tell her I'm sorry, you can't sit with us because I have to rifle through your friend's briefcase? God, this beer tastes so fucking good. You suck, Jake. I will get you back for that."

Jake laughed, his head falling back. "The look on your face was so funny."

Sean slapped at the table to get their attention. "Both of your faces are going to look funny if I don't get a decent explanation as to why this little mission of ours turned into a complete waste of time."

It hadn't been, but he wasn't willing to admit that. He'd enjoyed Grace's company far more than he should. She was sweet and funny and so smart. After they'd finished dancing, they'd sat with Adam and Jake and the others from the office who came in and crowded around Grace. Kayla had been there, but so had a bunch of men. Several of them had been watching Grace. She hadn't noticed at all, but Sean had made damn sure to stare them all down.

But he hadn't achieved what he'd come in here to do—give Adam and Jake time to go through Grace's briefcase and potentially download the contents of her hard drive. He'd known the second would be tough. Adam was supposed to take it with him into the bathroom, and if Grace said anything, he could claim to have just been watching out for it. But Adam hadn't gotten that far. They had sat in the bar for two hours, surrounded by co-workers. By the time Grace had declared it was time to go home, they had blown their opportunity. Sean knew exactly who to blame.

"Maybe you were just too busy hitting on the target to do your actual job." Sean was just about ready to throw down with Adam. Adam had done his damndest to steal Grace's attention away.

Adam slammed his beer down. "You practically fucked her on the dance floor. What was up with that?"

"Not even close. I kept my hands to myself." And that had been incredibly hard. All he'd wanted was to sink his fingers into her soft hair and tilt her head up for a kiss. After she'd relaxed and snuggled against him, Sean had remembered all the wonderful things about taking a submissive. Grace was wound too tight. She didn't give herself permission to enjoy anything. He could change that for her. She needed someone, someone with her best interests at heart. Getting to know her had proven to Sean that she was a natural submissive. She wasn't a pushover. She just placed almost everyone else's needs before her own. She required a strong partner who could watch out for her and make sure she got what she needed.

He couldn't be that man.

"That's not what it looked like from where I was sitting," Adam shot back.

Jake rolled his eyes. "Why don't you two just beat the shit out of each and get it over with? Sean, the minute Kayla showed up, I asked her to dance. You didn't notice that, did you? We were right beside you and Grace, but you didn't notice, so don't tell me we're the only ones who fucked this up."

"Eric Klein from HR walked up to the table just as I was getting ready to take the briefcase with me. He asked me a question, and by the time I was finished answering him, Kayla and Jake were back." Adam frowned as he loosened his tie. "After that, we were surrounded. You knew this wasn't a sure thing."

But he'd hoped. He'd hoped this would be easy and then he could step back from Grace since he seemed to be getting in over his head. But busting Jake's balls wouldn't help anything. Taking off Adam's might make him feel better, though.

Jake scooted out of the booth, his beer finished. "You know what you have to do, Sean. It won't be the first time you've taken one for the team. I don't understand why you're so reluctant. Seriously, if you don't want to sleep with Grace, we don't mind."

Adam's fist pumped in victory. "That's a plan, my brother. We're better equipped to do it anyway. One of us can keep Grace happily occupied while the other gets the job done."

Jake laughed. "Yeah, you just remember who takes care of communications. Have fun working, computer geek."

"Stop it, both of you." Sean knew he'd fucked up when every head in the place turned. He forced himself to smile. He lowered his voice. "You're not sleeping with Grace."

He wasn't going to allow that to happen. He could handle this. He could handle Grace. She wasn't different from the other subs he'd known. She was sweet and lovely, and he would walk away from her. She was just a job.

Jake shook his head. "Watch yourself, Sarge. You better not forget that she's involved in this."

"She is not," Adam replied. "That woman is not in league with a damn terrorist. You've lost your mind if you think that."

"Oh, she's involved," Jake said, picking up his jacket. "If Patrick Wright is here, Matthew Wright is working with him. If Matt is working with him, there's no way Grace isn't involved."

"Those are some big 'ifs,' Jake." Adam slid out, too. His face was set in stubborn lines. He'd picked his side.

Sean had picked his side, too. He just wasn't sure it was the right one. He'd been burned before. "She keeps that case close. How many admins have briefcases with locks on them?"

It was a quandary. Every instinct he had told him that Grace Hawthorne was just what she claimed to be. And Grace wouldn't be the first woman to figure out that sweet and submissive was an awfully good way to cover up criminal activities.

"I don't buy it," Adam said. "But I can see I'm the only one who hasn't given in to complete cynicism. I'm going home. I have an eight o'clock meeting. I hate sales."

Jake threw his hands up. "We're not going home, asshole. I set up a date with the bartender. I had to convince her that you were drinking the Cosmo as a bet. She was pretty sure you were gay."

Adam drew his hands over his chest. "Are you talking about double D's?"

"Yeah, the blonde with the huge rack and an open mind. We're due at her place in half an hour," Jake said. "Unless, of course, you have to get your beauty sleep."

"Fuck you, asshole. Damn, she's hot. I want the back door this time," Adam said eagerly. He was moving way faster than he was before.

And he was forgetting a couple of things. "You two better be careful. I don't give a damn what you do off the clock, but you be discreet. None of this better get around that office."

Jake held out a key. "Already thought of it. She wants us waiting for her."

Trust Jacob Dean to have gotten some random waitress to give him the key to her apartment in exchange for the promise of multiple orgasms. Sean waved them off. "Good night, guys."

They left, and Sean was alone. He took a long sip of his beer and thought about how Grace had softened against him. She'd tilted her head up, and he'd almost leaned over to brush his lips against hers. He'd wanted to order her to open her mouth and submit to him. She'd responded so well when he'd turned his Dom voice on and told her what he expected. She would respond the same way when he got her into bed. She would flower open for him once he'd trained her, and he would take care of her.

Damn it. He couldn't let that happen. He couldn't get close. He had to keep it light. He would get in her bed, but he wasn't about to open up to her.

No matter what happened, he had to be able to walk away. The trouble was, he was starting to think that he wouldn't want to.

Chapter Five

Three days later, Grace sank into the pool, sighing as the cool water covered her body. It was peaceful and quiet in her backyard. Her neighbors were elderly and rarely came out after dark, so Grace enjoyed the glorious solitude. Though the September days were ridiculously hot in Texas, the nights had started to take on a cooler, autumnal air. Grace looked up at the nighttime sky. For fourteen years, she'd called this three bedroom ranch-style house home. It had been her and Pete's dream house. She would have to sell it soon. It didn't make sense keeping it all on her own. She'd started swimming every single night she could when she'd had that revelation. The water would be too cold to swim in soon. Grace leisurely swam in the moonlight, her mind processing the last few days.

She'd tried to keep Mr. Sean Johansson at arm's length. He seemed intent on screwing up her perfectly rational plan. The day after they had danced together, he'd asked her to lunch. When she'd politely declined, he shown up in the building's cafeteria where she and Kayla were meeting. He'd promptly charmed the pants off Kayla, who announced that she'd take him if Grace didn't want him.

The big Viking seemed intent on wearing her down. He'd asked her out to dinner every single night, those blue eyes of his pulling at her. He'd followed her to happy hour and been really sweet to Kay and their new friends, Adam and Jacob.

That was the real problem with Sean. If he was just a pretty face and a hot body, she wouldn't be struggling. He was also…sweet. He talked to her. He asked her questions about her sons and what she liked to do in her free time. He seemed truly interested in her as a person.

The water felt silky and smooth against her skin. She loved this feeling. She'd left the swimsuit behind, getting out of it after she was in the pool and utterly certain none of her neighbors were in their backyards. Swimming felt different without a suit, sensual and a little forbidden. She swam to the deep end and sat down on the bench built into the side of the pool, her legs dangling as she considered the big Viking who was rapidly taking over her life.

Sean was everywhere. He was holding her chair out when they were in meetings together. He'd brought her a latte the day before when she'd had to work late typing up several proposals. He'd waited and walked her to her car because it was past dark by the time she was through. That had been the hardest invitation to turn down. He'd looked a little hurt when she'd explained she had to get home. He had asked again this afternoon, but she was becoming deft at refusing him. He'd tried to get her to attend a dinner meeting with Matt and some representatives from Chile. When he'd complained about not getting any decent home cooking, she'd breezily offered to feed him some of her famous lasagna one of these days. She'd said it with her patented flirtatious smile and tossed out something like he should drop by sometime. He didn't know where she lived, and he'd be gone in a week or so. She was safe.

But a part of her wished she wasn't.

There was only the small squeak of her gate opening that gave her warning she was no longer alone. With a little yelp, Grace pushed off the bench and clung to the side of the pool, her naked breasts scraping lightly against the wall.

"Grace? Are you back here? I tried your front door, but no one answered. Oh, there you are."

And there he was, a Norse god in the moonlight. And here she was…without her damn swimsuit. Grace prayed it was dark enough he couldn't tell. The pool had been built to have a lagoon-like feel. The granite was a dark blue-gray. She hadn't turned the pool light on, so it was possible he couldn't tell. Maybe. She prayed he didn't notice her suit lying on the deck.

"Sean, what are you doing here?" The question came out as a little squeak. Her nails ground into the tile on the edge of the pool.

He smiled. She could see his even white teeth in the moonlight as he walked onto the deck. He looked unbelievably sexy in a dark suit. His tie was gone and the shirt open at the neck. He carried a bottle of wine in one large hand. "You said you would feed me, woman. That place tonight was crap. I couldn't take another overdone steak."

"Matt tends to choose his restaurants based on the bar rather than the quality of the food," she allowed. Oh, she had to find a way to get him out of here. Though the water was the tiniest bit cold, her whole body flushed with embarrassment. The last thing this gorgeous man needed to see was her sagging boobs.

"You're telling me. See, if you had come with us, at least I would have had something pretty to look at." He held up the bottle of wine. "Instead, I come bearing gifts and begging you to feed me. Seriously, Grace, I'm not a man who enjoys restaurants every night. You don't even have to cook. Just let me use your kitchen. I'll come up with something. I'm quite good in the kitchen."

The kitchen sounded like an awesome place for him to be. The kitchen wasn't here, where he would be treated to the sight of her overly-large posterior. He could go play around in the kitchen and she would force the swimsuit back on. He would never have to know. "That's great, Sean. The back door is open. Help yourself to anything in the kitchen. I'll be out in a minute or two."

He started to turn toward the door and stopped. "You seem awfully accepting. I expected a bit of a fight."

"I never fight with a man who is willing to cook for me."

He took a few steps forward until his loafers were just against the edge of the pool. Grace was very thankful for the distance between them. She had the feeling if there wasn't water in the way, Sean would have gotten much closer.

"Are you okay?" He frowned suddenly, and the next question came out of his mouth on a low growl. "Do you have another man here?"

She felt her mouth drop open, and she turned, making sure the water covered her up to her neck. She kept one hand on the side of the pool for balance. "No. I don't have a man here, Sean Johansson, but if I did, it wouldn't be any of your business."

His gorgeous face turned slightly sheepish. "Would it make a difference if I told you I wanted it to be my business?"

"Sean," she started with a sigh. He was playing some sort of game. He had to be. No man that young and gorgeous would be desperate for a forty-year-old widow. "Don't play around with me. It's not kind."

He groaned and shook his head as though he couldn't figure out what she was saying. "Kind? What do you mean by that? Come on, Grace. What do I have to do? I've followed you around like a puppy for days. I've been perfectly charming to all your friends and gallant toward you. I'm standing here begging you to let me show off my culinary skills. I've decided maybe you'll take mercy on me if I feed you well enough. I'm playing by your rules, sweetheart. I'm keeping my hands to myself and being the perfect southern gentleman. I need you to tell me what's going to work."

"Nothing." She was going to have to be brutally honest with him. She wasn't going to be used. "I don't know how often this little act of yours works, but it's not going to work on me. I'm not going to influence Matt to give you a better contract. You're going to have to deal with him. Now, I would thank you to leave. From here on out, just be professional with me, and I'll treat you the same way."

His eyes narrowed. Grace shrank back a bit. It was as though she could feel his willpower filling the space between them. One hand was on his hip as he regarded her. His voice was deeper and smoother than before. "You are working under some serious misconceptions, little one. First, there's nothing at all professional about the way I feel about you. Second, I don't give a shit about the contract. It's a job, Grace. It doesn't matter. Answer me one question. If you tell me no, then I'll leave. Grace, do you want me as much as I want you?"

Grace swallowed. All she had to do was get that one word out. She just had to say no, and her whole life would go back to normal. He would leave her alone, and she could focus on her sons…who didn't need her anymore. They were off at college. She could focus on…her job? That sounded sad. Any way she looked at it, this big, blond man was the most exciting thing to happen to her since forever. Peter had been gone for so long. Her loneliness washed over her.

"I don't hear a 'no,' Grace." His voice was quiet, and she heard a well of emotion in it. "I need a yes."

He wouldn't move on without it, Grace knew. He wouldn't give her the easy way out. He would make her say it.

"Yes." She would regret it. She was absolutely sure of that. She would end up with a broken heart, but maybe that was better than having an empty one.

His smile lit up the night. His shoulders relaxed. There was a self-satisfied air about him that couldn't be denied. "I'm so glad. You'll see. Whatever job I'm doing has nothing to do with what's between us. Remember that." He held out his empty hand. "Come on. I was serious about my culinary skills. My mother didn't get the daughter she wanted. She passed her quest for the perfect pasta down to me. And this wine is heavenly. You're going to love it."

Grace shook her head. Just because she'd decided to spend time with him didn't mean she was ready to rise like Venus in front of him. He was still younger than she was, and she still had her insecurities. "You go on. I'll be there in a minute."

He considered the situation for a moment. It was clear to see he was not a man who was easily dismissed. A slow smile spread across his face and his foot started to tap. He leaned over, trying to get a better view. "What's wrong? Why won't you come with me? Are you skinny dipping? Did I catch you without your suit on?"

"No." It even sounded like a damn lie to her own ears. "I'm just shy."

He tsked her. He paced the side of the pool like a lion stuck in a cage. "You're not going to make this easy on me, are you? We can do this the hard way. That was lie number one. I'll keep count. I'd watch myself if I were you. There might be punishment later on."

61

There it was. Grace had to take a deep breath and acknowledge that what attracted her to the Viking wasn't just his good looks. He had the deep, authoritative presence of a Dom when he wanted it. At least he reminded her of the Doms in her books. Now she had a two-fold problem. She was naked and wet in a way that had nothing to do with the pool she was in.

Sean placed the bottle of wine on the table and shrugged out of his jacket. He looked around the yard, his eyes taking in everything. He finally turned and studied the box that controlled her pool. "Ah, there it is."

The pool was suddenly illuminated with a lovely blue light. It was a soothing color that also bathed her naked form in light. Grace gasped and tried to move away. There was nowhere to go, no place to hide.

Sean's breath was audible. He stood there for a moment looking at her, his eyes wide. "You really are naked."

Before Grace could protest, Sean jumped into the pool fully dressed.

"Sean!"

He swam toward her, his big body powerfully stroking through the water. He could hold his breath for a really long time. Grace moved to the very far end of the pool and thought about using the bench to get out. His hand was on her ankle before she could make the move.

His grin was a predatory slash across his handsome face as he surfaced and moved his hands to her waist. He stared at her through the water.

"What happened to being a gentleman?" Her voice was a breathy confection of yearning. She hoped she didn't scare him off. She searched his face. He didn't seem to be offended by what he saw. His blue eyes were taking in every inch of her.

"The gentleman has left the building." His hands moved up to cup her breasts. "God, you're beautiful."

She suddenly felt beautiful. It occurred to Grace that she had a choice. She could let her insecurities have their way and perhaps save her dignity—or she could let her dignity hang and have Sean. Her Viking won in a heartbeat. A light happiness filled her. She wanted. She hadn't wanted in so long that the very yearning was a pleasure in and of itself. She gave herself up to the feel of his hands on her. Her nipples were hard and aching. She wound her arms around his neck.

"That's right, Grace. Hold on to me."

He covered his mouth with hers as he pulled her to the middle of the pool. Grace's feet couldn't touch the bottom, but Sean didn't have the same problem. Five and a half feet worth of water couldn't cover up Sean Johansson. He pulled her away from the side. She had to wrap herself around him if she wanted to stay afloat. His lips were warm and soft against hers. He nibbled tenderly at her mouth and then rubbed his nose against hers. It was a sweet gesture that had Grace's heart as engaged as the rest of her. There was lust in Sean's eyes, but there was a wanting there that seemed like more than simple sex.

"You've made me crazy for days." He ran his tongue along her lower lip. She groaned in response. Every nerve in her body seemed to be coming alive. "You are the most damned flirtatious woman I've ever met. I swear if you use that honey voice of yours on the delivery guy again, I'll have to kill him."

Grace gave into the urge to run her fingers through that thick mop of his. He usually kept it ruthlessly slicked back, but now it was a sexy mess. She loved the silky feel of it under her fingers. She'd longed to be this close to him for days, and now she could see he was perfect even with no distance between them. His face was chiseled perfection. Even the shadow of his beard tickling against her cheek felt like a sweet sensation. "I don't mean anything by it."

She'd just always been a flirt. Pete hadn't really noticed. He hadn't been the jealous type. Sean seemed like the jealous type. If she belonged to him and he caught her flirting, he might not laugh it off. He might…he'd said there might be punishment later. That one phrase did all kinds of things to her libido. God, why had he said that? She wondered if she could talk Sean into spanking her. He might think she was a complete pervert. How would she explain that she read a lot of erotica and had a few wicked fantasies? She would have to settle for vanilla sex. It would still be so good.

"Why do you think I let that poor delivery guy live, baby? I know you're just being your sweet self, but Grace, I am very possessive. You need to remember that." His voice was light and teasing. He pulled her flush against his body, his hands cupping the globes of her ass as he walked them toward the shallow end of the pool. Now his chest was out of the water. The white dress shirt was plastered against his skin. It molded to the hard, ripped muscles of his chest that spoke of hours spent in a gym. He looked down at her, studying her face. "You look like you could eat me up."

Grace lowered her eyes, embarrassed to be so very open. It was hard to know how to play this. It had been so long since she'd dated. It had been twenty years since she'd been in an intimate situation with any man other than her husband.

"Hey." Sean set her on her feet. Without her heels, she came to the middle of his chest. He was so big he made her feel small and delicate. He cupped her chin and forced her to look up at him. The light of the pool illuminated his gorgeous face, making his light blue eyes seem darker, more powerful. "I love the way you look at me, Grace. It makes me feel ten feet tall, and I definitely want you to eat me up."

He lowered his mouth to hers, and this time there was no gentleness. His kiss dominated. His tongue thrust in and tangled with hers in a bold imitation of what she was sure his cock wanted. Grace softened against him, letting her hands explore his rock-hard chest as he kissed her. His mouth slanted over hers again and again. Their tongues slid in a silky dance. His five o'clock shadow scratched lightly against her, but she loved the feel of him. He pulled her into the cradle of his body, placing the long line of his erection against her belly. His hips rolled, a blatant invitation to play. It wasn't an invitation she intended to refuse.

She was lost, ready to wrap her legs around his lean waist and take him right then and there. Grace buried her face in the skin exposed on his chest. She kissed him there, her hands pulling at the buttons of his shirt, hating the fabric that kept his skin from hers. She wanted her hands on him, feeling the warmth of his flesh and the hard play of his muscles. She wanted to sink her nails in and leave her mark on him.

Sean pulled away abruptly. His sharp tone of voice cut through the soft haze of her lust. "No, Grace. You are not in charge."

Her feet found the bottom of the pool. She hadn't realized she'd been depending on him for balance. She felt vulnerable again, without the comfort of his body surrounding hers. She'd heard him, but the only words that really registered were no and not. She was making an ass of herself. How could she have thought he was serious? He was just being playful. He was probably really surprised she'd taken him seriously. She was a forty-year-old widow with sagging boobs and ten extra pounds that wouldn't go away. He was a Nordic god. Grace tried to make her way around him.

"Stop it." His voice was a sharp bark, and his arm went around her waist. "I'm not putting up with that. We're going to get the rules in place before we get started."

"Just let me go, Sean." She didn't want to hear about his rules.

"No." When Grace looked up at him, he seemed a bit savage. "Did you treat your last Dom like this, sweetheart? Did he let you manipulate him? That won't happen with us."

He picked her up and set her on the side of the pool. She could feel her face flaming with embarrassment. He'd mentioned Doms. Why would he do that? What had he heard about her? Only a few people knew about her fantasy.

The smooth tile was slightly cold on the cheeks of her ass. Her feet dangled in the water, leaving her feeling exposed and vulnerable. She quickly tried to cover her breasts. Her fence was high, but it felt wrong to be naked out of the water.

Sean's hands grabbed hers and pulled them away from her chest. "Don't you dare. You need to pick a safe word right now."

"What?" She felt her mouth drop open. He was asking about a safe word? "I don't understand."

How could he know? What would he think? He'd asked about her Dom.

He frowned. "Lie number two, Grace. Let me put this as plainly as I can. Me, Dom. You, sub. Pick a safe word, or I'll get out of this pool, carry you to that very nice bench over there, and we won't get up again until your ass is a stark red."

"Elephant." She spoke quickly. She wasn't afraid of the spanking. She was intrigued by it, but she wasn't sure how she felt about Sean knowing so much about her so soon. He didn't seem to be bothered by it. Grace let her eyes sink submissively down. From the books she'd read, she knew it should be a word she wouldn't use during sex. "Is that a good word?"

Her soft words worked some magic on him. His shoulders relaxed, and his hold on her grew gentle once more. "It's a very good word. Is that your usual safe word?"

She bit her bottom lip. He was under some mistaken impressions, but Grace wasn't sure if she should set him straight. She settled for honesty by merely answering his question. "No. I just made it up."

He smiled. "Excellent. I would prefer we start a fresh relationship. Now, I'm releasing these hands. Put them on the tile behind you and lean back. Then I want the heels of your feet on the edge of the pool. Do you understand?"

She glanced around, forgetting her game. She was a little panicked at the prospect of obeying him. "But Sean, people might see me."

"No one is out here, Grace." The impatience rolled off of him.

Grace shook her head and once again wished she'd kept her damn swimsuit on. Of course, by now, Sean would probably have pulled it off her. Grace was honest enough with herself to know that she would have let him, but there were several problems with the scenario. "I have a home owners association. I once got a three hundred dollar fine for leaving my garbage cans out two hours late. I can't imagine what the fine will be for leaving my ass hanging out."

He bit the words out like bullets. "No one can see your ass because you're sitting on it. As for that pussy of yours, don't think about it. All anyone's going to see is my face buried in it. So, all we have to worry about are those gorgeous tits. We'll just tell everyone you're French. Now, do as I told you, or we'll go to the bench."

She shivered, but it wasn't from cold. She'd fantasized so often about being placed over hard thighs and accepting loving discipline. Not even in her dreams had she expected it would come from someone like Sean. "You would really spank me?"

He stared a hole through her. "I'm very close to doing it right now. You have to make the choice. You can submit, or I'll stop right now, and we can pretend this never happened. I don't know if you're experienced or if you're just curious, but this is who I am, Grace."

"You're a Dom." Deep down she'd known. She had been sure he was all alpha male, but part of her had recognized a man who could completely dominate her.

His lips quirked up. "I believe I mentioned that. I've trained for years. I know a sub when I see one. Now, make the choice. Give in to me or say your safe word."

Everything she'd dreamed of was right there. She could explore something she'd always wanted with Sean if she was just brave enough to submit. Grace chose to give in. Sean was in charge. Grace let her legs fall open. This was what had attracted her to the lifestyle. She didn't have to worry about anything except obeying Sean. There was no place for insecurities with a Dom. Grace felt her body tremble in anticipation as Sean stared at her pussy.

"You're so fucking gorgeous. Look at how wet you are." His voice was a dark, warm blanket covering her and protecting her from the outside. It was safe here with Sean.

His fingertips grazed the inside of her thighs, making her shiver in anticipation. He ran his hands all along her legs, cupping her knees, caressing her flanks, running his fingers all the way down to her pink toenails and back up to the apex of her thighs. He moved a single finger from the top of her clit down through the wettest portions of her cunt. Very gently he worked that single, big finger deep inside her.

"This is better," he said, his voice still deep, but the previous bite was gone, replaced with a languid, sensual tone. "Let's go over a few things. Set some ground rules. I like to be called Sir when we're playing. I don't know if you've worked with a Dom before. Sometimes I'll ask you to keep quiet, but not tonight. I want to hear you. You have permission to make as much noise as you like."

"Thank you, Sir." She knew that much. Doms preferred Sir or Master when playing. They also liked to be obeyed. Luckily, he was willing to let her make noise. It would be hard to remain silent when everything about him made her want to howl. She gasped as he grazed her clit with the pad of his finger. "Oh, Sir."

"I love the way you say that." He moved between her spread legs. The height of the pool's side was perfect for his purposes. His face was right in line with her waiting pussy. He breathed in her scent. "You smell delicious. And I love this pretty, shaved pussy. It makes you look like a ripe peach."

Pete had asked her to shave it. She'd never gotten out of the habit. Now she was beyond glad for it. His mouth hovered over her pussy. She wanted more than anything to push up and force his tongue into her, but she was patient. After a moment, she felt the first gentle lap of his tongue.

"Oh, oh." She whimpered at the delicate feel of him on her clitoris. It had been so long. Tears formed in her eyes at the sweet feel of another soul touching her, adoring her. She'd missed this so much. She loved her children, but she'd longed for this.

He tormented her with little, teasing licks. His tongue darted from her swollen clit to her weeping slit, delving briefly in, only then to trace a line almost all the way to the rosebud of her ass. He kept it up for the longest time before she felt the pressure of a finger pressing against her anus.

"I'm going to fuck you here, Grace. Not tonight, but eventually. Have you been taken here before?" He rimmed her anus, but didn't press in.

"No." The feel of his finger against her ass was foreign and totally wicked. She wasn't sure if she liked the pressure, but she wanted to push her own limits. She wanted to please Sean. She pressed her backside against his finger.

He pulled his hand away, and she felt a short, sharp slap to her ass. She hissed slightly at the pain, but it quickly became a warm heat. "No. You take what I give you or I'll stop. Do you understand?"

"In theory," Grace admitted. She was careening between feeling intensely vulnerable and totally uninhibited. She was flustered and on edge. She found herself saying things she hadn't wanted to share. "I've only really read about BDSM. And it's been awhile since I...dated."

"You've never had a Dom before? Really? Your husband wasn't in the lifestyle?"

She shook her head. "No. He laughed when I asked about it. He said he didn't want to hurt me." He hadn't even been willing to try.

"And you haven't looked for a Dom? Not since he died?"

"I was busy raising my kids and working. It's hard to have any kind of relationship when you have two teenagers in the house. Sean, how did you know I was interested in…this stuff?"

"Years of training and very good instincts," he replied with a little kiss. "You attempt to please the people around you. You're not a pushover, but you gain a deep sense of worth from being valuable to others. You prefer to wait, to defer your own pleasure and needs if you notice someone else in need. You're a natural submissive, little one. You should be happy Doms don't grow on trees or else you would have been snapped up and collared a long time ago."

She couldn't help but laugh at that scenario. It felt right to be here with Sean. He'd seen so much in the few days he'd known her. He'd really studied her.

Sean was still for a moment. "Grace, how long has it been since you had sex?" The question was softer, the tone much closer to the everyday Sean she'd become accustomed to.

"I haven't seen anyone since my husband died, Sir. It's been six years."

He was quiet, but his hand traced a pattern against her pussy. "I am honored. I'm honored that you would let me show you this world. I promise I'll take care of you. I'm not interested in a one-night stand. I'll be very good to you. Starting now."

His tongue covered her clit, rubbing insistently as his fingers foraged deep. Grace's fingers bit into the stonework. It felt so good, yet she needed more. He worked one, and then two fingers, deep into her pussy, scissoring them when he found the proper place. Grace let out a little howl as he hit that perfect place deep inside her. He stroked her G-spot and her clit simultaneously, and she came with a fierce little cry. The orgasm spilled over her, curling her toes and making her very happy with the blond god who had made good on his promise. Her muscles shook with the tiny aftershocks as he licked her one last time.

Sean pulled her off the tile and back into his arms. Grace felt languid and happy. Her arms wound around his neck, letting him support her. The water felt cool now that her skin was so hot. It was a comfort to be surrounded by it.

"Why?"

Grace didn't pretend to misunderstand his quiet question. Honesty, she'd read, was the most important component of the relationship between sub and Dom. "I didn't want anyone until now."

He held her close, cradling her to his chest. He pressed light kisses on her forehead. "I'm very grateful for that. You won't regret it. Now, I need to get out of these wet clothes."

"Yes, you do, Sir." She put a little sexy growl on her words. He needed to get out of those clothes because it was his turn to come. She wanted to take him in her mouth. She wanted to learn every inch of that solid erection she'd only touched through the fabric of his pants.

Sean chuckled. "Oh, we'll get to that, but later."

Her head came off his chest, the pleasant buzz she'd gotten from the orgasm dissipating a bit. Her insecurities began to eat her again. "You don't want to?"

He seemed almost hesitant to broach whatever subject was bothering him. "I want to, but not until we get a few things straight. I don't know what you expect from a Dom. Since you're so new to all of this, I think we should talk about what each of us wants. Communication is the key to a relationship like this. I know what hasn't worked for me in the past. I want this to be easy between us, so I think I should explain. Grace, I want to dominate you in the bedroom, but I don't want a twenty-four/seven relationship."

Her heart felt like it would break. She really hadn't expected that from him. "You just want to see me for sex? You don't want to date me?"

His eyes widened with confusion. "What are you talking about? What do you think I've been trying to do? Grace, I ask you out three times a day. I go and get your three o'clock coffee. I sit like a lap dog at your desk, waiting to see if you'll deign to allow me to walk you to your car. It's hard on a man's ego. How can you say I don't want to date you?"

"You said you didn't want a relationship."

He sighed. "I don't want a twenty-four/seven D/s relationship, baby. Look, I have a brother. He's older than me. He's really hard-core and most of his friends are, too. I got into the lifestyle at a young age, but there are parts I'm never going to be comfortable with. I'm crazy about you. I want everyone to know we're together. I just…I don't want a slave."

She smiled up at him. Her relief surged through her like a wave. It had never occurred to her that he would want to take the D/s relationship outside the bedroom. "I'm glad to hear that. Sean, you should know that the first time you tell me what to do outside the bedroom, I'll probably take a skillet to your head." She cuddled back against him, happy they were on the same page. "My mama made sure I had a good cast iron skillet when I got married."

"Save me from southern women and their mamas." He started to walk toward the steps. His arm went under her legs, and he hauled her up. "I want you to think about this. I want to be utterly in charge when it comes to our sex life, but I want a partner. I want to depend on you as much as you depend on me. When we're in the bedroom or at a club, I'm the Master, but everywhere else, I want to be your boyfriend with all the stuff that comes with it."

He placed her on her feet. There was a towel on the bench. He wrapped her in it and started to dry her off with short strokes. Grace stood there smiling a bit. No one had touched her in so long, and now she had her own personal dryer. "What stuff comes with it, Sean? You'll have to forgive me, but I haven't had a boyfriend in twenty-two years. I married Pete when I was eighteen and had two kids by the time I was twenty. I'm afraid I don't understand dating."

"Hold your arms out." Grace did as Sean asked, and he wrapped the towel around her torso. "I think we should take it slow. Maybe we can have dinner tomorrow. Don't worry. We'll figure it out. We don't have to follow anyone else's rules. We can make them up as we go along." He leaned over and kissed the bridge of her nose. "Now, go get me one of those towels and turn on the shower. I'll clean up and then maybe get a look at your kitchen."

She nodded, but her doubts lingered as she walked through the cool house. She moved through the master bedroom and into her sunny yellow bathroom. It had become so very feminine over the years, she wondered at how out of place big, masculine Sean would look in it. She grabbed a towel, turned on the shower to heat up, and returned to him.

He'd taken off his clothes and stood there in the moonlight completely comfortable with his own nudity. Of course, who wouldn't be if they looked like that? Grace stared for a moment. He was a testament to masculine perfection. His shoulders were broad and his chest ripped. His abs formed a perfect six-pack, and she'd been right about his legs. They were long and powerful. There was the lightest dusting of blond hair across his chest. And then there was his cock. It stood up proudly, jutting from the *V* of his thighs. It was long and ridiculously thick. It lay almost flat against his abdomen, the head reaching his navel. Without a thought, Grace licked her lips. He was so hard it must be painful. Grace stepped forward, and her hand came out to touch him.

He stopped her by catching her wrist. "I didn't give you permission to touch me, Grace."

She felt herself flush with embarrassment. She took a quick step back and lowered her head so he couldn't see the tears welling up in her eyes. How could he not want her?

He released her hand and took the towel. He quickly wrapped it around his waist. "I thought I made myself plain. I'm in control of our sexual encounters. There will be times when I give you leave to do what you like. This is not one of those times. I'm going to take a shower and then we'll talk. Think about this long and hard. I might not be so easy to deal with as you think. I won't tolerate you manipulating me."

"I wasn't trying to manipulate you." Her fists were clenched at her sides. She didn't understand anything. If he didn't want her, why the hell was he here? "I didn't understand that I wasn't even allowed to touch you. Maybe I'm not cut out for this."

Maybe it was the kind of thing that only worked in a book.

He forced her chin up, his eyes fairly pleading. "I'm sorry, little one. I'm feeling a little savage. I need to calm down, and that means I need a few minutes to myself. I know you won't believe this, but I'm feeling my way through this, too. I haven't dated much."

She snorted. It wasn't a pleasant sound, but she couldn't help it.

His lips curled up slightly. "I didn't say I hadn't had an enormous amount of sex, but it didn't mean anything. Now, go open that bottle of wine. When I get out of the shower, we'll talk."

He turned around, and it took everything Grace had not to gasp. Sean was utterly perfect from the front, but his back was a mass of scars. She managed to keep quiet and not reach out to him. He was damaged. That was something she understood. He walked off, leaving her feeling more vulnerable than ever.

What had happened to him? The scars were white. They were years old, but told a tale of pain he'd endured. Grace wanted to go to him and wrap her arms around him. She wanted him to tell her what had happened and to promise that he wouldn't be in that position ever again.

She doubted that she was going to be able to sit patiently and watch him cook dinner as he explained why he was changing his mind about making love to her. It seemed to Grace that was what he was doing. She picked up the bottle of wine and walked back into the house, closing the door behind her. She would do as he asked her to, but she would do it in her way. And she would definitely find out how serious he was.

Chapter Six

Sean felt like beating his head against the tile of the shower. He had the water as cold as it would get, and the damn thing wouldn't go down. He looked at his recalcitrant cock. He was so hard, there was a drop of pre-come glistening on the tip. Wasn't it supposed to respond to cold by shriveling up?

The problem was, no matter how cold the water got, he couldn't forget about how hot Grace had been. She'd been soaking wet. Her little pussy had wept freely, just begging him to dip his cock in. Despite their obvious size differences, Sean knew she'd been so aroused he would have no trouble shoving his cock in all the way to his balls.

Stop. Stop thinking about it. Think about the fact that she doesn't even know your real name. She thinks you're Sean Johansson, boring negotiator for an IT company. She thinks you work a nine-to-five job that doesn't get you shot at on a regular basis. She doesn't know anything real about you.

But was that true? Despite her attempts to avoid him, he'd spent an awful lot of time talking to her over the last several days. She might not know all of the facts about his life, but he'd been honest about most things. It was always best to stick to approximations of the truth when undercover. He'd told her he'd spent time in the Army, though he hadn't mentioned he'd been in Special Forces. She knew he had a brother whose shadow he'd always been in. He'd talked about how hard it had been on his mom when his father had walked out. God, his mother would love Grace. His mother would admire her for the woman she was. He could just imagine Grace and his mom ganging up on him when he took on a dangerous job. Grace would even disagree with Ian. Grace would likely tell Ian off on a regular basis. He would love to see how his brother would deal with his sweet, strong-willed, southern sister-in-law.

Where had that thought come from? He couldn't be thinking about marrying Grace. That was crazy. He wasn't looking to get married. Sean took a deep breath and realized that the thought didn't make him panic the way it should. He was thirty-two years old. He wasn't some kid. Maybe it was time to think about settling down. Maybe it was also time to think about a career change. That thought had been ruminating for a long time. Grace had just crystallized his dream.

Of course, when Grace found out he was in her bed under completely false pretenses, he wouldn't likely be settling down with her. He would have a lot to answer for. The last thing he wanted to do was hurt Grace. He'd briefly considered completely pulling out of the job. He could claim trouble at the home office, and Ian could send someone else in. When the job was done, Sean could come back in as himself and start their relationship over. There was only one problem with that scenario. If Patrick Wright was really using his brother's business as a front, then Grace was in potential danger. He didn't trust anyone else to keep her safe. He would just have to deal with the consequences later.

Sean opened her bottle of shampoo. It smelled like peaches, like her hair. Lately the scent of peaches always aroused him. That damn shampoo did nothing to calm his cock down. His cock didn't care that Grace would be angry. His cock didn't give a shit that he was trying to build a relationship with her. His cock just wanted to get inside her.

Sean put the shampoo down and soaped up his hands. There was only one way to fix the problem. He wrapped his hand around

75

that unruly body part and started to stroke. His soapy hand stroked from the weeping head all the way to the base. He was going to maintain control. He squeezed and picked up the pace, thinking about how much nicer it would be if it was Grace's pussy clenching around him. He would hook her legs in his elbows and spread her wide. She wouldn't have anywhere to hide from him. She would give and give. She would take everything he had. She would scream out his name when he finally let her come just seconds before he allowed himself to let go. He would pump into her until he was completely empty. He would fill her up.

Sean stiffened at the image and let loose the breath he hadn't known he was holding. Warm semen spat out of his cock and covered his fist. He pumped until he didn't have anything else to give. He finally relaxed, his muscles unbunching, his breath calmer. Now the cold water was doing its work. Now he could think a little bit.

Sean quickly lathered his body while he thought about the trouble he'd gotten himself into. He needed to back off a little. He'd been far too impulsive, a trait his brother had always said would get his ass blown off someday. His intention hadn't been to make love to Grace this evening. He'd intended to cook her a late night snack and impress her with his culinary skills. He would ply her with a good wine and get her talking. He'd meant to get closer to her this evening by asking about her sons and then finding a way to talk about her boss. The most he'd planned to do was an innocent little make-out session.

She'd blown that plan out of the water with her little skinny-dipping adventure. He hadn't been able to control himself. He'd been in the water with his hands exploring all that perfect skin before he could stop himself.

Perfect skin. He wondered if Grace had really looked at his back as he'd walked off. He soaped his shoulders. He could feel scars there though he couldn't feel the ones that went lower. After he'd come out of the hospital in Germany, he'd forced himself to look at it. His back had been an angry river of scars with multiple tributaries running off the long, deep scar that ran down his spine. Sean knew he'd been lucky. He'd survived the IED that took out his

Humvee, but he didn't like to think about it. Now he had to. Grace would have questions. He doubted she would accept his usual comment. He usually mentioned that if they thought he was bad, they should see his brother. Sean doubted there was a single piece of his brother that had been left unmarred.

Sean felt infinitely more in control as he dried off. He shut off the water and stepped into Grace's delicate little bathroom. It was a confection of feminine frivolity. He was surprised by it since Grace always dressed so austerely. This was a little peek into her soul, like those hot shoes she wore. Sean smiled at the neatly organized bath salts and bubble bath oils she kept in an antique bin next to the clawfoot tub. There was a stack of paperbacks on the window sill. He could tell from the flowery-looking covers that Grace enjoyed lying in her tub reading romance novels. He looked through the covers and quickly figured out they mostly featured BDSM. She would be very interested in what he could teach her. He looked at that tub and pictured her there.

Of course, a tub that big was really built for two.

Not going there. He didn't need to get his brain caught on the image of lying back in that tub with Grace cuddled up between his legs. He could wash her hair and then allow her to bathe him. *Nope.* He wasn't going there.

He wished he had been smarter. He needed the barrier of clothes between them. He would have to dry his clothes before he could get back in them. He checked in her big walk-in closet. All she had was her own pink fluffy robe that he doubted would cover his chest. He was stuck with the towel. It was only thirty minutes or so. He would sit down with Grace and tell her he wanted to slow down, maybe go out a few times before they had actual sex. Maybe if he didn't have sexual contact with her again before the job was over, she wouldn't hate him. Maybe he could keep some piece of himself apart from her.

Sean wrapped the towel around his waist and opened the bathroom door. He'd ask Grace if maybe one of her sons had left behind something he could wear. Anything would be easier than sitting around her kitchen almost naked trying to explain that he didn't want to have sex with her when his cock so obviously did.

The sight that met him when he opened the door made him stop in his tracks. Suddenly, every single thought of leaving Grace further untouched fled as his cock firmly took command.

Grace sat in the middle of her queen-sized bed. She was completely naked and on her knees. Her palms were up, lying on her thighs, and her lovely head gazed to someplace on the floor in front of her. Her eyes were submissively down, and long auburn locks flowed around her shoulders like a silky waterfall. It was the graceful position of a sub waiting for her dominant partner's command. Everything inside Sean responded to it. He'd seen submissives waiting for him in this position countless times, but his heart leapt at the sight of Grace. This wasn't some nameless sub looking for a good time. This was Grace. She'd never sat in this position for anyone else. Just for him.

"Not on the bed, Grace," he heard himself saying. "When you greet me, you do it on the floor."

She moved quickly and found the position again. She never looked up at him, merely followed his command. Her red hair flowed freely down her back. It was wild and wavy from the humidity. It went well with her nude body, making her seem primitive and tempting. He took in every inch of her lovely, feminine form. She was petite, but curved in all the right places. Her breasts were large and natural. Her waist flowed gracefully into full hips he could grip while he fucked her. She was the most desirable woman he had ever seen. As though he hadn't just had an orgasm, his cock fought the cotton of the towel, trying to break free.

He placed a hand on her head and gave up the fight. He would regret it. He knew he would. And he also knew he couldn't walk away from her. He let the towel drop. "Your form is next to perfect. Straighten your spine a little. Those novels you've read seem to have the right idea. Look up at me."

Her chin came up. Her lovely face was placid. Those big hazel eyes were perfectly calm, but the slight curve of her lips gave her away. She was thrilled with his response. She'd known what she was doing. His little one was going to try to top from the bottom. It would be an intricate dance between them for power. He was looking forward to many, many years of such a struggle. This was what you didn't get from a slave, this fire and passion. She would always surprise him. Perhaps it was time to surprise his little sub, too.

"Did you do as I asked?"

She nodded, though a little wariness entered her expression now. "I opened the wine, Sir. It's on the table."

Sure enough, she'd followed the letter of his command, but not the intent. The bottle was chilling in a little silver bucket with two wine glasses beside it on the bedside table. "Grace, I told you I wanted to talk. Did you have any intention of talking to me?"

"Oh, yes." Her response was bouncy as though she was happy he'd phrased it in a way she didn't have to lie about. "I think we should talk."

He would have to be more direct. He hid the smile that threatened. He was supposed to be in control. "Grace, are you trying to seduce me?"

Now her face fell, and her teeth sank into her full bottom lip. "Can I seduce you?"

He sighed. That was what this was about? Did the woman not have eyes? In the week he'd known her, he'd always had an erection around her. She was his fucking Viagra, and he'd gone way over the "erection lasting four hours" point. He didn't need a doctor. He needed her. He was far past thinking about the job. He was thinking about Grace.

And he needed to teach his little sub a lesson. "I believe you'll find you can seduce me, but first things first." He sat down on her bed. "Over my lap."

He didn't miss the hitch in her breath. It wasn't nervousness.

"I won't ask again. Right now, it's a count of five. Every second you delay, I add on to it."

Grace's gorgeous heart-shaped ass was across his lap in no time. Her stomach pressed against his cock. She wiggled a little, trying to get situated. Sean steadied her with his left hand. "Do you know why I'm going to spank you?"

"Because I was trying to manipulate you?"

"No, darling. I'm going to spank you because you'll like it." He brought his hand down in a short arc, the sound cracking through the silence of the room. Her skin was so pale it immediately pinkened, and her breath came out in a sweet little squeal. She squirmed slightly. His hand came down again, on the opposite cheek. "I'll allow your sounds this time. Know that in the future, I will tie you down and gag you if you disobey me again."

He planted a little slap to the center of her ass then let his fingers slip underneath to make sure he hadn't misjudged the situation. Sure enough, his Grace was sopping wet and getting more aroused by the second. She liked her spanking. He wasn't cooling off any either, though. He could feel his cock pulsing against her heated flesh.

He shoved two fingers straight into her cunt. She was so slippery, he slid in unencumbered. He watched her back rise and fall, uneven with every jerky breath. His sweet sub was trying so hard to follow his orders. Her skin was perfectly pink and hot to the touch. She responded so well to his discipline. He would have to be careful when he used a cane or a whip on her. He couldn't wait to tie her down and put his mark on her. He pulled his fingers out and smacked her ass again two times in quick succession. He was past the point of waiting. He needed her. He lowered her down so she knelt between his legs. Her face came up. She flushed with need. Her tongue darted across those full lips of hers, and Sean's cock throbbed.

"Open."

She didn't hesitate. She opened her mouth and allowed him to thrust his aching dick between her lips. Her tongue came out to swirl around his head, making him groan. He thrust his hands into her hair. Later, he promised himself, later he would spend an evening instructing her on just how he liked his cock sucked, but for now he was overwhelmed with the need to simply use her, to know that she was his.

Why this woman? Why now? He couldn't lie to himself. Grace did it for him. She was smart and funny and challenging. She was so sexy he couldn't think about her without getting hard. How had he ever thought he could play games with her and walk away?

"Wider, Grace, you can take me all the way." He held her ruthlessly, shoving his cock in and out. He peered down. The sight of his erection disappearing between her lovely lips was just about enough to undo him. When he pulled out, her cheeks hollowed as she sucked furiously, trying not to lose him. Her tongue rolled over and over his flesh. He let his cockhead just brush her lips before burrowing back in to that soft place at the back of her throat. One more thrust and he would spill his come down her throat. Sean pulled out. His cock came out of her mouth. He wasn't coming down her throat the first time. He wanted to be buried deep in that wet pussy of hers.

"On the bed. Spread your legs." His voice was harsh even to his own ears, but Grace didn't seem to mind. She scrambled up onto her clean, quilt-covered bed, and her legs were splayed in seconds. She was gorgeously spread out for his pleasure. His fist found his cock and stroked it as he prepared to climb on the bed and claim her. He suddenly wanted to punch a wall. "Damn it. Grace, I have to go out to the car for something." He hadn't intended to make love to her. His condoms were in the car.

She smiled a little weakly at him and pointed to the bedside table. "I've had college boys in my house for a couple of years and no desire to become a grandmother. I made sure there were condoms in the house."

And she'd thoughtfully brought them down. She'd manipulated him, and he couldn't resist her. He reached over and grabbed one. He regarded her with his most menacing stare as he rolled the condom over his grateful cock. "I should have spanked you more."

"Later. Right now, please fuck me, Sir."

He crawled over her, hooking her knees over his elbows, pushing her legs even further apart. She was completely open to him. Her perfectly shaved pussy was coated with cream. It was begging him to come in, and he couldn't resist the temptation one more second. He lined his cock up, swirling it in her juice to moisten it, and slowly, painstakingly began to push his way in.

She was so tight and hot around his cock. Her pussy was a sultry cave he needed to explore. Her eyes were closed and her mouth slightly open. She sighed as he forced himself in another inch. "Open those eyes."

There would be no hiding from him. He demanded honesty

from her even when he had none to offer.

They obediently fluttered open to pierce him with a look of pure lust. There was no coyness in Grace. There was only simple desire for him. "You're going to make me crazy, you know that?" He watched her hazel eyes widen as he pushed forward until he was seated all the way to his balls. Her shoulders shook as she tried to adjust to him. He gave her a moment, savoring the connection he'd wanted from the minute he'd seen her. "Fuck, you feel good. You feel so damn good."

He pulled out and thrust in quickly. Her cunt sucked at him, trying to keep him inside. There was no way he was going to last. Later, there would be time to fuck her for hours, to make her come over and over again until she begged him to finish it, but now he had to come.

Sean angled his body down, forcing her to take more of his weight. It felt right to be inside of Grace, as though some odd piece of himself had just fallen into place. He held nothing back. He was savage in his need. He pounded into her. Her breathy moans told him she didn't mind at all. When he felt the shiver at the base of his spine that told him he was about to go off like a rocket, he let one of her legs go so he could rub her clit. He ran his thumb over that sensitive bit of flesh and watched Grace come. It was a beautiful thing. Her eyes got wide and her mouth opened to emit a soft cry as the little muscles of her pussy suddenly bore down on his cock.

Sean let his head fall back. She'd been taken care of. Now was his selfish time. He thrust in again and again as the semen jetted out of his body in a wave of relief. He ground himself against her so she milked every last drop out of him. When he was finally finished, he collapsed on top of her. He loved the softness of her skin rubbing against his. Her arms wound around him, and her fingers found his hair. He buried his face in her breasts, perfectly content to spend the rest of the night there.

* * * *

There was a big gorgeous hunk of man in her kitchen, and he wasn't waiting on her to feed him. She stared at him for a moment, the previous evening's events washing over her, making her flush all over again. It had been perfect. She'd never felt closer to anyone as she'd felt to Sean when she'd submitted to him. A little wave of guilt threatened. She pushed it back. She'd loved her husband. She'd been faithful, but he was gone. She deserved a little bit of happiness.

Grace stepped out of the bedroom after carefully preparing herself for the day. Sean stood at the stove wearing nothing but his trousers. Her small skillet was in his hands and he flipped whatever was in it with the skill of someone featured on the Food Network.

"Good morning." His smile made her melt a little. "I made coffee." He gestured toward the coffee pot where he'd already placed a mug for her use.

Grace was grateful for the distraction. She poured a cup and wondered what the hell had come over her last night. She'd had some serious sex with a man who liked to dominate his lovers. She'd so enjoyed being beneath him, submitting to him. She'd thrown herself into bed with a man who had to be ten years younger than she was.

"How old are you?" The question was out of her mouth before she could think twice.

He slid an omelet onto a plate and turned to her. "Is that what you're worrying about this morning?"

"I'm not worrying. I'm just curious."

His dark blond hair looked so much longer now that it wasn't slicked back. It fell over his eyes and curled around his ears. His eyes narrowed. "I thought we decided you wouldn't lie to me anymore." He moved to the table and set the plate down. "I'm thirty-two. And you're hardly Mrs. Robinson. The only person who will make a big deal out of our slight age difference is you."

Grace doubted that. She was forty with two grown kids. Sean was just getting started in life. Grace eased into the chair at her breakfast table and took a sip of coffee. He'd made it perfectly, and the omelet was fluffy. There was also whole wheat toast with butter and raspberry jam.

"I had to make do." He sat down across from her as though it was something they did every day. "You're pantry is nearly empty. I won't even go into your fridge."

His easy manner settled something inside her. She had worried he would hurry out the door this morning. A part of her had said it would be for the best. She hadn't realized just how deeply she'd hoped it wasn't true until she'd seen him standing at the stove. "Well, it's just me, you know. It's hard to cook for one."

"I don't have a single meeting scheduled today." He said with a great tone of relief. "I think I'll go shopping. There's a *Coq au Vin* recipe I've been wanting to try. Mind being my guinea pig?"

Her breath caught. "You want to have dinner tonight?"

"Yes. I thought it would be nice. I thought now that I've allowed you to seduce me, you might think about having mercy on a man and condescend to date me." His smile faded. "Unless you were planning on a one-night stand."

"I wasn't planning anything. I just didn't know if you would want to see me again."

His hand came across the little table. "I told you I was crazy about you. I want to see you, and it has nothing to do with that contract I'm negotiating with your idiot boss."

She ignored the comment about her boss. He was an idiot, but she was far too loyal to vocally agree. She let her fingers entwine with his, loving the way her skin practically hummed where he touched her. It felt so right to touch him. "I would love to see you again tonight. How long are you going to be in town?"

His fingers tightened on hers just a fraction, then he let go and sat back. "Uh, I guess another week or so. I should have everything tied up by then." His mouth tightened as he seemed to think about the situation. "Maybe it will take longer. I'm meeting with people other than Wright. And even then, I would have to come back on a regular basis."

A week. She had a whole week with him. Grace didn't fool herself. She couldn't keep someone like Sean forever, whether she wanted to or not. It was for the best. She could hardly see him being a step-father to her sons. *And why not?* Why did she have to choose someone based on their suitability for her adult children? *So what,* that defiant inner voice said, *if her boys didn't like Sean?* She'd certainly not cared for a couple of their girlfriends. Grace took a bite of omelet. It was heavenly, like the man who had made it. If she only had a week with him, she wanted to make the most of it.

"Why don't you stay here with me?" She held her breath, waiting for him to reject her.

His blue eyes danced with mirth. "Instead of my crappy hotel room? Hmm. That is an interesting proposition. I have to think about it. Let's see, the hotel room has a mini bar where I can pay ten bucks for a coke, a crappy shower that doesn't work half the time, and no HBO. This is also the place where the next door neighbors blast mariachi music at four o'clock in the morning. It could be really hard to leave such comfort. What have you got here to tempt me?"

She thought about last night. She thought about swimming with Sean again, though this time, he would be naked, too. It was an experience she didn't want to miss. "Mermaids."

His smile was sultry, and she knew he was remembering the night before, too. "Naked ones at that. Mermaids definitely win. Do you have a spare key? I'll get my stuff from the hotel and then stock up your pantry. I promise to be a perfect house guest. I'll even do the cooking. I should warn you, I'm not that good at cleaning, though."

"I think I can handle it." If his dinner was as good as his breakfast, she would clean all night long.

Twenty minutes later, she hummed as she parked her hybrid and began the walk toward her building. The night before with Sean was playing through her mind. She had a lover, and he was magnificent.

The wind whipped through the streets of downtown Fort Worth forcing Grace to hold onto her black skirt for dear life. The wind was dry and hot like the blast from a furnace. It raced through the tall buildings playing some natural version of pinball. Up ahead, Grace saw the doors to her building open, and Evan Parnell stalked out. His face was bunched up against the bright light of day. He scowled at anyone who dared to look upon him in a friendly way.

What was going on? He had been in the office every day for the past month, bugging Matt and making a general nuisance of himself. His very presence in the office was enough to set people on edge. He couldn't have come back for another check. He was paid monthly, and she'd written his check for the month. Parnell looked up and down the street, but seemingly took no note of her. He was carrying a stack of papers. Parnell hadn't joined the digital age. She'd heard him saying one time that computers and PDAs could only get a man in trouble.

Another blast of wind whipped up just as an old van pulled up to the curb. It was dingy and dirty with tinted windows. The driver's side window was open, and Grace could see a dark-haired woman in the seat. She was frowning, her mouth turned down and her brows in a *V*, as she stopped the van. She was somewhat pretty, her beauty marred by the disdainful expression on her face. Parnell slid open the back door and hopped in. Grace was slightly shocked. She'd never seen Parnell with a woman before. This one was slender and much younger than him.

Grace watched as a single slip of paper got hoisted by the wind, up and out of the stack Parnell held onto. The van drove off. Grace chased after that piece of paper, finally catching it with the toe of her d'Orsay pumps. She recognized the paper. She'd ordered it herself. It was Matt's stationary.

It was a series of numbers and a single address. *2201 Mount Dale Ave.* No city, or post code, just the address written in a masculine hand. She thought about putting it away to give to Parnell the next time he came in and quickly shelved the idea. Maybe it was the fact that she'd been brave enough to reach out and take what she had wanted last night that made her more curious, but she knew something was wrong with Parnell. She also knew that Matt wouldn't admit if he was in trouble. It was becoming clear to her that if she was going to find out what was going on between her boss and that jerk, she would have to investigate.

Grace slipped the piece of paper into her laptop case and walked up the steps to the office. She wouldn't mention it to Sean. He was only here for a week, and she didn't want to ruin her time with him explaining her paranoid theories. No, she would keep silent about her little mission. She would work to save her boss during the day, but the nights were for Sean.

Up ahead she saw Jacob and Adam waiting on the elevator. They looked so cute together. It was a sin to women everywhere that those men liked other men. Jacob waved at her. By the time they reached the ninth floor, they had plans for lunch that included a little shopping excursion. It was time to get rid of some of this black. Grace thought she might look good in blue, something that matched Sean's eyes.

By the time she got to her desk, she was far more interested in shopping than that little note she'd shoved in her briefcase. The situation with Parnell could wait a week, she decided as she got to work.

Chapter Seven

Sean knew the instant he entered the house that he wasn't alone. He silently set down his bag and cursed the fact that this particular assignment didn't allow him to carry. He could have used his SIG SAUER. Of course, he could imagine the questions Grace might have if she hugged him and felt the outline of a gun pressed into a holster against his flesh. She might inquire as to why her IT boyfriend needed a loaded gun. Still, he felt a little naked without it.

He left the door slightly ajar. He couldn't be sure he could close it without a sound. He listened, standing in the hall patiently. Whoever was moving was doing it quietly, but he was in the bedroom. As Grace's car was still gone and there was no other car in the drive, Sean had to suspect that this person didn't want anyone to know he was here. Sean moved across Grace's hardwood floors silently. He stuck close to the wall. Even on the first floor of a house, hardwood could creak. It was less likely to do that closer to the wall. He crept forward, his breath steady, placing his toe down, and then his heel. He would make his way into the kitchen. He might not have his trusty gun, but he was damn lethal with a knife as well. He played the scene out in his head. He would grab one of the smaller knives. It would be easier to wield and throw if he needed to. He would work his way back to the bedroom and have it at the bastard's throat before the intruder knew he was no longer alone. Sean would then politely question the intruder. Interrogations had been one of his specialties as a chief warrant officer with the Green Berets.

Sean would have to make sure to bring the asshole on the tile if he decided to kill him. It would be a much simpler cleanup. He glanced at the clock. It was slightly past noon. He needed to get the damn chicken on or it wouldn't be ready for dinner. Maybe he wouldn't be so polite with the asshole. He was ruining Sean's meal plan.

"Hello, little brother."

Sean turned, and his breath stopped in his throat. "Fuck you, Tag!"

Damn it. He'd nearly jumped out of his skin. His brother moved like a wraith. Ian had always, always been able to get the jump on him.

Ian's lips curled into a satisfied smile. He sat in the den adjoining the kitchen with a book in his hand. His enormous body occupied Grace's leather armchair like he owned it. But then Ian always reminded Sean of a king on his throne, no matter where he was sitting. Ian could be on the cheapest folding chair, and he seemed to turn it into something powerful merely by occupying it.

"I was about to slit whoever is back in the bedroom's throat," Sean declared.

Ian shook his head. "Please don't. I would hate to have to bury Liam. It's in his contract that if he's killed, I have to haul his ass back to Ireland for burial. That bastard won't even let me cremate him."

Sean didn't want to hear about whatever was in the Irishman's contract. Liam was fairly new to the team, and Sean found him slightly annoying. He didn't like the thought of him pawing through Grace's belongings. "What are you doing here, Ian? I'm not supposed to check in until tomorrow."

"Well, I was checking out this little book. Seriously, Sean? She's reading a book called *The Submissive's Response*. Women read this shit? This is like fantasy BDSM. No real Dom does stuff like this. He lets her tie him up. This author needs a little time with a real Dom."

The last thing Sean wanted to do was discuss Grace's choices in literature. "Again—I ask, what the fuck are you doing here?"

"You were supposed to check in yesterday." His brother set the book down. Ian's hands steepled in his lap. He sent Sean a look guaranteed to remind him who was the big brother and who was the little one.

Sure enough, Sean couldn't help but feel defensive. "I left Eve a message. I was busy working. I had to put in time with Wright and then got roped into a dinner meeting. You know how rough a deep cover assignment can be."

Ian gestured around the comfy little room. "You're not exactly posing as a drug dealer deep inside a crime syndicate, Sean. You could have found the time to sneak away and call in. I expected you to call at ten last night. What were you doing?"

Grace. He'd been doing Grace, in the pool, and then in the bed. The image played in his brain. Then, when he should have been copying the hard drive from her computer, he'd been holding her while she slept. He wasn't about to mention that little piece of information to his brother. "I told you—I was busy."

"Obviously. So you're finally in the lady's bed." To Sean's mind that sounded a bit like an accusation. "It took you long enough considering the lady's choice in reading entertainment. You could have been in her bed a long time ago."

Sean hadn't wanted to push it. This whole line of conversation was making him uncomfortable. "We're friends."

Ian stared at him, his eyes like laser beams looking for something to cut. "She gave you the key to her house. I would say you're more than friends."

He wasn't having this particular conversation. He didn't want to discuss the more intimate portions of his relationship with Grace. It felt too much like a report. What had happened between him and Grace last night hadn't been about business. He certainly wasn't going to hold back when it came to anything important to the case, but Ian didn't need to know how right it had felt to hold her or how damn content he'd been when he woke up this morning pressed against her body.

"I'm working on it." Sean went back to the front door and picked up his bags. He set his suitcase down, and then started unloading the groceries.

"Work harder. You haven't found out anything we don't already know. If you can't get this job done, then I need to pull you out and send in someone who can."

Sean ignored his first violent impulse to leap over the bar and beat his brother to a bloody pulp. No one was going to take his place. If Ian thought he could simply tell him to back off and Sean would let someone else try to seduce Grace, he was insane. The only thing that kept Sean calm was the unwavering belief that it wouldn't work. Grace wouldn't be interested in anyone but him. She'd proven it by offering herself last night. He was the only man she'd wanted since her husband died. Sean was quiet, and his reply as pointed as an arrow. "I'll get the job done."

"See that you do." That wasn't his big brother talking. That was his boss. Sean knew the difference.

Ian stood up and walked to the bar. He leaned forward. "What are you making?"

"*Coq au Vin.*"

Sean could practically see his brother start to drool. "That sounds good."

"It will be if I ever get a minute to put it on." Sean pulled out the fresh chicken he'd bought and a cutting board. He picked up the knife he'd intended to slit Liam's throat with and put it to another purpose. "Has it ever occurred to you that I can't find anything because there's nothing to be found?"

Grace was so sweet. Despite his knowledge to the contrary, it was hard to believe she was really involved in this mess.

"The CIA guy doesn't think so."

"Oh, well, if the Agency believes it, then it must be true." Sean remembered many buddies and teammates who went down because the CIA got its intelligence wrong. Afghanistan had given the Agency plenty of opportunities to screw things up. Of course, it wasn't the screwups that really worried Sean. It was the fact that the Agency always protected the Agency. They would use the rest of the world as pawns for their games. When Sean was a Green Beret, he hadn't had a choice in whether or not to play. He would rather hold a hot poker in his hands than have anything to do with the CIA.

Ian's fingertips drummed along the top of the bar. He hopped up on the barstool and made himself comfortable. "I think they're on to something here. Mr. Black gave me a look at his file on Wright. Wright is escalating. Black thinks he's behind two arsons, one at a lumber yard and one that killed a couple of people at a real estate development office. He likes to hit corporate offices, especially ones in large cities. Unfortunately many of those are in high-rises. The last fire that he started affected a twenty-nine-story building. It caused millions of dollars in damage, and the locals called it faulty wiring. I don't buy it, and neither does Black."

"Then why hasn't he called in the cops? This should be handled by the feds or Homeland Security." Sean's hands worked quickly on the chicken. It occurred to him, not for the first time, that he would really be happier in a restaurant somewhere. Fort Worth was a foodie town. It might be a really good place to open a little bistro.

Ian's hand slapped against the bar. "Get your head in the game, Sean. What's wrong with you? I'm talking about catching a killer, and you're more interested in that chicken." He leaned over and looked at the spices Sean had purchased. "What is Coco Van anyway?"

Sean quickly corrected the way his brother butchered the French pronunciation. "Forget it. It's for Grace. Now what the hell are you really doing here?"

A cloud passed over Ian's face. "How deep are you in with this woman?"

"He's certainly sleeping with her." Liam walked out of the bedroom. He was dressed all in black, from his T-shirt to the denims and boots on his feet. He flashed two empty condom wrappers at Sean and Ian with a smirk. "Only twice, lover boy?"

Sean washed his hands and pulled out the pot he would need. Grace's kitchen was very well organized for a woman who rarely cooked. "Some of us like to talk to our lovers."

"I thought you and Big Tag there just liked to tie them up."

He wouldn't argue with that. He'd gone to more than one store this afternoon, but he wasn't about to tell Liam and Ian that he'd bought handcuffs, lubricant, and a vibrator while he was out. He settled for sarcasm. "Unlike Ian, I sometimes take the gag out and listen to what the lady has to say."

That got Ian laughing. "I trained you poorly."

Liam slammed the condom wrappers down on the counter. Sean was well aware that Liam viewed him as a little brother to be taunted on a regular basis. Normally, it didn't bother Sean. "Still, I thought you were good for more than just twice. Guess it's hard having to do an old lady."

This time, it bothered him. It was an instinct. Sean's fist came out and met Liam's nose with a bone-crunching snap. Liam hit the floor. Sean calmly went back to his prep work.

"What the fuck was that for?"

Sean knew Liam had been thrown off guard. Liam's Irish was up. "The" came out sounding like a slurred *de* and "that for" sounded like *dat fer*. Sean gave him back some of his own. "Dat, boyo, was fer talking dirty about a lady."

Sean was happy with his accent. It mirrored Liam's. If he said another word about Grace, Sean would be forced to do something else.

Liam was on his feet in an instant. His mouth hung open with shock rather than anger. "Damn me, Little Tag. Tell me you haven't fallen for the girl. Sean, this ain't a good idea."

Sean shook it off and tried to act casual. "This was the plan from the beginning. I always planned on getting close to her. Now that I am close to her, I have to say that she's an extraordinarily nice lady. I won't let you talk about her like she's one of your underaged hotties."

Liam stared at him open mouthed and then looked to Ian. "Pull him out now. He's compromised."

Ian pointed to the condom wrappers. "Obviously. My brother's virtue isn't what I'm worried about. Did you plant the bugs?"

"Aye." Liam seemed to hear himself and suddenly his accent was gone, replaced by the flat cadence of the Midwest. "Yes, sir. I have all her landlines bugged, and there are a few in strategic locations. If she makes contact with Wright here, we'll know. By now, Adam should have bugged the office and her car. Also, we'll know if Little Tag here breaks his record of fucking her two whole times." He held his hands up in submission. "Pardon me. We'll be able to hear their beautiful lovemaking."

Sean gave serious consideration to kicking his ass. It just wasn't worth it. Liam's head was too hard to knock sense into. "Is this really necessary?"

Ian inclined his head slightly, and Liam took it as his cue to leave. He disappeared out the back door. Sean was left alone with his brother. "It is. We need to monitor Grace Hawthorne as though she was a prime suspect. Sean, I'm worried about you. I think your girl is in this up to her neck."

Sean rolled his eyes even though he knew he'd made the same argument to Adam just a couple of nights before. "Don't be ridiculous. Grace isn't some ecoterrorist. She's a lovely widowed mother of two."

There was a little pause that let Sean know Ian had something serious to say. Big brother knew how to leave him waiting. "She was arrested back in the mid-eighties."

Sean's head came up. "What are you talking about?"

Ian looked pleased to finally have his brother's full attention. "The arrest was purged from the records because she was a minor, but Eve managed to dig up the files. She can find anything, you know. Grace Hawthorne, formerly Thornton, was arrested at a protest. She was charged with assaulting an officer. She was placed on parole and the charge purged from her record on her eighteenth birthday.

The knife in Sean's hand fell to the side. There was nothing in Grace's character that would lead him to believe she had a record. He would have bet his life on her being a perfectly law-abiding citizen. "What the hell was she doing assaulting a cop?"

Ian waved it off as though the reasons were inconsequential. It only mattered that she had been arrested. Sean knew that sometimes Ian saw the world in stark black and white, with absolutely no shades of gray. "Best I can tell she was trying to save a monkey or something. She tried to stop a van carrying primates to a lab that tested beauty supplies. She chained her liberal ass to the gate and refused to let the truck pass."

Sean breathed a huge sigh of relief. That he could see. Grace had a strong instinct to protect anyone she thought weaker than herself. It was one of the things he admired about her. Hell, if he'd been there, he would have helped her. "If she hit a cop, then the cop deserved it."

"Well, there might have been mention of some of the cops getting handsy with the female protesters."

"See, he had it coming."

"All right, I might give you that, but she's deeply involved in a plot to keep the gas companies out of this area."

"A plot? With who?" She hadn't mentioned anything about this. Of course, they hadn't spent an enormous amount of time talking. He'd been far too busy making her moan. That might be why it hadn't come up.

"Her homeowner's association. She's been pushing everyone to refuse to sign their mineral rights away."

The chicken was calling again. Ian was making a big deal out of nothing. Maybe his brother was missing his old black ops days. This was the real world, and not everyone had hidden motivations. "Well, call the cops, brother. She's guilty of giving a shit. Maybe she doesn't want a bunch of gas wells leaking natural gas into the air. You know those things are built as cheaply as possible. Give it up. You can't call her an ecoterrorist because she cares about where she lives. Grace wouldn't hurt a fly. Ninety-nine point nine percent of those greenies are the most non-violent people you'll meet."

"It's the point one percent I'm interested in." Ian's blue eyes were hooded as he regarded Sean. It made Sean a bit nervous to be under that unblinking gaze. He felt like an insect being studied. The only question was whether Ian was about to push a pin through his abdomen and stick him in a box for collection. Sean stood silently, knowing that whatever Ian was about to do, he wouldn't be able to sway him. Ian always made up his own mind in the end. "If I pull you out, you'll be right back here, won't you?"

And he was almost always right. "Only after I hand in my notice. I'll quit the firm, and I'll stay with Grace. I don't believe for a second that she's involved in this, but if something is going on around her, she could be hurt. I have no intention of allowing that to happen."

Ian's shoulders slumped, a sure sign of defeat. From the day their father walked out on them when Sean was barely ten, Ian had led the way. On only one occasion had Sean even thought about going against Ian's better judgment. Ian had wanted Sean to go into business after college rather than following him into the Army. There had been times in Afghanistan that he'd wished he had listened to Ian. But now, he knew Sean would whole heartedly tell the brother he loved to go to hell, and all over a woman. Not just any woman, he thought in a burst of revelation—the woman. Grace was the one for him. Last night had proven it to Sean.

"All right, I'll leave you in, but watch your back," Ian conceded. "Eve's profile of Patrick Wright is frightening."

It was good to get back to the case. Eve St. James had been one of the best profilers the FBI had ever trained. Now she worked for Ian. If she was scared, Sean wanted to hear about it. "Care to enlighten me?"

"It's all in the report I sent you, if you could be bothered to read your e-mail. I'll give you the gist. He's highly intelligent and willing to kill, though he will wait if the time isn't right. He isn't governed by passion. He was almost certainly abused as a child, probably by his father. He has large chunks of time in his adult life that are unaccounted for. Eve thinks he was either underground or perhaps working off the grid when he needed cash. She's a bit confused by some of his history, but she's absolutely sure that he's cold-blooded and utterly ruthless."

"I'll buy that."

"Furthermore, he's quiet and serious. He doesn't play games or have any real wish to be caught. He has no grand desire for acknowledgment. He probably has donned masks and costumes on more than one occasion and might have plastic surgery if he thought it would help him elude the authorities. That part really scares Eve. Most of the time, these killers are caught because deep down they want to be."

Sean nodded. He promised himself he would read the profile later tonight, but first he wanted to know one more thing. He knew exactly how Ian ran these ops and just what he would have Eve do. There would be a profile on everyone involved. "And what did Eve have to say about Grace?"

Ian's mouth flat-lined. "She says Grace is completely harmless unless someone she loves is in danger. Then she would be a tiger. She says Grace is the kind of woman who gives her full loyalty to a person and then it is very difficult to sway her. Grace is the kind of person who loves fully and well. Eve very much liked your Grace."

His Grace. He liked the sound of that. "I think Eve's summed Grace up nicely, so what's the problem?"

"Eve's been wrong before."

Eve had been very, very wrong before, and it had cost two FBI agents their lives. It had been the reason she left the Bureau and finally joined McKay/Taggart where her ex-husband Alexander McKay worked.

"She's not wrong this time. Trust me, Ian, it's going to be all right." Sean turned to get a corkscrew for the wine. When he turned back, Ian had vanished.

Sean shook his head. He would never be able to match Ian's skill, and he was long past wanting to try. He had his own talents. He put the sauce on and then set the chicken to cooking. This particular dish took a long time to properly simmer. It would only be fully flavorful if given the right amount of time to cook. It was a little like a relationship.

But Sean didn't have time. Ian wanted this done, and fast.

If Sean was going to keep Grace at the end of this, he would need to bind her to him, and quickly.

Sean set the heat to low on the stove and picked up his keys. It was time to move the heat up with Grace. Sean thought he knew just how to make her boil.

Chapter Eight

Grace slid into her office chair, perfectly content with the afternoon's excursion. Jake and Adam had been total sweethearts, helping her find three skirts, two blouses, and a dress that showed off her assets to perfection. They had found some swanky boutiques she hadn't known existed. It was good to get a male opinion. Adam had been sweet enough to go into the dressing room with her and help her in and out of the cocktail dresses she'd tried on. He'd missed his calling. Adam should have been a stylist instead of an account rep.

"Tomorrow we could do lingerie." Adam sat down on the edge of her desk. "I know there must be a store around here that sells Agent Provocateur."

"Or La Perla." Jake set down her bags. They had driven around in Jake's Jeep. Grace had decided he was the more butch of the two. He tended to take the lead. Rather like Sean.

"I'm not sure about that."

The way she'd read it, the Dom usually liked to pick out lingerie. Sean was in charge in the bedroom. She wasn't sure he would like another man picking out her undies, even if that man had zero interest in seeing her in them.

Sean. She couldn't get her mind off Sean. She couldn't stop thinking about the fact that her big, strong Viking was at her place puttering around in the kitchen, cooking dinner. He would be there when she got home. For the first time in over a year, since her youngest had fled the nest, she didn't feel a small sense of dread at the thought of heading home. It wouldn't be empty. She could drive up and not be assaulted by a darkened house with its dreary silence and obnoxiously neat rooms. The neatness bothered her. It proved the house wasn't really lived in anymore. For the last year, she'd merely existed there.

Grace hoped Sean was just the tiniest bit messy.

"Come on, Grace," Adam cajoled, pulling her from her thoughts. He leaned in and gave her a sexy little wink. "You would look awfully pretty in a corset. I would pick an emerald green full corset with a matching thong. You could wear those amazing Jimmy Choos we saw."

Grace snorted. Oh, she would love the Jimmy Choos, if she could drop three grand on a pair of shoes. She wasn't so sure about the corset. Sean seemed to prefer her naked. She knew that was the way she preferred him. Grace thought about the scars on his back. She wanted to run her hands along them and ask the story of each one. She knew he'd seen combat. She wondered if he still dreamed about the day he got those scars. She would kiss them, running her lips along each one, learning their touch and taste. Each scar was a part of him. She wanted to know them all, to commit them to her memory.

"So, happy hour tonight?" Jake was looking at the clock.

Grace followed his line of sight. It was a little after two. Three whole hours before she would see Sean. God, she was acting like a lovesick teen. Before she knew it, she would be setting up a Facebook page just so she could say Grace Hawthorne is "in a relationship." Her boys would love that.

"She's not going to happy hour. She's rushing somewhere to see that big bruiser she's screwing six ways to Sunday." Adam's elegantly arched eyebrow dared her to say otherwise.

She wasn't going to lie. She might be discreet with someone else, but she'd gotten close to these guys over the last several weeks.

They had become her confidants. "He's not a bruiser. He's my Viking."

Adam laughed long and hard. It was a husky sound that did strange things to her insides. Now that she was having sex again, she had it on the brain constantly. Sometimes, when Adam and Jake looked at her today, she almost thought they were sizing her up, and not in a purely aesthetic way. She was crazy, of course. Sean Johansson was turning her brain to sexual mush. Adam pulled her out of her chair and wrapped his arms around her in a friendly hug, though his hands were awfully close to her backside. He was all muscle under his designer suit, and he smelled clean and crisp. She could appreciate Adam Miles, but she longed for Sean.

"A Viking? I love the analogy, sweetheart. Tell me something. Did he plunder your goodies last night?"

"He's going to plunder yours if you don't watch it." Jake was shaking his head at his boyfriend's antics. It struck Grace that they seemed intensely bonded for two people who had only gotten together a couple of weeks ago. She had noticed it earlier. They had a whole silent subtext going on between them as though they communicated on a different level.

Before she had a chance to reply, Matt's door opened. He stuck his head out. His eyes were red, and he looked like he hadn't slept in a day or two. "Grace, if you're back from lunch, I'd like to talk to you."

Grace said goodbye to her friends and walked into Matt's office. He wore his weariness like a wrinkled suit. Though she had pulled back from him in the last week, she still felt a tug at her heart when she looked at him. For years he'd been her friend, and now he seemed a little lost. Grace didn't think for one second that Matt's offer the other night had been serious. He was just that guy who never noticed something until someone else had it. The minute Sean was gone, Matt would go back to taking her for granted and being her friendly boss. It was the way Grace preferred it, but for now there was a tension to their every encounter. "What's wrong?"

He shook his head as though to purge himself of thoughts. "Nothing's wrong. As a matter of fact, it looks like we're going to get a big contract. I think I finally nailed down the Bryson

Building's janitorial services."

"Seriously?" Grace let herself smile. Matt had been fighting for that contract for months. "That's good news."

She was happy for Matt, though she wouldn't have done any business at all with that particular building. It was one of the biggest buildings in downtown Fort Worth, and it housed the largest natural gas development company in Texas. Grace knew the building well. She'd dropped off a signed petition there not three weeks before.

He nodded, and his lips curled up, though the smile didn't touch his face. He was too busy gathering up his things. He picked up his cell and wallet and shoved both into his laptop bag. "I'm going to head home for the day. Maybe celebrate a little. Can you handle things here?"

"Of course." She hoped beyond hope that he didn't celebrate too hard. Sean would be pissed if she got a call at three in the morning. "Where's the contract? I'll type it up and get it out to the manager over at the Bryson Building."

He stopped, his face a perfect blank for a second. "Oh, it's not quite ready. I'll just work out the language I want to use and type it up myself."

"What?"

"I can type, Grace."

"No you can't." He was awful. He could barely text without screwing it up. He never typed his own contracts.

Matt drew himself up to his full height, his eyes going slightly hard. "Don't worry about it. I have it handled. I did function before I met you, Grace, and I'll be fine after you're gone."

Grace was startled by that statement. What was that supposed to mean? "I didn't know I was going anywhere."

Matt's eyes refused to meet hers. He stared at some space on the wall behind her. "You think I don't know you're seeing that asshole? You think I missed the glow on your face this morning or that giggling you did with Kayla? Tell me you didn't spend last night with him. You can't. If he has half a brain, he'll take you with him when he leaves."

Grace sighed. "He's not taking me with him, Matt. We've just started to see each other, and he's made it plain that he'll be going

101

back to Chicago in a week or so. It's just a fling."

Matt relaxed slightly. His eyes finally found hers. She was surprised at the depth of relief she found there. "I hope so. I would hate to lose you."

"I'm not going anywhere, so why don't you let me do my job?" She was interested in seeing the contract. At the last meeting she had sat in on, the manager of the building was asking for deep discounts, so deep it would make the job financially untenable. She wondered what sort of magic Matt had worked.

He clutched his briefcase. "I'll get it to you tomorrow. That will be soon enough. Hold down the fort. And Grace, start planning a party for Friday. I want the whole office to celebrate. Someplace nice, okay?"

"Friday? I can't plan anything big for Friday," she sputtered. Parties took time. Parties took planning.

"You'll do it, Grace, or I'll have someone else do it." He practically ran out of the office.

Grace stared at the door for a moment. It wasn't like Matt to offer to do work himself that she could do. He was a lazy man, and he genuinely enjoyed doling out work to other people. His status as the boss was very near and dear to his heart. Grace's curiosity was getting the better of her. She looked at Matt's neat desk. It was neat mostly because Grace kept all the paperwork perfectly organized, and Matt asked for what he needed. That was the way they had worked for the last six years. What was different this time? She thought about the contract. It was for janitorial services.

Evan Parnell would be the liaison.

With only a second's hesitation, Grace opened the top drawer of Matt's desk. She pulled out the first pencil she could find and gently brushed it across the notepad he had left behind. Luckily, Matt never did anything half way. She could easily read what he had written from the impression on the pad. Grace felt her eyebrows come together.

2201 Mount Dale Ave.

The same address that Evan Parnell had written down earlier today. What the hell was at that address? Maybe it was time she took a little side trip.

"So when the boss is away, will the secretary play?"

Grace gasped and flushed as though she'd been caught doing something bad. She opened the drawer and placed the notepad inside Matt's desk. Playing it cool, she straightened the rest of the desk as she looked up at the man. "Nope. Doing my regular ritual of making sure my boss can see his desk through the usual mess."

Sean was standing in the doorframe. He looked deliciously casual in tight jeans, a black T-shirt, and cowboy boots. Even from across the room she could see the sensual look in his eyes. He shut the door. Sean walked straight up to her and towered over her, leaving not an inch of personal space between them.

"Hey, I thought you were cooking." She knew she sounded breathless, but that was because he wasn't leaving her room to breathe. He looked slightly predatory as he leaned over. There was no mistaking the sexual tension he was exuding. Sean Johansson was hungry...for her.

"It's simmering. It's perfectly fine. It's a dish that requires all afternoon to prepare. I thought I would come here to see if I could get you to sneak away with me for your afternoon coffee break, but it looks like you already went out."

The bags. He must have seen her bags. Oh, it was hard to think when his mouth was hovering so close to hers. She could feel the warmth of his body. She wouldn't need a blanket when Sean was in her bed. His big body was a furnace. He was leaning over her, looking at her with his intensely blue eyes, and everything inside her was heating up to match him. How could he affect her like this? He made her forget everything. "I just went shopping with the boys."

His eyes narrowed, and his voice became a low growl. "Boys? I was unaware your sons were in town."

She shook her head. She backed up, seeking the tiniest bit of space. Unfortunately, she backed straight into the desk. Sean's hands cupped her hips, tightening to let her know he required an answer. "They aren't. I was with some friends from the office. They helped me pick out some new outfits."

A little smile curled his lips. "Did you feel a need to look pretty, Grace? If that was the problem, baby, you shouldn't be putting on clothes, you should be taking them off." His hands were pulling up the sides of her skirt, caressing the skin he uncovered. They felt so strong on her skin, Grace found herself hopping up onto Matt's desk, wrapping her legs around his waist. "I think that's how you look best."

She gave him a bright smile. "I'm glad, but Adam thinks I look best in greens and blues. He says I should wear jewel tones."

Sean's hands dropped from their long, provocative exploration of her thighs to rest on his hips. He looked down at her. "Adam?"

"Yes, Adam, from sales. You met him at O'Hagen's a couple of days ago. If you don't like him then you better get used to him, because he's my friend. He's my friend, and so is his boyfriend, Jake." She placed special emphasis on the word boyfriend to let Sean know he had no reason to be jealous. Just the fact that he was a little bit jealous made her heart rate speed up. She let her hands find the sides of his face, stroking him. "So don't get upset when I shop with them. Besides, if I took you, I bet you wouldn't help me out in the dressing room the way Adam does. You would probably spend the whole time wondering when we could go home."

His mouth dropped open. His face became a mask of masculine outrage. "He was with you in the dressing room?"

Grace reached out to pat him soothingly. It was no big deal. It was just Adam. If the room had been big enough, she would have invited Jake in, too. "I needed help with the zippers."

"That better be all he helped you with." Sean's teeth were clenched.

Grace laughed. "Silly, what else would he help me with? I told you he's gay. He's much more interested in the way my clothes fit than anything I have underneath them."

Sean muttered something under his breath that Grace didn't quite catch, though it sounded a bit violent. He took a deep breath, and his face was gentler when he moved forward into her arms. "Listen, I don't care if he's never touched a woman in his life. I don't want him touching mine. Indulge me. I have a possessive nature. Feel free to shop with Adam all you like, but he's not allowed in the dressing room with you. Hell, we can go on a double date with the boys if it makes you happy, but this naked body is for me and me alone."

God, when he talked like that he sounded like he was interested in much more than a week-long fling. She was setting herself up to get hurt, but she couldn't help it. She would rather know. "Sean, you sound serious."

"When did I ever say I wasn't?" He smiled slightly and tipped her head up. He reached into his pocket and pulled out a small object. He let it dangle in his hand. Grace stared for a moment at the small, gold heart falling from a gold chain. "Do you understand what this means?"

She kind of thought she did, but she'd rather hear it from him. "A present?"

"It's more than that. If I was taking you to a club, I would put a collar around your neck to let the others know that you belong to me. This isn't a traditional collar, but you can wear it during the day. It's a symbol that you accept me as your Dom. Grace, will you wear this?"

It was the almost hesitant way he asked the question that sent her heart reeling. He wasn't a Dom in that moment, just a man who was a little scared he was going to be rejected. Grace gave him her most brilliant smile and held her hair up so he could put it on. Sean worked the clasp, and the heart fell against Grace's skin just below her neck. She brought her hand up to touch it. "I love it."

And she was starting to love him.

Now the Dom was back. He looked down at her with a wholly-satisfied smile. "It looks good on you. So, no more intimate shopping trips with other men."

She knew a dictate when she heard it. And, if she thought about it, she wouldn't be comfortable with another woman helping Sean into his pants whether she liked men or not. Grace decided to bow to this rule, though he was already breaking his "I only dominate in the bedroom" speech. It didn't surprise her. He was an overwhelming man. She relished the challenge. "Fine. Adam doesn't come into the dressing room with me."

"Good, then we can move on to the more interesting portion of the visit." His tone went dark and deep. "Show me your breasts, Grace."

She swallowed hard. "What?"

105

He took a step back, and his eyes went hard and icy. He really didn't like to repeat himself. "I said show me your breasts. They belong to me. I want to see them."

Grace looked back to the door, wondering who would walk in. Normally Matt's office was off limits, but then she was also usually sitting outside acting as a gatekeeper. Anyone could walk in. Her heart sped up.

"I'm waiting, and I won't ask again."

Grace's hands went to the buttons of her blouse when she saw Sean checking out the office chair. She knew exactly what he was thinking. He was wondering how it would work as a place to spank her. She decided it would be infinitely more dignified to be caught showing him her breasts than with her bare ass in the air. Of course, she could always walk away. The little gold heart was pressed against her throat, a reminder of everything building between them. She didn't pause, but kept unbuttoning the blouse. She was never going to walk away as long as he still wanted her.

Sean watched her with hooded eyes. His tongue came out to moisten his lips when Grace finally undid the last button and worked the front clasp of her bra open. Her breasts bounced free from their constraints. She knew they weren't as perky as they used to be. They were forty years old and had fed two children, but when Sean looked at her like a hungry lion, she couldn't help but feel sexy.

He stared at her for a long moment, the caress of his eyes almost palpable on her flesh. Her nipples tightened in response, and she thrust her chest out so he didn't miss an inch. The waiting was almost unbearable. She wanted his hands on her, his mouth covering her flesh.

"You are gorgeous, little one." His big hand came out to cup a breast, molding it and squeezing gently. Grace sighed, utterly content at the contact.

Sean stood in front of her and took both breasts in his hands. He pushed them together and then held them apart. He played with her nipples, pinching them between his thumbs. He had them hard and rigid and ready when he pushed the right one up and bent over. Grace's head fell back as his hot mouth closed over her nipple. Her legs moved restlessly up and down his sides as he sucked. He licked and played with the breast as though he was a boy fascinated with a new toy. He didn't miss an inch, licking around the areola and finally nipping the brown and pink nipple between his teeth.

"Tonight, I'm putting these gorgeous tits in clamps. They'll jiggle while you ride me. I like to watch your breasts bounce."

The image made Grace's pussy clench in anticipation while Sean feasted on the other breast.

After giving her left breast the full treatment, his lips worked up her neck pausing briefly to kiss the small heart that now marked her as his. He reached her mouth, and his tongue plunged in, allowing not a moment for retreat. He pulled her into his erection, grinding that big cock against her, only his slacks and her skirt between them.

Grace pushed against him. She was so ready to take him. She no longer cared who walked in or where they were. She only cared that he not stop until he'd given her what she needed.

"Turn around." Sean's command was a harsh whip as he pulled away from her. He was working the fly of his jeans.

Grace did as he asked. She got off the desk and turned, bracing herself against the wood. She heard a small crinkling and knew Sean had come prepared. He pushed her skirt up.

"I don't think we'll need these." He pushed her panties off her hips and down her legs. She obediently stepped out of them, and he set them to the side. His hands caressed her bare ass, then moved lower. He ran his finger down to her cunt and played in the juices he found there. He slid his fingers around, parting her labia. "You are so wet for me. Tell me, do you want me?"

"God, yes." She was going to die if he didn't take her soon.

"What do you want me to do to you?" His fingers teased around her clit, rubbing tantalizingly and then scurrying away. Grace moved, trying to get his fingers back. His hands moved from her cunt to her breasts. He pinched a nipple hard, the pain rushing into sensual pleasure in an instant. "I asked a question, Grace. What do you want me to do to you?"

She gave him the only honest answer she had. "Fuck me, Sir. Please fuck me."

"Well, since you asked so nicely, sub." He gripped her hips and shoved his rock-hard cock straight up her pussy.

The force of the thrust nearly rocked her off her feet. Grace held onto the desk as Sean fucked her. She heard him grunt behind her and wished there was a mirror. She loved watching his face contort as he approached orgasm. He pounded into her, holding back nothing. Sean wasn't careful or gentle, and as he had given her no instructions to be still, she matched him. Grace pushed back against him, clamping down on his cock as Sean tunneled in and pulled out. This was what she had missed all day. She had missed the feeling of Sean moving inside her, possessing her. She had missed the connection of his skin against hers.

He fucked her for what seemed like forever. The only sound in the room was their mingled moans and the slap of flesh against flesh. The rhythm held, her every breath a note in the song they were creating.

Sean rubbed her clit over and over, his fingers sliding firmly over her pulsing flesh. She came three times. Each time the wave rolled across her stronger than before. She had to bite her lip to keep from screaming out. Finally he moaned, and she felt the moment he lost control. He bucked up into her, raising her onto her toes as he seemed to seek fusion between them. Grace cried out as his dick slid across her G-spot, and she came stronger than ever before, her nails digging into the wood of the desk. She slammed back into Sean, not wanting to lose him even after she'd reached her orgasm. Sean's hands tightened almost painfully on her hips when he held himself deep inside her and groaned. He thrust in once again and then fell on her, pressing her down against the desk.

She rested for a sweet moment. She loved the feel of his weight against her, his breath on the back of her neck. He kissed her there gently before lifting himself up with a sigh. He helped her up, wrapped the condom in some tissues and tossed it in the trash can. He zipped his pants back up, looking perfectly proper except for the lazy, satiated look in his eyes. Grace tried to straighten her clothes. Her shirt was hopelessly wrinkled, and her panties were a lost cause. There was no way she was putting them back on.

Sean's smirk did nothing to lessen his appeal. He held up the silky bikinis. "Shall I take them with me?"

"Gee, thanks." She kissed him and nearly ran to the bathroom to clean up. It was going to be a long afternoon.

The hours ticked away, but Grace's mind was on that address she'd found rather than Sean. Even after he'd gone and she'd retrieved the notepad, tossing out the top sheet and placing it back on Matt's desk, she couldn't help but feel that something was going on behind her back.

Chapter Nine

Evan Parnell went through his folder for about the hundredth time. The note with the address he'd written down was gone. He knew he'd placed it carefully in the folder. It was what he did. He wouldn't forget. He didn't make mistakes like that. He was careful. He was perfect. He had to be, with all the assholes after him. He wondered, and not for the first time, if this brilliant plan of his was going to unravel. That was the trouble with long games. You never knew when they were going to go wrong. It took patience and will to play a long game, but he'd been trained well. He wouldn't panic. He was far too close to the prize.

He shouldn't have moved his stash. He should have simply brought it back to his base and locked it in the safe. And that would risk one of his "soldiers" finding out he wasn't who he said he was. *Damn it*. What choice did he have? He was so close to not having to worry about this shit.

Evan went through the day in his brain. It played out in his mind like a movie. The morning had started the way every morning started. He'd woken exactly fifteen minutes before the alarm was set to go off at six a.m. He'd trained his body long ago to wake at that time. He'd eaten a breakfast of egg whites, turkey bacon, and mango. It was properly portioned. It was what he ate every day without fail. He'd spent an hour jogging and then headed into the city by train. He'd met with Matt and left before ten to prepare for his online meeting with his South American contact. There was no way they could ever outbid the Chinese, but it never hurt to let the Chinese know he had options. Melissa had picked him up at the office, and they'd gone back to the safe house. He'd spent the rest of the morning on the computer preparing for the meeting. He'd gone over the plans and schematics for the Bryson Building now that everything was in.

It was only as he sat down to his lunch served at exactly 12:30 that he realized something was missing from his case. He'd put it off, preferring not to break his schedule. He'd had a conference with his contact and verified that he had the funds he needed. Then, and only then, was he able to concentrate on the problem of the missing information.

He'd gone through his briefcase exactly ten times. He'd been careful and thorough. It wasn't there. He'd gone to the van and searched it as well.

It wasn't as if he needed that one slip of paper. He remembered the address. He remembered everything. Matt had been the one to write it down. Evan had been the one to tear it off that fucking notepad of his. The last thing any of them needed was a paper trail beyond what was absolutely necessary, but Matt was too stupid to see that. If only he didn't need his brother...

Evan let the thought go. He did need him, for now. Matt had all the charm Evan didn't, despite his lamentable drinking problem. Matt had always been the charming one. It was why Evan had been the one to get the majority of the beatings handed out in their household.

He pushed the bad memories away. He didn't have time to remember his childhood just this moment. If he hadn't lost the paper in the van or the house, then he'd lost it between the office and here.

He remembered the wind whipping around downtown this morning. Evan closed his eyes and the scene came back to him. He had hurried down the stairs, eager to keep his schedule. He'd passed the new salesmen his brother had hired. They were queer, but Evan didn't really care about that. He'd passed Grace Hawthorne. Now Grace was someone Evan did care about. Grace might not realize it, but she knew far too much about his dealings. She'd been walking up from the parking lot. He'd glimpsed her briefly and then kept moving.

What if he'd lost it and Grace had picked it up?

That bitch was too close to his brother. How many times was he going to have to explain to Matt that he couldn't trust Grace? He'd had a mini-breakthrough over the last week. Grace was apparently hot for some client, and it was pissing off Matt. Evan had decided then and there to use it to push the nosy secretary out of Matt's inner circle. She was too "concerned" for Evan's comfort. If he hadn't been sure it would make his brother turn from him, he would have gotten rid of Grace long ago.

"Boss."

Evan turned at the sound of Melissa's voice. Now there was a woman. Melissa was an obedient soldier. She was a true believer in the cause. In truth, Evan didn't give a shit about the cause, but he did find fanatics to be very useful. They were awfully compliant little pawns as long as they didn't figure out he was only playing a game.

He gestured for the lithe brunette to enter and waited for her report.

"I found something you might want to see on the camera you put in Wright's office. And, sir, congratulations on getting the deal on the Bryson Building finalized. It will be a glorious day when we take down that monster."

A little tremble caught him off guard. He hadn't realized that his brother's potential betrayal had the ability to hurt him. His years of work should have burned that emotion out of his soul. Everyone betrayed him in the end. Yet, the thought of his brother actively turning against him rankled. Evan didn't like the feeling. Still, he had a role to play.

"We should all be congratulated, dear. And it will be a glorious day when we bring it down. Now, what has Wright done? Anything that might compromise our mission?" In no way could he allow his connection to Wright to be known. Only he and his brother knew the truth.

"It isn't Wright. It's the secretary." Melissa smiled a bit. She didn't do it often, and that moderate curling of her lips never warmed her up. "It's nothing of importance. I just thought you might find it amusing."

"Did you send it to me?" Evan opened his laptop and had the e-mail screen working in no time flat. Melissa answered in the affirmative, but Evan was already watching. She'd cued it up perfectly. A cold chill went through Evan's body as he saw that nosy bitch going through the stuff on Matt's desk. She looked down at the notepad. Evan watched as she took a pencil and revealed the address Matt had written down. Grace Hawthorne didn't know it, but her Scooby Doo move had just signed her death warrant.

"Please don't forward any information at all to Mr. Wright. He's become a bit unstable. Treat him as a hostile but useful ally."

Melissa nodded as though she'd known all along. "There's more. You should watch it all the way through. I have some things to take care of, unless you need me."

Evan waved her off. She walked out, and he gave his attention back to the computer. He'd set up the surveillance on his brother as a precaution. Matt was weak when it came to some things. It was important to make sure he towed the line. Now, he could see that his plan had been brilliant for another reason.

The large man from earlier in the week walked into the frame. He stalked Grace like a hungry lion. He moved well. Evan hadn't noticed it before. Johansson was the name he'd given. This Johansson fellow moved *really* well. Evan backed up the tape and watched him again. His long limbs moved with a fluid grace that went beyond mere athleticism. Evan bet he moved silently, too, out of long practice. It was how the military trained their black ops to move. Sean Johansson—if that was really his name—was former black ops. Evan had no doubt about that. So what was a former Green Beret or Navy SEAL doing in Fort Worth, negotiating some pissant deal?

Evan's brain filtered through the possibilities. He could have left the life and gotten a civvie job. Evan watched Johansson. His attention seemed to be focused on Grace. He crowded the secretary.

He could be exactly what he said he was. Evan made a note to check into his background. Johansson was either an idiot who liked to fuck secretaries, or he was a plant. That notion gave Evan a rolling wave of nausea. There was only one person in the world who would have planted a soldier at the same temp agency Patrick Wright's brother owned. How had that fucker found him? Or had he? Was this a fishing trip or a hunt? Uncertainty gnawed at Evan. He would have to figure it out before he made his final move.

The scene continued as Johansson flipped up Matt's secretary's skirt and fucked her right there on her boss's desk. At least one thing had gone right on this shitty day. A warm feeling spread through Evan's chest. *This must be what happiness feels like.* It was right there, the final wedge he would drive between Matt and that little whore.

He would be able to kill Grace Hawthorne with his brother's full approval.

And then he would work on that Johansson bastard. He was just a pawn, like all the rest. Evan knew he could take him out and then concentrate on the power players.

* * * *

Sean entered the bedroom after making sure the kitchen was clean for the night. Despite his earlier claims that he didn't clean, he'd been happy to stand beside Grace and load the dishwasher. It had been a familiar domestic scene that tugged at him in ways he didn't want to contemplate given his earlier conversation with Ian. Still, he'd enjoyed the evening far more than he'd expected. Grace was witty and smart and had a wicked sense of humor. She also knew when the Dom was back in the house. Sean had deepened his voice and told her to wait for him in the bedroom. She'd gotten up and walked off to obey without an argument. She'd merely looked at him with those "love me, protect me, take me" hazel eyes of hers and disappeared behind the door.

He was an asshole. He was going to burn in hell for what he was doing to her. He called himself every nasty name in the book and still went to the laundry room to make sure the alarm was off.

He didn't need to unlock the door. He'd passed Jake the copy of the key he'd made. He'd given his partner the key to Grace's house, a perfect copy of the one she'd handed him in complete trust and love.

Grace was in love with him, and he was letting wolves into her home.

It was all for the best. It was all to protect her. His heart hurt, but he opened the door to the bedroom anyway.

Sean looked down at Grace and a rush of arousal flooded his system. He was always aroused around her, but seeing her like this made him feel like a giant among men. She was a soft bit of heaven waiting for his command. As he had ordered, she was waiting for him on the floor of the bedroom in her submissive position. Sean ran a hand through her hair and was satisfied with her little sigh. She reminded him of a kitten when she made that sound. She purred when he stroked her. Only one thing marred the perfection of her waiting for his command. The way Grace had reacted to him walking into her boss's office made Sean uneasy. She'd been nervous, and Sean couldn't figure out why. She'd been startled, as though he'd discovered her doing something she shouldn't. He'd thought about rifling through Wright's desk while she'd gone to the bathroom, but she'd left the door open and the office had been crowded by that point in time. What was she hiding?

She looked utterly guileless. Sean let his worry slip away. He had a job to do.

Sean's job had been given to him in the plainest English possible. Distract the girl. Ian had been very clear on that point. Sean was to keep Grace occupied and then let Jake and Adam into the house when she was safely asleep. They hadn't been able to quietly copy her hard drive. It was too risky at the office. Grace's desk was out in the open. Even when Sean had distracted her earlier, they hadn't gotten the job done. It had to be tonight.

"Undress me."

Grace was on her feet in an instant. Her hands went to the buttons of his shirt, carefully undoing each one. She was meticulous. She unbuttoned one, pushed back the material, and moved down after kissing the flesh she'd exposed. After she did the first one, she'd looked up to him for permission. He said nothing, but let his lips tug up to give her the answer she wanted. When she reached the bottom of the shirt she pushed it off and folded it neatly, laying it on her dresser. She came back and got to her knees to unbuckle his belt.

Oh, yes, he wanted a kiss there. His cock was already rigidly erect and those butterfly kisses she touched to his shaft did nothing to help the problem. His slacks and boxers hit the floor as she gave his balls the same attention. God, they felt heavy. They were ready to go off at a moment's notice, but he held back from shoving his cock in her mouth. She would let him, but tonight wasn't about that. Tonight was about showing Grace he could handle her.

Guilt gnawed at Sean's insides, but his cock didn't seem to care. All his cock knew was that Grace was willing to play a little game. She kissed his balls one last time and then folded the rest of his clothes and put away his shoes. She sank back to her position and waited. Sean walked around to the bedside table where he had stored his purchases from earlier in the day. He took out the lovely clamps he'd bought with her coloring in mind.

"Up." He only needed the one word, and Grace moved from the floor to the bed. She faced him on her white quilt. "Hands on your ankles, little one."

Grace did as he asked. She couldn't possibly know how much her trust meant to him or how very little he deserved it. She leaned back and clutched her ankles. It left her body completely open to him. Her breasts thrust out, and her knees opened wide giving him the loveliest view of her pussy. It was already creamy, and he hadn't touched it yet.

He felt a satisfied smile tug at his lips. All he had to do to get Grace hot was feed her. Of course, he'd fed her himself. He'd made sure she was naked and then sat her in his lap and fed her each bite. He'd made sure she got an excellent meal along with a fine wine, and now it was time for dessert. Grace was definitely on the menu. Looking at her spread out like a feast for his taking, his guilt was getting crowded out by desire. God, he'd never wanted a woman like he wanted this one.

He reached out and cupped her breasts. The weight of them in his hands was already a thing of comfort and familiarity to him. Her skin was luminous in the low light of the bedroom. She looked so gorgeous it almost took his mind off what he had to do tonight. Sean looked over at her wine glass. It was half full. Sean wondered if that was enough. He couldn't be sure.

He'd never drugged a lover before.

Sean took her nipple in his hands. It was already a hard point. It stood at attention and practically begged for him to take it between his teeth and tug. He wasn't playing that way tonight. Sean rolled the pert thing between his thumb and forefinger and quickly attached the clamp. Grace gasped as the pretty clamp with small green crystals bit into her flesh. Sean methodically attached the matching clamp and looked at his work.

She would look pretty with rings. If he convinced her to pierce those gorgeous nipples, he wouldn't have to take them out. They would always be there for him to play with. He could tug on them with his fingers or his tongue. He could run a small chain through them or attach little weights to stimulate them. He could walk her around a club wearing nothing but the jewelry he placed on her body.

For the first time in his life, Sean understood his brother's fascination with totally immersive D/s. As he sat looking at his sub, he thought about owning her completely. If she was his slave, he would simply order her to quit her job and keep her safe at home where he could make sure no asshole like Matt Wright ever took advantage of her again. He could shield her from the world.

"Beautiful." He ran a finger from the base of her neck down her chest. He ran his finger over her warm flesh across the sweet little swell of her belly and down to that soft pussy. Grace shuddered slightly as his fingers swirled in her wet folds. The crystals on the clamps quivered slightly. Sean gave in to his fantasy. For tonight, she belonged to him, body and soul. "Who do you belong to, sub?"

"I belong to you, Sir."

"And who do you serve?" His middle finger gently circled her clit. He made sure not to actually touch the pouting little pearl.

"I serve you, Sir." The hitch in her breath let Sean know she wanted nothing more than that one touch he was denying her. Anticipation was the key to pleasure, that and patience.

"How do you serve me?"

"Any way you like, Sir."

He couldn't help but smile. She meant it. She would serve him any way he asked because she trusted him to never hurt her. He never would, not in any physical way. Her heart was another story altogether. Would it make a difference if he told her how deep he was in with her? That he'd never felt this much for another woman? Or would she just see it as one more lie he'd told her?

Sex. He'd bind her to him with sex. She'd be pissed when she found out the truth, but their relationship would have grounding. He was her Dom. He'd tell her to listen and she would, but only if he wrapped her in pleasure she knew she couldn't get anywhere else.

He decided to start where he already was. He allowed his thumb to firmly rub her clitoris. That plump little nubbin quivered, and her cream coated Sean's hand. Grace was biting her lip. He knew that his little sub was thinking of anything to get her mind off coming. She didn't have permission, and she was obviously trying to be so, so good.

"Come for me, but quietly. I want not a word to pass those sweet lips or we'll have some discipline." He circled her clit, and her hips shook as she allowed the sensation to take her. Her breathy moans told him she'd enjoyed her orgasm. It was just a little starter orgasm, nothing compared to what he could give her, but the night was young. Grace was so responsive. He'd have her screaming by the time it was over. Then he'd get to discipline her. All just another part of the game.

Sean pulled his hand away and without really thinking about it, brought his fingers to his mouth. He loved the tangy taste of her. He licked his fingers then decided that little appetizer didn't suit him. He needed more than an *amuse-bouche*.

Grace let out a breathy cry as he got down on his stomach and shoved his face in her pussy. He licked her from her pulsing clit to just before the rosette of her ass where he firmly intended to spend some time this evening. He gently ate at her tender labia, his tongue swirling, lapping up the cream that poured out of her. Her pussy was plump and ripe and ready to go off again. He brought two fingers up, coated them in her arousal and gently pushed them inside her cunt. His tongue set a firm, quick rhythm against her clit. He fucked her with his fingers and tongue until his sweet, obedient sub gave up and cried out over and over. Sean didn't stop until her shaking did. Her whole body jumped as he gave her clit one last lick. Aftershocks.

Sean got up from the bed. Grace fell back with a little cry. He waited patiently for her to open her eyes. It took a moment, but those hazel beauties were round when she finally sat up.

"I know I wasn't supposed to make a sound. I'm sorry, Sir."

She wasn't. He could tell. Again, another part of the game. He liked playing with Grace because she really was playing. She wanted the spanking he'd promised her. She would enjoy it thoroughly. He could play with her like this in the evenings and during the day she would turn her tart tongue on him and put him on his ass when he needed it. It was the best of both worlds. A submissive in the bedroom and an utterly reliable partner in the outside world.

"Hands and knees. Present that ass to me."

She wiggled it a little as she followed his command. She was saucy even when she was playing the game. She thought she knew what was going to happen. It was time to trip her up a little, to let her know she couldn't count on her Dom to follow the rules.

"Discipline doesn't always involve a spanking. Sometimes it's much worse."

"How much worse?" She turned her head back, and Sean was happy with the bit of trepidation in her eyes.

"I hope you enjoyed those orgasms, sweetheart. They're the last you'll have for a bit."

Sean got the vibrator he'd bought and carefully cleaned. He took up a position behind her and set it on a low hum. Grace's pussy was wet with anticipation when he gently worked it into her. "Hold it in place, Grace. I'm not done showing you your toys yet."

Her hand came up to hold the vibe in place. She wobbled for a moment but maintained her position. Sean took out his next little gift. A nice-sized plug. He chuckled as he lubed it up. Grace was already groaning. The vibe was starting to work back and forth, harder and faster in her pussy.

"Don't you come, sub." It was an order given with every bit of bite he'd have put into ordering around his old unit. The vibe's motion slowed. "I swear I'll have you tied to the headboard and feet in a spreader, and you'll have to sleep that way. You won't come for days, but you'll suck me morning and night. Is that understood?"

"Yes, Sir." She sounded like it was hard to concentrate. He intended to make it almost impossible.

"Now, when I say so, I want you to push back against me."

Grace groaned and muttered a curse word under her breath. She seemed to know what was coming.

Sean smacked her ass. "Watch your language." He took the perfectly lubed plug and placed it against her tight little asshole. He worked the pink plug in just a bit. She was tight. Sean's dick throbbed in anticipation. She was going to be like a vise on his cock. He rimmed her hole and started to thrust the plug into her ass in short strokes. Gradually his patience was rewarded as she began to flower open for him.

"Push back."

Her backside obediently flattened out and pushed back against his hand. The plug slid home, deep inside her ass, opening her for his later use. Grace let out a shaky breath. Sean sat back on his heels and looked at her. The plug was a sweet little sign of his possession. Sean leaned over and kissed the dimples in her lower back. He ran his hands along the globes of her ass. She was so feminine. There was nothing bony or boyish about his Grace. She was made for a man to enjoy. Sean intended to be that man—the only one.

He reached down, and his hand replaced hers on the vibe. He fucked her gently, making sure to stop every time she approached orgasm. He used one hand on the vibe and let his free hand tug on the clamps, pulling and plucking her nipples like he was playing an instrument. Grace was shaking with the need to come after the time ticked on and on. Her head fell forward, and he knew she had reached her boundary. This was what a Dom did. He pushed his sub to find her limits and bring her the greatest pleasure she could experience.

"Beg me, Grace."

She didn't hesitate. "Please. Please, Sir. Please let me come."

He decided it was time to give in. He picked up the condom

he'd laid out and rolled it on his dick. "Since you asked so nicely. But not without me. Hold the vibe."

Her hand came up to keep her pussy filled. His balls drew up painfully at just the thought of what he was about to do. Sean gingerly pulled the plug out of her hole. The little rosette puckered and clenched as though trying to keep its prize. He had something bigger in mind. He squirted warm lube on his hands and stroked himself from bulb to base, making sure he was slippery. He heard Grace moan, and her hips shook. He could feel her heat from here. His hands were a little shaky, too. It had been so long since sex had been more than a physical itch to be scratched. There was so much more than his cock involved in this.

But his cock wanted its way now. Sean gripped her glorious, curvy hips and lined his dick up to her rosy ass. He couldn't contain his groan as he pushed in, battling the little muscles he found there. Her anus clenched around him, sucking him in and pushing him out all at the same time. She felt so good. Without needing to be told, Grace pushed against him, aiding him. Inch by fiery inch, he tunneled his way in until there was nowhere further to go, until his balls were flush against her. Sean held himself there for a moment, enjoying the sensation of being balls deep in Grace's ass.

"Please." One little word that did strange things to his heart because it came out of her mouth.

"Yes, love." Sean reached down and took the vibe, pushing her hand away. He wanted control. He wanted to be the one filling her from both ends. He flicked the little button that dialed the vibe up and then started fucking her.

Grace was gone. She moaned and thrust back against him, bucking and thrashing in her attempt to get what had been denied her so long. He knew exactly what she was thinking because he was the man who had led her there. Sean stopped holding back, too. There was no place for finesse now. He pounded into her ass. He pulled out and shoved back in, the tight hole fighting him deliciously all the way. He moved the vibe in and out in time to the motion of his cock, flicking up to ensure the little rabbit head rubbed her clit. Grace screamed as she came. The sound was primal and entirely feminine. It filled Sean with pride and caused his balls to draw up even tighter. Grace thrust back against him, and the fight was over.

Sean released the vibe and gripped both of her hips savagely. He pushed her on and off his cock with no thought now except his own pleasure. Fire sizzled across his balls, and he groaned as come shot from his cock. Sean didn't even try to hold himself up. He allowed himself to fall against her, his weight pressing her into the bed. His whole body felt languid as the blood pulsed through him. He wrapped his arms around Grace and was surrounded by the softness of her skin and the sweet smell of her body. Her red hair tickled him, and their legs tangled as he rolled off her, but kept her close to him. Grace laid her head across his chest. So sweet. So trusting.

"I'm going to draw us a bath and get you another glass of wine, little one." The words were out of his mouth. He'd pushed them through.

Sean forced himself to move. He got up and went to the bathroom, disposed of the condom and cleaned himself off. He needed a minute. That hadn't been sex. That had been something more, and he was a bit unsettled by it. God, he had a job to do. He didn't want to do it. How long would the drug take? Not long, he hoped. He prayed Alex had prescribed the right dose. If anything happened to Grace, he would never be able to forgive himself. Sean went back in the bedroom. Maybe the damn drug would have done its work. He didn't want to give her another dose. Damn it, he wouldn't. If this dose didn't do its job, then they would make it another night. He knew Ian would have his hide, but Sean didn't care.

"Are you all right, Grace? I didn't go easy on you."

She had a dreamy little smile on her face as she looked up at him. "Yes, Sir."

Sean kissed her forehead then climbed back in with her. He had a bit of aftercare to take care of before he went into professional mode. Grace rolled over so she was flat on her back. She was so gorgeous, a goddess in repose. With a little sound of regret, Sean reached over and gently detached the clamps on her nipples. Grace's lovely face pinched a little against the pain the rush of blood caused.

Sean leaned over and kissed the affected area before moving on to the second nipple. He lowered his head and kissed that one as well. This time Grace's hand moved to his head. Her fingers tangled in his hair.

"I love you." She breathed the words, but they still hit him like an out-of-control locomotive slamming into a little bug in its path. He stopped and was perfectly still as the reality hit him.

Grace loved him. She'd said the words. Grace had said the "L" word, and not the one that always made him a little hot. She'd said the one that scared the holy crap out of him. His heart pounded in his chest as he realized he was really expected to say something back to her. What was he supposed to say? He knew what he was supposed to say, but she wouldn't believe him. She would believe him now, perhaps, but later she would think he'd lied. He didn't want to lie to her. God, did he love Grace? He knew she was the one. He just didn't know if he actually believed in the concept of love.

Grace sat up, lightly pushing him away. "Wow. That'll teach me to speak without permission."

Sean looked into her eyes. They were wide and wouldn't quite catch his own. She looked down at her hands. "Grace…"

Her smile was far too bright when she finally looked at him. "You said something about a bath? I think a shower is more in order. I have a really early day tomorrow, and I'm feeling a little woozy. I should probably get some sleep."

She started to scramble off the bed. Sean's hand came out to grasp her wrist. "I said a bath, Grace. Are we or are we not still in the bedroom? I'm still in charge here."

"I don't want to play anymore, Sean."

"I'm not playing. The sex might be a game, but the feelings are real. I'm honored that you feel that way. I'm crazy about you, too."

He pulled her back into his arms. She was stiff at first. He was patient. He ran his hands along her back, tracing the curve of her spine. He tangled their legs together, completely unwilling to give up their intimacy. His lips found her mouth, and he insistently found his way in. He groaned when she softened under him and submitted. He rolled her on her back and covered her body with his. He wasn't going to let her go. He was never going to let her go. She was his.

Without a single thought to anything except branding her, Sean forced her legs apart. His dick was already at full attention again, something of a miracle. He'd always needed a bit of rest between bouts, but not with Grace. His hunger for her seemed insatiable. He placed his forehead against hers and thrust into her pussy.

"Oh, Sean." No Sir this time. Sean knew she wasn't playing. This wasn't a game.

Sean pulled out and thrust back in. She felt perfect around him, so hot, so tight and needy. He couldn't say it. He couldn't tell her he loved her. But he could show her. He could give her this. Sean let his body lay on hers, forcing her to take every bit of his weight. She could handle it. She was his mate. Rather than protesting the rough treatment, Grace held on. Her legs wrapped tightly around his waist, and her hands dug into his back, urging him on. The first time had taken forever. This one was already racing to the conclusion. It felt too sweet to be inside her with nothing between them. Vaguely, alarm bells rang in Sean's head. He wasn't wearing a condom. He was going to come. He was going to come deep inside Grace. His balls drew up as though they completely agreed with that bad decision.

He didn't pause. He shoved his full length deep inside. His pelvis ground down onto her clit. Grace moaned as she came, her legs a vise around his waist. Her pussy clamped down on his cock, and the deed was done. Those tiny muscles milked him. His eyes watered as he pumped come into her. He never wanted the sensation to end. He spasmed as he gave up the last of his semen and slumped forward into her arms. He laid there listening to the steady beat of her heart.

He was so fucked.

It didn't matter. She wouldn't believe him, so it didn't matter what he said. He could be honest.

"I love you, too, Grace."

He looked up so he could see her reaction, enjoy a little time with the only woman he'd ever said the words to.

Grace was asleep. The drug had finally done its work. It was time for Sean to do his.

Chapter Ten

"Took you long enough, man. I thought you were going to go another round." Jake pulled away from the shadows, his lean body moving like a ghost. It was his special talent. Jacob Dean had been a ghost in Sean's unit. Jake had been the one he sent in when the situation called for an invisible man. His old friend grinned at him, even white teeth showing through the low gloom of Grace's living room. "And I thought Adam was going to die from the desire to be in your place."

"He still might." Sean was feeling a little savage. The last thing he needed was to be reminded that the ménage boys would love to take his place with Grace.

"Liam said you were taking it easy on Grace." Adam followed Jake into the living room. He carried a small case with him. "That's not what it sounded like from out here."

Sean felt his jaw clench. He'd forgotten Liam had bugged the bedroom. He couldn't stand the thought that they'd been listening to Grace's breathy moans, her cries of pleasure. Those were for his ears alone. "You're going to destroy that tape, Adam."

He held his hands up. "Don't blame me. And I don't have the tape. It's on a computer, and Eve already downloaded it." Adam's dark green eyes turned startlingly sympathetic. "You gotta watch it, man. I know she's an amazing lady, but you can't tell her you love her. She's going to be hurt. She's already crazy about you. She's not some agent who's playing a game. She's a real woman, and she'll take you seriously."

"She was already drugged when I said it. She didn't hear me." Sean had to take comfort in the fact. The truth was the drug had been working in her system long before that. She probably wouldn't remember she'd said I love you. That would be best for both of them. He didn't want to talk about this. "Can we get this over with? Or have the two of you completely forgotten how to hack a system?"

Adam's eyes narrowed. "I think I can handle it."

"Yeah, like you handled it this afternoon when you were supposed to do a simple download so I didn't have to fucking drug her?"

"Hey, asshole, I didn't get a chance. Kayla walked in and wanted to talk. What was I supposed to do?"

Sean was well aware he was taking his anger out on his friend, but he couldn't seem to help himself. "Maybe you can take her shopping, asshole. That's all you seem to be good for lately."

Jacob's sigh filled the room. "I told you that you were pushing him, Adam. He isn't like us. He's very possessive. You need to keep your hands to yourself this time."

"I just played with her a little." Adam sounded a bit like a child who'd had a toy taken from him. He marched past Sean with a petulant look on his face. By the time Sean followed Jake, Adam was setting up his system. Sean went to the foyer and grabbed Grace's bag. Within a couple of seconds, Adam had the systems set up. He stared at the computer, his hands flying across the keys. "It was just flirting. And maybe a little light make-out session."

"Excuse me." The words felt ice cold as they left Sean's mouth.

"He's joking." Jake smacked his partner upside the back of his head. "Stop tugging the tiger's tail or I'll let him eat you. Do your job."

"Fine," Adam growled. "She has it password protected. What are her sons' names?"

"David and Kyle." Sean had spent a portion of his afternoon looking at the pictures on Grace's mantel. When he wasn't plotting the way he was going to betray her, he'd stared at the two attractive young men she'd raised. There were pictures from their graduations and some family vacation photos. There was an old picture of a smiling, dark-haired man with glasses. He didn't look like a man who could land a woman like Grace. She had deeply loved her husband.

Now she loved him.

"Not working. Okay, husband's name is Pete. That's a no. She seems to change it every week." Adam glanced back at Jake with a knowing look in his eyes. "You think?"

Jake shrugged as he stared at the screen. "Worth a try."

Two seconds later the screen cleared, and they were in.

Sean was curious. "What was the password?"

"My Viking."

Sean looked between his friends. It was obvious to Sean that they were sharing some joke that he didn't get. "Viking? Like the football team?"

Adam gave him a smirky grin. "No, Sven, like the long, flowing-haired plunderers of lovely females. You remind her of a Viking."

And she reminded him of a fertility goddess. Sean felt his stomach turn. *Fertile*. He'd taken her without a condom and with no thought to pulling out. He'd just taken her and spilled himself in her hot, tight pussy. That wasn't right. He had thought about it. He'd thought about stopping. He just hadn't. What if he'd gotten Grace pregnant? The butterflies in his stomach calmed a bit. If he'd gotten her pregnant, then she couldn't turn him away when she discovered his lies. A baby would be a permanent link between them. God, he was an asshole, but the thought didn't scare him.

Adam closed the computer and unhooked the laptop. "Done. Now you can go hop back in bed with Grace."

Sean smiled, but it was an outward sign of his inner beast. Now that Adam had done his job, Sean could feel free to have a discussion with his friend. "Are you sure you're finished? Got everything you need?"

Adam looked smug as he packed up his equipment. "I have everything on that system down to her latest solitaire game. I'll go over it at my leisure."

"Try doing it with one eye, asshole." Quick as he could, Sean popped him, drawing his fist back and landing it squarely across his friend's left eye.

"Fuck!" Adam bowled over, his hands covering the offended body part.

"Don't you ever take advantage of my Grace. She's mine. I hear you get her in a position like that again and I swear to god, Adam, I'll take your head off next time." Sean looked over to see if Jake was about to defend his best friend. Jake Dean was infinitely more dangerous than Adam in a fight. Adam was the brain, while Jake was the deadly brawn. Jacob was merely shaking his head as he watched.

"I told you he was going to kick your ass when you walked into that dressing room with her."

Adam looked up, his eye puffing up already. "I was doing my goddamn job. I was told to keep an eye on her and let me tell you I got an eyeful."

Sean took another step toward the asshole and gave serious consideration to killing the fucker.

Jake rolled his eyes and came between the two of them. "Don't even try to justify your actions, Adam. You knew exactly what you were doing when you talked your way into the dressing room with her." Jake turned to Sean. "Let's go get some ice. I'd like to keep the swelling down, otherwise the talk at the office tomorrow might be that I abuse my boyfriend. Or did you forget our cover?"

Sean sighed and surveyed the damage. Jake had a point. "Damn it, Jake, I didn't think about it."

Jake shook his head as he studied Adam's eye. "No, but I can see you're not doing a lot of thinking at all, Sean. Maybe you should take a step back. It wouldn't be strange at all for Sean Johansson to get called back to corporate. It might give you both a little breathing room."

Sean wasn't going anywhere, but it was easier to just nod and mumble something about Grace's fridge. Jake shoved Adam toward the kitchen.

"He's not my sergeant anymore. I don't have to follow his orders. I got kicked out of the fucking Army, remember?" Adam complained as he walked out.

Jake's voice was low and soothing. "I know, buddy. I know. Let's get your eye fixed up."

The duo shuffled off, and Sean was left with a strange sense of loneliness. Jake and Adam had each other's back, and had for many years. Sean wasn't alone, per se. He had his family, but no one who was always on his side, and now he felt that oneness. If someone punched him in the face, no one was going to take care of him. His brother would tell him he deserved it and send him on his way. Grace wouldn't, though. Grace would probably try to baby him. If he'd been punched, she would have an ice pack in hand and stand there cooing over him trying to make him feel better.

Sean picked up Grace's laptop and placed it back in her case. He crossed the living room to the foyer and put it back where she kept it, ready for her to dash out the door tomorrow. He'd make her think about going in late or maybe taking the day off. He liked the idea of just keeping her out of the office. He'd make her French toast and sausage. He'd cuddle with her and take a long hot shower for two and make love to her again. It would be nice to play hooky. They could shut off the cell phones and pretend the outside world didn't exist.

A piece of paper slipped out of the briefcase and fell to the tiled floor. Sean knelt down to pick it up. His blood went cold. He recognized the paper. It came from the personalized stationary Matt Wright kept on his desk. Grace had shoved a pad of that stationary in Wright's desk as Sean had walked in the office. This note wasn't written in Grace's handwriting. A strong, clean masculine style was on the note. How was Grace connected to this damn address? It was innocent. It had to be. It was something he would have to figure out later. He quickly took a picture of the note with its address and account numbers of some kind. He sent the photo in an e-mail to Eve.

A cell phone trilled, and Sean heard Jake talking quietly.

"Yeah, Tag, he's here. Hold on, I'll let you talk to him."

Sean met Jake as he was walking out of the kitchen. Sean had turned his cell phone off before he'd joined Grace in the bedroom. He hadn't wanted any distractions, but now he got to deal with big brother's lecture. Jake shook his head as he handed Sean the phone. Adam sat at Grace's bar, a bag of frozen peas over his left eye. In the course of forty-eight hours, Sean had punched both Liam and Adam. He really had to stop beating the shit out of his teammates. It was becoming a habit.

"Yeah, what's up?" The only way to deal with Ian was to brazen his way through it.

"I need you to get your ass down here, Sean."

Big brother sounded dead serious. He was in full-on CO mode, and Sean had been in the service long enough that a bit of obedience was ingrained. "Yes, sir." But only a bit. "I mean no. Ian, just tell me what you need. I can't leave right now. I had to give Grace a little sleeping pill. I don't think it's a good idea to leave her alone."

His brother's low growl pulsed into his ear. "That's exactly what I'm talking about. You get your ass into Dallas. I want you standing at my desk in an hour. That is an order, Sean. Leave Jake behind if you can't stand the thought of Sleeping Beauty being left alone."

"Fine." Sean knew when his brother had become an immovable object. If he didn't get out to the office, Ian would come after him, and he couldn't risk that. He would go to the office, take his lecture and be back to Grace long before she woke up. She would be a bit foggy in the morning, but he could blame the wine. It would be an excellent excuse to keep her away from the office. "I'll be there in thirty minutes."

He left Jake and Adam in Grace's kitchen with express orders to make sure she was safe. He didn't feel right about leaving her unprotected. He'd been the one to put the drug in her system. He wouldn't leave her alone. Sean hopped into his borrowed Benz and was glad he knew his way to the office with his eyes closed. He was fully on auto-pilot, his world narrowed down to one thing and one thing only—Grace Hawthorne. For the first time in his thirty-two years, he was in love. There was no question in his brain about it now. He loved Grace Hawthorne, and there was a ridiculous part of him that wanted to shout it to the world. He'd found his other half. He loved to talk to her. He adored how kind she was and how quick she was with a comeback. And god, he loved the way she submitted to him in bed.

He'd tried to hold himself apart, but he just couldn't. He wanted her too much.

He thought about the note in her briefcase. Ian would make a big deal of it. Ian was a paranoid asshole. Sean loved his brother, but he was practical when it came to him. Ian had been through a lot. He didn't trust anyone he didn't have twenty-four/seven control over or a blood connection to. Ian held himself apart from everyone on the team. Ian was all about the job in a way Sean had never been.

Sean got on 183 driving east toward the building in downtown Dallas that housed McKay/Taggart. This was his last job. He knew it deep down. After this job was done, he was going after what he really wanted. He was going to culinary school. Everyone would laugh, but it was a goal of his. Grace wouldn't laugh. Grace would support him. Grace would kick his ass when the going got tough and pick him up when he wanted to quit. Grace would be his taster, his cheerleader, his partner, his biggest fan. Grace would be the reason he reached for what he wanted. And what did he want? He wanted to cook, and he wanted a family with Grace. He wanted that stupid ass white picket fence and a couple of kids.

He wanted everything.

It was all too soon that he was pulling into the parking garage and sliding out of the Benz. He hoped Grace wasn't used to the Benz. His real car was a classic 1972 Scout. He would trade it in for a minivan if she wanted him to. Well, maybe not trade it in, but he would buy a minivan if that was what she wanted.

The elevator ride to the fifteenth floor happened in the blink of an eye.

"Hey, Sean. How are you?" Eve stood waiting in front of the reception desk, her arms crossed over her chest. She was wearing jeans and a button down shirt, a sure sign that she'd been called in from home. Eve usually dressed to the nines for work. She was all about the power suit.

Eve standing there waiting for him put him on high alert. Eve was the PhD on the team. She was the freaking shrink. Sean stared at her, utterly wary of what she was about to say. "I don't know how I'm doing. Why don't you tell me?"

Her smile lit up the room. Her blonde hair was pulled back in a ponytail that made her look years younger than the thirty-eight she actually was. "Oh, dummy, I am so happy for you." She threw herself into his arms. Sean found himself hugging her despite his confusion. "Grace is lovely."

"I think so." He pulled back. It looked like he'd seriously fucked up. Everyone knew he was head over heels for Grace. He'd need to talk his way out of this and fast. "What does the big guy want?"

She frowned and shook her head. Sean caught sight of the scar that started just under her right ear. It was a large pale scar from a knife Sean knew had to have been huge. He'd only seen it once. That scar ran a good length of her torso, a gift from the only time the former FBI profiler had really fucked up. Now Eve shifted self-consciously and tucked the collar of her shirt close to her neck. "You need to talk to him. I think he's wrong, but he does have a point. Whatever happens, don't give up on Grace. She's not what he thinks."

Ian stepped into the lobby. His huge presence filled up the room in a way no one else's could. Ian put his hands on his hips, every muscle in his body tense and shouting to Sean that he was in trouble. "My office, now."

Without waiting to see if he was being obeyed, Ian turned on his heels and marched back down the hallway.

Sean felt like he was twelve again and getting called out by his brother/substitute father. He followed Ian down the long hallway. Growing up, his mother had conceded control of the house to Ian after their father had fled. Ian had been a teen, but he'd never faltered. He'd managed a job, high school, and helping his younger brother with homework without ever uttering a single complaint. Ian had been the rock they'd clung to. Ian had been the mountain he could never, ever climb.

Sean entered Ian's perfectly kept office with his spectacular view of the Dallas skyline. It was a power office that screamed out the owner's success. "What's this about?"

Ian sank to his chair. His big hands were on the top of his desk clenched into fists. He took a deep breath before he began his assault. "You love her? You fucking love her? She is a suspected terrorist, and you spend your time telling her how much you love her?"

Sean felt every muscle in his body go tight as though Ian were pounding him with his fists rather than mere words. "She's not a terrorist. This is completely ridiculous. She's a secretary. God, Ian, if you spent two seconds with her you would see it."

It was obvious to Sean that Ian didn't see past his file folder. He'd made his decision. "She's in this up to her neck. You can't expect me to leave you in after what you did tonight."

Sean's blood went cold. While he didn't believe that Grace was involved, he was damn sure that something was going on with her boss. "You can't take me out. She's in danger. I won't leave her."

"You are coming in. She is the fucking suspect, and you told her you love her. You are compromised in every way possible. You're coming in, and you won't see her again until this mission is over. If she isn't in jail or some fucking foreign country being questioned by the Agency, then feel free to take her to the movies and share a bag of popcorn."

Sean wasn't even going to argue with his brother's distaste for normal dating rituals. Ian had his kinks, and Sean wasn't going there. Sean tried another tactic. "Have you ever heard of lying? I told the lady what she wanted to hear. She'll comply with what I say. She's a sub, Ian. Imagine that bit of luck. She's a sub, and she's accepted me as her Dom. I put a collar on her this afternoon. She'll do what I tell her to do."

She wouldn't. Grace would fight him every inch of the way if she thought he was wrong, but Ian didn't need to know that. If Ian thought she was compliant, maybe he would leave them alone.

Ian studied him. "Bullshit."

"What is that supposed to mean?"

Ian's arms crossed over his chest like a shield. "It means you're coming in."

He felt his teeth grinding together and that need to punch

133

someone rising again. "I am not coming in."

Ian took a long breath. He sat back in his chair, and his hands came up to his chest, steepling together as he regarded his brother. Sean could see plainly that Ian was trying to decide the best way to "deal" with him. Sean was a problem to be solved, and Ian's brilliant brain would come up with a way to fix him. Ian had obviously decided that intimidation wouldn't work, so he was changing tactics.

"Could you be logical for one minute, Sean?"

Not where Grace was concerned. Logic didn't have a place where Grace was concerned. "Of course."

"Think about what you've been doing, Sean. Have you conducted yourself in a professional manner?"

Ah, the voice of reason. Well, he could be reasonable, too. "If you're talking about sleeping with Grace, we all knew that was probably going to happen. You sent me in because you wanted me to get close to her. Well, I got close. I couldn't possibly get much closer. I brought you some info we wouldn't have gotten if I hadn't been sleeping with her. Did you get the picture of the note I found? The one with the address? You wouldn't have touched that laptop of hers tonight if I hadn't made it happen."

Ian didn't look particularly convinced. "You gave me one address. It's hardly a revelation. I'll send Liam to check it out tomorrow."

"Don't bother. I want to see it for myself. There was a series of numbers on it, too."

Ian flipped open his computer. He quickly found what he was looking for. His blue eyes stared at the screen for a second. "They are account numbers. Cayman numbers, I suspect. Where did this come from?"

Why had he mentioned that? There was nothing else to do but tell him the truth. "I found it in Grace's briefcase."

Ian's fingers ran roughly through his long blond hair. Normally it was pulled back in a queue, but tonight it was around his shoulders. Sean often thought his brother had let his hair get long for one reason and one reason only—to distance himself from the soldier he used to be. "So let me get this straight. Grace controls the money at Wright Temps."

"Sort of. She writes out the checks. She's not the accountant."

That single eyebrow arched, and Sean got the feeling he was being herded. "According to Jake, accounting reports to her. She writes the checks, and she's walking around with a bunch of account numbers for banks in the Cayman Islands. Your girl is laundering money, Sean."

"You don't know that. Besides, the fact that accounting reports to her is just for show. As far as I can tell, she simply sends that on to Matt. She's just the gateway to the boss." But even he was starting to think now.

Ian's fists slapped against his desk and he stood, his tense body a testament to his rapidly declining patience. "How naïve are you?"

"Hey, he's not naïve, he's just studying all the angles like you taught him to." Eve stood in the doorway. She leaned against the door frame, her lovely face the only calm thing in the room.

Ian frowned at her. "I didn't request your presence at this meeting. I merely called you in to discuss your profile of Grace."

"Understood, Ian, but you'll be grateful for my meddling when you don't completely alienate your brother." Eve sighed as she looked at them. "Sean, Ian is worried about this case. There are several things that don't add up, and he would rather you came in. That sixth sense of his is working overtime."

Ian's instincts tended to be impeccable. He had an eerie habit of knowing when things were going bad and being able to dodge the bullets that came his way. It was what had made him the Army's go-to-guy for tough ops, and the nation's intelligence gatherers still kept him on their speed-dials. When Ian said something was up, Sean listened. "What's wrong, bro?"

His face opened slightly as he put a hand on a stack of file folders. Sean had the feeling he'd been pouring over them all night. "I don't know. Some things don't add up. Why is an ecoterrorist laundering money? Eve's profile reads like a biography of the Unabomber, so why is he hanging out with corporate types? I just don't like it. Something else is going on, and I don't trust Black."

Sean didn't either. He never trusted anyone who came out of Langley. Unfortunately, Mr. Black was the client. Ian seemed calmer now that they were talking about the case again, rather than Sean's involvement with Grace. The situation was deflating. "Have we rechecked all the information we got from Black?"

"Of course, and it all checks out. But you know that's meaningless, too. If Black wants to hide something, he has the resources to do it. When Adam gets a minute or two, he's going to run a deep trace. He's going to look for any trace of someone tampering with Patrick Wright's records. Of course, that is if I can get him to stop talking about how amazing Grace Hawthorne is."

Sean groaned inwardly because he knew exactly where Ian was going. He was not the most trusting of souls. "She's not some Mata Hari, Ian. She's not trying to seduce your team."

Ian's mouth became a stubborn, flat line. "That's not what it looks like from where I'm standing. I'm just glad Jake seems to be able to retain his common sense around the woman."

Sean could be stubborn, too. "The only way to figure this out is to stay close to Wright. The way to stay close to Wright is by staying close to Grace. I'm the closest one to Grace. I'm in the best position to watch her."

Ian turned to Eve. "Tell me, Eve, if I leave Sean in, will he be able to behave in a professional manner?"

"Of course." There was no hesitation in Eve's manner. Sean relaxed slightly. At least he had someone on his side.

But Ian wasn't done. "Around Grace? Will he be able to make logical judgments concerning his own safety and the safety of the members of his team when weighed against the welfare of Grace Hawthorne?"

Eve's shoulders slumped forward slightly, and Sean knew he had just lost the battle. "No. He meant what he said. He's in love with her. You should pull him."

Ian nodded slightly. "Jake is erasing all traces of him at that woman's house even as we speak."

"Fuck you, Ian." Sean felt his face go stubborn, his jaw clenching, his eyes narrowing. *That woman?* It was utterly insulting, and he wasn't about to put up with it. "I quit. Now I'm not your employee. Try keeping me away from her now."

Sean turned to walk out the door, no thought at all except to get back to Grace. Ian's next words made him stop in his tracks.

"Then I'll call in the cops and have her arrested now. With the evidence Black already gave us on the company combined with those accounts that I'm sure Grace writes checks from, she'll spend some time in jail, just being questioned if not actually arrested."

Sean turned and faced his brother. "You wouldn't."

"If you can say that, then you don't know me at all, little brother. I'll fabricate evidence against her if I think it will keep you alive. Here's my offer. I'll let you stay on the case. You brought me the address, you can go check it out. You can also take over surveillance on Grace. That way you can watch over her. You are not to contact her in any way. The minute you do, I call the cops in. Jake and Adam will take over the close cover."

Rage choked him. He stood there in the doorway, his mind racing, trying to find a way out. The trouble was Ian never left a way out. Ian would do it. Sean could do nothing but take his brother's offer. He had to protect Grace. She wouldn't be able to handle prison, even for the short term. His brother was a righteous bastard. "I will never forgive you for this, Ian."

"I know, but if I'm right about what's going on, then at least you'll be alive to hate me."

Sean strode out the door, glancing back only momentarily. His brother stood there like a chunk of granite, completely immovable and without a bit of emotion. Eve tried to stop him, but Sean pulled away from her. "Can't stay for a therapy session, Eve. I've got to go sit in a van and listen to our 'prime suspect' take a shower in the morning. I wouldn't want to miss that. I'm out when this is over, Ian. Do you understand that?"

Ian nodded, as though Sean's resignation had been a factor he'd weighed and found an acceptable loss. "It's for the best. You're not cut out for this."

Sean slammed the door behind him.

Chapter Eleven

Grace came awake in a bit of a haze. She sat up in bed and looked around trying to get her eyes to focus. Her mouth felt a bit dry. How much wine had she had last night? She thought it was only a glass, but she had to be wrong, right?

There was a glass of water on the nightstand. She smiled a bit before drinking a good portion of it down. Sean was a thoughtful man. The memory of last night washed over her like a cold rain. Now she was awake and just the tiniest bit mortified. What had possessed her to tell him she loved him? Grace let her head fall to her hands. She knew why she said it. She'd said it because she meant it. She loved Sean Johansson. She also knew that he was leaving, and that would be the end of their relationship. The most she could hope for with him was a few hot weekends, and then he would find someone younger and fall in love and get married. He had that whole phase of his life ahead of him.

Grace shook it off. He'd been sweet. He'd told her he was crazy about her. She remembered that much. He'd made love to her again. It was okay. They could move on and pretend like she'd never said it. They could enjoy the rest of the week.

She breathed in deeply, wondering if he was already in the

kitchen making something scrumptious for breakfast. She didn't hear the shower running. Tossing off the covers, she reached for her robe. Every muscle in her body protested. And she was sore in places she had never been sore in before. The floor beneath her felt wobbly. She wasn't drinking again. She couldn't handle it apparently.

"Sean?"

No one called back. Grace padded out of the bedroom and into the kitchen. No Sean there and no signs of an impending breakfast cooking session. The kitchen was pristine. Every dish had been washed and put away. The whole house was silent as a grave.

A sinking feeling threatened to overtake Grace. She turned back to the bedroom and, sure enough, his small suitcase was gone. When she looked at the bar, his keys were missing. He'd placed them beside hers the night before. She'd stared down at those side-by-side keys, a sweet intimacy invading her veins. Now tears filled her eyes. He wasn't out getting something or taking a jog. She felt it. He was gone. He'd left in the middle of the night without even waiting to say goodbye.

All because she'd been dumb enough to say I love you? That seemed a bit harsh. Grace managed to find the edge of her bed. She sank down as the tears started to fall. She knew Sean didn't love her, but she'd thought he'd liked her enough that he wouldn't just walk out. She sat on the bed for the longest time, going over everything she could remember about the night before. In no way did he seem like a man who was ready to run. He'd been sweet, and he'd made love to her like she was the last woman on earth. It had to be because she'd said she loved him. He probably envisioned a clinging vine pulling him down. Of course he didn't want a declaration of love from his week-long fling.

Grace forced herself to move, to turn on the shower, to brush her teeth. She walked through her morning routine like an automaton. Her legs worked, her arms functioned, but her brain was somewhere else. It was stuck in a loop of regret, recrimination, and no small amount of self-loathing. What had she been thinking? She'd thrown herself into a D/s relationship with a man she barely knew. She'd let him do things her husband hadn't even done to her before, and she'd begged him to do it. She'd been a complete moron.

And worse, she already missed him.

The phone rang after she'd dressed for work, and her heart leapt. For the first time that morning, she moved with purpose. She grabbed the phone. Relief felt like a drug in her veins.

"Hello." Of course he would contact her. He'd just gotten called away. He had a job after all and a life in another state. He didn't want to wake her. He was probably calling her from the airport.

"Hey, mom." The sunny voice of her youngest son filled her ears.

Normally it would buoy her spirits. Now she found herself forcing a light response out of her mouth as her heart fell. She stood there murmuring all the right things, but she wasn't really there. After listening to a couple of stories about what was going on in Austin, she promised to send him some gas money and hung up.

That was when she saw it, a small piece of paper hanging from a magnet on the refrigerator. Grace pulled it off with shaky hands.

Grace – Got called back to Chicago. Had a great time. Thanks for everything. Sean.

Fourteen words. No promises to call. He'd been the one to say their relationship could go beyond the week he was here. He'd been the one to point out that he would be back. Why had he done that?

To make it easier to get you in bed, idiot. He wanted you compliant and you were. You were everything he wanted right up to the point when you said you loved him. No guy that hot really wants a forty-year-old girlfriend.

That awful voice filled her head. It whispered to her. It spouted its terrible doubt all the way to the office. She heard it when she sat in on a meeting with Matt. She heard it through her coffee break with Kayla. It roared at her every time she passed a mirror. She skipped lunch, preferring to work at her desk.

"Hey gorgeous, are you going to happy hour with the rest of us losers or are you meeting that hottie of yours?" Adam Miles sat down on the edge of her desk looking young and filled with an energy she couldn't even comprehend today. She'd been hanging out with too many young people. That was the trouble.

"No, I have some work to do." Her voice sounded flat to her own ears. She forced a smile on her face. "Some other time." In the very, very distant future.

Adam's eyes seemed to bore through her. "What's wrong?"

"Just a headache. You know we old ladies get those."

He paled visibly. "You're not old, Grace." His hand reached out, grabbed hers, tangling their fingers together. "You're the loveliest woman I know. Hell, I'm thirty. I'm not that much younger than you. And you know women outlive men by like seven years or something. That makes me practically perfect. And Jake. He's thirty-one. We're the perfect age for you."

It was the first thing she'd found amusing all day. "That's good to know. If I ever need a gay husband, I'll be sure to let you know."

That seemed to startle him for a moment. He looked thoughtful as he stared at their entwined hands. "Doesn't every girl need a gay husband? And hey, sometimes Prince Charming comes in a strange package. You never know what's around the corner, Grace. Come out with me. Look, I'm wounded. You can't deny me."

Grace took a long look at him. He seemed to have tried to conceal it, but sure enough his eye was slightly swollen, and his nose looked rough, too. Her self-pity took a momentary backseat. She put her hands up to frame his bruised face. "Oh, sweetie, what happened to you?"

"I got mugged. I got mugged by a stupid, overly possessive asshole." His sensual mouth was pouting a little. He really was heartbreakingly attractive. He was leaner than Sean, but there was no doubt Adam Miles was fit.

Someone had gotten him good. "How do you know if your mugger's overly possessive? The asshole part is obvious."

"Well, he seemed awfully possessive to me when he was beating the crap out of me over something that doesn't really belong to him. Anyway, let's forget about him, love. Come out with us. If we can tempt you away from that big hunk of man meat, I promise to show you a civilized time. We'll get a couple of drinks and then go heckle some romantic comedy at the theater. It'll be fun."

She shook her head and then stopped. What was she planning on doing anyway? Was she planning on going home and crying her eyes out? Yes. That had pretty much summed up her plans for the evening. She would go home, stare at the television for a while and then try to eat something. After that she would go to her empty bed, if she could stand to sleep there, and cry. Couldn't she go out with her friends and then go home and cry her eyes out? Maybe, if she spent some time with the boys, she wouldn't need to cry. Maybe she wouldn't feel that overwhelmingly oppressive loneliness that threatened to swamp her. Maybe that damn voice would go away.

And why should she cry? It wasn't like Sean loved her. He'd made that plain last night. No man who really even cared about her would have left without saying goodbye. That stupid note didn't count.

"Okay." She was hesitant, but she managed to get the words out. Before Sean, she'd been forming a nice little friendship with Adam and his boyfriend, Jake. It would be comforting to not spend every evening alone. Sure she was the third wheel with Adam and Jake, but at least she wasn't alone, crying into her wine glass.

Adam's face lit up, and he looked younger than his thirty years. "Awesome." He leaned over and kissed her lightly on the cheek. "I'll go make reservations. I'll be back here at five, okay?"

Reservations? "I thought we were going to happy hour."

"We will. Some place nice. Now that we have you all to ourselves, we should celebrate." A long, slow smile crossed his handsome face. He reached out and touched her nose playfully with his index finger. "It's all going to be okay, Gracie. It's for the best, you'll see." He winked and strode from the room, already on his cell phone.

What had that been about? What was for the best? *Men*. She didn't understand any of them. Gay, straight, vanilla, Dom. She would never be able to get into those odd brains of theirs and come out with any form of logic. Saying I love you wasn't like asking for a commitment. She hadn't asked him to marry her. She'd just muttered something affectionate in the middle of some truly filthy, mind-blowing sex. It shouldn't have sent him scurrying halfway across the country just to escape her.

Damn it. She was going there again.

Matt's head popped out of his office. Grace noted that his eyes were bloodshot again. She would have sworn that he was wearing the same suit he'd worn the day before. Unlike Adam, Matt looked far older than his years. "Could I see you in here for a minute?"

Grace picked up a notepad and followed her boss into the office. Her heart hurt as she remembered the last time she was in here. Sean had ordered her to lean over the desk, and he'd had his way with her. Of course, he'd pretty much had his way with her any way he'd wanted. She could still feel his hands on her hips as he pushed that big dick of his into her pussy. He'd filled her up until she couldn't remember that she'd felt lonely before. It had been so much more than sex for her. That was what hurt. It hadn't meant the same thing to him. Not even close. She would remember him forever, and he'd probably already moved on to the next woman.

"Are you working on the party? I'd like to see the plans." Matt's voice brought her out of her memories.

She tried to shake off the vision of Sean's big body taking hers. She had a job to do. She needed to concentrate on that. "I called a caterer."

"And the venue?"

"I thought we'd use the Ashton." It was a gorgeous Art Deco hotel in the heart of downtown. The ballroom was the perfect place for corporate parties. Grace had thrown the Christmas party there two years before.

Matt was quiet for a moment, his eyes still as he seemed to consider her plans. "All right. That's a nice place. Close to the freeway. That will work."

Grace wasn't sure why he cared, but the street the hotel was on was close to I-35. "Yes. I got a good rate. I'm using their kitchens. Luckily they had a cancelation, so they could fit us in. I thought it would be nice to do an Asian buffet."

His nose crinkled up in distaste, but he shook it off. "I don't care about the food, just make sure everyone comes. Send out invites to everyone and their significant others. And invite the other tenants in the building. This is a big deal, Grace. This is going to take us to a whole different level."

"I understand." The Bryson Building deal was big. It made sense that Matt wanted to celebrate. It was just that he said all the right things, but Grace could see he was unmoved on an emotional level. He seemed so very disconnected.

"Good." He sat back down at his desk and started to go through the papers there. Grace waited for a moment. He didn't look up at her when he spoke again. "I got a call from Kelvin. They decided to go another way."

Sean wouldn't be coming back. He was gone. "I'll cancel your meetings with Mr. Johansson." The words tasted like ash in her mouth, but she managed to get them out.

His eyes came up to search hers. "And what about your meetings with him?"

"I didn't have anything scheduled with him." She hadn't thought she needed to. He was living at her place.

"All right. It's for the best, Grace. You'll see. We don't need that contract. We'll be rolling in money, now."

She was happy he was sure of it. She still hadn't seen the contract and wouldn't hold her breath. He hadn't put it on her desk this morning. He was holding it close to his vest for some strange reason. A couple of questions started to play at the back of Grace's brain.

"It's a good thing you didn't get serious about that playboy, isn't it?" Matt had a superior little smirk on his face.

A flush stole across Grace's skin. It was a damn good thing she hadn't run around the office proclaiming her conquest. Only Adam, Jake, and Kayla knew she'd been seeing him away from work. At least she thought that was all. God, she couldn't handle it if everyone knew she'd played around with a younger man and got dumped after only a few nights. It was a good thing he wasn't coming back. She didn't think she could handle seeing him back in the office, potentially hitting on someone new.

"Yeah. It was just casual."

He pinned her with a glare that made her wonder how much he knew. "I'm glad. Maybe now you can concentrate on work. Let me know how the party planning comes. I want this to be perfect, Grace."

Grace nodded and was relieved to find herself dismissed. She slunk out of Matt's office. It wasn't surprising that he would call her out. He'd been against her relationship with Sean from the beginning. He'd been the one to tell her she should be cautious. Cautious? He'd told her flat out Sean wouldn't stay, and he hadn't.

The rest of the afternoon centered around calls to caterers and plans for the big party. At three, Evan Parnell strode into Matt's office after giving Grace a smirk. He'd never actually looked her straight in the eyes before. The contact unsettled her. It also made her remember that slip of paper he'd dropped the day before. Following her instincts, Grace looked up the address on the Internet. It was to a mail facility that offered safety deposit boxes as well as mail collection services. She thought about that long list of numbers. Some of them she recognized now. She'd checked them against bank accounts that Wright Temps used and matched three of the numbers. One of them, though, was too short to be an account number. Grace wondered if it was a box number or a locker code.

When Evan Parnell left Matt's office, Grace was a minute behind him.

It was stupid. She knew it as she followed him out to his truck. She had zero business playing the private eye, but the longer this thing with Parnell went on, the more she suspected he was blackmailing her boss. Matt was getting markedly worse, and he almost always went on a bender after meeting with Parnell. Logic told her Matt should have dumped him as an employee long before. So why was Parnell still around?

Grace tried to follow at a distance. She lost him twice, but caught sight of the black truck at the bank. Parnell parked in the parking lot and went in. He was in the bank for ten minutes. He came out holding an envelope and immediately crossed the street.

Grace checked the name of the street. Mount Dale Avenue.

Grace put the car in park and slipped out to follow Parnell into the Addison Mail and Storage Center. The storefront was new, and the center appeared to take up most of the small strip it was located on. From the street she could see that Parnell was talking to the clerk. They spoke for a moment and then Parnell was allowed behind the desk and led to the back of the store.

What did Evan Parnell need with a storage locker? He had a large storage facility for his janitorial supplies. She doubted he was keeping mops and brooms here. Now that she knew the name of this place, she remembered the check she had written out. Matt had told her to pay it. It was for a small locker here. She'd paid for the full security package for a year. She'd assumed it was for Matt. Why was Matt paying for Parnell's storage with Wright Temp funds?

Grace glanced down at her watch. She would have to hurry to meet Adam and Jake. She briefly considered canceling on them, but decided not to. The thought of going home to her lonely little house and thinking about Sean all night was too much.

Besides, she had a mystery to solve. That alone could take her mind off her almost-lover. Whether Matt wanted it or not, she was going to save him from the clutches of one Evan Parnell. She was going to figure out just what kind of hold the man had over him.

* * * *

It was late when Adam and Jake dropped her off at home. Adam parked her little hybrid in the driveway. Despite her protestations that she was more than capable of getting herself home, the boys had insisted. Adam had stolen her keys at some point and refused to give them back. Jake had followed her. He pulled his Jeep in next to her. Adam shut off the car and was out and opening her door before she could get her seatbelt off.

"Thanks." She put her hand in Adam's and let him help her out of the car.

The evening had been pleasant. She'd genuinely enjoyed the time she'd spent with them, but her heart still ached at the thought of Sean. Was he back in Chicago now? Did he already have a date? He probably had two or three. And she bet they weren't gay.

"Keys?" Jake held out his hand. Adam passed them to his boyfriend and led her up the little walkway to her door. Jake had the door open. He frowned. "Don't you have an alarm?"

Yes. It was obnoxious and emitted the nastiest sound when she couldn't get to it in time. She set her briefcase down. "It's a nice neighborhood. My sons insisted on having it installed when they went away to college. I try to remember to set it when they're home, but otherwise, I'd just as soon not deal with it. Would you like some coffee?"

Sean had made her set the alarm. He'd been upset to discover she didn't use it on a regular basis. She had agreed to be more thoughtful about it. Of course, he had his mouth over her pussy at the time. She would have agreed to just about anything.

"You should set the alarm, Grace. I don't care how nice the neighborhood is, bad things still happen. If your sons love you enough to want to protect you, you should let them." Jake stood over her. He was bigger than Adam and quieter. Adam was all light and fun. Jake was a broody hunk of man. He was the authoritative one in the relationship. His voice was dark and deep. Grace almost found herself nodding and agreeing with him simply because of his voice.

Nope. Not going there again. She managed to shrug. "I have a baseball bat, and I know how to use it. Don't worry about me." She strode into the kitchen. She was done with domineering men, even if they were just doling out good advice. She started the coffee pot. She had taken care of herself for a really long time. A couple of days as Sean Johansson's sub didn't change that. Besides, he had only wanted her for sex, so she had been on her own anyway. "Maybe I'll get a dog. Or a gun."

"Dear god, no." Adam looked perfectly horrified. "To the gun, love, not the dog. We'll find you a nice big Rottweiler."

"Adam is right," Jake agreed. "A gun would more than likely be turned against you, or you would shoot someone you didn't want to shoot."

She chose to ignore the big man. Jake towered over her. His dark eyes always seemed to be assessing his surroundings. It was easier to concentrate on Adam, who had a much sunnier nature. She passed him a mug. "I might take you up on the dog. I don't want a Rottweiler, though. I'd greatly prefer a Lab."

Adam snorted as he took his coffee. "Yes, a nice Lab would lick your intruders to death."

Grace laughed it off and left the room to hang up her sweater. The rest of the evening was nice, but all too soon the boys were leaving. Grace walked them out, Adam lingering for a moment.

"Turn on the alarm, Grace." Jake's words were thrown over his shoulder as he walked toward his Jeep.

147

Adam winked at her, his light happiness buoying her spirits. "You should do what he says. He likes to be in charge."

Adam leaned over to kiss her cheek but lightly brushed her lips instead. He pulled back almost shyly. He was probably embarrassed he'd missed her cheek.

"Good night, Adam."

"Adam!" Jake barked at his lover, his tall form rigid in the moonlight.

"Now I'm in trouble. Goodnight, love." He didn't seem worried as he joined the larger man.

Grace sighed and closed the door. She turned the locks and walked back into the living room. Loneliness weighed on her. Despite her early attempts at forgetting, Sean's presence had clung to her all evening. Adam and Jake had carefully avoided the subject of her love life. They had talked about Jake's brothers and his artist parents. They had talked about the office and movies they liked. And everything brought her back to Sean.

Pete's picture on the mantle caught her eye. It was a picture they had taken on their trip to Hawaii shortly before the car accident that had taken his life. Grace pulled the picture down and tears clouded her eyes. She didn't even have a picture of Sean. Grace put the picture back and silently went to bed.

Chapter Twelve

"Tell me he didn't kiss her." Even from a distance there was no mistaking that motion. That fucking bastard Adam was at it again. Sean felt a need to race across the street and beat the living shit out of one of his oldest friends.

"Calm down." Liam shook his head. The van that served as a surveillance station was already cramped, but he pointed to the video feed from outside the van. Jake was stalking down the street toward them. "It's like Grand Central Station in here. Why am I here?"

"Because it's your shift," Sean said absently.

She had kissed Adam. Grace had stood there, not a day after he'd left, and kissed Adam.

Liam sat back in his chair and regarded Sean with a frown. "None of us needs to take a bloody shift. You won't leave. You need to go home and take a shower. Your stink alone should alert the world we're here."

Sean growled and opened the door to the van. Jake climbed inside. His hands were already out in a conciliatory fashion. "Just hear me out, Sarge."

He'd like nothing more than to get his hands wrapped around

Adam's throat. He could feel them there even now. It would make him feel infinitely better to choke the life out of someone. He'd spent the entire day following Grace around, skulking in the shadows while that fucker held her hand. While Sean had spent the last twenty-four hours with a hollow place in his stomach, Grace had sure moved on fast. She hadn't even spent one single night mourning him. She'd gone to work and hadn't skipped a beat. She'd been at happy hour like he'd never existed. She'd smiled and laughed, flirting with Adam.

"Where's Adam?" Sean was surprised at how evenly the question came out of his mouth. A coldness was settling around him.

"I left him in the car. I thought I should keep the two of you apart for a while."

Bitterness filled Sean's brain. She'd let another man kiss her the day after he put a collar on her. He'd been wrong, and Ian had been right. Sean sat back in the small chair that barely contained his bulk. His knees were practically up to his chin. First she'd followed Evan Parnell this afternoon. That was suspicious in and of itself. He'd called that in and had Eve working on the Parnell connection. Now she was romancing yet another agent. And he was beating up his team over her.

"It's fine, Jake." Sean forced himself to nod. He had been played like a fool. It was time to get a little bit of his pride back. "Someone needs to stay close to her. Might as well be Adam. Tell him she likes a little bite of pain."

Jake's eyes widened. "I certainly will not encourage him. Look, I know you're pissed off, but he's having some trouble. His dad is dying and none of his asshole brothers will let Adam in to see him. Adam's got it in his head that he's lost his family, and he wants to make a new one. I swear he has a fucking biological clock. We've always talked about finding a woman for the two of us, but now he's obsessed with it."

Sean shrugged. In his head all he could see was Grace standing there as Adam kissed her. She hadn't shoved him away. She hadn't protested that she didn't want him. She'd accepted his kiss. How much more had she accepted from him? "Dude, seriously, I don't care. I told you like I tried to tell Ian, it was an act. She's hot, I'll give you that. And she's very submissive. She's exactly my type, but she's too old for me. If Adam doesn't mind the age difference, good for him."

Jake shook his head. "Bullshit."

It was a word he was getting used to. There was nothing to do except push through. "Believe what you want, man. I'm heading home. I need to get some sleep. I have to follow her around tomorrow. Hey, do me a favor and have Adam move this little relationship of theirs along. If he's sleeping with her, I won't have to pull so many hours." The thought of Adam in her bed made him see red, but he plastered what he hoped was an easy smile on his face.

"Hey, Sean, maybe you should ease up." Liam had a halfway serious look on his face. He had one ear bud in his ear and offered the other one to Sean. "Why don't you listen in? She talks to herself a lot. You could learn a thing or two about her. I'll be honest, I've started to come around on her."

Sean shook his head. He'd made enough of a fool of himself. He was a professional. He'd trained and fought and bled to get where he was today, and he'd almost tossed it all away for some chick he'd been banging. That was all it was. It was sex. Ian had been right about that, too. He should have been going to the club and regularly taking a sub. If he'd taken care of his business, he wouldn't be in this situation. He would have been able to see Grace Hawthorne for what she was. "It's your shift. Don't pawn your work off on me, Liam."

Jake reached out to him. "Sean, don't do this. Whatever Ian said, she's not involved."

"You aren't the one who watched her tail a guy today." His hand was on the door. He didn't need to sit around and listen to another man who had fallen into Grace's web.

Jake's eyebrows climbed his forehead. "Really? Who?"

Sean spit out the information. Just an hour earlier, he'd wanted to keep it all to himself. It had seemed like more crap that made Grace look bad. He couldn't ignore it any more. "She followed the guy who runs the janitorial services to that address we found in her briefcase. It's some sort of storage and mail place. She tried to be careful that he didn't see her. It was very obvious what she was doing. And she's got some weird shit on her computer. I talked to Eve earlier. She says there's a surveillance video of the Bryson Building. It's very detailed. It covers entrances and exits and everything in between. If she's not involved, then why would she have something like that on her system?"

"That proves nothing except that she backs up her boss's computer," Jake argued.

"Why the hell would you think that? What does Wright need with a surveillance video?"

Jake leaned back against the side of the van. "Adam told me the name of the file is 'thumb drive my boss is going to lose.' As far as Adam can tell, she hadn't accessed that file. It was just sitting there on her drive. She definitely didn't watch the video on her media player."

None of which mattered if she'd made that tape. "Maybe you and Adam are the ones we should pull. The two of you seem awfully ready to believe anything that woman says."

Jake took a long breath. "That woman? Wow, you are going to regret this, Sean. There are some things in life that are way more important than a job. You have given me some good advice over the years. Let me give you some now. Tell Ian to go to hell. Whatever he threatened you with, you can handle it. Walk out of this van and go get your girl. If you knock on her door tonight and come clean, she'll forgive you. If you wait too long, there won't be any going back. Sean, if she's the one, you have to go get her."

Everything in Sean wanted to do just that. He could walk up to her door, force his way in, and take her. The caveman inside demanded that he do just that. He could fuck her so long and so hard she wouldn't remember anything but him. Whatever she'd done before, he would handle. He would make damn sure she towed the line from here on out. She would be his sweet, obedient wife or there would be hell to pay. She wouldn't flirt with every man alive. She wouldn't get involved with people like her boss or this Parnell person. Sean was shocked to realize that if he had his way, he would keep her barefoot and pregnant and locked away from the world. What had that woman done to him? He'd never felt so savagely possessive in his life.

Liam looked up from his surveillance. "This goes against everything I stand for, but I gotta agree with Jake. Maybe you should go talk to the girl."

"You are under the assumption that I give a shit about the girl." He did. God, he loved her. It was stupid, and he wouldn't give in to it. He was ping-ponging between loving her and hating her. It had to stop, and the only way he could stop was to power through. He turned his attention back to Jake. "It was a job, that's all. I lost my head because she is hotter than hell in the bedroom. Give her a try, man." If she got in between the ménage boys, then hate would rule. He could handle that. "Tell Adam he has my blessing."

Something infinitely cold crossed Jake's face, and Sean wondered if he hadn't just lost a friend. "She's our responsibility. Got it." He turned to Liam. "If you see anything weird, give us a call. Adam and I can be here in a couple of minutes. Liam, I want her protected. She's our op now, and I call the shots."

It rankled. He wasn't in charge of Grace. The idea bit into Sean like a rattler leaving noxious venom in his veins. "Good luck with that."

Sean left the van, slamming the door behind him. He didn't give a shit if someone heard. He jogged down the street. It was a nice, suburban street, just the kind he'd always dreamed of living on when he and Ian were growing up in their trailer park. He loved Grace's house. It was a far cry from the starkness of his apartment. His place had a big screen TV and a sofa, a bed, a whole lot of cooking equipment, and nothing else. That wasn't true. It also had things like hooks in the ceiling and spreaders that would lay Grace out for his delectation. He could tie her up at his place in a way he couldn't at hers. Of course, if he got her to Ian's, he might never leave the dungeon. Ian's dungeon was something he aspired to.

Stop. He wasn't going there. He wasn't going to get a white picket fence and two point five kids with Grace, and he wouldn't have her counting it out on a St. Andrew's Cross, either. He was done. He wasn't playing Grace's lap dog anymore.

He made it to his Scout. He'd happily given Eve back her Benz. He'd been too confined in the little luxury car. He greatly preferred his big-ass SUV. He slid into the car and took off immediately. He didn't turn toward his apartment. He wasn't going home to sleep. He was heading out to the small building Grace had tracked Parnell to.

It was late. The streets were quiet, but Sean parked down the block anyway. This part of the city was all about business. Though the lights were all on, no one was home. His feet made absolutely no sound on the sidewalk beneath him. Sean was still for a moment, letting his senses open to the world around him. The night was silent save for the normal sounds of the city. An air conditioner coughed to life. Somewhere he could hear a sprinkler system working. Nothing else. He'd been trained by the best. Though he'd been out of combat for a long time, the rhythm always came back quickly. He moved efficiently, and before he knew it, he stood at the back door of the Addison Mail and Storage Center. He had circled the place a couple of times to be certain no one was working late.

It was time for a little breaking and entering. It would be easy because Sean knew the simplest way into any building was to have the key, or in this case, the key card. He'd cased the place after Grace and Parnell had left. It was a simple thing to flirt with the girl at the counter and bump into her. He'd lifted the card out of her pocket and palmed it before she knew what was happening. Now he just had to hope no one had changed the codes.

He slid the card into the reader at the back door and a green light came on. *Bingo*.

Sean moved through the building, keeping to the shadows. His body hugged the wall despite the fact that he sensed he was alone. He looked around and found what he feared. A red light blinked from the corner. Security camera. It wasn't swinging, so it was stationary. It was set up to catch people coming in and out, but not people moving around in the building.

His eyes quickly adjusted to the dark. He was in a mailroom. The smell of slightly molding paper assaulted him. He moved freely through the mailroom and into a small office. No cameras here. There was a computer and a ton of paperwork. Sean shuffled through until he found an invoice list. No Evan Parnell. No Matthew Wright. *Fuck*. Grace. According to this paperwork, Grace paid the bill on box 115. He had to stop his hand from shaking. What the hell was he going to do? Could he really turn Grace in?

According to Mr. Black, the Earth League was targeting polluters. The Bryson Building housed the corporate offices of one of the world's largest natural gas companies. It was the same gas company Grace had signed a petition against. What exactly was she involved in? Was she really planning on blowing up that building? It seemed incomprehensible, but all roads were leading back to her. There was only one way to make sure.

He made his way to the door on his left and there it was. Another room, this one just rows and columns of boxes set into the walls. And another camera. This one swung around, but it also had its blind spots. Patience was the key. Most thieves would panic and either run or try to take out the thing, thereby alerting whoever was monitoring it that there was a thief. Sean wasn't a thief. He was something more complex, and he knew that patience would prevail.

One, two, three…the numbers made a staccato rhythm in his brain. Fifteen seconds to the right and then it started its sweeping swing. It wasn't the most high tech of units. Its range wasn't great. It was adequate, but not all encompassing. The question was, where was the box Sean needed to get into?

When the camera made its swing, Sean stepped into the blind spot and made his body as small as possible. Box 220. The box he was looking for was 115. *Damn*. It was on the other side. It looked like it was in a corner though. The other blind spot.

Sean let the camera swing by twice, getting the motion and timing correct. He hoped that he was right about the security code. There was only one number on that sheet he'd found in Grace's briefcase that might work. 115-36-2-12. The box number was 115. The rest had to be the code. Taking a deep breath, he followed the camera, staying in the blind spot. Counting, he waited and when the camera swung back, stepped out and located the box, about halfway up. He punched the code in, and the box popped open. He pulled the long metal box out, hugged it to his body and stayed close to the outer wall. In a few minutes, he was back in the mailroom, opening his prize.

And freaking out, just a little.

He was going to kill his brother, his goddamn, closed-mouthed, keeping-secrets brother. This wasn't about terrorists. And Mr. Black had lied to every one of them. Once again, the Agency was playing a game, and they were the pawns.

They were smack in the middle of a spy game.

* * * *

Evan was perfectly satisfied with the way his brother's face flushed as he watched the tape. Matt had been mad at first when he entered the office. He'd been angry to discover Evan had been spying on him. *Amateur*. It was what he did. He'd been a spy for so long, it was second nature to him. Thanks to the good old USA, he wasn't comfortable unless he knew for damn sure what the people around him were doing.

"What do you want me to do to you?" Johansson's voice came over the tape. Evan knew what came next.

"Fuck me, Sir." Grace's breathy moans made Evan's dick hard.

He'd never really thought much about his brother's assistant except for the trouble she could cause. She was a good front on several levels. She wrote out checks without really asking questions. He'd managed to get her to pay the bills on several storage units he didn't want ties to. But he'd never seen her as a woman. That had been a mistake. She was a total freak. He'd never suspected that. If he had, he would have fucked her a long time ago. Maybe if he had taken her to bed, he wouldn't have to do what he needed to do now.

"How could she? She barely knows him." Matt's face was a mask of pain. His hands clenched on the top of his desk, the same desk where his lady love had screwed the hell out of another man.

"Some women are just natural whores." Evan shrugged. And some merely required a firm hand. He suspected Grace was the latter. Damn, he should have seen that. He'd always had more trouble reading women than men. "You have to see that she's not worth your trouble."

His brother was much easier to manipulate than most women. Matt had always ignored what sat in front of him until someone else wanted it. The minute someone else wanted the toy, or car, or a girl Matt had been ignoring, he bristled up with angry possessiveness. It made him terribly easy to predict.

"Bitch." Matt's jaw clenched, but his eyes didn't leave the screen. Evan looked over his shoulder. They were at the part where Johansson fucked her so hard her tits bounced and her face contorted. She was hot. It would suck to kill her. Maybe he could have a little fun before he did it. Evan quickly discarded the idea. He didn't have time. There was a lot of money at stake. His retirement was on the line. He'd find someone even hotter once he got to his place in Thailand.

Then there was the fact that she'd followed him today. He might be more worried about it if Sean Johansson was still around. She was curious. She was about to find out what curiosity did to naughty little cats.

Evan reached into his brother's file cabinet. It was where his alcoholic brother kept the whiskey. He poured him a glass, not the first of the night. Matt accepted it without question and downed it quickly. He sat in his chair as Grace came and the big, blond guy had his fun, too. Evan closed the laptop and looked seriously at his brother.

"She's going to fuck up everything, you know that, right?"

Matt's hand shook slightly. "I can't believe it. She screwed him. She's always been so stand-offish about touching, but she lets him toss up her skirt in my office."

Patience. Evan let his brother rant for a few minutes. He was completely missing the point, but then he hadn't commented at all on the fact that his secretary had obviously been snooping. While Matt raged, Evan pondered the problem of her boyfriend. Evan still wasn't sure he'd heard the last of him. Johansson, if that was his name, was trained. He doubted he was Agency trained. More than likely he was ex-Special Forces. Corporate spy? It wasn't unheard of, but his brother's company had nothing a spy would want...except access to other buildings. No, he suspected that asshole Nelson had caught up with him. He was sure Nelson had introduced himself as Mr. Blue or Mr. Green or whatever color he was hiding behind this week. The whole CIA was one big fucking rainbow.

It wasn't surprising. Nelson had been his handler. Nelson knew what he was capable of. When he'd disappeared at the end of the last op in Shanghai, Evan had left plenty of evidence that pointed to Patrick Wright's untimely death. He'd had another identity in place, and then, after a little plastic surgery, had finally settled into being Evan Parnell. It had taken the bastard almost five years to catch up to him, but Nelson was too late.

Evan had the package. He'd taken it last night after his "shift" at the Bryson Building. One fucking shift and he had the prize. Damn, it was good to be back in the States where the pickings were easy. If he had been in China, he'd probably be dead. One little badge and a human resources file and you were in over here. Now all he had to do was hold it together until the drop. Another couple of days and he'd drop the package at the party. His Chinese contact would pick it up. The Chinese government would gain about ten years of aviation technology research, and he'd gain twenty fucking million dollars.

If Sean Johansson and Grace Hawthorne didn't wreck it for him.

"So what are we going to do about it?"

Finally, an intelligent question passed his brother's mouth. Evan smiled his best "big brother" smile. "Well, I have some thoughts on that."

Twenty minutes later, Evan breathed in the night air. It smelled like rain to him. Tomorrow would be a good day for a storm.

Chapter Thirteen

The rain was coming down in sheets, pounding at the window beside her desk as Grace held the phone to her ear. The woman on the other end of the line droned on for what felt like forever before there was a chance to respond. This party was going to kill her. "Yes, I know it's short notice. Okay, if we can't do the spare ribs, what can we do? Dumplings sound good. Pork and chicken. All right."

The conversation dragged on and on. The hotel's catering liaison was a long-winded woman. She had a story about every single dish she offered.

Sean would just cook. She wondered if Sean cooked Asian. Probably. He'd seemed to really know his way around a kitchen. The French dish he'd cooked had been heavenly. She remembered the rich taste of the sauce and how he'd offered it up to taste from his fingers. Grace had sucked them into her mouth, loving the flavor and texture of him as much as the food.

Stop. Focus. She had to stop allowing thoughts of Sean to occupy her every moment. She'd spent most of the previous night crying over Sean Johansson. She hadn't slept at all. She was not wasting a perfectly good workday on him as well.

"Orange peel beef. Got it." She thought that was a yes on the beef. Maybe the woman had told her she couldn't. Damn it, she had to get her head in the game. She had mere days before this party, and Matt was already in a crappy mood. If this went to hell, she wouldn't be able to work with him.

"Listen, Sue, why don't you just e-mail me a list? I trust you, and I know you'll do the best you can on the time you have. As for the drinks, Matt wants an open bar." Big surprise there. Lately Matt's life seemed like one big open bar. "Can you take care of the bartenders?"

Twenty minutes and negotiations on how many bartenders they would need later, Grace managed to get off the phone. It had been a productive day so far. The party was going to be fine. The contract with the Bryson Building had already started, and hopefully the money would start rolling in. They would need it to cover the party.

"Hey, you." Kayla smiled down at her. She looked around the office. "Where's that hunk of yours? It's almost three. Shouldn't he be rushing in with your afternoon coffee so you don't have to hurt your dainty toes by walking? I haven't seen him around." She leaned in with a little grin on her face. "Do you have him tied up somewhere?"

He hadn't even tied her up. They hadn't gotten that far. Grace took a deep breath and tried for a casual smile. "He went back to Chicago."

Kayla's face fell. "Oh, sweetie, I'm so sorry."

"It's no big deal. It was a fling. I thought you would be happy. I'm slutting it up a little bit." She kept her voice light, trying to breeze her way through this encounter.

It was obvious her friend wasn't buying her tough chick act. Kayla pulled her out of her chair and hugged her. "You wouldn't even know how to slut it up, hon. If you were sleeping with him, you were involved. Are you going to see him again?"

Grace shook her head. There was no pretending now. Her eyes welled up, and she choked back the tears. "No. I don't even have his number. He left a note. It didn't say anything about calling."

"Asshole."

"It was just a fling." Grace shook her head. That was true. She had always known that was all it would be. Sean was always going to head back to Chicago. Grace had just thought she could hold on to him a little longer than she had. She had also thought that he would at least say goodbye.

"Not for you it wasn't." Kayla let her sink back into her chair. Kayla's face flushed with anger. "If he were here, I would stomp on his toe and then call it an accident. He's an idiot if he can't see how awesome you are."

Kayla looked cute in a sunny yellow dress and blue scarf that was completely incongruous with the weather. It was pouring rain outside, and the claps of thunder shook the building.

"He's just a guy. Seriously, Kayla, it's fine." The weather matched Grace's mood perfectly. The last thing she wanted was to have a heart-to-heart right here in the office with Kayla. She would end up crying, and she didn't want to cry anymore. She'd cried so much the night before her eyes were still a little swollen.

Kayla studied her for a moment. She frowned. "I doubt that. I'm pretty sure you need some retail therapy or at least some time with Señor Cuervo. But now that you're single again, we should see about setting you up. You have to forget that jerk and get right back on the horse." A startled look crossed Kayla's face. "Unless…didn't I hear that you went out with Adam Miles last night?"

She wasn't sure what that had to do with getting back on the horse. Not that she was getting on any horse, or man, anytime soon. She'd given the whole flaming hot affair thing a try, and she'd gotten burned. "We went out for dinner and a movie last night. He's a friend. And he's gay. Jake was with us." It couldn't be a hot date if the guy brought along his boyfriend.

"Holy crap. How exactly was Jake 'with' you? Tonya in HR says those boys are wild."

Grace felt her eyes go wide. "What are you talking about?"

"Tonya said she's never had a night like the one she spent in between those two."

"No. They aren't bi. They're gay. They just started a relationship. I can't imagine that they would do that." But she kind of could, in a totally hot, dirty way. They were two gorgeous men. The idea of them kissing had always done something for her. The idea of them kissing and then reaching out to the girl watching them really did something for her. "No. That has to be a rumor. You know you shouldn't pay attention to gossip."

"What else am I supposed to do? Work? That's horribly boring, Grace. I would much rather think about your suddenly raging, hot sex life. And I didn't mention anything about them being bisexual. Maybe, but according to Tonya, they were all about the girl. Has one of them made a move on you? I bet it's Jake. He's the dark, broody one. I bet he's the aggressive one, too."

"No, it wasn't Jake." She hadn't meant to say that.

Kayla's grin practically lit up the room. "Then it was Adam. OMG, Grace, what happened?"

"It was nothing." Wasn't it? It had just been a little kiss. And a whole lot of hand holding. And Adam's arm around her waist for a lot of the night. But he didn't mean anything by that. She wasn't so vain that she expected a thirty-year-old hottie to be after her. A hottie and his boyfriend. Although, now that she thought about it, she'd never seen them kiss. Maybe they were just shy. She shook her head. They couldn't be straight. "It wasn't anything. I don't know what happened with Tonya, but I'm strictly hag material, if you know what I mean."

Even the thought of two hot guys wasn't breaking through the sadness she felt about Sean. She could put together four, and they wouldn't be as stimulating as the thought of the man who she had briefly called Sir.

"I doubt that. You're not very self aware." Kayla got up and sighed. She pulled the scarf off her neck and began wrapping it around her hair, covering it. "There's nothing else to do. We need lattes. I'm going to brave the rain and get us some. You stay here. You've had a crappy day. You always go get the coffee. I'll do it today."

But she hadn't lately. Lately, her daily run to the coffee bar two streets over had been taken over by Sean. Until yesterday.

She'd always made her daily run to the coffee bar at exactly three p.m. But when she started seeing Sean, he'd show up with her latte, and then they would talk for a while. Yesterday, she had forced herself to make the walk. It had proven beyond a shadow of a doubt that he was gone and life was back to normal. "You don't have to, Kay. It's awful out there."

"It's letting up, and I need some caffeine. Give me your raincoat and your umbrella, and I'll be good to go." Kayla's hand was already out and waiting.

Grace sighed and stood back up. She hugged her friend. At least if she was back to normal, Kayla was with her. She needed sugar and coffee and girl talk. "Thanks. Get me a couple of cookies, too. I'm supposed to go to happy hour with Adam and Jake tonight. Want to join us? You can form your own opinions about my future ménage a trois chances."

Those would be zero, but she was willing to play along. Kayla was taking one for the team by going on the coffee run.

When she was fully geared up for the rain, Kayla gave her a jaunty salute and promised to return as soon as possible. Grace sat back. Matt had left earlier in the day after barking a few orders at her. He'd been in a terrible mood and obviously hung over. Now it was quiet. She thought briefly about visiting the storage place again and asking some questions. The weather made that decision for her. But there was something she could do.

Grace got up and walked to Matt's door. She was surprised to discover it was locked. She tried it twice before accepting it. He never locked his door. Confused, Grace walked back to her desk and pulled out her keys. Maybe he'd forgotten she had a set, or he'd just made a mistake. Either way, she was going in. She wanted to see that contract he'd signed, the big moneymaker they were celebrating on Friday.

It took her awhile to find the file. She shuffled through it, reading through each bid carefully. Twenty minutes later, she came to the final, signed contract, and then her jaw dropped open.

They were losing money on the Bryson Building deal. How was that possible? Why would he do that? What on earth had possessed him to make such a deal?

By the time Grace looked up, Adam was standing in the doorway, a smile on his face and his hand out to her.

* * * *

163

Sean watched her cross the street from his car. Her face was covered by her bright red umbrella, but he knew the raincoat she'd worn that morning. He checked the time. Exactly three p.m. It was the afternoon coffee run. It didn't look like a little rain was going to keep Grace away from her afternoon fix. What a miserable fucking day. He hadn't slept. Every time he closed his eyes, all he could see was Grace in between Adam and Jake right before Patrick Wright, former CIA agent, showed up to kill them all. It was so fucking nice of Mr. Black to not mention he was really hunting a rogue agent. Bastard.

After he'd driven back to Ian's and screamed at his brother for keeping him out of the loop, he'd handed over the copies of the evidence he'd made.

Sean slunk out of the SUV to begin his obligatory tracking of Grace Hawthorne. He knew where she was going, so he hung back. The last thing he wanted was for Grace to catch him. It would make him sink even lower in his brother's estimation.

At least he'd made up for a little of his fuckup with the info he'd brought in the night before. The box Grace paid for, and Evan Parnell used, had been full. There had been two passports, a plethora of credit cards in various names, cash from several countries. There had also been a very interesting file on one Eli Nelson, who looked an awful lot like Mr. Black. It seemed Evan Parnell, who was almost certainly Patrick Wright with a great deal of good plastic surgery, had a beef with the CIA agent. There were some serious allegations against the man. There was also evidence that Parnell had been selling corporate and government secrets to the Chinese and intended to do so again.

And Grace was smack in the middle of it all.

So, who was she? Sweet widow with a penchant for submission and really bad luck in jobs, or savvy co-conspirator? And did he really care? He'd been up all night thinking about her.

She had wound her way around his heart like a weed, and she just might end up choking the life out of him if he didn't do something about it. What could he do? Walk away? The thought churned his stomach. He'd made the decision last night that he couldn't leave Grace to the wolves. Whatever she had done, he would take care of it. When she realized how much trouble she could be in, she would come to him. When this was over, he would offer her his protection and once she was legally bound to him, he wouldn't allow her anywhere near this world again. He would get her the best lawyer money could buy, and they would put this behind them. He was quitting and going to culinary school, and Grace would be far from all of this.

He would never, ever, let her know how much power she had over him.

Ahead of him, Grace and her red umbrella turned down an alley. It was a shortcut to the coffee shop. Sean stopped. It would seem weird if someone followed her down the narrow alley. He ducked into the deli next to the alley and bought his own cup of coffee. She would be a couple of minutes. Sean stared out the window and thought about the latest fight he'd had with his brother. Sean had argued that they should bring Grace in and offer to cut a deal with her. Ian had pointed out that they weren't really in a position to cut a deal with anyone at all. Ian wanted to wait and see what happened. Sean knew what that meant. Ian had a plan, and he wasn't sharing it with anyone.

The coffee burned down his throat, but Sean welcomed the heat. It wasn't more than two days ago that he was running after Grace's afternoon coffee. He'd also spent the day cooking for her and preparing to take care of her when she got home from work. He was such an idiot.

Their relationship would be different this time around. Ian was right. He needed a twenty-four/seven sub. If Grace wanted his protection, she would accept him as her permanent Master. She would wear his collar and his ring.

No, she won't. She'll more than likely hit you upside the head with that cast iron skillet her mama bought her, Taggart. What makes you think she'll come to you when she's got the ménage boys?

Sean remembered the soft way she'd submitted to him. She might have lied when she said she loved him, but there was no faking her response to him sexually. She'd been so hot for him.

She'd been willing to do anything he asked. Sex would be the key to handling Grace.

He would tie her up and let her sweat a little. He was incredibly good with a single-tail. He would crack the whip and tease her until she begged him to take her. He'd think about it. It wouldn't do to give in too quickly, no matter how much his dick begged for it. He'd leave her on the St. Andrew's Cross for a while. He'd use a vibe on her pussy and clamps on those tits of hers. He wouldn't let her come until he was ready. He would be in charge.

Sean stared out the window as people walked by. Women with umbrellas, kids splashing in the puddles as their moms tried to haul them along, a couple of men rushed by the window. A man in a baseball hat caught Sean's eye. He wasn't rushing. He was walking patiently as though the rain didn't bother him. His face was turned away, but Sean had the vague impression he'd seen the man before. Someone from Grace's office?

He glanced up at the clock, surprised to see ten minutes had passed. She should have been walking back by now. A little frisson of fear crackled along his skin making goose bumps flare along his arms. Where was Grace?

He chucked the coffee and went back out into the rain. It was coming down harder now. Maybe she was just being sensible. She should wait in the comfort of the shop and enjoy her afternoon fix out of the rain. It made sense. So why was his stomach in knots?

The wind picked up, and Sean watched in dawning horror as Grace's red umbrella skittered across the pavement. The wind lifted it like a vibrant balloon escaping gravity. It rushed past him before hitting the street and rolling away. Sean ran. His feet seemed as though they were weighed down. It took forever to run the half-block to the little alley Grace had disappeared down. Time seemed ridiculously slow, and then it stopped all together.

Sean felt his stomach drop as he caught sight of the body in the alley. She was face first in the rain, her limbs at odd angles as though the body had tried to move, but discovered the task impossible.

"Grace." His voice was little above a whisper. He couldn't find the scream that should have come naturally.

Please answer. Please get up. Please, please fucking wake up. This is a dream, a really bad dream. I'm going to wake up and be sitting in the van outside Grace's house. Just wake up.

His hands started to shake as he moved toward her. She was so still, and then he saw the strange, red water rush by his feet down toward the storm gutter. He stared at it dumbly for a moment before realizing what it was. Blood. Oh god, Grace's blood was running down the street and into the gutter.

He ran, stumbling toward her, tears in his eyes mixing with the rain on his face. He hit his knees when he saw the knife in her back. The handle was simple and wicked at the same time. It was buried in her black raincoat. It would have cut through the gray blouse she was wearing today and made its way into her lungs.

She wasn't breathing. Somewhere deep inside, he knew she was gone. All of his training told him that wound was fatal. Still, he prayed. He didn't try to take the knife out. That would make things worse, if there was anything left to make worse. In the back of his mind, he realized he should be running after the man in the baseball cap. He'd been the one to kill Grace. He should be up and running to avenge the woman he loved. So why did he sit in the alley crying? Why did this wretched grief shove out all other thoughts? It froze him in place, and he wondered suddenly if he would ever be able to move again.

He couldn't take it anymore. He turned Grace's body over. They would find him here with her. They would find him crying in the freaking rain, and he didn't care. He stared down into her face.

"Grace?"

It wasn't Grace's eyes that stared unseeingly up at him. It was her friend, the funny, flirty one who had threatened him with grave bodily injury if he broke her friend's heart. Kayla. She'd pulled him aside that second day on the job and warned him. He'd been impressed by her ferocity. Kayla was dead, not Grace. Kayla, who was wearing Grace's raincoat and carrying her umbrella. Kayla, who had pulled her hair back in a scarf to protect it from the rain. He'd mistaken Kayla for Grace. Grace made her way to the coffee bar every day by the same route at the same time.

The man in the baseball cap hadn't been planning on killing

Kayla. He'd thought he was killing Grace. When he realized his mistake, he would try again.

The first call Sean made was to 911. He then quickly made his way out of the alley. No one had seen him. He was sure of that. He made his way back to his car and called Jacob Dean.

Whether Ian liked it or not, Grace was coming in.

Chapter Fourteen

Adam hustled her into the elevator, Jacob Dean close behind him. He held her hand firmly in his. Adam had discarded his jacket and tie and looked casually elegant. She doubted he could look anything else. She'd never seen him in jeans. He squeezed her hand in a reassuring fashion. "Don't worry about Kayla. We'll stop by the coffee bar. It's really coming down. She'll be happy to not have to walk."

Grace sighed and slipped her phone back into her bag. When Adam had shown up in Matt's office to take her to an early dinner, she'd argued that she should wait for Kayla. She'd tried Kayla's phone twice, but no one answered. She was almost an hour late. It would be easier to just go find her like Adam had offered. It was actually easy to take everything the handsome man was offering her. After the confusion of the afternoon, Adam seemed very solid and welcoming.

Jake stood beside them as the elevator descended, but didn't look like a man about to have a nice evening out. Jake seemed more tense. His eyes moved like he was searching for something. He had said very little, and Grace was beginning to worry that he was angry about something. Maybe he was angry that he couldn't get a night out with his boyfriend alone. Grace could understand that. Jake couldn't want a third wheel hanging around.

"You know what, Adam, I think I'm just going to head home. I'll stop by and find Kayla, and you two can go out." She offered him an encouraging smile. Maybe he would take the hint. She would miss his easy company, but she didn't want to come between him and Jake.

"We'd rather be with you, love." Adam looked up, watching the numbers descend. Now that she looked at him, he seemed a bit tense, too. What was going on with them?

She went up on her toes and whispered in his ear. "I don't think Jake wants a girl around tonight. You should go and have fun with your boyfriend."

Adam seemed startled as he looked down at her, and a slow smile crossed his face. He didn't bother to whisper. "Jake is perfectly fine with having a girl around, love."

The elevator doors opened. Jake turned to her. "Believe me, Grace, if things were slightly different, I would be more than happy to show you just how comfortable I am with having a woman tonight."

Whoa. Jake hadn't sounded like he was joking. His face had been perfectly serious. Before she had a chance to respond, Adam was pulling her along into the parking garage. Suddenly Jake stopped and put up his right fist. Adam's arm came around her waist, pulling her back into the hard plane of his chest.

"What?" Grace looked around trying to see what had caught his eye. She would protest, but it hadn't been that long ago that some jerk on a motorcycle had almost plowed into her, and that was in the outside lot. The inside lot had always given her the creeps. There were too many places for people to hide. It was too quiet and gloomy. She almost never parked in here. Now she was very thankful for her escort.

The staccato sound of footsteps echoed through the garage. They were distant but coming closer.

"Cover her." Jake's order came out as a low bark. Adam responded immediately. In two quick moves, her back was against a pylon, and Adam was taking up all the available space.

"What's going on?" She kept her voice low because it seemed like the right thing to do.

Adam's eyes looked down at her. "It's going to be all right, darling. Jake and I are going to take very good care of you."

"I don't understand." A tendril of real fear was taking over. What did she really know about these men?

"I'll explain everything when we can get the hell out of here. I promise, it's going to be okay now. We don't have to pretend anymore." Adam's body pressed against hers, and his mouth descended. Grace was too shocked to move. This wasn't a friendly mouth coming her way. This mouth was sensual and had purpose. Adam's lips closed over hers, pressing softly in. It was so different from Sean. It was sweet, but when Sean kissed her, she felt it in her womb.

"That's no big surprise." The cold words startled Grace out of her thoughts. She pushed against Adam because she knew that voice.

There he was standing in front of her, as though the universe had pulled him from her thoughts and made him reality. He was dressed in jeans and a T-shirt that was plastered to his chest from the rain. It clung to him, molding his every muscle. His hair was swept back leaving his face stark, with nothing to soften the planes. He was gorgeously masculine, and everything in Grace responded to him.

"Sean?"

His blue eyes stared a hole straight through her. Adam's arm came back around her waist, forcing her to stand with him.

"Where's the car, Sarge? I want to get Grace out of here as soon as possible." Adam sounded different. The teasing, playful tone of his voice had changed to something harder, more competent. "We'll take her back to our place and hole up there."

"I'm not going anywhere." Grace pulled away from Adam. Sean was back. He'd come back. And found her kissing another man. That wasn't good. "Sean, he's just a friend."

Sean's fists were clenched at his sides. Everything about him said "angry man." It was up to her to soften him. Doms probably didn't like finding their subs in someone else's arms. Grace's hand went to the necklace she was wearing. It might help to point out she was still wearing her collar. She hadn't had the heart to take it off.

Sean's eyes flashed down to the little gold heart at her neck and then back to Adam. "Oh, I bet he is, sweetheart. I bet he's a good friend. You're not going anywhere with him."

Sean's words were icy, but he held his hand out, and Grace took it immediately. She walked from Adam to Sean, placing herself as close to him as she could get. Her hand rested on his chest. She didn't care that he was cold and wet. A light joy filled her heart. He'd come back. "Of course I'm not going anywhere now that you're back. Though I should play harder to get than I am. That note was a terrible way to leave me, Sean."

His eyes stared down, still flinty and cold, but his hand came up and wound its way into her hair. He pulled her head back and crushed her mouth against his. His other hand grabbed her ass and held her to his body, leaving no mistake about his desire. His erection poked her in the belly as his tongue plundered her mouth. Grace let herself go very soft against him. Something was riding her lover, and whether it was catching her with Adam or something that happened in Chicago, she knew he needed this show of dominance.

When he finally came up for air, she touched the line of his jaw. "He really is just a friend. He didn't mean anything by it."

"He meant it." Sean ground the words out.

Adam's face was flushed. "Of course I did, Grace. I care about you. I care about you a hell of a lot more than Sean does. He gave you to me. Do you understand? He chose to leave you and then told Jake that we had his blessing to sleep with you."

"Now is not the time or the place to question my rights to my sub." Sean took a step toward Adam, and Grace wondered if she was going to have to stop a fight. What was wrong with Adam?

Adam didn't seem to have a sense of self-preservation. Grace could feel the pent-up violence in her Dom, but Adam just moved closer. "Oh, really? Your sub? Don't you mean slave, Tag? Sean Taggart doesn't have a girlfriend. He takes a slave. You should know he never keeps one for long, Grace."

"Jake, if you don't want your friend to end up in a shallow grave in East Texas, I suggest you get him to shut up." Sean growled the order.

Jacob Dean's head swung from one man to the other. "Are you seriously going to do this here? We need to go. Adam, hold your tongue before you make an idiot of yourself. He's back. She's made her choice. As for you, you fucking Neanderthal, can we get her to a safe place before you tattoo your 'property of' sign across her ass?"

There was too much going on. About three thousand questions slammed through Grace's head as Sean's hand tightened on hers. He started to drag her toward a row of vehicles. What were the men talking about? They were speaking in some shorthand she didn't understand. It made no sense. They barely knew each other. They had only met when Grace had introduced them a few days before. And who the hell was Sean Taggart?

Grace dug her three-inch J Renee heels in and pulled back. It was time to get some answers. "Stop. Why are they calling you 'Sarge' and 'Taggart'? And how do you know them? Why do I need to go to a safe place?"

Sean's face was set in fierce lines when he turned to her. If he hadn't had such a tight hold on her hand, she would have backed away from what she saw there. "Obey me. Get in the car." He gestured toward a monstrous SUV and tossed his keys through the air. Jake's hand came up and caught it. "You drive."

Grace didn't move. Sean's eyes narrowed on her. "I'm not going anywhere until someone tells me what's going on."

"You are wearing my collar, Grace. You will obey me."

She felt a stubborn look cross her face, her mouth firming, her eyes settling into a steely gaze. "You said that was just for the bedroom, Sean. We're not in the bedroom. I want some answers."

Instead of being reasonable, Sean simply leaned over and grabbed her, tossing her over his shoulder in a fireman's hold. Grace felt her world upend and dropped her briefcase as she was held firmly against Sean's shoulder. "I changed my mind. You'll obey me, or there will be hell to pay. I'm doing this to protect you, little one. The next several hours will go much more easily if you do everything I tell you. The first order of the day is complete obedience. You will look to me for guidance during the interrogation, and you will not lie. I discover one lie that crosses those sweet lips of yours and you'll be over my knee. I won't hold back. I swear you won't want to sit down for a week after I'm done."

"Interrogation? What kind of game are you playing, Sean? I don't want any part of it." Why was someone going to interrogate her? She was starting to get frightened. Her playful Dom was gone, and in his place was a cold, aggressive predator. The predator looked hungry, and Grace was afraid she was lunch.

"Very nice, Tag. The lady is scared as it is and you offer to beat her," Adam said, his disdain apparent. He carried her briefcase with him.

Grace heard a car door open and then another. She was shoved into the backseat. The minute her body hit the leather seat, she scrambled, trying to get out the other side. She wasn't sure where she was going. She just knew she needed to find out a few things before she went anywhere with Sean. It was plain to her that she didn't understand what was going on. She managed to find the door. Her fingers curled around the handle. She heard a click as it locked, and then Sean was pulling her back. Frustration flooded her as Grace pushed against him. "Let me go or I'm going to call the cops."

"With this?" Sean held up her cell phone. He must have taken it out of her case. He handed it to Jake, who was starting the car. Adam settled himself into the front seat beside him. "You don't want to call the cops. Trust me. With the evidence we have on you, they'll take you into custody immediately."

Grace felt tears well up. "What are you talking about? What evidence? What is going on, and who the hell is Sean Taggart?" She practically screamed the words, and they seemed to bounce around the cab of the vehicle as Jake backed up.

"I'm Sean Taggart, Grace. That's my name. Sean Johansson was a cover while my group investigated you and your boss." The sudden trill of a phone cut through the tension and then Sean was talking softly to someone on the other end.

"Yes, Ian, that's what I said." Sean continued as Adam turned in his seat. He looked at Grace with no small amount of sympathy in his eyes.

174

"My name really is Adam Miles. I don't have the service record Sean does, so I can go by my real name from time to time. Grace, I want you to know I don't believe you're involved in any of this. You just got caught up in it. I meant what I said earlier. Jake and I want to take care of you."

"Damn it, Adam, do you want him to kill you?" Jake snarled the question as he pushed some buttons on the console of the SUV. Grace was surprised to see several different views pop up on the mirrors of the vehicle. It looked like there was a camera in the back of the car, and the view was plain in the rearview mirror. Grace cocked her head and could see both of the side view mirrors had small monitors as well. Whoever was driving would be able to see anyone or thing coming toward the car from several angles. She doubted this was a standard feature.

"She deserves to know the truth. You don't believe she's involved any more than I do," Adam argued.

Jake shook his head. "That's not our call."

Sean seemed to be finishing up his conversation. "All right, but I won't let them take her, Ian. You understand?" He shoved the phone back in his pocket. His face was a block of granite as he looked straight ahead. "We're going to Ian's. He called in Black. The Agency wants to talk to her, but they've agreed to do it at Ian's. We'll be holing up there for the night, and tomorrow we'll figure out what to do."

Adam's face went ashen. "They're going to take her, Sean."

"Take me where?" Her hands had started to shake, and she couldn't stop the tears streaming down her face. Jake turned the car toward the freeway. The rain had started again. It pounded against the roof. Grace was grateful for it. Maybe they couldn't hear how hard her heart was beating.

"It's called rendition," Adam explained. "The CIA takes you to another country to interrogate you so they don't have to follow Geneva Convention rules."

"CIA?" What the hell had she gotten into? What did the CIA want with an administrative assistant?

"I'm not letting Black take her anywhere," Sean growled. "Damn it, Adam, do you want her panicked? Do you honestly

175

believe I would allow some Agency asshole to waltz off with my sub?"

"Well you certainly didn't have any problem walking away from her. You gave her to me. Jake told me you said we had your blessing to pursue her."

Grace could see Jake's hands tighten on the steering wheel. "I also told you he didn't really mean it."

"Screw all of you!" Grace screamed, startling the men. She was done listening to them argue. "Tell me what is going on, and tell me now, or I swear I'll fight. I'll kick and scream and punch whoever I can get my hands on."

Sean turned his cold blue eyes on her. "Nicely played, sweetheart. Are you going to seriously tell me you have no idea what's been happening right under your nose?"

Grace met his eyes. It was starting to sink in that she'd been used. These three men knew each other and had for a long time. They were playing some sort of game. Bitterness welled up. "Well, as I apparently have no idea who any of you people are, I think we can discount my intelligence. Treat me like a five year old. Give it to me in words I can understand."

Sean sighed and briefly closed his eyes. "God, you're going to play this out until the end, aren't you? You don't have to pretend, Grace. I'm the idiot who knows what you've done and still intends to protect you. After this business with Black is over, we're going to talk about the conditions of my help, but I'll play along with you for now. The CIA has been tracking a rogue agent for the last several years. When they first approached the firm I work for, they gave us his cover. It wasn't until we had solid proof that he used to work for the Agency that our contact admitted it. The man we're tracking has been working the underground as an ecoterrorist for several years. It's given him some inroads with certain groups that have proven useful to him. Is that where you met him?"

Grace felt like her whole world had turned upside down. She heard the words CIA and ecoterrorist, but couldn't come up with a single way either would have a connection to her life. "I have no idea what you're talking about."

His gorgeous lips quirked up in a disbelieving smirk. "Really?

We know about your arrest record."

"I was a kid. I got arrested for protesting on private property. My dad paid the fine, and the judge said the record would be sealed because I was sixteen. I never got arrested again. It was supposed to be expunged from my record." Grace remembered the day like it was yesterday. She remembered how both her parents had shown up at the jail. Her mother had cried, but her father had been royally pissed off. He'd died the next year, and she'd been married and pregnant shortly after her eighteenth birthday. It was her one and only attempt at civil disobedience.

"Nothing is ever really expunged, Grace. My group can find out anything. You can't hide from us. Did you meet Patrick Wright because he works with subversive underground groups? Are you affiliated with the Earth League? It's his cover. He's been hiding in what the Agency would consider plain sight. He's had many names, but then someone of his supposed nature would. From what I can tell, he's used his subversive activities to gather corporate and government secrets to sell to foreign agencies. He goes into corporations or buildings that house government entities and causes trouble. No one thinks anything beyond what he wants them to think. He copies the information he needs and everyone is so upset by the damage his 'group' has caused that they don't consider what really has occurred."

Grace's mind was racing. "Patrick Wright? Like Matt?"

"Yes, it's his brother." This came from Adam, who spoke softly, as though trying to soften the blows that had come from every angle since she'd walked into the damn parking garage.

"Matt's involved in this? I've never met his brother."

Sean was as sarcastic as Adam had been sweet. "Sure you haven't, sweetheart. We suspect that Patrick Wright had a great deal of plastic surgery after his time with the Agency was done. He would be going under an assumed name. You would know him as Evan Parnell."

"Oh, god." The secret meetings. The contracts that didn't make sense. What had Matt gotten them all into? "The Bryson Building."

"Yes, I believe we'll be talking about that."

"Sean, I don't know anything."

177

His eyes alone told her he didn't believe her. "That's why your computer is littered with surveillance and information a thief could use. Listen to me, you're going to tell us everything. You're going to give Parnell up, and then you'll be out of this."

Frustration was building inside her. How could he think she had anything to do with this? He knew her. She'd been more intimate with him than she'd ever been with a man. "I don't know anything. Evan Parnell is just a guy at work."

"You pay his bills. It's your name on the security deposit box he keeps."

"I am Matt's admin. I don't recall helping Parnell with anything, but if I did it was for the company. It's part of my job." For the last several years she'd been writing checks for all the things Matt needed. It was a bitch to keep up with considering everything else she had to do. Now that she thought about it, Matt had started asking her to pay for things out of a miscellaneous fund right around the time Evan Parnell had shown up. She didn't always ask questions when Matt asked her to write a check. It was never more than a couple of hundred dollars, maybe a thousand. Could she have been used to do something illegal?

Sean seemed to think so. "All of the evidence against you will be on the table when we get to where we're going. You'll see the case we've made, and then maybe you'll drop this ridiculous act. It will all go so much smoother if you're just honest with us. You're a little fish. Patrick Wright is the shark."

He was so cold, so unlike the warm man who had become her lover. It made sense. That man hadn't existed. He'd been a cover to get her to talk. It seemed incomprehensible to Grace that she found herself in this position, but there was no disputing that she was in a car in the custody of someone who didn't care about her, who would use her to his own ends. She looked at the man she had fallen in love with and didn't know who he was. She had been so stupid. What had she been thinking? How could she have thought for a single second that someone as gorgeous as Sean Johansson...Taggart could ever be interested in her? She was forty, and while she was still reasonably attractive, she wasn't anywhere close to his league.

"It will go so much easier on everyone if you just confess,

Grace." His judgmental tone was the last straw.

Grace retreated. She sank into herself and let the world around her become background noise. She curled her hands into her lap and made very sure she didn't touch Sean Taggart at all. It wasn't easy. He was a ridiculously large man, and he didn't seem very interested in respecting her space. Grace moved slightly so she was against the side of the door.

Sean's hand came out to grasp her forearm. "Don't try it. The doors are locked, and you can't open it from the inside."

She started to protest that she wasn't about to throw herself out of a moving vehicle, but kept silent. She didn't have anything to say to this man.

"Don't cry, sweetheart." Adam turned around and reached out to her. Grace moved away from him. He'd lied to her, too.

Grace felt the tears rolling down her cheeks. Damn it. She wished she was one of those people who could bottle up her emotions. She never had been. She'd always worn them on her sleeve, and nothing seemed to be able to toughen her up. The tears rolled down and suddenly the chill hit her. She was wet from pressing herself against Sean, and now the cold seemed to seep into her bones. Maybe it was the cold or the emotion, but Grace felt her teeth start to chatter as a fine trembling began across her skin.

Sean cursed, and she felt him move beside her. He reached into the back of the SUV and when his hand came back, he held a blanket. Grace sat motionless as he settled it around her shoulders. She stiffened when he pulled her into his arms.

"Stop it." He used his Dom voice on her, but she wasn't buying it anymore. It wasn't real. It was just one more trick he had used against her. He'd figured out her fantasies. The loving care he had shown her before had been the bait for his trap. She was across his lap, pressed against his chest before she could protest. Grace squirmed, trying to get away from him, but his arms were a cage around her. Like everything with the man, she was utterly helpless. "Calm down, Grace."

"I'd prefer to sit by myself." She wanted to be away from him. It was hard to think about anything but how big his body was and how protected she'd felt when she'd thought he cared about her. The urge to wrap her arms around him and cry her heart out was almost overwhelming.

"And I'd prefer you calm down and let me take care of you." He was quiet, whispering his words into her ear. "There's no point in fighting me, Grace. You can't win. You're caught. I don't care why you were doing it. Maybe you needed the money, whatever, but it stops now. So relax. I'm going to take care of it. I'm going to care of you."

He wasn't going to give her the dignity of sitting by herself. He seemed to want to take everything away from her. Grace sat stiffly in his arms, tears continuing to fall. She might not be able to get away from him, but he was wrong about the rest of it. There was a reason to fight. And she was going to give him hell.

Chapter Fifteen

Sean hated the stiff way Grace sat in his lap, as though she couldn't stand to be so close to him. What the hell was her game now? She wasn't very good at it. When she should have led him on a merry chase, she'd easily submitted. Now, when she should be doing everything in her power to appeal to his soft side, she gave him the cold shoulder. He should shove her off and let her shiver. Instead he pulled her close, unable to deny the need to be close to her.

He'd thought she was dead. He'd seen her body and known he would spend the rest of his life alone. Grace was his soul mate. Grace was the one woman he'd waited for. He hadn't known he was waiting, hadn't given it much thought before, but in that moment when he'd thought Grace was gone, he'd known that she was the one.

No matter what she had done, he wouldn't let her go. When he'd turned her body over and discovered that it was Kayla who had lost her life in that dank little alley, he'd decided on his course. Grace never had to know how much he loved her. It was better that she didn't. She'd been lying for so long, she probably wouldn't know the truth if it slapped her across the face. He wondered how long she'd known about him. She'd had the upper hand. Now the tables were turned, and he would be in charge. He would take care of her, but he would never give her a hint of the chokehold she had on his heart.

"Not long now." Adam's soft voice made Sean want to put his fist through the other man's face. He was looking back at Grace as though she needed to be saved from him. Sean stared at the man he'd known for years. He'd met Adam and Jake that first year in the Army. He'd known all about their penchant for sharing, and he'd kept his mouth closed. He'd saved their asses time and time again. This was how Adam repaid him? By coming after his woman? He and Adam would have another talk very soon that just might end with Sean having to hide a body. He could do it, he thought with a sort of savage satisfaction. He would love a long fight. His body was primed with unleashed violence. He couldn't go after Parnell, not yet. Adam would do.

"I'd like to call a lawyer." Grace was very quiet, but her words were even and controlled. Her hands were still a jumble of fine trembles, but she'd gotten the rest of her body under command.

He looked at her, wishing she would give him the same courtesy. Her eyes stared forward. "I'll get you one if it becomes necessary. I don't think it will."

He intended to make sure she never had to deal with anything like that. Patrick Wright, a.k.a. Evan Parnell, was the one they were really after. They didn't need to prosecute Grace. Hell, they probably wouldn't prosecute Patrick Wright. It made for bad headlines when the CIA lost one of their own. Rogue agents were bad for business. Patrick Wright wouldn't get the courtesy of a trial. The Agency would want this all swept under the rug. Sean just needed to make sure Grace was protected when the cleaners came.

"Do I get a phone call?"

He sighed. "You aren't being arrested. I'm trying to keep that from happening."

Jake turned down the long, winding road that ended in Ian's very private estate. Ian lived outside the city where there was still breathing room. Of course, Ian didn't really care about breathing room. He did care about privacy. Ian had selected this little country estate of his for its lack of nosy neighbors. As Jake carefully navigated the road, Sean knew his brother had already been alerted that they were on their way. Ian's security measures alerted him to anything and everything that made its way onto his property.

"And you're not the cops?" Grace asked.

"We aren't cops. We're a group of ex-Special Forces that works as private security and does occasional government work on the side."

She sniffed, a derisive little sound. "So you're a mercenary."

It didn't bother Sean. He'd been called worse. "Use whatever name makes you feel better about yourself. The important thing is we've handled just about every situation you can think of. We can get you out of this. You just have to trust us."

Adam had taken off his seatbelt. He had an umbrella in his hand. Sean had no doubt he would be right there ready to escort Grace inside.

"Yes, I'll trust you. You've proven yourselves so worthy of trust up to this point." Grace turned her head to look out the window.

Sean followed the line of her sight. He could see Ian's big farmhouse coming up quickly. It had an enormous wraparound porch and the grounds were gorgeous. Ian had done very well for himself. All he could offer Grace was a crappy apartment that was far worse than her house. He had money saved up, though. He just hadn't had anything to spend it on up until now. It would be better to put it into the restaurant he wanted to open, but if Grace needed a nicer place to be happy, he could do that. If he didn't have to spend it all trying to keep her out of jail. "It's my brother's place."

She turned and looked at him for the first time in twenty minutes. Her hazel eyes were puffy from crying. She didn't cry prettily like some women. When Grace cried, it showed everywhere. He wanted nothing more than to press his mouth to hers and make everything go away. He forced his hands to remain still on her skin. They were restless with wanting to caress her and comfort her. Her tongue came out to moisten her lips, and he felt that little swipe in his balls. It had been too long. He had to get back into her bed. He wouldn't feel sure of his hold on Grace until he was deep inside her.

"So your brother wasn't a lie?"

He didn't like the guilt that lashed through his heart when she looked at him as though he was the one at fault. "No, Ian's real, and you're about to meet him. I didn't lie about everything. I was honest with you about most of the facts of my life. I just didn't tell you my real name or what I do for a living."

"Or that I'm some sort of suspect."

"Yes, I left that out, too." Once she was in bed, he could make her purr. She hadn't faked her response to him. He just needed to reinforce those bonds, and he would have her. "When you meet Ian, don't be scared of him. He can be intimidating. I just want you to trust me to take care of you."

She turned away, but not before he saw the distrust in her eyes. It made him angry. He wanted to smash through that reserve of hers and force her to accept him. The car rolled to a stop. Even from his vantage point, he could see his brother, Eve, and Liam standing on the front porch. Ian had his arms crossed over his huge body. He watched the vehicle with that stare that told Sean he was in trouble. He would have to protect Grace from Ian. Ian could be ruthless. If his brother thought Grace was bad for him, Ian would do whatever it took to get rid of the threat.

The doors unlocked, and Grace scrambled off his lap. Sean would have preferred to carry her in. It was muddy and she could fall, but he doubted Grace would allow it. Sean followed her out. Adam already had the umbrella over Grace's head. He pressed it into her hand and opened a second one for himself. Apparently Sean got to fend for himself despite the fact that it was his car and his umbrellas.

Sean raced ahead to get out of the rain. Grace and Adam took things a bit more slowly. They had cover.

Ian was frowning when Sean got up the steps. "Tell me no one saw you snag her."

Jake was right behind Sean, shaking the rain off his hair. "Of course not. They didn't see Sean at all. Adam and I just talked her into leaving work a little bit early. As far as anyone knows, she's at happy hour with her friends. She'll hear the news about Kayla sometime tonight, and that buys us some time. Trust me, the way gossip works at that office, someone will call her and leave a message on her cell. No one will expect her to be at work tomorrow."

"She doesn't know?" Eve's eyes watched the ground behind Sean, probably trying to get her first good view of Grace.

"I didn't want to tell her like that. Kayla was a really good friend of hers. She has to be eased into it." Sean knew he should have mentioned it, but he would rather wait until they could be alone. He needed to be able to hold her when he told her someone was trying to take her life. Maybe then she would cling to him. "Is Black here?"

Ian's head shook, and a small smile crept across his face. "Not yet. It's a good thing, too, since our little suspect seems to be very slowly getting away."

Sean turned and saw Grace walking, or rather slogging, down the yard. Her heels seemed to be sinking into the grass, but she kept on with her head held high. She wasn't running, merely walking with a stubborn stride. The little umbrella was perfectly erect over her head. Adam was walking beside her. His words were muffled by the rain, but Sean was sure he was trying to convince her to come back with him. He just didn't understand that Grace required a firm hand.

Sean jogged back down the stairs and out into the driving rain. His long legs ate the distance up quickly. He didn't care about the rain pouring down. Grace was already disobeying and already causing trouble. "Grace!"

She stopped briefly and turned to him. She looked strangely prim and proper in her skirt and gray buttoned up blouse. It would look better if she unbuttoned a few of those little pearls, but Sean wouldn't complain. He didn't want other men looking at her breasts, either. Her face was pale as she regarded him. "I'm going home. You aren't the cops, so you don't have any right to keep me here. I'll call the police when I get home, and they will sort all of this out."

A slow boil was starting in his veins. She was pushing him hard. He needed to calm down. "This is for your own protection. I'm not doing this to have fun."

"It really is important, sweetheart. I'll stay by your side," Adam offered in a voice that rankled Sean's every nerve. The other man's pretty-boy face was entreating Grace sweetly. Sean wondered how Adam would look after his balls had been ripped off and shoved down his throat.

"Get the hell out of here, Adam." Sean recognized he was invading the other man's space, but then Adam didn't seem to have a problem with boundaries. He'd been stepping all over Sean's for days. "This is between me and my sub. I don't see her wearing your collar, so step back."

Grace's hand immediately went to the gold heart around her neck. In one smooth move, she pulled the delicate chain off her body and tossed it in his face. "I don't belong to you. Either one of you. And if either one of you follows me, I'll call the cops as soon as I can flag down a passing car, and I will press charges for kidnapping."

She turned and started walking again.

Sean reached out and grabbed her elbow. At the same time, Adam pushed his shoulder back, causing Sean to lose his balance. He and Grace went down in the mud. The umbrella tumbled away. Grace fell onto his body, the length of her pressing down into him. His cock responded immediately. Her face came up, so close to his he could kiss her without really trying. And then Adam was pulling her up, his hands circling her waist protectively.

"Grace, I'm so sorry."

Not as sorry as he was about to be. Sean was done. Without a single sound, he moved from his place on the ground and pounced. There was no yell, no warning. One moment he was on the ground, and the next, Adam was the one in the mud.

Sean pulled his fist back and planted it squarely in his rival's face. He could hear Jake yelling in the background. Let him come. He'd take that fucker down, too. Adam kicked up, trying to roll Sean off him, but Sean had the advantage. One hand wrapped around Adam's throat and squeezed. Adam gasped, abandoning his attempts to throw off his opponent. Both of his hands came up to try to pull Sean's fingers from his throat. Rage was riding Sean. He'd been through too much. Loving Grace, losing her—first to her own betrayal and then to a killer—had his nerves on edge. She was alive, but somehow she seemed even further away from him than when he'd feared she was gone. He felt completely out of control when it came to Grace, but this…oh, this he could do.

And then his control was taken away when something hard smacked him brutally upside the head. He lost his grasp and toppled over onto the muddy ground. Adam leapt up, never one to miss an opportunity. Sean was holding his head when he realized Adam's fist was coming toward his face. There was a flash of silver and black, and Adam went down, too, joining him on the wet ground, his previously pristine suit a mess of mud and blood.

Grace stood over them both, the umbrella folded now, and she wielded it like a club. She was a curvy, avenging angel looking down on them. Her hair was plastered to her head. Her blouse was soaked, and it was obvious she was cold. Her breasts heaved as she dragged air into her lungs. Sean suddenly knew what it felt like to be a barbarian. She was his mate, and she had defied him.

"Grace, I've had enough. I'm telling you to get your sweet ass into Ian's house, or we're going to have trouble."

Adam was getting to his feet. He opened his mouth, but Jake had his hand around his best friend's neck. "Not a word. I swear, Adam, if you pursue this, I am going to advise Ian to fire you. If that doesn't work, I'll convince Eve that you aren't fit for duty."

Adam's jaw dropped open. "Some fucking friend you are. I am doing this for us. She could be the one. You want her just as much as I do."

"No, you're doing it for you. You're being a selfish little prick. I have been your best friend for years. We've been through some shit that most people wouldn't have made it out of sane. We did because we were a team. We're a part of this team, too. This team has been our family for years. You are being a traitor to this team. All feelings, wants, and desires are secondary to the team and the mission. So, Adam, the question is, are you still a member of this team or are you going to walk away now?"

Adam threw off Jake's hand and stalked toward the house, his decision plain. Jake nodded to Sean and followed, leaving Sean alone with Grace. At least someone knew how to handle Adam.

Grace's eyes were wide as though she had finally realized just how much danger she was in. She shrank back, holding the umbrella across her chest. Like that little thing could stop him.

"Are you coming inside, Grace?" The question was even and calm. He stood very still, making no move toward her. He didn't have to. When he wanted her, he would take her, and there would be nothing she could do to stop him.

"I told you, I'm going home. I took off that stupid collar, Sean. You can give it to the next idiot who's dumb enough to trust you."

His blood was starting to thrum through his system as anger turned into something else. They would never get through an interview session with this much tension between them. Maybe it was time to follow his instincts. "I won't ever take another sub. You're mine, and it's going to stay that way."

"Not in this lifetime, Sean," she snarled the words at him, every movement of her body just begging him to force the issue.

"You have a safe word, Grace," he offered magnanimously. "Are you going to say it?"

"Fuck you."

He practically growled. "Not your safe word, baby."

He was on her in a second.

* * * *

What the hell was she doing? She was tugging the tiger's tail, and she couldn't seem to stop. Ever since the instant she had discovered Sean's lies, something wicked had taken up in Grace's chest. For a while it had been drowned out with sorrow and self-doubt, but now it flared to life and demanded to be heard.

"You have a safe word, Grace." Sean was so gorgeous. His blond hair was dark now that it was wet, and his clothes clung to his body like a greedy, worshipping lover. His eyes were firmly focused on her, leaving no doubt as to what his intentions were. The rain was coming down in sheets, but there was no mistaking his low growl for an offer of amnesty. He wanted her to submit. He wanted her on her knees waiting for his command. If he couldn't have that, he wanted her to admit she couldn't handle it and walk away. "Are you going to say it?"

The words were out of her mouth before she could judge the wisdom behind them. Oh, she was in so much trouble and still that safe word was buried with absolutely no hope of ever being said. "Fuck you."

A fierce grin lit his face. "Not your safe word, baby."

Sean moved almost faster than her eye could track. He was so quick and graceful. There was only time to try to bring the umbrella up again, but before she could strike, his hand wound around the handle. It was tossed away. Grace attempted to turn, to prolong the fight. The outcome was inevitable. She would go down, but she wasn't going down easy.

Grace pushed against him as he hauled her into his arms. Her breasts pressed against him. His hands tightened around her arms forming manacles she couldn't escape. His mouth slammed down on hers.

Yes, a voice deep inside her said. This was what she had pushed him for. This was what she needed. She couldn't ask for it. Her pride demanded that she stay away from him, but her heart was willing to push him into giving her what she wanted. She wanted Sean. She wanted him inside her with a ferocity that surprised her. Sean's tongue dominated. She felt small and helpless compared to him. He plunged into her mouth as the rain came down, and there was nothing she could do but feel his desire.

And yet…Grace attempted to shove against his chest. He had used her and would continue to do so. What was she thinking? Why couldn't she use her safe word and be done with it?

"Don't fight me." He murmured the words against her lips. "I want to be gentle. I want to show you how it can be. If you keep pushing me, I'll take you to the dungeon and there won't be any tenderness."

But she didn't want his tenderness. That had proven to be false. His passion though, she would take that. Grace brought her foot down on his. He hissed in pain as the stiletto made contact and dropped her hands for a moment. Grace turned to try to run. She was face first in the mud with Sean's big body pressing her down before she could take a second step. She was caught between the soggy earth and Sean's hardness.

"I told you." His words were shouted as he held her down. She struggled, but he was far too heavy. She felt him moving, squirming, and then he rolled her over in one smooth move, recapturing her quickly. He had his belt in his hands. Before she could protest, that strip of leather bound her hands together in front of her body, and Sean hauled her up like a calf he'd just roped. "You can walk with me, or I can drag you through the mud. Your choice, Grace."

Or, she could say her safe word and be done with it, done with him. She started to walk behind him, his hands tugging her along, but the shoes stuck in the mud, and she stumbled. Sean cursed, and in a second she was cradled in his arms being carried toward the big house. Her bound hands sat in her lap. She shivered from the cold, but a part of her was heating up. What kind of a woman was she that he could use her, and she practically begged him for more?

Sean didn't pause as he hit the steps. His eyes stared straight ahead.

"Later, Ian," he growled as they passed a huge blond man who had to be Sean's brother. There were others there, but no sign of Adam and Jake. Grace was grateful for that. This was between her and Sean.

Sean kicked open the front door.

"Sean, what the fuck do you think you're doing?" Ian asked, following them.

Grace could see him over Sean's left shoulder. He looked just like Sean, only harder and more dangerous. Ian Taggart didn't look like a man who was used to being ignored.

"Are there towels in the dungeon?" Sean didn't stop. He moved with great purpose down the hallway. Grace's heart skittered. *Dungeon.* She'd never seen a dungeon before.

"Sean, this is utterly ridiculous."

"And yet it's happening," Sean shot back. "Are you going to come between me and my submissive?"

Grace heard Ian's sigh. Sean seemed to have said some magic words that made him back off slightly. "You need a monitor. Does she even have a safe word?"

Something wicked was riding her. That big, blond guy who

didn't even know her was acting like she was an idiot. "Yes, it's 'screw you!'"

Sean barked his laughter and walked through a set of French doors. She could hear Ian talking to the blonde woman who had been on the porch. He was saying something about how his brother had gone insane.

Then Sean slammed the doors shut, and Grace wasn't thinking anymore. His mouth covered hers, devouring her. Grace closed her eyes and gave herself over to the feeling. This was real. It might be the only real thing left in the world. Sean tore his mouth away from hers, and Grace felt the loss. The doors opened again, but Sean didn't seem to care. She could hear the other people talking as Sean strode to the middle of the room. He set her on her feet, but before she could move, he had her bound hands attached to a hook in the ceiling. Grace could still stand, but just barely. It made her feel vulnerable and terribly aroused. She shivered, and she wasn't sure how much of it was from the cold.

Sean's hands were all over her. He crowded her with his presence. His fingers unbuttoned the top she wore and immediately delved under her bra. Her nipples, already stiff from the chill, grew painfully erect. He pinched them, the sensation bolting from her breasts to her pussy. God, she needed this. She needed him.

"You're cold." He stepped back. He didn't take his eyes off her, but held out his hand. "I need a knife."

Grace noticed the fine tremors running through her body. Ian was frowning as he pressed a wicked-looking blade into his brother's hand. Grace noticed that both he and the blonde woman were in the room, and the doors were shut. Grace wished her hands were free so she could cover herself, but Sean seemed utterly unconcerned with their audience.

"Sean," she whispered. "We're not alone."

His eyes came up. "Yes, I was aware of that. Welcome to the dungeon. This is how it works. If I want to take you in front of an audience, it's because I'm showing off my lovely property. You know what to do to make me stop."

He kept taunting her with that damn safe word. And she just kept making the choice to keep her mouth shut.

The woman was bent over pulling something out of a drawer. The far wall was covered in shelving units. When she stood up, there was a towel in her hand. She handed it to Ian.

Ian was frowning at his brother with a barbaric ferocity. "You don't need a knife. You need to have your head examined."

Sean snorted his brother's way, and then went to work on her blouse. He obviously had no intentions of allowing her to properly undress.

"Damn it, Sean, I like this blouse." Grace squirmed as Sean cut through the material at the shoulders and sleeves.

His blue eyes bore through her as he tossed the blouse away and went to work on her bra, cutting her out of it. She was naked from the waist up with no way to cover herself. A flash of heat went through her system. She saw the room for what it was—a private dungeon. Sean hadn't lied about that. There was a large X on the wall with leather bindings. She searched her brain. St. Andrew's Cross. She'd glimpsed a big bed as he'd carried her in and a wall with all sorts of paddles and crops, whips and bindings. He really did live in this world she'd only read about. Sean pushed her skirt off her hips, but used the knife to flick at the strings of her bikini panties.

"Was that necessary?" Grace asked. He could have pulled them off with her skirt.

"You won't need them again." He took the towel from his brother and began to dry her off. He was soaked to the bone, but he took care of her first. Grace knew she should be spitting out her safe word, but she couldn't. If she said that one word, it would all be over. Sean would be done. He wouldn't touch her again.

Ian stood at the back of the room as though there was a line he simply wouldn't cross. "Are you thinking at all, Sean? Black will be here soon. We need to move her to the interrogation room."

Sean seemed to grow a couple of inches. "Are you telling me what to do with my submissive?" When Ian wouldn't come to him, Sean moved toward Ian. He went toe to toe with his brother.

"Well, someone has to. You don't seem to be able to handle her."

Grace had had just about enough of Ian. She might be pissed at

Sean, but by god this was between them, and she was sick of other people putting their noses in it. She was the one standing here cold and naked in front of complete strangers. She didn't need for Sean and Ian to have it out now. "He handles me just fine. Get out."

Ian's eyes widened, and his chest puffed out. Sean stepped firmly between them. "Not going to happen. She is not yours to discipline. You heard her. Grace, he's worried about you. Tell him what you call me."

"Mostly, right now I call you asshole."

Sean growled.

She decided to get it over with. The sooner Ian left, the sooner she wasn't showing him everything she had. "Fine, Sir. Master. Whatever, this is between us."

Ian shook his head. "You have one hour. No more. Come along, Eve."

He started out of the dungeon without another look back at the woman named Eve. They didn't appear to be intimate partners, though the blonde had seemed perfectly comfortable in the dungeon. Eve turned her head and smiled, giving Grace a little thumbs up before the door closed.

Sean turned to her. "You're manipulating me again."

Grace pulled at the leather belt, but there was no give to it. "Again? Me, manipulating you? I think it's the other way around, Sean."

"No?" He pulled off his own shirt, much calmer now than he had been before. "You're angry about my deception. You're angry I caught you. You want to get me just as pissed as you so I'll take you without any kindness, and then you can hate me."

"What makes you think I don't hate you already?" She deeply feared she didn't. Maybe she was trying to do exactly what he said.

"Well, your defense of my person, for starters. Then there's the fact that we're here. You might be angry, but you know this is between the two of us. There's no place for anyone else in this relationship." He picked up the towel, and she held back a sigh as he started to rub her body with it. He began with her outstretched hands.

"We don't have a relationship, Sean. We have a bunch of lies you told me."

His hands moved the thick towel across her in a sensual glide. He paid close attention to her breasts. The lush towel moved over and around first one, and then the other. When he was through, every inch of her breasts felt sensitized.

"Really? Besides my name and my vocation, what lies have I told you?"

Her skin tingled as he moved down. The chill was gone, replaced with a slow heat. He got to his knees, still in the stiff denim he was wearing. He paused at the apex of her thighs. Grace bit back a groan as he gently patted down her pussy and went to work on her legs. She had to stay in control. It would have been so much easier if he'd just stayed pissed off. "You said you cared about me."

"Not a lie, little one."

She didn't buy it, but it had been easier to completely disregard that he was anything but a liar when they were fighting. Now he was at her feet, wrapping them one by one in his hands. He was still soaked to the bone, but she was getting warm and dry. "I don't believe you. You're just saying that because you want to control me during this interview thing."

Sean got up from his knees, his hands going to the fly of his jeans. Grace couldn't help but notice the way his big cock was already tenting the denim. She ached to touch him. She was suddenly very glad her hands were tied above her head. Sean pushed the soaked jeans over his hips and briskly dried off his magnificent body. He seemed infinitely more comfortable since he'd walked into this room. He was at home in the dungeon. He was back to being a Dom.

He invaded her space. His naked body pressed against hers, the connection humming all along her skin.

"I'm doing this to protect you." His hand trailed from her neck down to her straining nipples. "I'm going to get you out of this, Grace. Trust me."

Trust him? Tears filled her eyes. "How can you ask me to do that when you don't trust me at all?"

His bright blue eyes became hooded. "This is neither the time nor the place for this. We'll get to the evidence against you soon enough. Now I need something, and I know you do, too." His erection prodded her belly.

Grace pushed against him as much as the restraints allowed her. "I need you to leave me alone."

He sighed heavily. His hand touched her neck, tracing the line where her necklace used to lay. "That's the last thing you need."

"Don't tell me what I need." He was frustrating her to no end. She brought a foot up to kick at him, anything to get him as out of control as she felt. She didn't even make contact. His hand shot out to catch her.

"Don't try it again. I'm being patient. At the next infraction, I get out the crop, Grace."

His calm voice did her in. She was a roiling mass of emotion, and he was perfectly calm. It wasn't anywhere close to fair. She kicked out, finally catching his leg. He stepped easily back and disappeared from sight.

"Get back here and fight with me," Grace snarled. It sounded like he was opening drawers. She knew exactly what he was looking for and part of her was so grateful for it.

"I don't want to fight with you." His words were clipped as though he was losing some of that patience of his. "Damn it. Apologize or use your safe word. Otherwise, it's a count of twenty, sub." He held a crop in his hands. Grace stared at it. It was roughly the length of Sean's forearm and the tip looked like soft leather. What would it feel like?

He brought her head up, his fingers gentle against her chin. His eyes held hers for a moment. "I don't want to do this. I would rather take you down, unbind your hands, and make love to you."

He wanted to make love to a woman he believed capable of all manner of crimes? He hadn't even laid out what he wanted to accuse her of, but he wanted her to lie back and welcome him into her body? She wanted him, but not like that. This was the end. She wouldn't touch him after this session, and she wanted none of his tenderness. "I hate you."

His eyes closed momentarily as though the words brought him pain. He was a spectacular actor, but then she already knew that. "If this is what you need…count of twenty, sub."

The crop came down across her ass in an arc of flame, licking her skin, making her gasp. Her skin burned, and then the heat sank in.

"I need a count, Grace." His words were heavy, weary even.

"One."

Immediately the crop came down again, the sound cracking through the room like thunder. Tears pooled in her eyes, making the world a soft, watery place. She let her head fall forward as the second stroke lashed across her. "Two."

She'd always wondered. She'd always dreamed of this. She knew it was a perversity, but something about the way the pain became heat and the heat became pleasure made Grace feel free. This was what she'd been looking for. It wasn't about the pain, exactly. It was about trusting him enough to give over. She didn't have to think or worry in this place. She was only allowed to feel.

Sean had perfect rhythm. He seemed to know exactly what she needed, and Grace was strangely grateful to him. After so many years of bottling up the need, she let herself float.

"Five," she said as the fifth stroke came. She bit her teeth against it and then let the heat flow.

The crop came down over and over. Her count continued, moving past ten and eleven into twelve. Her own voice seemed far away now, as though it wasn't really a part of her. Now she was in a place where nothing mattered but that sweet heat and the rush of arousal that caused her pussy to throb. The world and all its worry receded, and she could concentrate on feeling.

"Nineteen."

She panicked a little, coming out of her safe place. One more and she had to give him up. One more and she had to be alone again. The crop came down, and she couldn't say it. She couldn't give him that final number that marked the end of them.

He didn't wait for it. She heard the crop hit the floor and felt his hands skim the cheeks of her burning ass.

His lips pressed into the curve at the base of her spine, and it felt too sweet to fight. He ran his mouth all along her back, depositing kisses along the way. When he got to the nape of her neck, his mouth nuzzled her. His body cradled her. He cupped her breasts, his cock nestling in the cheeks of her ass. His mouth found her earlobes and licked and teased them.

"I need you, Grace." He plucked at her nipples, the sensation making her moan. He rubbed his cock against her. "I need you so much." His hands skimmed down her body and found the V of her thighs. "You're so wet. You're so wet for me."

His fingers slid easily into her pussy. She was soaking wet. Her clit quivered with every pass of his hand. He fucked a single finger into her as his cock pressed between her cheeks.

And she couldn't fight him. She wanted him. She wanted one last time with him. She protested when his hand came out of her pussy. It earned her a nip to her ear, an erotic little torture. Sean knew just how much pain to give. He knew just how to make her feel. He opened her heart in ways she thought impossible, but he didn't feel the same way about her.

She would never find another man like him. Despite everything he had done, Grace was going to miss him for the rest of her life.

He pulled her hands off the hook above her head, and in a moment the belt was gone and she was free. He ran his strong fingers all along her arms, making sure she hadn't lost circulation. When he was done, he pulled her close. His gorgeous face was so serious, it was hard to believe this was just a game to him. "I…I'm going to look after you."

"But you don't trust me." It wasn't a question. She knew the answer. The knowledge was a bitter pill, but she had swallowed it.

His jaw tensed, and his hands tightened around her. "It's going to be okay. I'm going to take care of you."

He lowered his lips to hers, and his tongue licked the seam, demanding entry. He licked her lips the way he would a decadent dessert. She opened beneath him. She knew she should fight, but she couldn't. She wanted one last moment with him. After this, she would be alone with only memories of him to keep her warm. She allowed her arms to wind around him as he lifted her up.

"Wrap your legs around me. I can't wait."

His big dick unerringly found her pussy, and Sean pushed his way in, filling her up, making her moan. He pushed her down onto his cock and held her against him, forcing his way in. She held on for dear life as he walked them to the bed. He never lost their connection. He tipped them over and came down heavily on top of her. She was caught between the silk of the sheets and warmth of his skin.

His hands came out and framed her face. "Are you all right?"

She nodded. She didn't care about her sore skin. It was just one more sensation to be had at this point.

"Thank god." Sean lifted his torso up and stroked into her. "Oh, you feel so good." His eyes were heavy with desire. "So fucking right."

He used long, slow, maddening strokes on her. He worked his way in to the hilt and held himself there for a moment before slowly pulling almost all the way out. Grace tightened her legs around him, not wanting to lose him. Over and over he pressed in and pulled out. He filled and retreated with purpose. Grace tried to push her hips up. She wanted to force him to lose that iron-willed control of his. He simply growled and let his weight hold her down. She had no choice but to take everything he gave her. His cock pressed deep, and Grace thought she would go crazy if he didn't finish it. Every millimeter of her pussy was aching.

"Please." It came out unbidden.

His mouth curled up, and Grace knew she'd made a mistake. He'd been waiting for her to beg. He was a game player to the end. "If this is what you need, then I will give it to you."

He slammed his cock in. He came up on his knees, his hands on her thighs forcing them apart so every inch of her pussy was exposed and open to him. Sean looked down, and Grace knew what he was doing. He was watching his dick plunder her pussy. He was watching as he fucked what he felt belonged to him. He pounded into her. His face flushed, and his breath came out in ragged draws. He pushed up into her, hitting that magic spot. Her pussy came alive, and she went flying. Sean's thumb dragged across her clit, sending her into spasms of pleasure. She barely heard his strangled groan as he held himself against her and flooded her with his come.

He pushed into her even though she could feel his dick softening. It was as though he didn't want to lose the connection. After awhile, he slumped down, holding not an ounce of his weight off of her. His face found the crook of her neck, and he lay cradled against her body.

"Mine." She heard the whisper, felt the possessive kiss he bestowed on her neck.

But she wasn't. And she wouldn't be again.

Chapter Sixteen

Sean watched through the two-way mirror and thought briefly about what a complete pervert his brother was. How many people had a room with a two-way mirror and a viewing area in their homes? Ian Taggart did. He found it useful when training Doms and subs. Now Ian had moved out all of the sex toys and installed a very boring looking table with folding chairs. It looked like the set of any procedural room on television, right down to the nervous-looking suspect and the overbearing interrogator.

Except Grace didn't really look nervous. She looked tired and withdrawn as she sat, coldly ignoring everything Ian said. Eve was sitting in the room with them, but she was watching Grace rather than participating in the interrogation. He'd watched as Eve's face went from wary to concerned to downright sympathetic. The profiler of the group seemed to think Grace was an innocent bystander. Anxiety started to pulse through Sean's system, making him edgy and restless.

What if he was wrong? What if he was allowing his past to color the current situation with Grace? If she was innocent, then he had a lot of apologizing to do.

There was a fine tremble in her right hand as she lifted it to her neck. She was reaching for something. Damn, she was reaching for the necklace he'd given her. In the few days she had worn it, it was obvious she'd become used to playing with it, possibly rubbing the little heart between her thumb and forefinger. It would have given her comfort. Now she reached for it, and it wasn't there anymore. It was still outside, lost in the muddy yard. He would find it, fix it, get it back to her.

And she would potentially throw it right back in his face.

Her hazel eyes seemed focused on some point behind Ian's head. Her mouth was tight, and the little lines around her eyes seemed so much more pronounced than usual. Sean wondered when she'd last eaten something. He'd pushed her hard, and now Ian was doing the same. He wanted nothing more than to walk into that room, haul her into his arms, and take her home. He would feed her and bathe her and cuddle her against him while she slept. He wanted this whole thing done with.

"She doesn't seem very helpful."

Sean felt his stomach tighten. Mr. Black. He'd shown up just after Sean had escorted Grace out of the dungeon. Sean had showered with her and taken care of her pink backside. He'd gotten dressed and was ready to go find her some clothes when Eve had brought him a bag. Someone had driven out and found Grace a skirt, shirt, and fresh underwear. Probably Adam, since the sizes were perfect, but Sean was grateful anyway. The whole time he'd taken care of her, Grace had just stood there like a doll, listless and lifeless. She was in a complete post-scene plunge. She followed all of his instructions, but she wasn't with him. She was someplace else, someplace where she didn't have to deal with him. He needed to smash through that wall.

"Maybe she doesn't know anything," Adam said.

Adam, Jake, and Liam stood in the back of the small viewing room. Sean had done his best to tolerate the man. Jake had asked him to be understanding. There had been some talk about something Adam was going through, but Sean didn't care. If Adam made a move on Grace again, he was a dead man.

"I doubt that, Mr. Miles. The evidence is clear." Black stood beside Sean, not bothering to look back at Adam. His cold eyes were clearly fastened on Grace Hawthorne. Black didn't try to hide his identity this time around. He was dressed in an expensive, probably hand-tailored suit to match his expensive shoes. His dark hair was fashionably, though conservatively, cut. He was attractive but bland, the kind of man it would be easy to look past. His brows lifted quizzically as he turned toward Sean. "You got a look in his safe box? Taggart said you were the one who found proof I was fudging the truth."

"You were lying. It's what you do." Sean still didn't trust the man. He never would as long as Mr. Black worked for the Agency.

Mr. Black merely shrugged. "It's a living. Did you find out what he's trying to steal this time?"

"Something from the Bryson Building. How long has Parnell been doing this?"

Black chuckled, but the sound was oddly cold. "Parnell? Sorry. I still think of him as Wright. I was his handler, you know, though he was always a stubborn one. Damn fine agent, but then the rogue ones usually are. He's been at this for at least three years. He faked his death five years back. It took me a little time to track him down. I never thought he would involve his brother. He didn't have a close relationship with his family. His father was somewhat rough with him. No close family ties is one of the reasons we recruited him. He's smart and cautious. We need to handle him carefully or he'll run."

If Sean thought for a moment Parnell would run and forget all about Grace, he would give the man a pair of sneakers. But a man like that would tie up his loose ends. Kayla's body proved that beyond a shadow of a doubt. He turned his attention back to the interrogation room.

"I don't know." Grace was shoving a piece of paper back Ian's way. Sean strained to see what it was. It looked like her signed checks for the security deposit box. Ian, or perhaps Mr. Black, had pulled some strings and gotten copies from the bank. Her voice sounded tinny and tired over the speakers.

"You have to know, Ms. Hawthorne. Is that or is that not your signature on the checks?" Ian pointed to the signature, his voice hard and unrelenting.

"Yes. I signed the checks."

"For Evan Parnell?"

She shrugged. "I didn't really know what it was for. Matt asked me. I pay out petty cash and all of his personal stuff. It's his company, his money. If he wants to pay seventy-five dollars a month for a box somewhere, I guess I thought that was his business."

"But the box was in your name."

She bit her lip and remained silent.

Ian went on.

Black leaned in. "You know, Wright was always good with the ladies. He always kept one or two on his string to do his bidding. He never liked to leave his mark when a pretty woman could do it for him. Of course, he tended to kill them when he was through, but he enjoyed them while it lasted. She's probably in love with him."

"She isn't sleeping with him." Sean spat the words out. He didn't believe that particular accusation for a moment. "He hasn't touched her."

Black now turned to him, giving Sean his full attention. "Really? And you know this, how?"

Sean forced his voice to remain even. It had been a mistake to react. Black might be the client right now, but he was still Agency. He could turn in a second. Ian would be pissed if he knew Sean had given Black information like that. "I've had Ms. Hawthorne under surveillance for several weeks. I think I would know if she had a lover."

The only lover she had was him. He was sure of it. She hadn't lied about that.

Black's eyes narrowed, but then he turned back to the interrogation room. "Wright can be tricky. You just never know with him. So, this woman he killed today, you think he was after Hawthorne and got her friend instead?"

This he could talk about. "I believe so. Kayla Green was following a pattern set by Ms. Hawthorne. She was wearing Grace's coat and carrying her umbrella. They're roughly the same height. It was raining pretty hard. In the rain, I would have mistaken Kayla for Grace. Hell, I did. I followed her. He probably realizes his mistake by now. I have no doubt he'll try again."

A reptilian smile crossed Black's face. "Yes, I believe he will, too."

A cold feeling settled in Sean's gut as he watched Black. The man seemed very content, and that wasn't a good thing. Sean could tell he was already trying to figure out how to use Grace to his advantage.

"What did Ms. Hawthorne say when she learned her friend was dead?"

There was a moment of complete quiet before Adam spoke up. "We haven't told her yet." He paused. "We thought Sean should do it. He's the best one to handle her."

Sean glanced back at Adam. He seemed to want to talk, but knew that now was not the time. They didn't air their dirty laundry around the clients. Sean nodded slowly and turned back to Black. "She's a little fragile right now. I thought it best to get her through the interview before I brought that up."

"Unless she already knew Wright was gunning for her and that was why she sent her friend out there."

"Not a chance." The words were out of his mouth before he could call them back.

Black studied him carefully for a moment. "It's a simple thing, you know. What was this daily ritual she had her friend perform instead of her?"

"Coffee. She always makes a latte run at three in the afternoon."

Black shrugged and waved a hand. "All she has to do is cry a little. Pretend she's had some trauma in her life. Women are very susceptible to little dramas. She's a widow. She could say she missed her husband and felt a little blue. A female will do a lot to make a friend feel better, even walk through the rain to get her a cup of coffee when, I'm sure, the break room probably has one."

"I don't believe it," Liam said, speaking for the first time since the interview had begun.

Black stared at the Irishman. "Why? Are you an expert on the woman? I thought Mr. Taggart was the one assigned to…take care of her."

Sean didn't like the way he said it, but Liam was already

responding. "After listening to her talk for days, I can definitely say I feel like an expert on the woman. She talks to herself. A lot. Nothing she's said, no conversation she's had over the phone or thing she's murmured to herself while getting ready in the morning has given me a single hint that she's capable of what you're accusing her of. I'm going with Eve on this one. The lady is innocent. We should remove her from the line of fire and move on."

Black was like a dog with a particularly juicy bone. "Perhaps she knows you're listening."

Liam's eyes rolled. "Not a chance. If she had, she wouldn't have sung the soundtrack to 'Wicked' while she was vacuuming. The girl can't carry a note. She's truly awful. Trust me, no one sings like that if they know they're being listened to. Also, she talks to her breasts. She asks them why they won't sit properly in her bra. Who does that?"

"She could be very savvy." Black wasn't listening to a thing anyone said.

A strange calm settled over Sean as he listened to Black. Black made perfect sense. Grace could have used her breakup with him as an excuse to send Kayla out as cannon fodder. If she was a ruthless thief, it would be easy for her to send her friend out to take the knife for her. Sean's brain worked overtime as he watched Grace. She was so lovely sitting there. She was perfect, and that was the problem. He didn't trust his instincts. Grace seemed perfect, therefore there must be something wrong with her. Black went on. Somewhere Sean could hear the man talking about how Grace could be fooling them all, but Sean was finally calm enough to ask the pertinent questions.

Who was Grace Hawthorne? Grace Hawthorne was the type of woman who could easily write out a check for something when she wasn't sure exactly what she was buying. She would do it because she trusted the people around her. Grace Hawthorne was the type of woman who was loyal to a man who had given her a chance even when that man was a wretched alcoholic. Sean felt his heart twist inside his chest. Grace was the type of woman who would follow a man she thought was cheating her boss even though it put her in danger.

God, he hoped Grace was the type of woman to give a man who loved her a second chance.

"She didn't have anything to do with this," Sean said, a deep calm settling inside him. He trusted Grace. It was far past time he shoved aside his role as an employee. He wasn't an agent anymore. He was Grace's lover, her Dom, and it was time to protect her. He brushed past Black.

"About damn time." Adam sighed as he walked past.

Sean took the ten steps from the small viewing room to the interrogation room door. He slipped in the room, and ignored Ian's wide-eyed stare. Grace turned to him, her eyes bright and focused for the first time in an hour. He pulled up a chair and sat down beside her, sliding his hand onto hers. "Go on. Answer the question. It's going to be all right."

They needed to get through this. It wouldn't go away, and there was no way to hide her from it.

Grace's face contorted sweetly. She stared at him for a moment, but she didn't move her hand away. After a brief pause, she turned back to Ian. "I don't know Matt's brother. He talks about him, but mostly after he's had a few, if you know what I mean."

Sean squeezed her hand. It was the most animated answer she'd given the whole interview.

Ian's eyebrow arched aristocratically. "So you're telling me you didn't know that Evan Parnell is really Patrick Wright?"

Grace's eyes widened, and she clung to Sean's hand. "No. Until Sean told me, I had no idea. I don't see how I was supposed to know. I've seen pictures of Matt's brother. He doesn't look anything like Evan."

Sean leaned toward her. He was painfully aware of Black stepping into the room. "Babe, he probably had a lot of plastic surgery. Some criminals with cash change their appearance to get away from the law, or in this case, his former employer. He probably did it in Central America. He seems to have some ties both there and in Asia. Wright is trying to avoid the law and the Central Intelligence Agency."

"So Evan Parnell is related to Matt, but he never told me?" She chewed on her lower lip.

"I'm sure he didn't want you to know. When exactly did Parnell show up?" Sean knew the answer from the paper trail, but he was curious to see it from Grace's view.

"A couple of years ago. We ran into some serious trouble moneywise. I never got a real explanation as to why. The books all seemed good. Matt said it was the economy, but we had contracts rolling in. I always suspected Matt had done something he shouldn't have with the money."

Sean nodded in what he hoped was an encouraging fashion. That was exactly what they suspected had happened as well. Matt Wright liked to gamble when he drank. He played deep and not well. "So Parnell came to your boss a couple of years back?"

"Yes. He said he was trying to take his custodial service to another level. He'd done some work in the Northeast, but had to move. He didn't have any contacts in Dallas. We hadn't offered custodial services before. I was surprised. Matt's a bit of a snob. He liked that he repped IT services. It had a cache in our world."

"But an IT temp would be watched, Miss Hawthorne." Black eased into the chair beside Ian. "They would be very restricted in their access to the systems and the building."

Grace leaned over, her shoulder brushing against his. Sean could practically feel the anxiety rolling off her. "Who is he?"

Black frowned and leaned forward. "I'm the man who will decide your fate, Miss Hawthorne."

Grace turned to face Sean. "I have a fate?"

Sean checked his chuckle. He leaned in. "He's a drama queen. He can't help it. He's with the CIA. They take a class or something."

Sean caught his brother's brief smile before Ian covered it up.

Eve didn't bother. She laughed out loud. "Grace, this is a man who calls himself Mr. Black. He works for the CIA. He used to be Patrick Wright's handler."

Black turned his stern expression on Eve. "Thank you for the introduction, Ms. St. James. I might have preferred to keep some of that information to myself. Ms. Hawthorne doesn't need my biography to answer my questions."

"You're on American soil, Black," Sean interjected. "She

doesn't have to answer any of your questions. She could just get a lawyer."

"Sean..." Ian's warning was interrupted.

Mr. Black leaned forward. "I don't think that's a good idea. If she does that, I'm afraid she'll be implicated in the death of Kayla Green. That's the kind of thing that doesn't go away. Once the press gets a hold of that story, it will follow you, Ms. Hawthorne."

Grace's hand went slack in his, and Sean watched all of the blood drain from her face. "What did you say?"

Sean tried to pull her hand back in his, but she moved away. If Sean could have killed Black in that moment, he would have.

Black smiled the smooth smile of a predator who knew he had the upper hand. "I was talking about the death of your colleague. She was found murdered in an alley. It was by a coffee shop."

"Grace, I meant to tell you." Sean's words felt impotent.

Grace wasn't listening. "Kayla's not dead. I saw her this afternoon. She just got stuck in the rain."

"How could you tell her that way?" Eve sounded outraged.

"Black, this is neither the time nor the place." Ian's jaw tightened.

"Oh, but it is. It's obvious to me your group isn't what I thought it was. You're supposed to be the baddest of the bad, but you're treating this suspect with kid gloves." He turned back to Grace. "Your friend is dead. I believe she's dead because Patrick Wright mistook her for you. As to the method of her demise, Wright was always a big proponent of knife play. He preferred it to a gun. You should ask your gallant swain there. He is the one who found her body."

Now Grace was looking at Sean. Her hazel eyes accused him. "You knew. You knew what happened to Kayla, but you didn't tell me?"

He kept his voice low, trying to keep the matter between the two of them. "Grace, I was going to tell you, but when we were alone."

"We just spent an hour alone, Sean. It didn't occur to you to tell me then?"

It hadn't. It hadn't even crossed his mind. He'd been too

concerned with making love to her, with marking her as his. He hadn't wanted to deal with anything but the need to be close to Grace. "I was going to tell you tonight, when we go home."

"I'm not going anywhere with you, Sean. Either you thought I would know because I had something to do with it, or you decided it was up to you to control whether or not I knew my friend was dead." She turned back to Black, obviously dismissing Sean. "Why would Parnell, I mean Wright, want to kill me?"

Sean wanted to wipe the smug smile off that son of a bitch's face.

"Well, Ms. Hawthorne, I suspect you know more than you're telling us, or more than you think. Did you care for your friend?" Black asked.

"I loved her." Her voice was soft. What she said was true. There was no question in Sean's mind. She loved her friend, and she was falling right into Black's trap.

"Then the only way to help her now is to catch her killer."

Sean was on his feet in an instant. "That is not going to happen."

Black wasn't paying attention to his show of righteous anger. He leaned toward Grace. "I believe you're the only one who can make this right."

Grace threaded her hands together. They made a tight fist on the table. "What do you need me to do?"

* * * *

There was a brief knock on the door, but Grace didn't bother to bid the person to come in or stay out. She knew who it was and nothing so simple as words would keep Sean Taggart out when he wanted in. She would have locked the door to the big bedroom she had been shown to after the "interview" was over, but she suspected Sean would have used a key or simply kicked the door in. He had skills she had never dreamed of.

Over the last few hours, she had learned an awful lot about her lover. He was former Special Forces. Sean Taggart had been a decorated Green Beret working the most dangerous missions the

Army had in Afghanistan. He'd worked for the CIA before, while he was in the Army, and as a contractor in the States. He was a dangerous man.

He was also a man who knew a whole lot of cuss words. He'd used some words Grace wasn't even sure were English on Mr. Black when Grace had agreed to help. Then he'd used a few on her.

Grace sat on the bed while the door opened, and Sean entered carrying a huge tray. It hurt to look at him. He was so gorgeous. He was a solid presence in a world that now seemed completely off kilter. She wanted nothing more than to toss this whole problem in his lap and allow him to solve it for her. It would be easy to do. He would let her. All she had to do was give the word, and Sean would take over. She would be hustled off someplace safe. He would handle it.

And he wouldn't look at her the same way again. She remembered his words that first night they had made love. He wanted a partner. Even though she didn't intend to be that partner, she couldn't bring herself to say the words that made her just another clinging sub to him.

"I brought you dinner." He stood at the foot of the bed, his words small and seemingly cautious.

"I'm not hungry." The thought of food…then the smell hit her. She looked down at the tray he set on the bed. It was as elegantly set as any restaurant she'd been in. There was silverware, a china plate containing a small, crusted serving of something that smelled delicious, a salad, a wine glass, and a carafe of white wine. "Is that a pie?" It didn't smell sweet. It was savory and reminded her she hadn't eaten in hours and hours.

"It's comfort food. It's a chicken pot pie."

"I don't like that." They always tasted like cardboard and bland soup.

"That's because you've never had one from scratch." He set the tray down and climbed onto the big bed beside her. He cut into the pie and held out a forkful. "Open."

Her mouth was open before she thought about it. He'd used that Dom voice on her. Grace was about to close her lips when the taste swept across her tongue. Her eyes closed in decadent surrender.

She could hear the satisfaction in Sean's voice. "See. It's very different when you use fresh ingredients. And the pastry is my mother's recipe."

Grace gave in. She took the fork from him. He seemed slightly disappointed, but gave it up. He was such a mass of contradictions. He was a big, strong warrior who knew how to handle a gun and make a piecrust from scratch. He was a Dom who took such loving care of her, but had thrown her to the wolves.

She mustn't ever forget that last part.

Sean poured her a glass of wine. Grace reached for it and then remembered the last time he'd served her. Something about that night didn't sit right. That night she'd had exactly two glasses of wine and passed out. Grace knew she wasn't a heavy drinker, but she'd spent enough time at happy hour to be able to handle some wine. She slid a narrow glance at Sean. "Is this one drugged, too?"

He flushed. Grace was pretty sure he didn't do that often. "No. I won't ever do that again, Grace. I promise. If it helps, I thought I was protecting you at the time."

Grace took a tentative bite of salad. She didn't really want to eat, but she had to keep her strength up. She had to walk back into the lion's den in the morning. "Not really."

She set the fork down as the events of the day washed over her again. How could Kayla be dead? How the hell could Kayla, sweet, vivacious Kayla, have met her end in an alley? Tears welled up.

Sean swept the tray and all its contents off the bed in an instant and was back to her, his strong arms pulling her to his chest. He cupped the back of her head, his fingers sinking into her hair. "Oh, baby, it's all right. Go ahead and cry. I'll take care of you."

It was easy to sink into his warmth. She let her hands wrap around his neck as he pulled her into his lap. She was wearing someone's, probably Sean's, old T-shirt. It was enormous on her, coming to her knees. The material rode up, allowing Sean's big hand to cup her knee. His nose nuzzled into her neck. There was nothing inherently sexual about the touch, just two people who were intimate taking comfort in closeness.

Grace sobbed against him. She let herself go. She cried for Kayla and all that she had lost. She had been so young. She cried for

211

herself, for losing Pete, and then Sean. She cried because she'd been strong for so long that it felt good to let go. Grace cried for Matt, who was so lost. And she cried because she was so scared. What Mr. Black wanted her to do was to put her life on the line without any training or know-how. She was going to play a game she didn't even know the rules to, but there was no backing out now.

All the while, Sean held her close, sometimes murmuring soothing words in her ear, sometimes just rocking her against him. After a long while, she heard the strong beat of his heart as she began to come back to the world. He was a solid, warm body to cling to. She knew what she should do. She should push him out. She should be strong, but she seemed to have used all of that strength up accepting Black's offer.

She was going back to work tomorrow, but not as Matt's admin. That was now her cover. She was going back in as a spy.

"Grace." Sean's voice was soft and close to her ear. They were curled around each other like puzzle pieces. "Let me get you out of here, baby. I can get us by Ian's security. We'll get in the car and just drive. I have some money saved up. Let me take you away. We'll drive for a while, get new IDs, and then we can go anywhere we like."

"I thought you were under the impression I was guilty as sin."

His turnaround had been surprising. Ever since they'd come in from the rain, he'd been much more tender with her. It was unnerving. She preferred the righteously angry Sean to this man who treated her like she was made of glass. It was easier to hold herself apart from him.

Sean's blue eyes grew soft, and he ran his hand through her hair. Everywhere he touched, she felt the connection to him. "I was an idiot, baby. My only excuse is you knocked me on my ass. I've never been in this position before. It threw me for a loop. I'm much more used to people lying to me. It's the nature of the business." He was quiet for a moment and seemed to come to a decision. "You know the scars on my back?"

She nodded. She'd intended to kiss each one when she'd thought they were just lovers. She'd wanted to run her lips across all the places he'd been hurt. Without thinking about it, her hand went to his shoulders where she knew some of the large, silvery scars started to wind their way down his back.

"I got those in Afghanistan. My CO, who I trusted more than anyone besides my mother and my brother, sent me and two others on a mission to this small village just outside of Taliban-controlled territory. We caught an IED ten miles from the village. I'm the only one who survived. Turns out we had bad intelligence. The Agency didn't take credit, so my CO got called up. He tried to pin it on me and the two men in my unit who died in the explosion. He tried to say we didn't have authorization to be there. He claimed we stole the Humvee and were going on a drug run. It happens. I was court-martialed. Ian found evidence that proved I was just following orders and, well, he also has some pretty badass connections in that world. Needless to say, I was exonerated, but it didn't exactly boost my trust in my fellow man. Three months later, Jake and Adam got busted for fucking the wrong person...at the same time, of course. They were good soldiers. They got set up. The Army was my life at that point. Then there was my dad, he walked out." Sean sighed and shook his head. "What I'm trying to say, Grace, is that I'm not a man to take things at face value."

"I understand. I guess I feel the same way."

He chuckled. "You are an entirely different creature, Grace. I finally came to terms with that. You're a woman who trusts and loves with an open heart. You have to forgive me for not recognizing something I've never had."

"Yeah, well, my open heart gets pummeled on a regular basis, so I think I'll close it off a little bit." Maybe it was time to toughen up.

His hands tightened. "There's no need now. I told you I would protect you, and I mean to do it. The first way I can protect you is by getting you away from here. You are not cut out for this game. We'll go somewhere and never look back."

It sounded perfect. They could find some tropical island and be two completely different people. They never had to come back. And she wouldn't see her sons again. Grace sat straight up as a horrible thought occurred to her. She understood that Parnell hadn't meant to kill Kayla. He'd been coming after her. But he could do far worse things than merely killing her. "My boys. He can get to my boys."

Sean tugged her back down, shaking his head. "No, he can't. By tomorrow morning, they'll both have twenty-four/seven security. Liam is on his way to Austin even as we speak. He's going to pick up your sons and take them to a safe place until this is finished. Ian and I already spoke to them. Your oldest son has quite a mouth on him."

Grace laughed a little. David was always careful around his mother, but she knew he could cuss a blue streak when he got angry. He was also very protective. Kyle was sweeter, but he would be just as concerned. She didn't want to bring them into this. They had their own lives. "What did you tell them?"

"I explained the situation. I told them you're in the middle of something dangerous and that I would protect you. I had to talk really fast, or I think they would have been on a plane to get here. That's not a good idea."

Grace agreed. She didn't want her babies anywhere near her right now. They could end up like…

"It wasn't your fault." Sean pulled her close as though he could read her mind. More than likely, he was just really good at reading her face and body language.

Grace shook off the emotion. If she dwelled on Kayla, she would dissolve again. "So this Liam guy is going to protect my boys? Is he any good?"

Sean's lips quirked slightly up. "Well, several European governments think so." He looked at her seriously and cupped her face. "Liam is deadly, babe. He's smart and fast. He's never let me down before. He'll take care of them. I had to promise that you would call them in the morning."

It would be good to hear their voices, to know they were safe. She could answer their probably numerous questions. "What else did you tell them?" Surely he wouldn't have mentioned anything but the case.

"I told them I was going to marry you."

"You said what?" Her screech reverberated through the room.

Sean merely shrugged and reached out for the wine glass he'd set on the nightstand. He took a long sip and then passed it to her. "I told David that I was going to marry you, and he shouldn't worry. I think that was a miscalculation on my part. He still seemed very worried, though now about me in addition to the situation we're in."

Grace took the wine. It looked like she would need it. She tried not to think about the fact that Sean's lips had touched the same place hers had. It was one of those intimate things couples did. Grace scrambled out of bed and started to pace. "I can't believe you told him that."

Sean lay back against the ornate headboard looking ridiculously hot in jeans and a T-shirt and no shoes. Even his big feet were sexy. "Well, I thought it was better than telling the boy I was engaging in superhot D/s sex with his mother. Besides, it's true. I do intend to marry you. I thought that putting my very good intentions out there would ease his mind. I don't understand kids. After I explained I would marry you, he threatened to cut off my penis with a rusty knife and shove it someplace where a heterosexual male doesn't want a penis stuffed, though I suspect a gay man wouldn't want his own penis shoved up his ass, either. It's a truly pansexual threat." He gave her a slow smile. "Though if you want to experiment, babe, I'm willing. I've never tried it myself, but I've heard it can be pleasurable."

She gave him what she hoped was a savage smile. "Yes, I'm thinking of experimenting on you right now, Sean." Maybe her son had the right idea.

"Try it, little one. I dare you. I'll have you bound to this bed before you can lay a hand on me, and then we'll see who gets tortured. Do you know what I want to do to you?"

Don't go there. Stay the hell away from anything having to do with sex when around Sean Taggart. She wasn't stupid. It was how he pulled her in. Every time she started to get away, he turned those blue eyes on her, and she was caught. "What?"

All her good intentions didn't mean a damn thing to her pussy. When had that part of her body taken over? Pretty much the minute she'd met Sean.

His deep voice pulled at her. "I want to tie you to the bed. It wouldn't be hard. Ian has his whole house decked out for play. I'm sure there are ropes in the dresser behind you. My bag has a few

215

toys I picked up for us. I've been waiting to use them on you."

"What kind of toys?"

"A pretty little plug for your ass. This one is a little different than the last one. This one is made of glass. It's made for sensation play. I can make it cold. How would that feel against your asshole? Or I could warm it up and it would slide into your ass like a hard, hot dick. You liked it when I fucked your ass. I'll fuck you with the plug for a while, but I won't be able to hold out for long. I'll have to lube up my cock and work my way in. I'll fuck that ass of yours until you forget what it's like to not have me in there. I'll strap a butterfly to your clit. You'll be caught between my cock in your bottom and that vibrator on your clitoris. The point is, once I get you tied up, you'll be mine. You'll be my gorgeous slave, and I'll do exactly what I want with you."

His voice played across her skin. She wanted nothing more than to give in and let him do all of it to her, and yet something kept her away. She was wary. He'd pretended to be interested once before to get her to do the things he wanted her to do. He was a savvy agent. If it had worked once, why shouldn't he try it again? If he knew her at all, he had to know she couldn't walk away. That man had killed her friend. She couldn't look at herself in the mirror if she let him get away when she could stop it. Beyond the things Patrick Wright had done to her personally, he was a threat to the country. Who wouldn't step up when all of that was at stake? Yes, all of the talk of taking her someplace safe could just be more of Sean's well thought out script.

"You don't believe me."

She wished he couldn't read her. "You have to admit, it makes more sense that you're just playing me."

"I deserve that. But we're in this position because of you, Grace." His Dom voice was coming out again.

"Me?"

"Yes, you. You manipulated me into this position and don't try to deny it. I came by that night to have dinner with you. I had no intentions of ending up in bed. What happened in the pool was my fault. You were far too tempting to let go, and I had wanted you for days. But I'd decided to leave it at that, because I knew I wanted more. What were your instructions that night?"

She felt her face flush. She knew exactly what he was talking about. "I was supposed to open the wine. You never said where I should wait for you. I opened the wine."

"And met me naked in a gorgeously submissive position you knew I couldn't turn away from. Classic brat behavior. I knew it would get me in trouble, and I took you anyway. Now I'm paying for it, aren't I?" He frowned her way. "You wouldn't be so angry at me if I'd kept that small but necessary distance between us."

He was probably right, but Grace also knew that if he had rejected her advances that first evening, she would have retreated from him. He really had been in a tough spot. She wasn't about to admit it to him, though.

He waited, but sighed when he seemed to realize she wasn't replying. "Fine. We both know what you did. We're both culpable, baby. You for topping from the bottom, and me for letting you. It won't happen again. Take your clothes off, Grace. Assume the position."

She hated the way her heart raced. "You can't expect me to play with you after everything that's happened."

"I'm not playing. This is serious. This is something I think you need. Tell me you don't need me tonight, and I'll walk out the door. I won't go far because there's no way I'm letting anything get near you while this case is going on, but I'll let you alone for the night. Otherwise, do as I told you."

Again, he put the choice in her hands. Again, she chose him despite her better judgment. The thought of spending the night alone and without him left her cold. He was right. She needed his arms around her, his voice commanding her, or she would spend the entire night in worry and despair. Grace pulled the shirt off and dropped to her knees.

Chapter Seventeen

Sean had to concentrate to get his jeans off. His dick was rock hard and aching. It had been since the moment he'd climbed onto the bed with Grace. She'd been hurting at the time, but his cock hadn't cared that she was emotional. It had only known that she was close. Now he could give them what they both needed so much.

She was the most beautiful thing in the world to him, her head bowed, waiting for his command. She trusted him in this at least. He placed a hand on her head, acknowledging and accepting her submission. "Stand up, little one."

She rose with a little difficulty. For someone untrained, Grace seemed to know what to do, but often the little things tripped her up. He was looking forward to formally training her. He would take her to the club and show her off. He would be so proud to be her first Dom, her only Dom.

She stood before him, her hazel eyes looking up. The sadness, the uncertainty was still there. He wanted it gone. He let his hand trail softly along her skin starting at the curve of her shoulders. He moved from her shoulders down the curve of her chest. Her breasts were round and heavy. He loved the way her nipples puckered sweetly under his gaze and practically begged for his touch. He cupped her breasts, enjoying the weight in his hands. She sighed and let her head roll back. Sean got to his knees and licked at one pouty nipple. He sucked the little bud into his mouth and lavished his affection there. He pulled and sucked at the nipple, his hands circling her waist and cupping that gorgeous ass of hers.

Sean changed to the opposite breast, not wanting to leave it out. He tongued her and already he could smell the sweet scent of her arousal. She was so responsive. He brought his thumbs down and slid both into her juicy pussy. Her whole body quivered as he massaged her clit, his thumbs sliding over and around her labia. Everything about Grace was soft, from her pink pussy to her glorious breasts to her heart.

How had he ever considered she could be involved in something that might hurt someone else?

Sean kissed his way down her body. He let his tongue delve into her navel and past the little curve of her belly. He rubbed his nose in the *V* of her thighs, letting her scent and her taste surround him. She was the best person he'd ever met. He wasn't going to let her go. He was going to treasure her and protect her, one way or another.

Sean finally allowed his tongue to have its way. He gave that juicy peach a long lick and was rewarded with a heartfelt shudder from his sub. "On the bed. I want you on your back, legs spread, arms over your head."

Grace rushed to comply. She settled herself on the fluffy white comforter and parted her legs for him. Sean took a moment to look at his submissive. Her hair made a stark contrast to the white of the comforter. Her eyes looked up at him with desire. She wasn't thinking about the events of the day now. She wasn't worried about tomorrow. She was in the moment, and that was the gift he could give her.

"You're fucking gorgeous."

A small smile played on her lips.

He felt his eyebrows rise. He could read her. She was a freaking open book. He'd just been too blind to accept it. "You don't believe me?"

"Sean, I'm older than you, and even if I was ten years younger,

I wouldn't be in the same league."

He leaned over and kissed her knees. "I don't know what league you're in, but I like it. Whatever you think of me, know that I have never lied about wanting you." He kissed a path up her leg. "I wanted you the moment I saw you and haven't stopped since. I love your legs and the way they wrap around me when I'm shoving my cock into you." He kissed her belly. "I love how soft your skin is here." He chuckled as he cupped her ass. "I don't have to tell you the way I feel about this part of you." He moved on and buried his face in her breasts. "I want to sleep right here, Grace. I want to fall asleep every night buried deep inside you, with your breasts cradling me." He sighed and reluctantly moved on. He nuzzled her neck. "I think you're the most gorgeous woman I've ever met and don't try to call me a liar." He'd reached her mouth and now his cock was perfectly placed. He kissed her sweetly as he thrust his dick inside. "God, I can't lie about this. This is my home."

And it was. Sean was aware he was playing none of the games he had promised her, but they could get to that later. They had all night. Sean let his face fall to the curve of her neck as he thrust in and out of her tight pussy. She clenched around him, the little muscles inside rippling against his cock. She wrapped her legs and arms around him, and he was enveloped by her. Sean picked up the pace, completely overcome with love for this woman. He had never believed in it before, that there was one person for him, but Grace had proven him wrong. She was his. He was hers. And it was perfect.

He thrust for the longest time, putting off that moment that signaled the end. He was careful. He made sure his pelvis hit her clit with every sure thrust. He read all of her signs; the way her legs tightened, her breath became ragged, and how often she called out his name. She came three times, crying out her pleasure before he finally gave in and let it take him. He gripped her hips and held himself against her as he came and came.

A light joy overtook him. It was just the first. He'd shown her tenderness, now he could play. Now he could do all the things he had promised her. She was his lover, his future wife, and his sweet submissive. He could do anything he wanted with her.

"I love you, Grace." He breathed the words like a mantra against her skin.

"Elephant."

The word cut through his bliss, and his head came up instantly. She couldn't have said it. "What?" The words sounded dumb to his ears.

Her hazel eyes were wide and filled with tears. "I said elephant."

Her arms fell to her sides, and her legs unfurled. She withdrew as surely as though she had walked across the room.

Sean felt a flare of panic. She didn't believe him. It was the only explanation. "Grace, I love you. I love you so much."

Her face contorted. She was losing control. She pushed at him. "I said my safe word. I want you to go."

His heart pounding, Sean got up. Despite his every muscle protesting, he pulled his body from hers. He stared down at her, impotent against the weapon she had against him. "Baby, don't do this. I love you. You have to believe me."

He wanted to stay with her. The alpha male in him wanted to force his way back inside her. He could make her accept him. The Dom took a step back.

Grace curled into a ball and turned away from him. "I asked you to leave. I want to be alone, Sean. I used my safe word."

"I love you. I won't not say it because you're scared." He gathered his clothes, his heart as heavy as a rock. "I love you."

Closing the door between them was the hardest thing he'd ever done.

* * * *

Grace sat up in bed. The clock on the nightstand read 3:00. She knew immediately that it was a.m. She ran a hand across her face. She'd been crying in her sleep. Would she ever stop crying? Her body felt heavy, every muscle tired. Her mouth, on the other hand, was parched beyond belief. Grace stared at the door that led to the hallway. Was she locked in?

She pulled on the robe that had been left for her. She was going

221

to find out. If she was a prisoner here, then they had better be prepared for her to make a few complaints. The only thing she had to drink in this room was the wine Sean had left behind. Though getting drunk was tempting, Grace decided it wasn't a good idea. She needed water.

She caught a glimpse of herself in the big mirror over the dresser. *Wow*. She looked tired. Her eyes were puffy and red. She wasn't a woman who cried prettily. She stared at herself and wondered how Sean could have told her she was gorgeous. She patted down her hair, trying to make it seem less like a rat's nest. There wasn't anything she could do until morning. Then she would demand that someone take her home. She had to be at the office. She had to act like everything was normal.

Tentatively, Grace put her hand on the doorknob and tried to turn it. To her surprise, it immediately opened. She nearly tripped over the body in the doorway.

Sean sat up and stared at her. Even in the dark hallway, she could see that his face was set in mulish lines. The left side of his face was deeply creased as though he'd been lying on something. "Where are you going?"

"To get a drink of water. What are you doing here?"

He rolled his head around and groaned at the pain. He stretched, apparently trying to get the circulation back in his limbs. "I can't leave you alone. You won't let me in our bed. This is the closest you would let me get, so I'm sleeping here."

She wanted to laugh, but stopped herself. He looked so serious and boyish at the same time. His hair was falling in his face, softening the normally harsh lines. She wanted more than anything to believe him. When he'd said I love you, she'd panicked. It had hurt so much when she'd realized Sean had lied that she simply couldn't do it again. She'd spent the last several hours thinking about what a relationship with Sean would be like. They were too far apart. He was just starting his life. Though there was only eight years between them, there was a wealth of experiences he hadn't had. He'd never been married, never had children. She had two in college. Could she start over?

Of course, it might be a moot point. They hadn't been careful.

He'd taken her a couple of times without a condom. The thought didn't panic her the way it should, but his job was enough anxiety to send her running. Even if he was telling the truth, she didn't think she could live with him knowing that every day could be his last. His job was dangerous. She had already lost one man she loved. She didn't think she could go through that again.

"So, are you going to let me by?" It came out more grumpily than she intended.

He was on his feet in an instant. Where a sleepy boy had been before, now an intensely alert man stood in his place. He gestured down the hall. "The kitchen's that way."

She heard low voices as she got closer to her destination.

"Looks like you're not the only insomniac." Sean pushed at the swinging door that led into the gorgeous gourmet kitchen. Everything about the room was shiny and modern. Jake and Eve sat at the island in the middle of the room. It was covered in pretty, black granite. They each had a mug of something in front of them and a sandwich. They were talking in low tones. They both looked up and smiled when the door opened.

"Hello, Grace." Jake nodded her way. "I was just getting Eve's opinion on how to keep my best friend alive."

"Keep him away from Grace," Sean said under his breath.

Eve looked between Grace and Sean, her eyes seeming to read the body language. "I was telling Jake that once Adam realizes Sean is dead serious about Grace, he'll move on. Now that Sean has announced he's going to marry Grace, I think Adam will accept it."

Sean sighed and crossed to the cabinet. He shuffled around behind her.

"We're not getting married," Grace replied with a frustrated huff. How many people had Sean told? Had he sent out invitations?

Jake grinned, the curling of his lips lightening his brooding good looks. "I think I might take that bet. The Sarge is used to getting his way."

"He could have been a bit more subtle, though. Sean, next time throw a nice party when you have a big announcement," Eve said. "Just about anything would be better than the way you announced it."

"What did you do?" Grace asked the question with a sort of breathless anticipation.

Jake laughed. "What he always does. He punched the shit out of his brother and told Ian he was marrying you, and he could like it or fuck off."

Grace turned, shocked at Jake's words. She'd gotten the idea that Sean was close to Ian. "You got in a fight with your brother?"

He shrugged and handed her a glass of water before kneeling to look for something in the bottom cabinet. He came back up with a small pan. "He pissed me off. Omelet or grilled cheese?"

"Grilled cheese," she said automatically. She shook her head, not willing to give up the conversation. "Why would you hit your brother?"

Jake sat back on his barstool. "It's a thing they do. Some families hug or have long discussions, Ian and Sean Taggart beat the shit out of each other. It's their way. You'll get used to it. Thanksgivings are fun. You should see what happens when Ian starts to give Sean menu advice."

"I don't tell His Highness how to run his business, he should keep his nose out of my kitchen," Sean growled.

Eve was shaking her head. "That is such bullshit. Little Tag tells Big Tag how to run his business all the time."

"Little Tag?" Grace had to ask. They couldn't be talking about six-foot-three-inch, two–hundred-twenty pounds of pure muscle Sean.

Sean flushed slightly as he ducked into the huge double-door fridge.

"Ian's bigger and older," Jake explained. "From what I understand, everyone's called them that since they were in school."

She couldn't imagine anyone calling Sean little, but Ian did have a couple of inches on him. Of course, Sean was way more handsome. "They should call them Sexy Tag and Sexier Tag."

Sean slid the most decadent smile her way. He winked. "Thanks, babe."

"And how do you know I'm not the sexier one?" Ian's deep voice startled Grace. Grace noted that Eve and Sean didn't flinch, as though they had known he was there all along. The six-foot-five-inch man filled up the doorway. He was in a pair of pajama bottoms and nothing else. He still wasn't as hot as Sean.

"I know." Sean gave his brother a superior look and went back to his frying pan. Already Grace could smell something heavenly. "I know my Grace. You're not her type."

Grace nearly laughed. Though they were practically twins, Sean was right. There was something dark about Ian Taggart that simply didn't exist in his younger brother. Sean could brood and emote with the best of them, but there was always a light in his eyes. Ian looked a bit like a man who never laughed.

"I thought you were dealing with your subs," Eve said, staring at the big man. There wasn't a bit of desire in the lovely blonde's eyes, merely the teasing look of a little sister. "What's wrong, Ian? Did the pain sluts finally realize you're never going to collar them?"

Grace leaned close to Eve. "There was more than one?"

Eve's lips turned up in a conspiratorial grin. "Almost always. They call him all hours of the night and beg him to spank them."

"They have names, Eve." Ian glared down at her.

"Do you remember their names?" Jake asked.

Ian's brows slashed together in an intimidating *V*. "How about we keep the discussions of my private life to a minimum around the newcomer?"

Eve rolled her eyes. "She's not vanilla, Ian. She's not going to have heart palpitations because she hears that you like to spank women. I think she's figured out that it's a family trait. Besides, it's best to get it all out in the open now before she runs into your groupies and they start calling you Master."

Ian's eyes narrowed. Grace felt the weight of his stare. "That's not what she calls Sean."

Sean flipped the pan with the ease of long practice and caught the sandwich on the other side. He shot a look back at his brother. "Is that seriously your problem with her? Your problem with Grace is that we're not in a twenty-four/seven relationship? When was the last time you were in a serious relationship, Ian?"

Ian's icy eyes slid across her. "She doesn't even have a collar, Sean."

Eve sighed. "I'm afraid Ian takes his lifestyle very seriously,

Grace. You find yourself in the middle of a family argument. Think of it as a belief system. This is Ian's belief system, and he's passed it on to his brother. Ian practically raised Sean, you know. Ian's worried his brother can't be happy in a vanilla relationship."

"He's thinks I'm a brat or a SAM." Grace looked pointedly at Ian, who seemed a bit shocked she knew the lingo. SAM stood for smart ass masochist. A brat was pretty much the same. Both were a type of submissive a serious Dom would avoid. She wasn't completely ignorant. Sure, she'd gotten a lot of her information from romance novels, but she'd been on the Internet, too.

Sean slid the sandwich on a plate. "I told you she's not a tourist. She's already accepted me as her Dom. Just because Grace and I choose not to be twenty-four/seven doesn't mean we're not practicing in private. And it's hard for her to wear her collar when she throws it in my face."

He patted a barstool and put the plate down. He looked at her, a challenge in his eyes. She thought briefly about telling him to go hell and then practicality set in. Her stomach growled, and she really wanted that sandwich. Also, she couldn't embarrass him in front of his brother. Openly disobeying him when they were having a discussion about Sean's ability to handle her seemed a bit mean. She didn't like Ian poking into their business, either.

"Thank you," she said as sweetly as possible. She hopped onto the chair.

Sean's satisfaction was an almost palpable thing. He kissed her forehead and urged her to give the sandwich a try. "Besides, she doesn't need a collar. She'll have a ring on her finger as soon as we pick one."

Grace opened her mouth to protest because she wasn't going to marry him to soothe his pride. Sean quickly shoved the sandwich in before she could get a word out. Grace would have spat it out, but it was heaven. The bread was crisp and buttery while the cheese was perfectly melted. She had been so wrong. She had thought sex was Sean's weapon against her, but damn, the man could cook.

He grinned down at her. "It's not your normal grilled cheese. I used a smoky Gouda on whole wheat and fried it in a little bit of truffle oil. I like to take comfort food and give it a gourmet flare.

One day I'll make you my version of mac and cheese."

Eve's eyes glazed over. "Seriously, it's amazing. It's nothing like what comes out of a box. If he weren't like my brother, I would have been all over him the first time he made that spaghetti thing."

"Lobster *Alsace*. I got the recipe from a restaurant in Venice." Sean turned and started to clean up.

"You know, Sean, as long as you're cooking..." Ian looked down at Grace's plate. She pulled it closer, not willing to share.

"Kitchen's closed. I used all the cheese on Grace's sandwich." Sean turned his back on his brother. Grace could sense the tension between them. What had Ian said to get Sean to hit him? She was sure it was about her.

Ian placed both hands on the island countertop and stared at Grace.

"Are you going to be able to get through tomorrow?" His tone suggested he believed she wouldn't.

"Of course." Grace had the story down. She'd gone over her cover endlessly with Mr. Black. She had left work early with some friends and then Sean Johansson had called. He was back in town, and he'd wanted to see her. She'd spent the night with him and didn't know about what happened to Kayla until that morning. Once someone told her, she could give way to her real emotions, but she owed Kayla this.

"Because if either of the Wright brothers gets a hint that you're lying, I have no doubt that we'll lose them." Ian looked like a man who didn't appreciate having a rookie in on his operation. He had mentioned that to the CIA guy a couple of times. "If Evan Parnell goes to ground, we'll lose our chance. We have to work on the assumption that Parnell has the information he wants to sell. He won't just e-mail it to them. The United States scans for that sort of thing after 9/11. He'll make a drop after he's sure his money is secure. We have to catch him in the act. That's the only way to take Parnell and the foreign agent down."

"I understand." Grace knew the risks. That was why she had to keep it together.

Sean was suddenly at her side. "Or we could just take Grace out of the equation all together. I'll sweep in and take her away for a romantic getaway. She'll need it. Everyone will understand. Her friend died. She needs some time."

"I'm not leaving, Sean," Grace said wearily. Now that she had some food in her stomach, she was getting sleepy. So much had happened, she wanted to rest and maybe she'd wake up and it would all be a dream. Sean would be a boring IT director, and they could have a normal life. Until that happened, she had a part to play. "It's going to happen at that party, I just know it. Matt's been so insistent on us celebrating a contract that loses money. Why else would he push me so hard?"

The party on Friday was the key. Parnell had to drop the information off in order to get paid. The party was perfect. There would be plenty of people and loud music. It was in a hotel, so no one would be surprised that there were strangers milling around. Of course, it all depended on her. She was the one who would make that party happen. Just as he seemed to use her for everything else, Evan Parnell was pulling her strings to cover his actions.

"I agree with Grace. He's making contact at that party. If he's working with the Chinese, then he'll have one shot. They don't give you a second chance. He'll need to make his drop at the appointed time, or risk losing his contact." Ian crossed his arms over his massive chest.

"Yes, he could get desperate. Another reason I don't want Grace involved." Sean's voice was tight, and Eve's fingers drummed across the table.

"Boys, you had this argument earlier," Eve pointed out. "It ended in violence, like everything between the two of you does. Grace has made her decision. Shelve it."

Ian didn't seem interested in listening to the psychologist. "If you don't want her to do it, then tell her no. Put a collar around her neck, or a ring on her finger, and tell her what to do."

Jake groaned and let his head fall to his hands. "You're all stubborn bastards, you know that, right?"

Grace's stubborn bastard ignored Jake. Sean took a step toward his brother. "Maybe that would work with your subs, but Grace has a mind of her own."

"I think that's probably the reason Ian has a problem with her,"

Jake interjected.

Ian turned on him. "I can fire you, you know."

"Promises, promises," Jake said with a sigh. "I'm going to bed before this turns into another fist fight."

Ian ignored Jake, too. "My subs might not be permanent or even exclusive, but they are much more obedient. They follow the rules of our contract or they aren't my subs for long. It's why your relationship with Grace will most probably fail. You have no contract and no rules."

"Hey," Grace started to defend herself. Eve held out a hand.

The blonde got in between Sean and Ian, turning her face up to Ian's. "You haven't been tested the way Sean and Grace are being tested. You have no idea what you would do in their situation. You know I love you like a brother, Ian, but you're wrong right now. You should back off. He's not going to be swayed away from her."

"I wouldn't be in a situation where I had a sub who refused to obey me." Ian's voice held the surety of a man who knew his own limits.

Eve shook her head. "Grace isn't doing this to be stubborn. She isn't doing this because she wants revenge. She's doing this because she knows she won't be safe until this man is taken out, and Sean will do anything to make sure she's safe. Sean's in danger, too. You are misreading her, Ian. Grace loves your brother. Oh, she might not admit it because he acted like an ignorant ass, but she does. I can see it in her eyes."

Ian's jaw had tightened the instant Eve had mentioned the woman from his past. He straightened up. "Just see that she doesn't fuck up this op, Sean."

He turned and walked out, every muscle in his body tense.

Eve's shoulders fell. "Well, I screwed that up. I think I'll go to bed, too." She turned to Grace. "Give Ian a little time. Sean is all he has. He's very protective."

Sean paid no attention as Eve walked out. His eyes were steady on Grace. "Is what Eve said true?"

Grace had no intention of going there. It had been too long a day to make that decision. She needed time and sleep. "I just want to go to bed, Sean."

He nodded slowly and followed her out. She felt him behind her and wondered if he really intended to sleep on the floor in front of her door. She couldn't stand the thought. She opened the door to the bedroom and turned to him. He looked as tired as she felt. "Come to bed, Sean."

He had his clothes off and was under the covers before she could change her mind. Grace crawled in beside him. Despite her hesitations, she was happy he was beside her.

"I love you, Grace." He made no move to touch her, but his words were caress enough.

"I can't right now." She couldn't. She couldn't say it yet. She might never be ready to say it.

"I love you enough for both of us. I'll say it until you believe it." He rolled onto his back. "Will you let me hold you? Nothing more, little one."

Grace fell into his arms. "You're the only one who calls me that. I'm not exactly little."

His chest moved as he chuckled. His hand stroked her hair and the strong beat of his heart was a lullaby to her ears. "You're small compared to me. You're just right for me."

Grace let the warmth of his body sing along her skin and sank into sleep.

Chapter Eighteen

Evan Parnell, formerly Patrick Wright, watched the bitch walk through the door. He sat on the sofa in the small outer office that served as Matt's reception room. The door swung open, and she breezed in as though he hadn't tried his damndest to murder her not twenty-four hours before. A man in slacks and a dress shirt followed her speaking animatedly. Adam Miles. Grace Hawthorne dumped her laptop bag on her desk and smiled up at that queer who always seemed to be around her. Something about that fellow and his lover had made warning bells go off in Parnell's brain, but he quickly let it go. They moved well, but they probably took Krav Maga classes because it was trendy. They also weren't as demonstrative as other gay couples he'd met, but it still offended him. He didn't like queers, and he certainly wasn't afraid of them. If they were dangerous at all, it would be because someone had trained them. Most agents came from the military. The Army tended to weed those pansies out fast.

Sean Johansson was another story, and he was back just in time to really fuck things up.

Johansson strode in carrying a cup from the coffee house that stupid friend had been on her way to. The knot in Parnell's gut tightened. If Grace had just followed her daily routine, he wouldn't be so worried. She would be on a slab in the morgue, and Evan wouldn't have to put up with his brother's whining. First Matt was okay with killing Grace because she was a faithless bitch. Now Matt loved her and couldn't imagine a world without her and why, oh why, did they have to kill anyone?

It was enough to make him want to wrap his hands around Matt's throat and squeeze until he couldn't whine anymore. Couldn't his brother see how close he was to the prize? He just needed to hold it all together until Friday night.

Parnell had tried to get a hold of his contact. Something was wrong. He felt it deep down. He needed to move the drop, but the damn Chinese weren't answering. Those fuckers played a deep game and didn't like to have the rules changed on them. If he didn't make the drop at the appointed time, they would more than likely decide he'd sold to another buyer and come after him. He would have two governments out to kill him and no twenty million dollars. He had to make that drop no matter what.

"Mr. Parnell?"

Grace's voice pulled him from his thoughts. He looked up. The secretary had finally stopped staring at the men around her long enough to realize she had someone in her office. Those big hazel eyes pulled at him. It was when he'd looked into the other one's eyes that he'd realized his mistake. He could still remember the thrill of hunting her down, shoving the knife in and turning her body around so she would know who had killed her. He had so looked forward to the shock in those pretty green and gold eyes. The brown eyes that had stared back at him had been a terrible surprise.

"I'm just waiting on the boss man." Evan showed none of his gut-churning anxiety. He kept his face peaceful and used his best "man of the people" tone. He had been playing this particular role for several years now. He had it down pat. "We have a problem at the Bryson Building."

"Sounds boring," the queer said with a dramatic sigh. He gave Grace a little wave. "See you for lunch, dear?"

The big blond man frowned. His chest puffed out like a gorilla about to defend his territory. Didn't the idiot know the other man was gay? "Not today. I'm afraid I'll need my fiancée this afternoon, Adam. We're picking out rings."

Another unpleasant surprise. It didn't suit his purposes to have the asshole back in town at all, much less hanging all over his victim. What the hell was that man's game? "You finally snagged a man, Hawthorne?"

She didn't take the bait, merely sighed. "I guess so. I can't seem to get rid of him." She opened the appointment calendar on her desk as the gay guy exited to go do whatever gay guys did for a living. She was frowning when she looked back up. "You don't have an appointment."

He shrugged. He'd never made an appointment. Grace might not know it, but he was the freaking boss and had been since the day he'd walked back into his brother's life. "Don't need one."

She drummed her fingers in an impatient tattoo along the oak of her desk. Something was different about little Grace. She seemed far too sure of herself. "You know, all of Matt's other direct reports make appointments to see him. He's a busy man."

Yes, Matt was probably busy getting his ass sloshed at nine in the morning. Evan felt his anger on the rise. What right did she have to question him? He forced himself to stay in check. She would get hers. "I just need a minute of his time."

"Fine. I'll pencil you in, but I would prefer if you would do me the courtesy of making an appointment from now on." Her lips thinned as she picked up a pencil and wrote his name in the appropriate box. Johansson sat on the edge of her desk, his big presence the only thing that kept Evan from finishing the job he'd fucked up yesterday. Parnell knew a brief moment's gratitude for the big, besotted idiot. He still wasn't sure that Johansson wasn't an agent of some kind, but he did know now was neither the time nor the place to deal with Grace.

Matt chose that moment to drag his red-eyed body into the office. He was wearing a suit that looked pressed and fresh, but the rest of him looked like he'd been steamrolled. His eyes were bloodshot, his hair mussed. His skin was a sallow yellow. He stopped and stared at Sean for a moment.

"You're back."

Johansson smiled. It was the type of smile that annoyed other men. It was a smile a man only used on a rival to let him know he'd already won everything they had fought over. "Don't worry about it. I'm not here on business anymore. I'm just here for Grace."

Evan stood up. It was time to get down to business. He couldn't let Matt get involved in this little love triangle again. "I need to talk to you."

His brother slid him a sullen look. "In a minute. I need to talk to Grace first."

His temper ticked up another notch, headed straight into the danger zone. "This is important."

Matt's hand was on the door. Grace was already walking toward him, laptop in hand. "So is this. I have to talk to Grace. Something terrible has happened. I'll see you in a minute."

The door closed behind them before Evan could get another word out.

Johansson's smile was smug as he sipped on his fiancée's coffee. "Nice weather we're having, huh?"

It was stormy outside. It was nothing compared to the storm Evan intended to bring down on all their heads.

* * * *

"What's he doing back here, Grace? I thought you got rid of him."

Matt's words cracked through the air, and the hope that they could have a civil conversation was blown to smithereens. Grace set the laptop down, not bothering to open it. It didn't look like they would be doing any work today. It occurred to Grace that if he fired her, she wouldn't have to go through with any of this. She could walk away with a clean conscience. And Sean would stay on. No matter what he said, he had a job to do, and he would do it. His brother was counting on him. Despite the small feud they were in, Grace knew Sean loved his brother.

"I didn't get rid of him, Matt." Grace sat down, hoping to ease the tension in the air. "He got called back to his office." She stuck to their cover. "He went back to Chicago, got some loose ends tied up, and took a sabbatical. He's just back here to spend some time with me."

"You're sleeping with him." The accusation was ground out of his mouth.

Grace held her temper. If she shouted the way she wanted to, Sean would be in here laying out Matt, and that wouldn't help anyone. "That's none of your business, Mr. Wright. If you feel it is affecting my performance, then I will discuss it with you."

He slumped into his chair. "Damn it, Grace, I thought we were friends."

"We are, Matt. You know you can tell me anything." *Tell me about Parnell. Tell me you aren't involved in this. Please ask for help.*

His face fell, mouth drooping, eyes watery. "I do have to tell you something."

Grace leaned in, her hopes soaring.

Matt took a moment, and even when he spoke, he was quiet. "Something happened yesterday. I got a call from the police."

Grace felt tears well up. She had known this would happen. At least she didn't have to really act now. Her emotions were real. "About what?"

"Grace, I know you were friends with Kayla Green." He closed his eyes as though he couldn't stand to look at her. "I'm so sorry to tell you this. She was killed yesterday. The police think it was a mugging gone bad."

Grace let herself go. She finally allowed the tears to flow. She listened to the bullshit Matt was spouting and for the first time realized her boss was in on this. She knew him. She knew his tells. He was feeling guilty, and there was only one reason for that. He had known his brother was going to kill. He had known his brother wanted to kill her, and he'd let it happen. A cold chill crossed Grace's skin.

Matt got up and crossed the space between them. He got down on one knee and looked up at Grace. "Sweetheart, I'm so sorry to be the one to tell you. She was so young. I still can't believe it myself. I talked to her just yesterday."

But now Grace recalled that he had barely been able to look her in the eyes. He'd left early, and he'd been very short with her. He had known what was supposed to happen. Grace wanted to smack him. As a second option, she would run screaming from the room. She could do neither. She had to suffer through his clammy hands sliding over hers, his red-rimmed eyes looking up at her. "I just can't think about her being gone."

She forced herself to be still, to accept his "sympathy."

"I know." His voice was low. "But these things happen. I guess it was just fate. But, Grace, sometimes fate can save us, too. Sometimes, it can stop us from making a terrible mistake."

His hand moved restlessly on top of hers. She couldn't take it anymore. She pulled away and stood. "I don't think Kayla would have felt that way. And I certainly don't think it was fate. It was some wretched man. It was some person who didn't care who he hurt."

Matt stood, unsteady on his feet. "Yeah, I guess. But sometimes things aren't so simple." He walked up to her and invaded her space. "Grace, tell that asshole to go back to Chicago. You promised. You promised you would give us a chance."

His hands were on her hips, and she could smell the whiskey on his breath. She crossed her arms over her chest, trying to get some distance between them. "Matt, we're just friends."

His eyes narrowed, and his hands tightened. "You promised."

She had to stop herself from shoving him away. "I told you I would think about it. I don't love you, Matt. Not that way. I'm so grateful for the chance you gave me, but I just don't have those feelings for you."

"Because of him," Matt practically spat. "Everything was fine before that meathead showed up."

"You didn't even look at me before Sean showed up." And she'd been perfectly fine with that. She'd been more than happy to be his admin/keeper who he utterly took for granted.

A little smile played on his lips. "Is that what you're upset about? Darling, sometimes it takes a little jealousy to force a man to step up. I've always seen you. I was just waiting until I was ready to commit. Now I am." He got serious again. "I can save you, Grace."

"Save me from what?" She knew, but she wanted him to say it.

He hesitated, his eyes sliding away from hers. "From that bastard Johansson. What else could I be talking about? Can't you see he's just going to use you? He doesn't love you. He can't love you the way I can. He couldn't possibly. He's going to use you and leave you. He'll never marry you."

"He already asked." She didn't bother mentioning that she'd told him no. That wasn't part of their cover. Grace tried to pull away from Matt. His hand wrapped around her upper arm.

"What?"

Grace bit her bottom lip. "You're hurting me."

"And what the hell do you think you're doing to me? I love you, Grace. I gave you a job when no one else wanted to hire you."

"And I'm damn good at it." She wasn't a charity case. She'd run this office for years. Resentment bubbled through her. "You're hurting me."

"Yeah, you're hurting me, too." Matt growled at her, shaking her slightly. "What about me?"

"Well, you'll have your head taken off if you don't get your hands off her this instant." Sean's low voice was menacing, and Matt immediately backed off.

Sean stood in the doorway. He didn't move to intercept Matt, but the threat was in his stance. His gaze was on Matt, and the other man wouldn't meet it.

"Sorry, Grace," Matt muttered.

"Grace, sweetheart, I just heard some disturbing news." Sean's voice was back to being even and smooth.

She nodded and collected herself. The blood was still pounding through her system. "Yes, I heard about Kayla."

Sean crossed the room. Matt went to his desk as though he needed to put some distance between them. Sean pulled her into his arms, and she felt safer than she had all morning. They didn't have to pretend when it came to this. It was part of their cover. Grace buried her head in his chest.

"You'll understand if I take her home. She's too emotional to stay for the day." Sean's hands smoothed down her back as he spoke.

"Sure. Take her home. Is everything ready for Friday?"

Grace turned to her boss, her former friend, the man who hadn't bothered to warn her that she was going to be murdered. "Yes, I can make the calls I need to make from the house, and I'll do the walk-through tomorrow. The invitations are already out, and the hotel is booked. Don't worry. You'll have your party."

"Then you should go home. I can handle things here." He sat down at his desk. "Send in Pat...Parnell on your way out. I'll see you tomorrow."

Sean took her hand and led her out. She gathered her things as Parnell watched. All the way, she could feel Parnell's eyes on her.

Sean was quiet as they waited on the elevator. He used his phone, his fingers typing out a message. She was sure he was informing Jake and Adam that they were on the move. Things between Sean and Adam were tense, but at some point they must have reached a truce. They were working together to ensure her safety. She'd received a stern outline of all her safety protocols from the Taggart brothers before she was allowed to go into the office. Both Sean and Ian had promised violent retribution should she stray from the protocols. She had been informed that she was to obey not only Sean, but Ian, Adam, and Jake. She had sat there wondering if the absent Liam would have been topping her, too, if he weren't out protecting her sons. When she'd pointed out to Sean that she didn't have his collar on anymore so he didn't have the authority to boss her around much less allow his friends to, she'd been met with a long, dangerous, unnerving stare. She'd decided not to push her luck. They were the experts, after all.

The elevator doors opened, and Sean pulled her inside. The minute they closed, his hands ran along the skin of her arms. "I swear to god I will kill him if he left a mark on you."

His face was fierce and now she realized just what it had cost him to play the game. He'd wanted to tear Matt up for touching her. Grace let him inspect her then pressed her body into his, softening instinctively against him. "I'm fine, Sean. He just got a little handsy."

It was up to her to calm him down. She might have protested earlier that she wasn't his submissive anymore, but the argument was sounding weaker and weaker. It was starting to be sheer stubbornness. She ran a hand through his hair.

His fingers sought her hips. His entire body relaxed as she touched him. His face lost its ferocity as he touched his lips to her forehead. "I don't want you alone with him."

This was the dangerous part. She wasn't so sure Sean wouldn't toss her over his shoulder and simply lock her away until this was over. That wouldn't suit her purposes or the mission's. She had to keep his caveman firmly in check. "I promise. I'll avoid him like the plague. There's just today and tomorrow, and then I'll spend all of Friday at the hotel. I won't be alone with him."

"Just know that someone is always watching, or listening." He gently touched the brooch she was wearing. It had a small camera and listening device imbedded in amongst the jewels. He'd hooked it into her sweater himself and made sure it was functioning before he would drive her to work this morning. Grace knew that Ian and Eve were listening in from somewhere in the building. "All you have to do is say the word, and the cavalry comes riding to the rescue."

"And I will." Though only as a last resort. She wanted to keep Sean safe. She didn't want him using his body as a shield. "Now, let's go and check out the event site."

He nodded, though he didn't seem to like it. He was thoughtful all the way to the hotel.

* * * *

Two nights later, Grace knew she had to make a decision. She sat at her table, watching him as he worked in the kitchen. Some heavenly aroma filled the house. The last couple of days with Sean had been strangely peaceful. The odd normality of their daily routine had set Grace on edge. She should be worried about the party coming up tomorrow. She should be planning and practicing, but all she could think about was the fact that it would all be over and she would have no real hold on Sean. She had been friendly with him, but she'd held him at arm's length, unwillingly to open her heart to him again. At night he slept beside her, but they kept to their own sides of the bed. He seemed to be waiting for her to come to a conclusion.

What was she really afraid of?

For Sean's part, he had been nothing but sweet. He'd backed off, but spent as much time with her as she would allow. He'd cooked breakfast and dinner and showed up to escort her to lunch. At night, they watched TV or read in companionable silence. Grace had received a phone call from Liam and was able to talk to her sons. The night before, David had asked to speak with Sean. She'd handed the phone over, and he'd promptly left the room. She wasn't sure what David had to say to Sean that took thirty minutes, but Sean was quiet the rest of the evening.

Now he concentrated on his work. His easy smile had been replaced with a tenseness that didn't go away no matter what they were doing. She wondered if he was thinking about the same thing she was. After tomorrow, there would be no reason for him to stay here with her. The job would be over. She would be safe. He could go home.

And Grace could look for a new job. She could try to find her way back to normal. She could take her friends' advice and try dating again, maybe fill out one of those online matchmaking surveys. They might be able to find the perfect man for her. Or she could acknowledge that the perfect man for her was currently frying tortillas not ten feet away.

But that was a dangerous thing to accept. Her heart raced at the thought. She could offer herself to him only to find out that he really was just staying close to her because he had a job to do. He could be interested in her only as a submissive partner. The sex would wear off eventually. He could decide he wanted a fresh young thing to marry. He could never want to get married at all, despite what he had said. He'd been feeling guilty at the time. Or, worst of all, he could be perfectly serious. He could love her. He could marry her. And he could die.

Grace sipped the wine Sean had placed in front of her not twenty minutes before. She had loved Peter Hawthorne with all of her heart, and he had died on her. He had been killed in a car accident. There was nothing in the universe that promised her this time around would be different. Sean had a dangerous job, but even if he was the IT guy he'd said he was, accidents happened. It all came down to one question. Tears filled Grace's eyes as she asked herself the question she'd been dreading.

If she loved Sean Taggart, didn't she owe it to herself and him to be brave enough to risk her heart?

Sean was putting the finishing touches on his enchiladas when Grace stood and walked to the bedroom. She heard the oven door open and close as she shed her slacks and sweater. When she was naked, she fell to her knees and assumed the proper position on the floor. Head down, palms up, she waited.

It was only a moment or two before she heard the door open. "Grace? Sweetheart, dinner should be ready…" His voice fell silent, but after a moment his shoes came into view, and she felt his palm on her head. "Grace, if this is your version of goodbye, I do not accept it. You seem to believe that I'll disappear after tomorrow and your life will go back to normal, but I'm telling you, it won't. I'm not going anywhere. I love you. I'm going to say it until you believe it. If you toss me out, I'll sleep in your doorway again."

She was well aware that tears were flowing down her cheeks as she looked up at him. His face was red with emotion, his jaw tense. "I think I prefer having you in bed with me, Sir, rather than tripping over you as I leave in the morning. Besides, I've gotten used to having someone cook for me."

He shook his head and got to his knees, face to face with her. "No. No more Sir." His hand disappeared into the right pocket of his slacks. He pulled out the small gold chain with the heart he had given her and she had thrown in his face. "I sloshed through a lot of mud to find this, little one. I want it around your neck, and I won't be called Sir anymore."

She nodded and held up her hair. She knew what he wanted. He clasped the necklace around her throat. "Thank you, Master."

He cupped her face, framing it with his big hands. "My Grace."

He leaned in and took her mouth. Grace softened under his onslaught. Sean was fierce. His tongue plunged, demanding her response. His hands were suddenly everywhere. He cupped her breasts and ran them along her curves. He traced the curve of her back and curled his fingers around the cheeks of her ass, pulling her against his rock-hard erection.

He finally pulled her gently back, his hands twisted in her hair. His blue eyes were dark with passion, and his face a mask of barely leashed desire. "You will marry me, Grace."

She almost laughed. It was the best she would get from a Dom like Sean. In essence, it was a question. She would accept or not, and that would be her answer. There was no reason to make him wait. "Yes, I will."

"We're getting married, and I'm quitting the company. I'm going to culinary school, and then I'm going to open a restaurant when the time is right."

Tears pooled in her eyes again. "You're quitting?" She clutched his arms to stay upright, her relief was so great.

He frowned, obviously misunderstanding. "Yes, and it's not negotiable. I have plenty of money saved up. I'll sell my condo and move in here with you. I have enough to take care of you. You won't have to find another job."

"I like to work, Sean. I don't mind. I'm just happy you won't be risking your life."

His eyebrows drew up, and he chuckled. "You were worried about me?"

"Every day since I found out what you do," she admitted. "I'm glad you're quitting. I know you're good at what you do, but it isn't your passion."

"You're my passion, and you like to eat. I'm only doing it to please you, little one." He grinned down at her and sighed as he pulled her close and nibbled on her earlobe. "When I'm ready to open the restaurant, you can help me run it."

A little shiver of anticipation went through her. "I would love that, Sean, but until then…"

He slapped her ass, the little pain causing her pussy to gush with arousal. "You will do as I say."

Aroused or not, they were going to settle this here and now. "I thought you didn't want to be twenty-four/seven."

He had the good sense to look a little sheepish. "Maybe I've come to the conclusion that Ian's right. I think I didn't care enough before, but now I want to be responsible for you. Grace, I don't want to fight. I want to spend the night inside you. If you insist on working, then we'll find something suitable, but I won't let you work for a man like Matt again. We'll compromise. All right?"

She had the feeling that all the concessions would be heavily in his favor on this subject. And that she could push him if she really wanted to. Her relationship with Sean was laid out for her. They would struggle and fight for control, and it would be challenging. Every moment would be worthwhile. "Yes, Master."

She would compromise. They would find a way that worked for both of them. It was the way their marriage would work. He would set down the law, and she would work to find a way around it. Ian had been right. She had a little brat in her.

Sean's eyes narrowed. "I know when I'm in trouble. At least give me some obedience tonight. On the bed. Hands and knees."

Grace scrambled up, eager to obey. In this, she would never question him.

She heard him opening the bag he'd placed by the bed the first night they had returned from Ian's. It was a small leather bag, and Grace had no doubt it was the kit he'd specially prepared for her. It contained the toys he'd bought for her. Her eyes closed in sweet anticipation.

He parted the cheeks of her ass, and she shivered as he squirted lube onto her anus. She bit back a groan when she felt the plug breach her hole. "Push back." Grace gently pushed her backside onto the little piece of plastic. "That's beautiful," Sean said as he seated it firmly.

"Oh, god," Grace moaned as she felt the soft vibrations begin. Sharp prickles of sensation swamped her.

"That's just the beginning," Sean promised. "And, Grace, you are not allowed to come."

She closed her eyes. That was going to be near impossible. Already every nerve ending was begging for release, and he wasn't finished playing with her. His hands circled her waist and she felt a small object being placed right over her clitoris. A butterfly. She would never last. He connected the little straps around her waist and then pushed the button that started the vibrations.

"Damn it, Sean." Her pelvis was awash with humming pleasure.

He smacked her ass. "No cursing, and you use my title when I'm fucking you, love."

A perverse thrill went through her. She could play with this man to her heart's content. "Fine, damn it, Master."

He smacked her other cheek. "I can do this all night." He shoved two fingers up her pussy. "You come without permission and I swear I won't fuck you for a week. Is that understood?"

"Sean!" She practically cried because he was setting a near impossible task.

She heard the rustle of him undressing. "I didn't say how long I would make you last, little one. But if you disobey, there will be hell to pay. You'll wake me with a blow job, and you'll suck me again before we sleep. You'll get nothing in return." He walked around the bed, and she could see him. His proud cock jutted from the *V* of his thighs. He stroked himself leisurely, his hand running from the thick base to the bulbous head. "It's nothing more than you deserve. You've been topping from the bottom since I met you. It stops tonight. I get even a hint of manipulation, and I'll have you tied to a St. Andrew's Cross taking the lash. Is that understood?"

"Yes, Master." It wouldn't work to argue with him. He was in charge in the bedroom. Anywhere else was a power play, but here he was king.

"Good." Pre-come was dripping off his cock. "Lick the head."

She leaned forward and dragged her tongue across the weeping slit. She was rewarded with a groan from her man. She was able to concentrate on licking and sucking the big cock in her mouth. Her pussy and ass were humming, but it was sweet background music. She whirled her tongue around the head of Sean's dick, lavishing affection on it.

"That's right. Suck me in now." He pressed into her mouth, filling it with his flesh. One hand tangled in her hair as he fed her his length.

Grace reveled in his taste and feel. He filled her mouth. She relaxed her jaw to take him further. He was pressing the remote on her vibes and making it hard for her to concentrate. The vibrations were driving her toward orgasm, and she was determined that wouldn't happen. This was a battle. She teased the sensitive *V* on the underside of his cock. She used the tip of her tongue on it and then sucked him deep, taking him to the back of her throat.

"Oh, fuck yeah." Sean's head was thrown back, the remote in his hand seemingly forgotten as he lost himself in the pleasure of her mouth. "Swallow me. I'm going to come. You take every drop."

He dropped the remote and concentrated on fucking her mouth. Grace softened her throat as he forced his way in. His hips pumped, and his heavy balls hit her chin. Grace whirled her tongue on the underside of his cock. He was too big. She couldn't circle him, but when she pointedly swallowed around him, he roared as he started to fill her mouth with salty come. Grace drank him down. She licked him clean with long, loving strokes of her tongue.

His hand softened in her hair, stroking her gently as he continued to thrust against her. After a long moment, he pulled out. "Very nice. Spread those legs now. I want to fuck my pussy."

She felt a fresh rush of cream coat her pussy. He was going to fuck her, pack her full of cock and toys. Patience, Grace told herself. She had to be patient. He walked around and she felt the bed shift as he got in between her spread legs. His fingers stretched her pussy.

"Do you want to come?"

How could he ask her that? It was all she wanted. "Yes, Master. Please."

She held herself back. It was hard to be still when all she wanted was to buck against his fingers, to shove her pussy back against him until she exploded. All she could do was beg. He had the power, and it made her so hot she couldn't stand it.

He held his hand still inside her pussy. "I could leave you like this, baby. I could bring you to the edge again and again and not quite let you go over. I could do it until you're willing to give me what I want."

"What do you want?"

The words came out of his mouth on a tortured groan. "You safe, Grace. You out of this altogether." His fingers came out, and Grace knew a moment's fear that he would do just that. Then his hands tightened on her hips, and she felt the head of his rejuvenated cock at her entrance. "But I love you. I don't want you any other way, baby."

He sank into her, and Grace almost sobbed at the sensation.

Her hands clutched the quilt under her. "Master, please."

"Yes," he growled behind her. He fucked her hard, slamming his length into her. "You can come. Oh, you're so tight. I can feel that plug vibrating against my cock." His cockhead slid against her G-spot, and Grace screamed as she came. The orgasm rolled over her like a wave of sensation. It was more than mere pleasure. She felt their connection so keenly. Her head fell forward and everything inside her released.

Sean fucked her ruthlessly. Even as she came down from the first high, he brought his hand over the butterfly, pressing the vibrator tightly against her clit, causing her to come all over again. This one was long and started in her womb, vibrating outward until her skin hummed happily, and her blood pounded.

Grace lost control of her arms and fell forward. Only Sean's strong hands held her up. His cock jerked inside her as he slammed in and groaned when he let go. Grace felt the hot wash of his semen coating her pussy and womb and sighed in contentment.

He lay skin to skin with her for a moment before peeling away and gently easing the toys from her. He cleaned up and was back in her arms. He cradled her to his chest, and she could hear the pounding of his heart.

"My wife," he whispered holding her close.

Yes, he was her husband. She pushed away thoughts of tomorrow. For tonight, they were together, and the future seemed perfect.

Chapter Nineteen

Grace looked around at the throng of people milling about the Ashton Hotel's ballroom. The ballroom was located on the top floor of the hotel with a spectacular view of the city at night. Her eyes went to the large balcony. It was lit with twinkling lights and came with a big bar where attendees could sip wine and enjoy the lights of Fort Worth. The inside was just as nice. The whole space had been turned into an elegant, Monte Carlo-style casino. At least four hundred people gathered in the ballroom. It was wretchedly hard to keep up with who was going where. She had to hope Ian Taggart knew what he was doing.

She caught sight of him as he offered a finely dressed couple a selection of pan-fried dumplings. Ian looked elegant in black eveningwear. He proved charming when the occasion called for it. He was a perfect waiter. Even the head of the wait staff had commented on how she would hire him for any event she had. Every female eye watched him as he made his way through the crowd.

Of course, Ian's little brother had his share of admirers, too. Grace felt her eyes narrow as one of the HR girls tried her hand at flirting with her Viking. He looked up suddenly, as though he knew she was watching. A small smile played on his sensual lips, and her jealousy vanished. Sean was hers. The other women could come on to him as much as they wanted, but he would always come home to her. She looked down at the ring he'd placed on her finger that morning. It was a full-carat princess cut diamond, and the matching wedding bands, both his and hers, were sitting in the jewelry box on her dresser.

"You said yes." Matt's tight voice startled her from her thoughts.

She turned to find him standing beside her, his eyes fixed to the ring on her finger. He was dressed in a suit, but it was already rumpled, and he was working on his fourth Jack and Coke. At least Grace thought it was his fourth. She might have lost count.

"I love him." Her hand went up to play with the other sign of Sean's possession. Her fingers curled around the gold heart he'd crawled through the mud to retrieve for her.

"You barely know him."

Grace wasn't taking Matt's crap tonight. She had been very careful around him. She'd avoided going into his office as per Sean's instructions. The one time she'd had to, she'd called Jake Dean before going in. He'd been sitting at her desk when she'd come out. She was sure Jake had been listening at the door the entire time, waiting to pounce if she'd needed him. "I know him enough to love him. And Matt, you should know that I'm turning in my two week notice on Monday."

If there was a company to go back to after tonight. No matter the outcome of this evening, she wouldn't go back. It was time to start another chapter of her life. If Matt came out of this, he would need a new administrative assistant.

His whole face fell. "You're quitting."

"It can't be a surprise to you, Matt, after everything that's gone on the last several weeks." She crossed her arms over her chest. "I think it's best if we both move on."

His chin firmed, and an ugly glare gleamed in his eyes. "You're right. I need someone younger, anyway."

She could feel herself practically glowing. Sean hadn't let her out of bed until this morning. He'd managed to save his enchiladas, but they'd eaten the decadent meal in bed, in between raucous sessions of sex. Her Master had reveled in their commitment, and she was happy for it. And a little sore. She might need to take up yoga.

"He's ruined you." Matt growled and invaded her space a little. "You used to be sweet. Now you act like a slut. My brother is right."

"Brother?" He must be drunk. He hadn't mentioned his brother in anything but the past tense for years. Before she could follow the line of thought, though, Adam was at her side.

"Hey, hon, I think the caterers need your help." Adam's hand was at her elbow pulling her a good foot away from Matt.

"Are you all right?" Sean was at her other side. Unlike Adam, he didn't have to pretend. He was her fiancé. He had every right to look concerned. He glared at Matt.

"Of course." Grace laughed off the whole situation. It was obvious she was safe here. She couldn't move without one of the agents being on top of her. Even now, she could see Eve dressed in a slinky cocktail dress watching the scene play out. Jake Dean's eyes were watching the room from his seat at the Blackjack table. She was sure Ian was just waiting for a chance to kick some ass. And somewhere in all of this, Mr. Black watched with his dark eyes, waiting for the chance to take out his old agent.

"I'm fine." She laced her fingers through Sean's and gave him a reassuring squeeze. "I was just about to ask Matt here where his buddy Evan is. They seem so close lately. I thought he would be here."

Sean's hand tightened around hers in an unmistakable warning to not push it.

Matt laughed, an ugly sound. "Oh, I assure you, he's here somewhere. I think he'll seek you out, Grace. I know he wanted to have a word with you. Yeah, don't worry about Parnell. You'll see him soon enough."

Matt turned and started to walk away. Sean released Grace's hand, and she didn't like the look in his eyes as he began to follow Matt. Adam put a hand on Sean's chest.

"Not the time, Sarge."

"He just threatened her."

"And he'll get his," Adam promised. "She's got eyes on her.

She'll be fine. Ian is watching, trying to ID the foreign agent. Almost everyone else has eyes on your girl. We're going to make sure she comes out of this. Now, go calm down, and don't kill Wright until you have a damn good alibi."

Adam seemed to get through to Sean. Her Viking leaned over and gave her a lingering kiss. She knew better than to pull away. She didn't even want to. Sean released her, and she could see the worry in his eyes. He still turned to Adam. "Fine. I need to check in with our guest, anyway. He's getting anxious."

Sean had not been happy about bringing Black along, but the CIA agent had insisted. As he was paying the bills, Ian had been forced to allow it. Black was in a room on the floor below them, watching the ballroom through security cameras. Ian's partner, Alexander McKay, who she'd just met a few hours ago, was with him. It was hard for Grace to believe that funny, sweet Eve had been married to that bull of a man. He was just as bleak and uncommunicative as Ian. Sean stalked off to make his contact. Adam watched him, shaking his head.

"You have that poor man in knots, love."

Grace took a deep breath, coming down from the adrenaline high of having it out with Matt. "I'm surprised he left me with you."

Adam shrugged. "We've come to an agreement. I keep my hands off you, and he lets me live." Adam's handsome face twisted in a bit of self-deprecation. "I'm sorry I pushed so hard. I really thought you were attracted to us."

He said us, and Grace now understood he meant him and Jake. They were a package deal. Sean had told her about their background. She softened a bit. "I was attracted to you two even when I thought you were gay. How could I not be?"

"But you love the Sarge." It wasn't a question and required no reply. It was a statement of fact, and it seemed Adam had accepted it. "My only excuse is that I thought you were perfect for us. We're not getting any younger, you know. We need to find our third so we can get started."

"Started on what?" She was more than curious. Adam seemed to have a vision of how his life should work out. He didn't seem to think that sharing a woman with Jake was just for fun.

"The normal stuff. A family, kids, a house, and a dog. I know we're weird, but that doesn't mean we don't want all the normal things."

Grace looked over at the very darkly handsome Jake Dean. Women were all around him, but he didn't seem to notice. Jake didn't seem to be looking for something permanent. And he'd never really looked at her at all. What if Adam and Jake had different tastes in women? That would make finding one woman for the two of them pretty damn hard.

Then Sonja Patton from payroll walked by. She was a brunette with soft curves and an even softer face. She was maybe ten pounds overweight, but there was something lovely about her. Jake's eyes trailed after her.

"Yes, dear, he has a type." Adam chuckled as though reading her thoughts. "He was very attracted to you. He's just better at hiding it than me. Look at the women trying to get his attention. They're all perfectly model thin and hard as nails. Women. I don't understand you. You starve yourselves to gain a man's attention when what most men want is a little softness. Have you looked at a *Playboy*? Those aren't the same women you find on the cover of *Cosmo*. Don't worry about me and Jake. We'll find our heavenly bit of femininity. She'll probably steamroll both of us, just like you did with Sean."

Grace smiled up at her friend. The woman who got caught between Adam and Jake would be one happy girl. Unfortunately, Grace was far too in love with one Viking to ever consider it. Grace gave the room a once-over. Everything was running perfectly. It was a good party. Maybe she should go into party planning after this was over.

A thin woman dressed in gray slacks and a black sparkly top caught her eyes. The woman with dark hair pulled back in a bun looked strangely familiar. Grace tried to remember where she had seen her before.

"What is it?" Adam asked, following her line of sight.

She shook her head. "Nothing." She must be a girlfriend of one of the employees. That would explain it. She turned back to Adam. "Now you said something about a problem with the caterer."

Twenty minutes later, she had the dumpling issue sorted out and everything was running properly again. The band had taken to the stage, and the dance floor was hopping. Grace couldn't help but remember how good it felt to be wrapped in Sean's arms when they had danced together.

She caught sight of Matt out of the corner of her eye. The woman who had seemed familiar to her earlier passed him by and nodded. His eyes followed her briefly. Grace sighed. She really hoped Matt wasn't about to get in trouble. The last thing she needed was to have to deal with a drunk, horny boss hitting on some employee's girlfriend and starting a fight in the middle of her successful party.

She was grateful when Matt turned away from the woman and walked off toward the big balcony terrace. He passed a large potted palm tree. Grace noticed something fall out of his pocket as he opened the door and walked out onto the softly lit terrace.

Grace sighed. He never, ever changed. He was forever losing stuff.

Or was he?

Grace stopped in the middle of the room. She hadn't seen hide nor hair of Evan Parnell. Was that really a surprise? If he was as smart as everyone said he was, why would he show his own face at the drop when his brother could do it for him?

Grace looked around the room and thought about running to Adam or Jake. Would she lose the package? Was she the only one who had seen it? What was she supposed to do? Sean had gone downstairs to check in with Alex and Mr. Black. What if they missed their chance?

Heart pounding, Grace walked across the room. *Play it cool. Pick the damn thing up and then run for Adam.* She would run as fast as her four-and-a-half-inch heels would carry her. She would hand it off to Adam, and then she and Sean could go home and this nightmare would be over.

A sudden vision of a dark-haired woman in a van waiting outside the building floated across her brain. The woman in the gray slacks! She had been in the van that picked up Evan Parnell that day. Now Grace could see it clearly. It was the day she had chased down the little paper with the address of the mail place. Parnell had stood outside of the building, and the van had driven up. Grace could see the woman's dark hair and her slightly pinched face as she pulled up and waited while Parnell hopped in. She hadn't turned to look at him, like she would a friend or lover. There had been no warm greeting between the two.

She was his employee. Parnell had more than one person working for him tonight.

As quick as she could, she leaned over and grabbed the thumb drive. Grace straightened up and started toward Adam, pushing her way through the throng of people headed toward the buffet which had just opened for supper. She could see him up ahead and started to call out to him when she felt someone pull at her elbow.

"Don't call out." Something pressed into her side, and she saw Parnell's partner standing next to her. The dark-haired woman had one hand on Grace's elbow. Grace looked down to find a small pistol being shoved close to her ribs. It was pushed painfully against her side. Every nerve in Grace's body went on high alert. "And don't try to get the big bastard's attention, either, unless you want me to start shooting these fine people. I'll kill you first, and then I'll start in on everyone else. I'll do it if I have to."

"What do you want?" Grace kept her voice low as the woman started to maneuver her toward the back of the room. There was so much going on she wondered if anyone noticed. They probably looked like two women having a talk in an overly loud room.

The other woman's voice was a harsh snarl in Grace's ear. "I want the planet to be a nice place. It's corporate types like you who mess everything up for the rest of us."

"I'm an admin." She needed to stay calm, keep her talking. Sean was downstairs where they had all sorts of surveillance equipment. He would look for her. He would come after her.

"You work for the man. You take their money, you can share their fate. We're bringing down the Bryson Building and the gas company in it. I'm not going to let you stop us."

They seemed to be making their way to the door in the back of the ballroom that led to the stairs. She wanted to shout out, but she was afraid this woman would do exactly what she threatened. And the band was playing so loud. Grace doubted anyone would hear her over the roaring party music. She tried reason. "Your boss has been lying to you. Evan Parnell isn't interested in the environment. He's ex-CIA. He's been using you and your group as a cover to make money selling corporate and government secrets to foreign governments."

The woman snorted. "That's ridiculous. I've followed Parnell for two years. I know my mentor. He taught us everything he knows about bringing down the polluters."

Grace tried to drag her heels. "Look, I don't know what he's told you, but whatever interest he has in the Bryson Building isn't about the gas company. He wanted in that building for something else."

The gun pressed in so hard it made Grace's ribs ache. "Move. Don't try anything or I'll shoot. Now open the door."

Grace opened the door and almost immediately was assaulted by the quiet in the stairwell. The minute it closed behind them, it was like they were in another world. She could barely hear the music, and it seemed far too bright. There were stairs going down immediately in front of her, and to her left were a set that led to roof access.

"We're going up." There it was again, the press of steel against her side.

"Why, what's up there?" Grace was stalling but she wasn't sure what else to do. She wasn't an action hero. She was terrified. It took everything she had just to stay upright. She had to stay alive until Sean got to her.

"That's for me to know and you to find out."

She tried to pull Grace along, but her heels slid on the smooth surface of the industrial floors. Grace tried to stay on her feet, but tripped forward. Her captor cursed. She slipped toward the bank of stairs going up, and then the report of a gun filled her world with a single bang that seemed to echo on forever. Grace was suddenly covered in a fine spray of red stuff.

Blood. Oh, god, she'd been shot. She felt her side, trying to find the hole that was surely in her abdomen. It didn't hurt the way she would have thought. She couldn't feel anything at all. A strong hand pulled her up.

"Are you all right, Grace?"

Grace clung to Adam as he pulled her to her feet. She had a glimpse of the woman who had taken her, a single, neat bullet hole in the middle of her forehead. She stared down. "How?"

Adam's voice sounded far away, but she could understand him. He had a gun in his palm, the gun he'd used to kill her captor. "I saw her start toward you. When I realized I couldn't get to you before she did, I figured there were only two places for her to take you, out the front or down these stairs. Jake is watching the front, and I ran down to the floor below. It was too easy to hear me if I followed you from directly behind."

"You were fast." Her hands were shaking. She turned away from the dead body. Adam looked like a different person. Gone was the happy, funny friend she'd come to know, and in his place was a deadly warrior.

"Yes." Adam replied with a clipped, harsh tone.

"But I'm faster." The words came from above, and Adam reacted violently. He shoved her back, covering her with his body.

"Get out of here, Grace." He started to move back toward the stairs going down, but her whole world was filled with terrible explosions and suddenly Adam went down. Grace watched in horror as Adam's white dress shirt blossomed with blood. He hit his knees, a sad look on his face.

"Go," he shouted with what had to be the last of his breath.

He fell forward, but not before she saw the bullet hole in his gut.

"You're not going anywhere, Grace." Evan Parnell had his gun trained on her. He was dressed in black from head to toe. Even his hands were covered in black gloves.

Grace tried to move to get to Adam. A red dot was suddenly on her chest right over her heart. Parnell came down the stairs, moving with the grace and care of a man well trained.

"I said stay there, Grace. I meant it." Parnell sounded different now. The gruffness that was always in his voice was gone. This man was smooth and competent.

"Let me help him," Grace pleaded. She wasn't a nurse, but she was willing to try anything.

"He's past help." He gave his dead assistant a single glance, and then kicked Adam's body over as he joined Grace on the landing. "Still alive, you faggot? Is the Army letting your kind in these days?"

There was blood coming out of Adam's mouth. He looked up at the man who had shot him, defiance still on his face. "Got kicked out of the Army, asshole. Best day of my fucking life. But sorry to correct you, I'm not gay."

Parnell shrugged. "The whole queer thing is a good cover. I totally underestimated you. If you hadn't been so concerned with the girl over there, I doubt I would have gotten the drop on you. As it is, thanks for taking care of Melissa. I was going to kill her myself, but I hate to wreck my karma, if you know what I mean."

"Fuck you," Adam spat.

"Please let me help him." Grace could feel tears running down her face. Adam was dying right in front of her. She needed to call someone. She needed to get him help. The reality of the situation was starting to flood her and panic threatened to take over. She pushed it down. It wouldn't help Adam, and it wouldn't help her. "What do you want from me, Patrick?"

She used his real name, hoping it would throw him off.

His eyes widened, and he hissed. "Son of a bitch found me. Damn it." He looked down at Adam, whose hand covered the hole in his gut. "I should have known. You CIA?"

"Contractor. I hate spooks. Can't trust 'em." Adam gritted his teeth with each breath.

"At least you got that right. And if you think you can trust Nelson, you're wrong. He's as dirty as I am." Parnell turned his cold eyes to Grace. "As for what I want from you, well, you dumb bitch, I want you to pay up on the twenty million you just cost me."

"What are you talking about?" Graced asked.

He pointed toward her pocket. "The thumb drive. You just had to pick it up. Luckily I had Melissa watching the drop to make sure nothing went wrong. At least I didn't lose the package. If the Chinese won't buy it, then I know some Venezuelans who will. Your man is an idiot, you know. I can't believe he sent you in to do his job. Now, you're going to come with me, or I'll put a bullet through this one's head."

"Grace, I'm dead anyway. You run." Adam's eyes pleaded with her.

Grace didn't have a choice. She couldn't watch Parnell kill him, not when there was the slightest chance that he could live. Jake would realize something was wrong. He could get here in time, but only if she walked away with Parnell.

"Okay, I have the drive and I'll go with you." She held her hand out and let Parnell pull her to him.

He chuckled against her ear, the sound jagged and disturbing. "You're a dumb bitch, Hawthorne. I could still kill him. I won't. He'll provide a very nice distraction." He started to walk her toward the stairs, pressing her forward. "You see, a regular agent would walk right by his body on the way to get to me. I have the feeling this group will get all huggy-huggy, save my buddy. It will make it so much easier to pick them off one by one. Or to make a deal. You're my one-way ticket out of here, red."

He pushed her up and up. When Grace reached the roof, she wondered if it was the last place she would ever see.

* * * *

Sean slammed into the room. Alex McKay had called him to come down here, and Sean knew he had to obey. He comforted himself with the fact that Adam and Jake were on Grace babysitting duty. Sean had made it clear to his teammates that Grace's protection was more important than anything else. It wasn't a conversation they had included Ian in. In some ways, Sean would always be Jake and Adam's CO. After everything they had gone through together in Afghanistan, they had bonded in a way that was hard to break. He and Adam had had it out and reached a sort of common ground. Adam was going to keep his hands off Grace, and Sean promised not to use him for target practice.

"What's up?"

Black stood in the back of the suite watching the bank of black and white televisions feeding the images from the tiny surveillance cameras they had set up across the hotel.

"Mr. Black believes he's identified at least one of Patrick Wright's accomplices. A woman named Melissa Lowe. She's a known member of the Earth League. She's at the party. She's attempted to make contact with Matt Wright." Alex handed him a printed photo of a thin young woman. Alex was dressed in sweats and a T-shirt. He looked more like a linebacker in the off-season than a former FBI agent.

"All right, you track her." He pulled out his SIG SAUER and checked the clip. "Any idea who the foreign agent is?"

"Ian took him out ten minutes ago. He was Chinese." Alex said it matter-of-factly. He pointed back to the bathroom. "We used facial recognition software. I think he was quite surprised by it. He's trussed up and waiting transport to the nearest facility. All we have to do is watch for the drop, pick up the package, and hope Wright shows his face. If not…"

Black's face looked ghostly in the light from the monitors. He never looked up. "If not, then the Chinese will assume he's a double agent, and he'll have two governments trying to kill him. But I want that package."

"Do we have any idea what it is?" Sean was curious.

"There is a small aerodynamics firm in the Bryson Building," Black said. "One of the engineers there is working on certain instrumentation upgrades that would greatly benefit our current drone programs."

Drones were changing aerial warfare. Drones flew at ultrahigh altitudes and could bomb targets and gain intelligence without risking human lives. If the US was making a leap technologically, the Chinese would pay big to keep up. "All right, I'll buy that." He took the picture Alex handed him. "I'll make sure everyone knows about Melissa Lowe."

He heard Black sigh. "No need. I think everyone knows now."

"What?" The hair on the back of Sean's neck stood up. Something bad was happening. He could feel it. The little voice that always spoke to him right before the bad shit went down was whispering. He strode past Alex and stared at the monitors. The one in the center was the only one that mattered.

"Shit, is that your Grace?" Alex leaned in behind him.

Sean watched as Parnell's accomplice herded Grace toward the back of the ballroom. Horror built in his system, churning his gut. They disappeared from one monitor only to show up on the next. The dark-haired woman had something pressed into Grace's side, a gun no doubt. Grace's face was tight as she looked around.

God, she was probably looking for him. She was in danger, and he was downstairs.

Sean watched as Adam Miles took notice of Grace and signaled to Jake. Seconds later, Adam raced out of the room, and Jake followed at a more leisurely pace. Sean approved of the plan. One to watch the front, another to go up the back way but from below. Adam would either meet them on their way down or follow them up. If they turned back, Jake would be there.

"I'm going back." He would follow the same path Grace took. He understood why Adam had done what he did, but Sean would just go through with guns blazing. He wasn't going to let Parnell get away with her.

"I'm going with you." Alex was following him out.

Sean shook his head. He leaned in. "No. You have to stay and coordinate. I don't trust him." He gestured back toward the CIA agent.

Black turned to him. "I need Patrick Wright alive. He has information that this country needs. He has contacts. If you kill him, we lose everything."

"I'll try." Sean looked to Alex.

Alex nodded, but his face was bunched with worry. "You just be safe. And…"

"I'll watch out for Eve." He was out the door before Alex could thank him.

Sean wasn't an idiot. Alex and Eve could spit at each other all they liked. They might be divorced, but he knew neither one of them dated. He put thoughts of them out of his mind and concentrated on Grace. He bypassed the elevator and went straight for the stairs. The minute the door closed behind him, he heard the sound of shots being fired. He checked his first instinct—to scream Grace's name and run into whatever was waiting for him. He called on every bit of training ever given to him and let his blood run cold. The gun in his hand became a mere extension of himself. He moved silently up the stairs and prayed the gunfire had been Adam taking out Parnell's accomplice.

If it wasn't, then he would spend the rest of his life hunting the man who killed his mate. It would be the only thing that kept Sean alive.

Sean stopped as he entered the stairwell and opened all of his senses. Every nerve he had was on high alert. When he heard Grace's voice, a piece of his soul relaxed.

"What are you talking about?" Her shaky voice was the sweetest sound he'd ever heard. It meant she was still alive, and he had a shot at saving her.

Parnell said something about a thumb drive. He must mean the package. Parnell knew that the deal was off, and he seemed to think he could use Grace as a ticket out. He heard Grace offer to go with him, and Adam tell her he was already a dead man. *Shit*. He might be pissed at Adam Miles, but he wasn't about to let some asshole rogue agent kill him. When he heard the door close above him, Sean moved quickly. He took the stairs two at a time, adrenaline flooding his system. He stopped in his tracks when he reached the ballroom landing.

"Fuck."

Adam lay on the cold concrete floor, his guts half torn out. There was another body slumped to the side, but only Adam mattered.

"You're telling me, Sarge." Adam looked up at him with weak eyes. "You go. He's got Grace. He's going to kill her. No question about it. You can't just go after him. You have to find a way to sneak up on him. There are plenty of vents that access the roof. Alex has the plans."

Sean pulled out his phone. It was set to contact Alex. "We have a man down. Adam's down with a GS to the abdomen. He's in the stairwell. Wright has Grace on the roof. I'm going in. I need you to guide me to one of the vents on the roof. I need to come in very quietly."

He couldn't stay. He cared about Adam, but he was responsible for Grace. In the short time he'd known her, Grace had become his whole world. He looked down at the man who had fought beside him for years, practically begging him for forgiveness.

"What the fuck are you waiting for?" Adam tried to sit up but fell back to the floor.

Sean moved toward the roof and prayed they all came out of this alive.

Chapter Twenty

The night had a crispness to it that signaled autumn was close. All Grace felt was the chill. Parnell pushed her out onto the roof. Grace shivered slightly in her sleeveless cocktail dress, thinking about how Sean had zipped her up and laid a possessive kiss on her shoulder. She'd felt happy and loved.

"You look beautiful," he had said. Grace had felt beautiful.

She was going to die here. She wouldn't feel Sean's arms around her again. There was no way Parnell would let her live.

"Move over there." Parnell pointed toward the side of the building. At this height, she could feel the slight sway of the building. Maybe it was just her imagination. She could hear the chatter from the terrace below. The wind was blowing the sound toward her, which meant anything she said would probably go the wrong way. Maybe if she screamed really loud…

"Don't think about it." Parnell pointed the gun at her. "You'll be dead before you can scream."

Her hand tightened around the small thumb drive. He hadn't forced her to give it up yet. He seemed to want something more, but she was afraid to think what. He herded her to the side of the building. The roof was dotted with vents and air-conditioning units. The wind whipped around this high up. Her stomach churned as she looked down.

"You cost me a lot, lady."

"I didn't mean to." Her back hit the concrete wall that separated her from the twenty-five story fall to the ground below.

"I don't care." He grunted as he pointed the gun her way. "You fucking the CIA agent they sent after me?"

She shook her head. "He's a contractor." She remembered the word Adam had used. "He works for a private security firm. His brother runs it."

"Which firm is that?" His right eyebrow rose as though daring her to challenge him.

He was severely underestimating her will to keep him talking. Every minute he talked was another minute she lived. It was another minute for Sean to come find her. And he would. She knew it. He would move heaven and earth to get to her. She had to be ready when he made his move.

"McKay-Taggart. They have an office in Dallas." She hadn't seen it yet, but she intended to help her fiancé move out of it. He was going back to school, and she was going to help him. He was getting out of this world. They were going to have a family.

Tears pricked at her eyes. They could have it all, if she lived.

"Never heard...fuck. Ian Taggart?" He spat out the name like a curse.

Grace nodded her head.

"Goddamn it." Parnell, Wright, whatever his name was took a long breath and slammed his foot into the ground. "That fucker sent Taggart after me. Do you know who Ian Taggart is?"

"He's Sean's brother." That was really all she knew about the man. Well, she knew some of his sexual proclivities, but she didn't see how those fit into her current predicament.

Even in the moonlight, she could see that Parnell had gone a little green. "He's a legend in the business. He's the one you go to when the wet work gets too wet, if you know what I mean."

She didn't. She didn't know anything. She didn't understand a thing. She just wanted Sean. She wanted his arms around her.

"Ian Taggart is a fucking assassin. He kills people." Parnell shook his head. "That is just like Nelson to send a fucking assassin after me. After everything I did for him. Taggart is a piece of work. If he says he's running a security company, it's almost surely a cover for his real work."

Grace tried not to think about that because she could see Sean moving very quietly on top of the roof behind Parnell. Her heart nearly stopped when she saw him in a vent on top of the roof, moving as the air conditioner came on to cover the noise. He moved far more fluidly than a man that big should move. For the first time, Grace had to acknowledge that her man was a trained killer, and she was very thankful for it. Hope soared in her. Sean was here. He would take care of it.

"You're wrong about Ian." She had to keep him talking. She had to give Sean time. She took careful inventory of her surroundings. There was a large air-conditioning unit just a couple of feet to her left. She would need cover when Sean made his move. He wouldn't be able to do anything until he knew she was safe.

Parnell sneered at her. "I'm not wrong. He's the worst of the worst, and he's using all of you. I bet he's working with Nelson. Damn it. They're probably all working with Nelson. What's he calling himself this week? Mr. Black? Mr. Gray? It's all the same. You're all the same. That means you're just a pawn, and no one will come for you."

He was wrong. She knew it because her man was edging his way toward her. He just needed a little more time. She was the only one who could give it to him. "I'm marrying Sean Taggart. He'll come for me. He'll make a deal with you."

"Not if his brother doesn't allow it. A man like Ian Taggart will just kill him if he gets in his way."

"No. Sean is his brother. Ian loves his brother."

Sean moved toward her, his boots making no sound on the surface beneath him. He had taken off his jacket and tie. He was an elegant panther making his way toward his mate.

In the moonlight, Parnell's eyes looked black as night. "Ian Taggart doesn't love anything. Trust me, sweetheart, when you've seen as much as Taggart and I have seen, it doesn't matter anymore. I poisoned my brother not twenty minutes ago. He should be keeling over right about now. It was easy."

"Matt?" Her throat practically closed up at the thought. He'd been awful the last few days, but he'd been a good man once. The thought that he was dead pained her. How many of the people in her life were going to die before this was over?

Patrick Wright's face became a mask of disdain. "Yes. I never intended to share my score with him. He made it damn near impossible to get this job done, and now you've managed to fuck it up. I have to find my contact and try to convince him I didn't double cross him."

"That's going to be difficult, Wright." Sean was on his feet and had the enemy firmly in his sights. "Move it, Grace."

As Parnell turned, Grace obeyed. She dove for cover. She settled behind the metal case of the air conditioner as Parnell snarled at Sean.

"What is that supposed to mean? And why did your brother send in the scrubs? Is he not man enough to meet me himself? Or maybe he wants me to do his dirty work for him?"

"My brother is busy handling your contact. Ian's already taken him out. I have no doubt he'll be riding into the rescue as soon as he can." Sean sounded very sure of himself.

Grace was terrified. He was out there with a known killer. Grace got to her knees and tried peeking from behind her cover. The two men seemed to be in some sort of standoff.

"Your brother is making a deal."

Sean's head shook. "I don't buy it, Wright. I know my brother. He doesn't like the CIA any more than I do."

"Your brother was an agent for ten years, idiot. I'm not sure he isn't still an agent. He's using his little company as a cover."

Sean stopped. He didn't drop his gun, but Grace could see Parnell was getting to him. "That's not true." He firmed his stance again. "I'm taking you in."

"Never going to happen," Parnell swore, and he pulled the trigger.

Grace screamed as she saw Sean's shoulder fly back. He didn't miss a beat. He rolled and took his shot. Parnell looked down at his chest. His gun dropped, and he hit his knees.

Grace was upright in an instant. She chucked her shoes and ran to Sean, who was already back on his feet. Grace was careful, but she inspected the wound. There was a neat little hole in his dress shirt, and his shoulder was bloody. It was his left arm that had taken the bullet, and he held it close to his side. His right kept a gun trained on Parnell.

"Go back down, Grace." Sean's face was set in fierce lines as he approached his fallen opponent.

Grace merely followed behind him. It wouldn't do to argue, and she wasn't about to leave him.

Sean held the gun at Parnell's head and turned him over. It was a repeat of what had happened with Adam, though Parnell was shot through the chest. Blood bubbled up through the small but deadly wound. Grace knew she should feel something, but he'd killed Kayla and Matt and probably Adam. Satisfaction that he'd gotten what he deserved was the only emotion she had.

"Son of a bitch, I knew I should have killed you when I had the chance." Parnell choked on the words.

Sean's face was devoid of sympathy. "Who are you working for?"

Parnell laughed, a terrible sound that rattled his chest. "The only person I can trust, asshole, me. You'll learn. Maybe not. If you're working for Nelson, you're as dead as I am."

That seemed to disconcert Sean. "Was Nelson your handler?"

Parnell's voice got farther away. "He taught me everything I know. Now he'll teach you. You deserve everything he gives you, you son of a bitch."

Parnell's head fell back, and he was gone.

"What does that mean?" Grace looked up at Sean. She needed to believe this was over. The look on Sean's face didn't give her much hope.

"Are you okay, brother?"

Sean seemed to deflate a little as his brother stalked onto the roof. He had a gun in his hand, and his eyes darted around the area, looking for new threats. He was still dressed in his waiter uniform. It didn't look like the man had even wrinkled his clothes when he apparently took down a foreign agent.

"Is he down?" Ian nodded at Parnell's body. His face showed absolutely no emotion.

"I got him, but he won't be available for interrogation. I know I was supposed to bring him in alive, but he didn't leave me much choice." There was no pride in Sean's declaration. He was merely answering a question.

"How bad are you?" Ian's voice was tight as though he was only capable of using the absolute minimum number of words necessary.

"He's shot in the shoulder," Grace said quickly. Sean allowed himself to slump to the ground. He groaned as he tentatively touched his shoulder. Grace followed him down, getting to her knees beside him.

"It's not a big deal. Adam's worse." Sean's breath came out in pants.

Ian nodded and lowered his weapon. He seemed satisfied the danger had passed. He pulled his phone from his pocket. "Yeah, Alex, we need another bus. Sean. He's fine, but he'll need someone to dig out the bullet." Ian looked down at his brother. "Adam's still hanging on. Jake and Eve are treating him. The ambulance should be here in a minute. And the cops. Do we have the package?"

Grace touched Sean's good shoulder, needing the connection. "I have it."

Ian held out his hand. "Good. Give it to me."

She looked to Sean who nodded. She was just about to hand the thumb drive over when she saw another figure darken the doorway. He raised his gun and fired.

Ian Taggart moved like a cheetah. One minute he was the man's target, and the next he was gone. Grace pulled back the thumb drive. She had never felt more vulnerable in her life. She looked around for cover, but she couldn't leave Sean. Sean struggled to get to his feet. His arm came up, but he was slow. The man in the door wasn't injured. Grace screamed as the night cracked around her again, and Sean went down for a second time. Grace crawled to him, her knees scraping over the rough floor. Sean's right thigh was torn open. Blood seemed to be coming from everywhere.

"Good evening. Young Taggart, if you raise that gun, I'll shoot the female. Toss the gun away, and she might live through this." The man with the gun was backlit. She couldn't discern the features of his face, but she knew that voice. Mr. Black. Evan Parnell had been correct in his assessment that his old boss would turn on the team.

Sean's face twisted bitterly. Grace looked around, trying desperately to figure out where Ian had gone. He couldn't have simply left them. Sean tossed the gun toward the doorway with a curse.

"You should get out of the business, Little Tag. Your brother is much more suited for it than you are." He came slightly out of the doorway, and Grace could see Mr. Black's urbane face. If he was worried about betraying the team he'd hired, he didn't show it. "And I know you're here, Ian Taggart. Did you think I didn't know you were on to me? I knew. But you're a game player to the end. And you used your brother and his little woman to try to catch me. I admire you, Tag."

Grace felt Sean stiffen under her. He was trying to move, trying to force her behind him.

"I'll take the package, Ms. Hawthorne," Black said with a smile that didn't reach his eyes.

If she gave up the package, they were all dead. She could see that now. She looked down, and Sean's face was tight. He was trying so hard to move, but his body simply wouldn't. He practically vibrated with frustration.

"I would stay down if I were you, Mr. Taggart." The CIA agent walked out calmly. The gun in his hand was focused on Sean and Grace, but his eyes moved around the space, watching for threats.

"Get out of here, Grace," Sean pushed her away. He didn't seem to be able to use his left hand at all. He shoved her with his right. Even in the moonlight, she could see the desperation in his eyes. "Go. Whatever you do, don't give him the package. Find Ian."

She couldn't do that. She wasn't even sure if she trusted Ian at this point. Panic threatened to swamp her. It boiled up like bile in her throat. She was the only thing standing between Black and Sean.

"Oh, dear, I'd rather you didn't run." Black took careful aim and put another bullet in Sean's leg, this time the left.

Grace had a hand on Sean's body when the bullet hit his thigh. She felt his every muscle jerk and twist. Sean groaned as the blood started to flow again. Tears streamed down her cheeks making the world a watery mess. How much more could he take? Black was playing with them. When he was done, he would simply put a bullet in Sean's heart, and she would watch him die. What could she do? Sean's whole damn life, every day he might have from here on out, depended on her.

"Don't shoot again or I swear I won't be responsible for my actions." Ian walked out from behind the brick enclosure that held the doorway. It didn't matter now because Black was on them. Grace moved to put her body across Sean's. He couldn't take another freaking bullet. She tried to cover as much of him as she could. Her body was the only shield she had. She buried his head in her chest.

He tried to push her away, his right hand coming up weakly. She looked down at him. He was so beautiful. Her heart was filled with him. He couldn't die here.

"Oh, that's sweet." Black was standing next to her. "And not something I can allow."

Grace gasped as Black's hand tangled in her hair, and he pulled her up. Every nerve in her scalp lit up with pain, but she forced herself to fight him. He hauled her up anyway, like a rag doll in a child's merciless hands.

Black held her tight. "Now, Tag, I'm taking my package and getting the hell out of here. This is my retirement. You can shoot me, but I'll take out your brother's little girlfriend, and I might be able to get him, too. What's it going to be, Tag? You let me leave with the girl, and your brother lives to see an operating table. Otherwise…"

"I will never forgive you," Sean vowed with a shaking voice. Grace didn't think he was talking to Black. His head was up, his eyes staring at his brother as though he could will Ian to do something. "Do not do this, Ian. You know what I want."

Ian's face remained a stoic mask. He didn't glance down at his brother. His eyes were steady on Black. "Take her."

"Good choice. He can always find another girl."

Grace held tightly to the thumb drive as Black dragged her to the wall. She craned her neck to look down. There was an empty balcony below, a twin to the balcony where the party was still going on. That balcony was lit with twinkling lights. It seemed like it was worlds away from her now. The balcony below was dark and quiet. It was the only real escape route Black had. Ian had called for an ambulance. There were going to be cops and paramedics in the stairwell, and any minute they would show up here. She was sure Black was in good physical shape, and he was probably very athletic. But damn, that was still a long fall. Once he had them both on that balcony, he would kill her. He didn't need her, only the package. She would be dead weight after he had that.

"Grace!" Sean had managed to turn over and was trying to crawl toward the gun he'd tossed away.

He wouldn't stop. Her Viking would die before he let her go. It would have worked. It would have worked between them. She could have had a whole rich second life with Sean as her husband. All of the reasons to be afraid vanished in the face of his struggle. Love for Sean was all that mattered now. He wouldn't stop fighting for her. She owed him the same.

She had seconds before he got to the gun, and Black was forced to kill him. She had one shot at saving the man she loved. She understood why Black hadn't gone for the package before. She had it, and he had her. They were at a stalemate. Ian couldn't shoot because he didn't want to hit her. If she didn't have the package, Black would kill her in an instant.

But he'd overestimated her will to live in a world where Sean was gone. Perhaps this time chaos would be her friend.

"You want the package?" She drew her arm back and tossed it over her shoulder as hard as she could. It went sailing over the wall. "Go get it!"

The minute the package left her hand, all hell broke loose.

"Fuck," Black cursed and leapt to the wall as Ian started running toward them. Grace tried to move away, to get to Sean, but Black caught the neck of her black cocktail dress. It bit into her flesh, choking her. She was still his shield. Ian couldn't get a shot that didn't hit her. "If I'm going down, I think I'll take you with me."

And Grace went flying. The world seemed to slow down. Ian ran toward her, but she was moving faster. Her stomach lurched as she fell backwards, watching the building and safety and Sean get further and further away.

She heard Sean's scream, but it seemed a distant thing. She fell for what seemed like forever. At some point, Black let go of her collar. When she hit the balcony, she landed with a sickening thud that knocked the breath out of her. She looked up at the black night. Nothing hurt. That was bad.

She had a vision of Black running by, and then Ian Taggart landed on his feet. He knelt down beside her. His face was the only thing that seemed real in the world. He looked so much like his brother. Sean. Her Viking.

"Grace?" His hand came out, his fingers resting against her throat.

She tried to move, to tell him that she was fine, but nothing seemed to work. She wanted to speak, to tell Sean she loved him, but the words were trapped inside her.

Sean was still screaming. She wanted to hold him. Oh, she was going to miss him. Tears slipped helplessly from her eyes. She couldn't move. Why couldn't she move?

Ian looked up, a frown on his face. His body twitched as though he was fighting some instinct. His prey was getting away, Grace realized. Then he set the gun down, his decision obviously made.

"It's going to be okay." He pulled her hand into his. "Damn it, Grace, you have to live. Please live. He won't ever forgive me if you die."

The last thing she heard was Ian's voice calling for another ambulance. Then the world went dark, and all its horror winked from existence.

* * * *

Grace came back to consciousness slowly. It happened for seconds at a time. She would become aware of a terrible, debilitating pain, and then she saw a flash of a face. A gorgeous Viking was watching over her. He was saying something, and then it was all gone and darkness took her again. There were times when all that seemed real was the warmth of a hand in hers, squeezing her flesh, begging her to come back.

But the world was warm here. It was safe here. The darkness wasn't a bad place to be, and she could stay here forever if she wanted.

And still the Viking called to her.

"Please," he pleaded.

He was the only thing that kept her tethered. He wouldn't let her go.

Her children were grown. They would miss her, but they didn't need her, not really. It was okay to go. It was okay to hide from the pain.

"I love you." He whispered it over and over. He never let up.

Gradually, Grace realized eternal peace would have to wait. Sean wasn't letting her go.

When she finally opened her eyes, it all seemed like a strange dream. Her body ached, and she looked down at the man sleeping with his head on her chest. He held onto her hand, his big body stuffed in a hospital chair. That's where she was. She was in the hospital. The events of the night she was injured rushed back. It played like a horror movie in her head, but the end result was sleeping beside her. Sean was alive.

She wiggled her toes. Oh, they moved. Her whole body was a bundle of pain, but at least she felt it. She embraced the ache in her bones because it meant she was alive.

"Sean?" Her mouth was dry, her voice rusty.

"Mom?" A familiar voice was heard. She turned to see her sons on the other side of the room. Her head swam for a moment.

There was a mad scramble as Sean woke up, and suddenly David and Kyle were at her side.

"Mom? You're awake. Thank god, you're awake." Kyle rushed off, yelling for a nurse.

"How long?" Grace asked.

Sean's eyes filled with tears, and he didn't even try to stop it. He let the tears wash down his face. Grace stared at him. He was so perfect.

"You've been in a coma for ten days." He put his forehead gently against hers. "I thought I lost you."

She let her fingers find the gold silk of his hair. She was weak, so weak, but touching him gave her strength.

She looked up at her oldest baby, who had a hand on Sean's back. Kyle ran back in the room, and the nurses took over. She had all her men in one room.

"I love you, Grace."

She smiled through the pain. Everything she wanted was right here. "I know. I love you, too, Viking."

* * * *

It was three days before Ian Taggart snuck into her room.

The whole team had been to visit. Adam and Jake had shown her all of Adam's cool new scars. They were puckered and red, the staples having just come out. Adam had been close to death, but he joked about it. Eve had sat with her, telling her everything that had happened. She was the one who had explained just how close Adam had come to dying. Sean had to be sedated before he would allow anyone to take him into surgery. He'd been determined to wait on Grace. Now Sean had a couple more scars on that glorious body of his, but he was on the mend. Liam had shown up bearing flowers and a big fluffy teddy bear. Alexander McKay had brought magazines, but no Ian.

Ian had waited until Sean and her sons had gone out for something besides hospital food. Then he glided into the room like the ghost he was.

"Would it help at all if I said I was sorry?"

She didn't pretend to misunderstand. She looked at her giant soon-to-be brother-in-law. "Are you?"

"Yes," he admitted. His arms crossed over his massive chest. "And I would do it again."

He would choose his brother. She could handle that. "I understand."

His face softened slightly. "But, Grace, I underestimated you. You are good for Sean. You're much stronger than I gave you credit for."

She shrugged. "And now I have a metal plate in my head." And she would have to grow back the hair there. Her skull had shattered in some places. It had been a close thing. "I think it makes me tough."

He laughed a little. "And an automatic pat-down at security gates. You'll be hell on metal detectors."

Grace frowned. There might be body cavity searches in her future. "I hate that man."

Ian's face went dark. Grace was beginning to understand it was the face he made when he thought about his prey. "I'll get him, Grace. If it's the last thing I do. I will kill that man. He's dropped off the radar. He's gone rogue, but I'll find him. The good news is that we found the package before he could. It was all the way down on the street. That's quite the throwing arm you have."

Grace didn't care. Sean was sure Black or Nelson or whatever his name was wouldn't come after them. There was no reason to. They were out. That was what mattered. "I'm glad we have the information. As for Black, I'm sure you'll do what you have to. Do you still work for the CIA?"

Ian's eyes widened, and for a moment, she worried he wasn't going to answer her. "No. I got out a few years back. I never really was on the payroll, so to speak. I was a contractor. And the Army loaned me out. I won't ever work for those bastards again. I don't know what Black said about me, but everything I have ever done has been for the good of my country."

Grace believed him. There seemed to be a core of integrity to Ian.

And now Ian seemed awfully willing to chat. No one would talk about the case with her. Any time she asked, they changed the subject as though worried it might tax her broken brain. "Is Matt really dead?"

Ian nodded. "Yes, Grace. He's dead. The police found him in a bathroom. It looked like a heart attack, but we know that's not true. The toxicology report will tell us what kind of poison was used on him. The District Attorney is pouring over Wright Temps. The Earth League has broken up, and the FBI has officially taken over the investigation. It will take them a while to sort through the mess Patrick Wright left behind. I want to assure you that you've been cleared of any wrongdoing. I've talked to both the FBI and the CIA.

You're out of this, Grace. You and Sean are free and clear."

A knot eased in her chest. She was happy to hear that she had been declared innocent, but knowing Sean was out of the line of fire really eased her mind.

Ian was quiet for a long moment, looking over the lilies Sean had filled her room with. "I knew a woman who loved lilies. She's gone now, too."

There was a long silence as he stared at those flowers, and Grace knew she was seeing a piece of Ian Taggart's soul very few people saw. He was opening himself to her. He was accepting her as his family. He turned to her, and there was a certain humbleness in his stance she had never seen before from him. "I need something from you, Grace. I know I have no right to ask."

She wanted to ask him about the woman, but the moment had passed. "I'm listening."

"Come to work for me."

That wasn't what she'd expected. "Why?"

She hadn't even started to think about work. She really was going to need a job. She and Sean had gone over their finances the night before. He had money saved, but they would need cash to start his restaurant later on. And culinary school wasn't cheap.

"Because I need someone to run the office." He stared at her, waiting patiently.

She stared back. That was a bullshit answer.

He sighed. "Fine. Sean won't talk to me. He won't take my calls or let me anywhere near him. He won't forgive me. You're the only tie I have to my brother. I don't want to lose him. I know I made mistakes, but I love him. I don't want to lose my family."

Now that she believed. If anyone in the world needed a strong family to ground him, it was Ian Taggart. As she was about to become a member of his family, it was an idea that deserved consideration. "What if Sean won't let me work for you?"

She had to admit, she found the idea intriguing. And that group really needed someone to look out for them.

A small smile tugged at Ian Taggart's face. "I think you'll find a way. You subs always do."

Grace grinned back. Yes. They always did.

Epilogue

Six months later

"Guacamole again?"

Adam stared at the bowl on her desk. Sean was setting up her little lunch. He had Fridays off from school, and every Friday he brought in a gourmet picnic. Every Friday, Adam showed up to mooch. He claimed that since getting gut shot, his appetite had increased threefold. Grace couldn't tell from the cut of his suit. He was as fit as ever.

"I never argue with pregnant ladies," Sean proclaimed, grinning as he broke out the tortilla chips. "She can't get enough avocados. The baby is going to come out green."

Grace plucked a chip out of her husband's hand. She really did crave them. She wanted avocados on everything. Baby girl loved them. She let the taste flow over her tongue as she settled her hand over her expanding belly. Sean covered her hand with his and dropped a kiss on her lips. She was four-and-a-half months pregnant. For some reason, she was just sure this one was a girl.

"Can't pregnant ladies like cookies?" Adam snagged a chip and some dip anyway.

"I am not a pastry chef." Sean said it like it was the worst thing a person could be. Sean had become a terrible food snob.

Grace was just happy Sean and Adam were friends again. "I'll make some chocolate chip cookies tonight. We need some sweets. Savory boy over there would feed me protein day and night."

Sean shrugged. "Practice makes perfect."

Adam ambled off after enjoying a healthy portion of chips and guacamole. Grace sat back and enjoyed the view as her husband bent over to pull out the rest of her feast. Damn, he looked fine in a pair of jeans. He looked even better naked. The only thing she craved more than avocados was her Viking. She was just about to reach out and pat that hot ass when Ian walked by. He nodded at her on his way into the big corner office. He did not stop to talk to Sean, but she didn't miss the way he looked at his brother. Ian missed him, but he wasn't pushing.

She liked being the office manager of McKay-Taggart. She especially enjoyed going toe to toe with her brother-in-law. Sean had progressed. He was talking to Ian again. Oh, he was only using four letter words, but Grace had high hopes.

She had no intention of the baby not knowing her uncle.

"I'm going to go heat up the soup." Sean kissed her again. He did it all the time. He always had his hands on her. "Don't go anywhere."

"Not a chance, baby."

After a few minutes, she could smell the heavenly aroma of tortilla soup coming from the break room.

"Hello?"

Grace looked up. A pretty woman in a green sweater and blue jeans stared down at her. She had a mass of curly brown hair and clutched an oversized handbag in front of her. She was lovely in a very soft, feminine way. She had an hourglass figure and big green eyes. "How can I help you?"

The woman, who Grace pegged as late-twenties, early-thirties, bit her bottom lip nervously. "I need to hire a body guard. My agent recommended your firm."

"And why do you need a bodyguard?" It wasn't an unusual request, but it certainly wasn't one they got from walk-ins. In fact, they almost never had walk-ins.

The woman laughed, but it was a nervous sound. Her eyes turned down sadly. "I know this is going to sound silly, but someone's trying to kill me."

It was a terrible thing to hear, yet Grace found herself smiling. She knew just how to play this one. "Oh, dear. We can definitely help with that. And why take one bodyguard, when you can have two?"

Sean was coming back in from the break room when she placed the call to Jake. She had a feeling about this one. Jake's eyes widened when he came out to escort the lovely Serena Brooks to his office.

"Matchmaker," Sean accused as he set the bowl in front of her.

His eyes were hot on her as he sat down. She knew that look. She was going to get pulled into someone's office for a little play. Her pregnancy hadn't slowed Sean down a bit. He still was her hungry Master. Thank god.

"You know what they say about newlyweds. They can't stand for anyone to not be as happy as they are."

He winked at her. "Then Adam and Jake should watch out."

Yes. If they were anywhere near as lucky as she and Sean, they had better.

* * * *

The McKay-Taggart security team returns with *The Men with the Golden Cuffs*.

Sign up for Lexi Blake's newsletter
and be entered to win a $25 gift certificate
to the bookseller of your choice.

Join us for news, fun, and exclusive content
including free short stories.

There's a new contest every month!

Go to www.LexiBlake.net to subscribe.

Author's Note

I'm often asked by generous readers how they can help get the word out about a book they enjoyed. There are so many ways to help an author you like. Leave a review. If your e-reader allows you to lend a book to a friend, please share it. Go to Goodreads and connect with others. Recommend the books you love because stories are meant to be shared. Thank you so much for reading this book and for supporting all the authors you love!

The Men with the Golden Cuffs
Masters and Mercenaries, Book 2
By Lexi Blake
Out Now!

A woman in danger...
Serena Brooks is a bestselling author of erotic fiction. She knows how to write a happy ending but hasn't managed to find one of her own. Divorced and alone, she has no one to turn to when a stalker begins to threaten her life. The cops don't believe her. Her ex-husband thinks she's making the whole story up. She has no one left to turn to except a pair of hired bodyguards. They promise to guard her body, but no one can protect her heart.

Two men in search of love...
Adam Miles and Jacob Dean are halves of a whole. They've spent their entire adult lives searching for the one woman who can handle them both. Adam is the playful, indulgent lover, while Jacob is the possessive, loving Dom. When Serena comes into their lives, Adam is certain that she's the one. But Jacob's past comes back to haunt them all. He is suspicious of Serena's story, and his concerns are driving a wedge between him and Adam. But when the stalker strikes, they will have to come together or lose each other forever...

* * * *

"Who is Master Storm?" a low voice asked.

She shrieked like a five-year-old girl. Jake Dean had somehow gotten into her bedroom and behind her when she wasn't looking. "You have to stop that! God, you're going to give me a heart attack."

"He's good at that. It's one of his great life skills." Adam leaned negligently against her doorframe. Mojo sat beside him, their enormous bodies blocking her escape route. Mojo's tail thumped and his mouth hung open, tongue panting. At least her dog found them amusing.

They were both here in her small bedroom. It was the most

straight-man attention this bedroom had gotten in years.

"Don't sneak up on me like that." She forced herself to look at Jake. Between the two of them it was obvious Adam would be easier to deal with. Jake was the hard-ass. She didn't deal well with hard-asses.

A single brow arched above his model perfect face. "I didn't sneak up. You weren't paying attention to your surroundings. You were far too busy telling your agent to fire us."

Adam's face fell. "What? But we just got here. Look, sweetheart, I know the whole breaking-in thing was scary, but we did have a point. Your security system sucks. And, in our defense, we did call and ring the doorbell. We can't do our job standing on your front porch waiting for you to finish with the dancing thing. That was adorable by the way."

She flushed. God, she hated the fact that a part of her wanted to believe he wasn't insulting her. His teasing tone was soft and cajoling. When he smiled, the most gorgeous dimples showed up on his face. Adam Miles was just about everything she could want in a boyfriend. He was charming and smart, and he came with a built-in alpha-male partner.

Stop right there, Serena Brooks. Your imagination is running wild. The world doesn't work that way.

"I don't think this is about the break-in. She said we were making fun of her." Jake's brows drew together in a serious expression as though he was working through a problem. "I didn't make fun of her. I told her to stop yelling. I have excellent hearing. I can't stand yelling."

And he apparently thought she was dense. "You know I wasn't talking about you." She turned to Adam. It had really hurt coming from him. She'd expected someone like Jake to think less of her for what she wrote, but Adam had seemed more tolerant.

"What? Me? Are you serious? How did I make fun of you?" He seemed to really struggle with the idea.

"You obviously read some of the titles of my books. Look, I get that you wouldn't read a book like that, but I won't listen to anyone denigrate the choices I've made in my lifestyle. You might not understand or accept it, but I will demand that you respect it."

Jake actually laughed. "The little sub thinks we have problems with BDSM."

Adam's eyes rolled. "Yeah, uhm, you do have some problems, sweetheart. How long have you been in the lifestyle? Or are you a little tourist who likes to rage against the machine?"

"I had to take off my leathers to come here. I was at a club called Sanctum." Jake's face had softened a bit. "Adam knows my limits. I don't like pretty subs spouting filth at me in anger. He has a smart mouth, but he would never ridicule you. Lightning would strike."

Adam smiled at her. "And the earth would shake. Seriously, we don't think that way. We're far too odd on our own. And I haven't read any of your books, but I would like to."

Jake's whole body went on wary alert. "We actually need to. From what I understand, this is about your books, correct?"

She was caught between relief and a dangerous joy. She believed them. They really didn't care. In fact, Jake seemed to be involved in the lifestyle. She didn't know many men outside the lifestyle who would use the term leathers when talking about a pair of pants. The thought of Jacob Dean in a pair of leathers, his cut chest on display as he nodded to the floor, silently requesting that she kneel at his feet, made her heart pound. About a million questions popped into her brain, but she forced herself to keep to the questions asked.

Thieves

A new urban fantasy series by Lexi Blake

"Author Lexi Blake has created a supernatural world filled with surprises and a book that I couldn't put down once I started reading it."
Maven, The Talent Cave Reviews

"I truly love that Lexi took vampires and made them her own."
KC Lu, Guilty Pleasures Book Reviews

Stealing mystical and arcane artifacts is a dangerous business, especially for a human, but Zoey Wharton is an exceptional thief. The trick to staying alive is having friends in all the wrong places. With a vampire, a werewolf, and a witch on the payroll, Zoey takes the sorts of jobs no one else can perform—tracking down ancient artifacts filled with unthinkable magic power, while trying to stay one step ahead of monsters, demons, angels, and a Vampire Council with her in their crosshairs.

If only her love life could be as simple. Zoey and Daniel Donovan were childhood sweethearts until a violent car crash took his life. When Daniel returned from the grave as a vampire, his only interest in Zoey was in keeping her safely apart from the secrets of his dark world. Five years later, Zoey encounters Devinshea Quinn, an earthbound Faery prince who sweeps her off her feet. He could show her everything the supernatural world has to offer, but Daniel is still in her heart.

As their adventures in acquisition continue, Zoey will have to find a way to bring together the two men she loves or else none of them may survive the forces that have aligned against her.

Thieves
Steal the Light
Steal the Day
Steal the Moon
Steal the Sun
Steal the Night
Ripper
Addict
Sleeper
Outcast, Coming 2018

About Lexi Blake

Lexi Blake lives in North Texas with her husband, three kids, and the laziest rescue dog in the world. She began writing at a young age, concentrating on plays and journalism. It wasn't until she started writing romance that she found success. She likes to find humor in the strangest places. Lexi believes in happy endings no matter how odd the couple, threesome or foursome may seem. She also writes contemporary Western ménage as Sophie Oak.

Facebook: Lexi Blake
Twitter: https://twitter.com/authorlexiblake
Website: www.LexiBlake.net

Sign up for Lexi's free newsletter here.

CPSIA information can be obtained
at www.ICGtesting.com
Printed in the USA
LVHW111345250821
696078LV00003B/32